My Soul is full of longing
For the secret of the sea
And the heart of the great ocean
Sends a thrilling pulse through me.

- Henry Wadsworth Longfellow

ABLE
SEAMAN

ABLE SEAMAN

The Sailing Anthology

JACK LONDON

circle up
stories

Printed in the United States of America. All rights reserved under International and Pan-American Copyright Conventions. Published in the United States by Circle Up Stories LLC, 522 Crafton Ave., Pitman, NJ 08071.

The "Circle Up Stories" logo is the exclusive property of Circle Up Stories LLC. Circle Up Stories is an imprint of Circle Up Stories LLC.

Text set in PT Serif and Playfair Display. Cover photo by Ave Calvar Martinez from Pexels with additional illustration by PipandJ Papery.

Library of Congress Control Number: 2021930544

ISBN (paperback): 978-1-7343702-2-5

ISBN (ebook): 978-1-7343702-3-2

www.circleupstories.com

Contents

INTRODUCTION

JACK LONDON (born John Griffith Chaney in 1876) traced his pedigree to "a tumbleweed family, blowing with the winds of failure" (Sinclair, Andrew, *Jack: A Biography of Jack London*, 1977), and his myriad life experience—as a pickle factory worker, hobo, sailor, and both an oyster pirate and a badge-carrying deputy of the California Fish Patrol tasked with catching those same poachers—served as ample fuel for London's literary creativity.

This anthology contains the short stories London wrote centered around sailing, starting with the submission that won him $25 as a seventeen-year-old, "Story of a Typhoon Off the Coast of Japan." On the whole, this collection is an iconic representation of the short story as a form, filled with stories of daring and tension.

But London's action-packed tales are pocked with out-and-out racist characterizations. For example, Chinese sailors, are belittled as yellow, unscrupulous, worthless opium smokers. As abhorrent as this characterization is, it is consistent with contemporary sentiment and would not have been surprising to London's readers. *The Yellow*

Danger, published out of Britain in 1898 by M. P. Shiel, cast the Chinese as "fiendishly lov[ing] cruelty... devilishl[y] cunning." For all the drama and allure, London consistently relies on and reinforces these prejudicial, discriminatory types throughout these and other writings.

Despite these deficiencies, London's work resonates now as it did then. Writing in 2011, literary critic Harold Bloom (1930-2019) wrote that the "worship of the wild... accounts for London's permanent appeal to readers throughout the world" (Bloom, Harold, *Bloom's Modern Critical Views: Jack London*). In the unpublished travel journal of a young visitor touring San Francisco in 1905, a man and his traveling companion took a ride on the Sausalito Ferry. One entry records this:

> *"John and I hustled out early this morning and got the Sausalito ferry for Sausalito. Fare 40¢ Frisco to Mill Valley on return. It is worth remembering that the Sausalito ferry is the opening scene in Jack London's new book,* The Sea Wolf. *It was a very pretty trip, but the heights were hid in fog, as usual."*

Jack London's *The Sea Wolf* (1904) was published just one year prior to this visit, but this private reference captures much of what is the lasting allure of London's work. With skillful treatment of even the most trivial, London exposed the world to quintessential American experiences that were otherwise inaccessible to most.

Typhoon Off the Coast of Japan

Typhoon off the Coast of Japan (1893)

IT WAS FOUR BELLS in the morning watch. We had just finished breakfast when the order came forward for the watch on deck to stand by to heave her to and all hands stand by the boats.

"Port! hard a port!" cried our sailing-master. "Clew up the topsails! Let the flying jib run down! Back the jib over to windward and run down the foresail!" And so was our schooner *Sophie Sutherland* hove to off the Japan coast, near Cape Jerimo, on April 10, 1893.

Then came moments of bustle and confusion. There were eighteen men to man the six boats. Some were hooking on the falls, others casting off the lashings; boat-steerers appeared with boat-compasses and water-breakers, and boat-pullers with the lunch boxes. Hunters were staggering under two or three shotguns, a rifle and heavy ammunition box, all of which were soon stowed away with their oilskins and mittens in the boats.

The sailing-master gave his last orders, and away we went, pulling three pairs of oars to gain our positions. We were in the weather boat, and so had a longer pull than the others. The first, second, and third lee boats soon had all sail set and were running off to the southward and westward with the wind beam, while the schooner was running off to leeward of them, so that in case of accident the boats would have fair wind home.

It was a glorious morning, but our boat-steerer shook his head ominously as he glanced at the rising sun and prophetically muttered: "Red sun in the morning, sailor take warning." The sun had an angry look, and a few light, fleecy "nigger-heads" in that quarter seemed abashed and frightened and soon disappeared.

Away off to the northward, Cape Jerimo reared its black, forbidding head like some huge monster rising from the deep. The winter's snow, not yet entirely dissipated by the sun, covered it in patches of glistening white, over which the light wind swept on its way out to sea. Huge gulls rose slowly, fluttering their wings in the light breeze and striking their webbed feet on the surface of the water for over half a mile before they could leave it. Hardly had the patter, patter died away when a flock of sea quail rose, and with whistling wings flew away to windward, where members of a large band of whales were disporting themselves, their blowings sounding like the exhaust of steam engines. The harsh, discordant cries of a sea-parrot grated unpleasantly on the ear and set half a dozen alert in a small band of seals that were ahead of us. Away they went, breaching and jumping entirely out of water. A sea-gull with slow, deliberate flight and long, majestic curves circled round us, and as a reminder of home a little English sparrow perched impudently on the fo'castle head, and, cocking his head on one side, chirped merrily. The boats were soon among the seals, and the bang! bang! of the guns could be heard from down to leeward.

The wind was slowly rising, and by three o'clock as, with a dozen seals in our boat, we were deliberating whether to go on or turn back, the recall flag was run up at the schooner's mizzen—a sure sign that with the rising wind the barometer was falling and that our sailing-master was getting anxious for the welfare of the boats.

Away we went before the wind with a single reef in our sail. With clenched teeth sat the boat-steerer, grasping the steering oar firmly with both hands, his restless eyes on the alert—a glance at the schooner ahead, as we rose on a sea, another at the mainsheet, and then one astern where the dark ripple of the wind on the water told him of a coming puff or a large white-cap that threatened to overwhelm us. The waves were holding high carnival, performing the strangest antics, as with wild glee they danced along in fierce pursuit—now up, now down, here, there, and everywhere, until some great sea of liquid green with its milk-white crest of foam rose from the ocean's throbbing bosom and drove the others from view. But only for a moment, for again under new forms they reappeared. In the sun's path they wandered, where every ripple, great or small, every little spit or spray looked like molten silver, where the water lost its dark green color and became a dazzling, silvery flood, only to vanish and become a wild waste of sullen turbulence, each dark foreboding sea rising and breaking, then rolling on again. The dash, the sparkle, the silvery light soon vanished with the sun, which became obscured by black clouds that were rolling swiftly in from the west, northwest—apt heralds of the coming storm.

We soon reached the schooner and found ourselves the last aboard. In a few minutes the seals were skinned, boats and decks washed, and we were down below by the roaring fo'castle fire, with a wash, change of clothes, and a hot, substantial supper before us. Sail had been put on the schooner, as we had a run of seventy-five miles to make to the southward before morning, so as to get in the midst of the seals, out of which we had strayed during the last two days' hunting.

We had the first watch from eight to midnight. The wind was soon blowing half a gale, and our sailing-master expected little sleep that night as he paced up and down the poop. The topsails were soon clewed up and made fast, then the flying jib run down and furled. Quite a sea was rolling by this time, occasionally breaking over the decks, flooding them and threatening to smash the boats. At six bells we were ordered to turn them over and put on storm lashings. This occupied us till eight bells, when we were relieved by the mid-watch. I was the last to go below, doing so just as the watch on deck was furling the spanker. Below all were asleep except our green hand, the "bricklayer," who was dying of consumption. The wildly dancing movements of the sea lamp cast a pale, flickering light through the fo'castle and turned to golden honey the drops of water on the yellow oilskins. In all the corners dark shadows seemed to come and go, while up in the eyes of her, beyond the pall bits, descending from deck to deck, where they seemed to lurk like some dragon at the cavern's mouth, it was dark as Erebus. Now and again, the light seemed to penetrate for a moment as the schooner rolled heavier than usual, only to recede, leaving it darker and blacker than before. The roar of the wind through the rigging came to the ear muffled like the distant rumble of a train crossing a trestle or the surf on the beach, while the loud crash of the seas on her weather bow seemed almost to rend the beams and planking asunder as it resounded through the fo'castle. The creaking and groaning of the timbers, stanchions, and bulkheads, as the strain the vessel was undergoing was felt, served to drown the groans of the dying man as he tossed uneasily in his bunk. The working of the foremast against the deck beams caused a shower of flaky powder to fall, and sent another sound mingling with the tumultuous storm. Small cascades of water streamed from the pall bits from the fo'castle head above, and, joining issue with the streams from the wet oilskins, ran along the floor and disappeared aft into the main hold.

At two bells in the middle watch—that is, in land parlance one o'clock in the morning—the order was roared out on the fo'castle: "All hands on deck and shorten sail!"

Then the sleepy sailors tumbled out of their bunk and into their clothes, oil-skins, and sea-boots and up on deck. 'Tis when that order comes on cold, blustering nights that "Jack" grimly mutters: "Who would not sell a farm and go to sea?"

It was on deck that the force of the wind could be fully appreciated, especially after leaving the stifling fo'castle. It seemed to stand up against you like a wall, making it almost impossible to move on the heaving decks or to breathe as the fierce gusts came dashing by. The schooner was hove to under jib, foresail, and mainsail. We proceeded to lower the foresail and make it fast. The night was dark, greatly impeding our labor. Still, though not a star or the moon could pierce the black masses of storm clouds that obscured the sky as they swept along before the gale, nature aided us in a measure. A soft light emanated from the movement of the ocean. Each mighty sea, all phosphorescent and glowing with the tiny lights of myriads of animalcule, threatened to overwhelm us with a deluge of fire. Higher and higher, thinner and thinner, the crest grew as it began to curve and overtop preparatory to breaking, until with a roar it fell over the bulwarks, a mass of soft glowing light and tons of water which sent the sailors sprawling in all directions and left in each nook and cranny little specks of light that glowed and trembled till the next sea washed them away, depositing new ones in their places. Sometimes several seas following each other with great rapidity and thundering down on our decks filled them full to the bulwarks, but soon they were discharged through the lee scuppers.

To reef the mainsail we were forced to run off before the gale under the single reefed jib. By the time we had finished the wind had forced up such a tremendous sea that it was impossible to heave her to. Away we flew on the wings of the storm through the muck and flying spray. A wind sheer to starboard, then another to port as the enormous seas struck the schooner astern and nearly broached her to. As day broke, we took in the jib, leaving not a sail unfurled. Since we had begun scudding she had ceased to take the seas over her bow, but amidships they broke fast and furious. It was a dry storm in the matter of rain, but the force of the wind filled the air with fine spray, which flew as high as the crosstrees and cut the face like a knife, making it impossible to see over a hundred yards ahead. The sea was a dark lead color as with long, slow, majestic roll it was heaped up by the wind into liquid mountains of foam. The wild antics of the schooner were sickening as she forged along. She would almost stop, as though climbing a mountain, then rapidly rolling to right and left as she gained the summit of a huge sea, she steadied herself and paused for a moment as though affrighted at the yawning precipice before her. Like an avalanche, she shot forward and down as the sea astern struck her with the force of a thousand battering rams, burying her bow to the catheads in the milky foam at the bottom that came on deck in all directions—forward, astern, to right and left, through the hawse-pipes and over the rail.

The wind began to drop, and by ten o'clock we were talking of heaving her to. We passed a ship, two schooners, and a four-masted barkentine under the smallest of canvas, and at eleven o'clock, running up the spanker and jib, we hove her to, and in another hour, we were beating back again against the aftersea under full sail to regain the sealing ground away to the westward.

Below, a couple of men were sewing the "bricklayer's" body in canvas preparatory to the sea burial. And so with the storm passed away the "bricklayer's" soul.

PLAGUE SHIP

PLAGUE SHIP
(1897)

"WHAT'S THIS! WHAT'S THIS! Do you wish to kill the man? Such treatment is too heroic. Bah! An emetic of ipecacuanha, fifteen grains of powdered calomel and as many of quinine, and then castor oil! Why my dear madam, you know absolutely nothing about medicine!" and the speaker glared indignantly at her.

She flushed, half hurt, half angry, but smothering her feeling, replied, "What do you take the case to be? Typhus?"

"No. It's merely a bilious fever, made the more severe by this d—, I beg your pardon, this infernal weather."

"Bilious fever! Ha! Ha! Ha!" They had withdrawn from the side of the sufferer, and she burst forth into merry peals of laughter.

"Yes, madam, I repeat it. Bilious fever. Bilious fever! Do you hear? Bilious! Bilious! Bilious fever!"

"My dear sir, though I do not know you, from the wondrous knowledge you display I'll call you doctor. Then doctor, let me ask you if you have ever heard of black vomit, or, if that does not come within your technical nomenclature, yellow fever?"

"What symptoms does the man evince. Madam Know-It-All?"

"Miss Know-It-All, if you please. Languor, chilliness, muscular pains, headache, fa—"

"Precursors of any febrile attack. You evidently do—"

"Face flushed, eyes suffused then congested, nostrils and lips red, tongue scarlet, temperature 105, loss—"

"Loss of appetite, hot skin, thirst, nausea, restlessness, and delirium—all the usual accompaniments of any high fever—go on Miss—Miss—"

"Miss Know-It-All. But all these militant symptoms have ceased and he is now in a state of prostration and collapse. This, the stadium, is as you know the great characteristic of yellow fever."

"Collapse! Bah! Convalescence. The man is recovering but weak, and here I find you have given him ipecacuanha, calomel, quinine and castor oil. Where's the ship's doctor? I'll have you out of here!"

"As for the ship's doctor, he's sick too, with bilious fever I suppose. And for you who are you pray? Don't rest under the hallucination that you are still walking your hospital, wherever it may be. I am as competent as you; nay, have a diploma as well as you: and as to this case, have had too much experience to be mistaken."

"Madam—A—A—Miss—I— I— I— I'll see the captain at once. You're a—a—a—don't know your business!" And in choleric wrath he left her in pursuit of the chief officer.

The steamer *Caspar* had left the West Coast, with a clean bill of health and in first-class order, for San Francisco.

But fortune had illy favored her and from the first day her voyage had been one of trials and tribulations. She had been fearfully overloaded with both cargo and passengers. So low did she float in the water that she seemed and behaved like a log. All buoyancy was lost: she was dead, plunging through instead of rising to the great seas she had met with. In this condition she had encountered a storm, broken her propeller shaft, and been blown hundreds of miles out of her course into the Pacific. The engineers had worked night and day but could effect no permanent repair. They would manage to run the engines a few hours, then their patches would give away and they would be forced to stop twice as long to again make ineffectual repairs. They were still far out of their course and even the captain did not know when they would get back. To make it worse, they had been blown into an unfrequented portion of the ocean, far from the beaten paths, and could look to no outside source for assistance.

There were 158 first class passengers and only berths for 95. Many of the ladies were forced to sleep on lounges and settees, while the gentlemen literally floored and walled the smoking saloon when bed time came. While it was thus rather hard on the first-class passengers, it was worse on the second, and in the steerage it was frightful. Some of second-class berths were directly over the screw and so close to the Chinese quarters as to be rendered almost uninhabitable by the fumes of opium and otherwise abominable stenches. In the after-lower-deck, it was more like a cattle ship. Four Chinese, half a score of Negroes, and quadruple as many white people, the majority of which were seasick, were crowded into this hole. So far down was it, that there was no ventilation save through the ports, which more often were bolted down than otherwise.

And now, in the fierce tropic heat of midsummer, to cap their misery, fever had broken forth. While many were hasty in proclaiming it the terrible yellow jack, the more clear-headed, cognizant of their horrible condition, naturally attributed it to that. The ship's doctor, a too efficient and too poorly paid man, had been the first to come down, leaving the passengers and men to take care of themselves. Their endeavors had been spasmodic and erratic. A fifth of the crew were down and the rest were on the verge of mutiny, threatening to take to the boats. The firemen and stokers were as bad, no longer yielding subordination to their officers. The Chinese, while none were taken ill, continued to stolidly smoke their opium, turning a deaf ear to the protests of the passengers and the commands of the captain, which they knew could not be enforced. The first officer, in despair, had taken to whiskey and was now locked up in a fit of horrors, while the rest of the officers were nearly crazy in their impotency. The passengers were just beginning to awake to their danger; but as yet, save for the isolated efforts of the couple that quarreled over the diagnosis, had done nothing.

Doctor Chandler, who maintained it was bilious fever, had yet to meet his thirtieth birthday. He was returning from an expedition to Peru, on which he had been absent a year. Long retired, in fact, except for his hospital experience, he had never taken up a practice; for the same hand that educated him, had, on its demise, endowed him with an ample fortune. Possessed of a scientific worship for good sanitation—it was his hobby—to the absence of it he attributed, under various names, the sickness which had fallen on them.

Miss Appleton, while possessed of a diploma, had perhaps not as much experience in hospitals, but of Southern origin, she had gone through an epidemic of yellow fever in New Orleans and was familiar with all its symptoms. She was a woman not more than twenty-five, beautiful as the word goes, but owing more to a pleasant, forceful personality than to her physical charms. Traveling with her aunt, as soon as the disease had manifested itself, she deserted her to the attention of a maid and threw herself into the breach. And thus, just as she had attempted her first case, had she encountered Doctor Chandler, who had similarly awakened and who was in search of his first patient.

Several days had elapsed and things were going from bad to worse. At last, everybody had been forced to acknowledge that the disease was yellow fever, even Doctor Chandler, who had become very contrite and usually begged Miss Appleton's pardon every other time they met. Though rather rash and headstrong, he was really a good fellow at heart, and soon the twain were on the best of footings. He was generous and self-sacrificing to a fault and devoted himself night and day to the struggle. Maud Appleton easily penetrated his brusque exterior and grew to understand and like him. Still, they occasionally quarreled over methods of treatment, nor, it must be confessed, was she always in the right.

In the meanwhile, the ship's doctor, several of the stewards and cooks, and quite a number of the passengers and crew had succumbed and been given hasty sea burial. The captain had caught the contagion and lay helpless in his stateroom, leaving only the second and third officers to manage the men whom every day saw the more unruly and boisterous. Save the two doctors and the dozen or so that had volunteered as assistants, the passengers were sunk in a state of lethargic horror. At first they had been panic stricken, but that had now subsided and they had become stolidly indifferent to the course of events. They recognized no ties except those of blood, and selfishly struggled for their individual creature-comforts—few, it must be acknowledged, they obtained, for each hour the discipline grew more lax and nothing could be obtained from the stewards and waiters without liberal tipping. In short, the plague ship had become a floating hell in which brute struggled with brute for survival.

Sick and giddy, Miss Appleton had staggered from out the fetid atmosphere below-decks, and now was leaning over the rail in a vain effort to catch some refreshing breeze. The *Caspar* lay in the trough of the sea idly rolling to the smooth swell. She had no steerage-way; the quartermaster had deserted the wheel; the engineers had given up the struggle; and despair had settled upon the ship. The heat was suffocating, and as Maud panted for breath, she was approached by the indefatigable Doctor Chandler, who had new cause of quarrel concerning the treatment of one of her patients. But they quarreled good-naturedly now, more in pleasant badinage and sharp repartee. Amid all their misery, it had become their one source of pleasure—a contest of wit and in which personality was lost in the keenness of professional zeal. Though their methods were quite diverse, he had lost as many patients as she, while in the number of recoveries she was one the better of him—the patient over which they had had their first dispute being now in the last stage of convalescence. This rankled the doctor, in a professional way, and did not in the least abate his faith in his treatment, while he ascribed her success to a phenomenal streak of luck, which gave her the patients that would have recovered any way.

But while they enjoyed themselves in their merry dispute, affairs of moment were approaching a crisis. The crew had long before deserted their stuffy fore-castle and camped on deck beneath sails spread as awnings. Later they were joined by the stokers, oilers and firemen, who brought along their sea-bags and blankets. Here, in full view of the terrorized passengers, they played cards, fought, cursed God and man, and refused all duty. Too powerful to break, the officers were forced to send their meals to them and to pray that they would not take to the boats. For all their lawlessness, however, they maintained a crude organization and enforced their rules with terrible penalties. Whenever one fell sick, he was carried away to the fore-castle and attended upon by shifts appointed for that purpose. Only this morning, the remainder of the cooks, waiters and mess-boys had deserted and come forward to join them. As the crowd of them, carrying all the paraphernalia for an improvised camp, came marching along the deck, they had received an otherwise than cool reception.

"I say, lads, what the—are we to do for cooks and mess-byes and grub?" queried one of the tars.

An instant sufficed for the mutineers to grasp the situation. With belaying pins and sheath-knives they drove the would-be deserters, bag and baggage, back to their duty, incidentally breaking a few heads and creating a momentary pandemonium. This incident had given the shifty second and third officers their cue, which they were soon to utilize with such disastrous consequence.

The mutineers quickly gave full intimation of their next procedure. They took possession of the boats; saw to it that they were seaworthy; and looting the hold, provisioned them. The passengers crowded the after-decks in a terror-stricken mass, while a few of the more clear-headed grouped round the officers and placed themselves at their service. As the day proceeded the panic grew: several mutineers they saw fall to the deck, overcome by the heat and the dread yellow jack. These were quickly carried away to the improvised hospital while their comrades worked the faster in completing their preparations.

Nor was this the only trouble which threatened. The three score Chinese between decks, who till now had manifested no discontent, were ripe for revolt. The contemplated desertion of the cooks and waiters had left them without food for twenty-four hours, and the officers had been forced to lock them in. Left to their fate, their yells and curses penetrated throughout the ship and at any moment they were expected to break forth. To add to the terror, the sick and dying, actuated by some subtle impulse, had broken out in loud cries and wailing.

It was at this moment that the officers put into execution the plan they had conceived. Why not turn these two destructive forces, which threatened them, against each other? The sailors were in just the mood for a fight, and as they never lost any love for their Asiatic brethren, it would not take much to precipitate one. The second officer argued that if they left the ship, those that remained would be at the mercy of the Chinese, and, since they were bound to take to the boats, it were best to be left behind in safety by cleaning the Chinese out. And again, he thought if the conflict were severe enough, the ranks of the mutineers would be so decimated, that he could conquer them with the help of the passengers, engineers, cooks and stewards.

Maud and Doctor Chandler had conducted their quarrel with the customary assurance of good comradeship and an agreement. Each was to choose a patient that had just come down and take exclusive control, brooking no interference and applying their own method in its extremity. As chance had it, they chose a pair which had just taken to their berths: a young Californian and his sister, returning from a visit to their father, an extensive mine-owner in Peru. She selected the young man, and he, the sister. Leaving the deck, they were elbowing their way among the passengers who had been sent below by the second officer. Amid the confusion on every side, as they entered the saloon, anarchy and hell broke forth.

The hub-bub which the Chinese incessantly maintained had ceased for a space; but now, redoubled in fury, it arose, amid the crashing of heavy bodies and the splintering of wood. They heard the rapid revolver shots of the two engineers set to guard them, followed by terrible oaths and shrieks of agony. Then the passageways were thronged and the yellow devils, inflamed with blood, were upon them. At this juncture, the door of the first officer's stateroom flew open, and he sprang out, an awful sight to behold, He was evidently suffering the tortures of delirium tremens: his eyes were set and dilated; his gigantic body convulsed with nervous spasms; his mouth a mass of froth and blood, Throwing himself into the doorway, armed with nothing but a huge battle-axe (some curio of his), he held the fiends at bay. The fleeing passengers blocked the other exit while those that remained beheld a wondrous struggle. Among the Chinese were some of the most redoubtable high-binders and hatchet-men of the coast—mercenary and trained fighters for the societies to which they owed their allegiance. Unlike the average Chinese, they were not cowardly: murder and bloodshed was their profession.

His battle-axe described flaming circles of steel as it flew back and forth, hither and thither, on its mission of death. At first, the marauders had rushed to their certain fate; but now they drew back, leaving several of their number beneath his feet. Into the narrow passage they knew he dare not pursue for lack of space in which to wield his great weapon. Stepping to the fore, their leader prepared to finish the struggle. It seemed as though David had come forward to face Goliath. His appearance belied his reputation as the wonderful Ah Sen, the fiercest of all hatchet-men: slender and effeminate of form, his delicate face seemed more that of a smooth-faced boy or woman, than that of a notorious desperado. Seizing the proffered knives of his men, thrice he cast one, full at his opponent. They leaped from his hand like rays of glancing light, turning half-way round in mid-air and burying themselves in the first officer's breast. Yet he seemed not to feel them. Again he tried; but this time, aiming at the throat, it hurtled past still intent on its mission and sank between the shoulders of one of the ladies, smuggling in the press at the other door. The highbinder, evincing not the slightest irritation at his failures, changed the method of attack. Seizing a hatchet, with the speed of the lightning, it pursued the path of its predecessors. Full on the forehead, it struck the giant, who swayed, tottered, sank to his knees: like a cat. Ah Sen followed his weapon to his fate. For one second the giant was endowed with the full vigor of his strength, and in that second, Ah Sen encountered him. There was no struggle. Rising to his feet and totally disregarding the knife which entered his side, he seized the slender-necked celestial by the head with both his hands—once—twice—his body whirled in giddying orbit round his head. There was a snap of bones and rending of flesh and Ah Sen sank to the floor, his neck wrung like a chicken's. The next instant he was joined by his antagonist, who fell beside him, literally hacked to pieces by a score of knives and hatchets.

In the meantime, the officers had been busy persuading the mutineers to do the one act of mercy before they left the ship. The celerity with which the contagion spread and its malignancy had put them in a fright, terrible to behold in strong, fearless men. They had been loth to listen, doggedly proceeding with the work of launching the boats, all bent upon their departure, but when the noise of the combat reached them and they knew that the Chinese were up, they forsook their tasks, hastily armed themselves with cutlasses distributed by the first officer, and sprang to the rescue.

Dividing into two parties, after killing a few stragglers which they caught murdering and robbing the passengers, they hemmed the remainder in the great saloon. Here, aided by the firearms of the officers, short but sanguinary conflict ensued, ending in the complete annihilation of the Asiatics.

Exhilarated by their success, their fiercest passions aroused by the battle and blood, all the brutishness of primeval man burst forth and the sailors were in the mood for any mischief. Bloodstained and panting, they grouped about the ringleader, who, qualified with all the attributes that go to make the sea-lawyer and popular demagogue, addressed them in a short but very trite speech:

"Ho! My lads! We've blasted the heathen and saved the ship—never say die says I—we've saved the passengers too—ain't it so? (Interruptions of "Aye, aye, that we have.") and in saving their bloody necks, we save their treasures too—what say ye? (An' where do we come off? Aye, that's the ticket!) Hold your jaw, Jack Gunderson: I'm coming to that. Yes, where do we get off? The company? (Ha! Ha! Ha! The skinflints! They'll pay us—see us with Davy Jones first!) Aye, my lads, that's not true enough: they'd see you in hell first, a-simmering like pork-chops in the galley. But here's the proposition: let the blasted passengers keep their bloomin' lives and us their treasure. What say ye, mates?" A burst of applause and cries of "A loot! A loot!" signified that it had been answered in the affirmative.

Charybdis had saved the passengers from Scylla to engulf them himself. It was not destruction, however, for quickly overcoming the officers and the remnant of their supporters, they assured the passengers of their good will and desire for suitable reward. The latter they at once proceeded to appropriate.

The sailors fell to their work with a vengeance, and in the scenes which followed, there was much mingling of the ludicrous and the tragic. Staterooms were ransacked, baggage of all descriptions turned upside down and inside out, and articles of wearing apparel appropriated; nor did they hesitate to personally despoil the passengers. Maud's aunt, an old lady, yet vigorous in body, mind and invective, led two of the tars, intent on her magnificent earrings, a merry chase. She finally sought refuge in the stateroom of the Senor Morella, an Honduras patriot, martial of aspect and afflicted with a wooden leg—a memento of his latest insurrection. He lay in his berth, dying, with his artificial limb unstrapped but near him. Seising this redoubtable weapon, she laid about her with such will and good purpose, as to down the robbers as fast as they stuck their heads inside. Quite a crowd ceased their looting to enjoy the fun. But the "old she-devil", as they delightfully termed her held her own against all comers.

As usual, the men broke into the spirit room, and while some became good-natured and jolly, others became the more violent. Fearing injury to her aunt, Maud hurried forward to persuade her into giving up her jewels, accompanied, of course, by Chandler, as protector. He was quickly dispossessed of his gold repeater and diamond links—little incidents which he scarcely heeded, so intent was he on guarding Maud. She, however, failed in her mission, barely missing being brained by her somewhat confused and belligerent relative. Though frustrated as a peacemaker, she well succeeded in involving herself and her protector in new troubles. One of the sailors, a big, hulking brute, rendered amorous by the too-frequent caress of certain plainly labeled bottles, threw his arm about her waist and drew her to him. Quick, full on the lips, he kissed her.

In that moment did the doctor become cognizant of a new sensation—a sensation he knew to be different from any he would have felt, had it been a woman other than her. A swift shoulder-blow, and the man lay in a heap on the floor. The next instant he was on his feet, cursing and glowering malignantly at the doctor, who in the heat of his anger made as though to repeat the performance. To Maud, events followed like a flash: the fellow's cutlass hissed through the air; a comrade interposed another; the blow was broken but still fell upon Chandler's head; and when she beheld the rush of blood, she experienced a strangely-intense and solicitous anxiety for him.

"A breeze! A breeze! My hearties! Fair wind for Mexico!" came a cry from above. A second saw the mutineers on deck, springing into the boats which lay alongside. The *Caspar* was deserted.

In the bloodstained cabin, amid the weeping and shrieking of women, the wailing of the fever-stricken, and the curses and groans of the dying combatants, Chandler, bathed in a baptism of blood, and Maud, flushed and fainting with what had transpired, sprang or rather tottered and fell into each other's arms. There, in that moment of horror, with all the hideousness of the present and terror of the future upon them, they confessed their newly-discovered and mutual love.

Many days had elapsed. Helpless, the *Caspar* drifted about with her cargo of misery and death. No help had come: none was expected, save through the safe arrival of the deserters in Mexico, which was merely problematic. In the absence of this disorderly element, the survivors had settled down to an orderly existence, systematized everything, isolated forward the fever patients, and were getting along far better than might have been expected from people in their condition. As a traveler in Yosemite loses all conception and appreciation of height and distance, so had they lost all horror of their situation. Continually facing death, they had come to fear it not; and great indeed must have been the occurrence which could have surprised them from out their placidity. They had not broken under the strain but merely accustomed themselves to it. In fact, they were progressing finely, and too much could not be attributed to the two doctors, who, while loving, still quarreled over methods.

Meanwhile, Maud and the doctor, while in no wise neglecting their other cases, devoted themselves night and day to the particular ones of the brother and sister. They had been very sick, but never, even in the worst of crises when the toss of a penny would have almost decided life or death, had the two physicians even dreamed of consulting each other. They had put into the fullest operation their favorite methods, and so strong was their professional rivalry that they abided the result with far more anxiety than is usually the lot of the patient to receive from its physician. In fact, so extreme had the contest become, that they devoted all their spare time to the nursing, scarcely seeing each other, save to quarrel about the merits of their respective schools or to twit each other, as the case might be, on any bad signs which might have been manifested. Still it seemed as though the superiority of either was not to be thus exemplified, for neither patient had died, and both were now fairly convalescent. Nevertheless, each had been surprised at the zeal displayed by the other, and now, when all danger was past, all doubts vanished, their surprise grew as their zeal flagged not.

The days took their allotted course, slipping silently, imperceptibly, each into the other, while no new incidents or happenings arose to vary the monotony of their existence. In truth, the gods had smiled upon them in their distress. The *Caspar* encountered no storms while the fierceness of the epidemic began to abate. Perhaps, because everybody, with the miraculous exception of the two physicians, had been either killed or cured. Everything was on the mend: nothing was apprehended except bad weather, and even in that the *Caspar* stood a fair show of remaining afloat. In case of storms, small sails had been prepared by which to heave to and ride them out. With the dwindled company and the great boilers, the engineers had no difficulty in maintaining the fresh water supply, while, as part of the cargo was composed of food, little was to be feared from starvation. Slowly the summer dragged on, but quickly the sick list grew smaller, till finally, amid great rejoicing and festivity, it had become totally negated and the ship thoroughly fumigated.

But while everything was so bright, Maud found herself tormented; by strange thoughts and discovered an inconsistent vein in her nature which she had never dreamed of. Again and again she summoned herself to judgement, but always to judge in vain, for in despair she invariably threw the case out of court. Sometimes she came to herself and was appalled at the thoughts which had risen uncalled in her mind, at the visions she unconsciously contemplated. Her life became one tangled mesh of self-analytical whys and wherefores, ifs and musts, pros and cons. The more she endeavored to reason with herself the more entangled and confused she became. Cold memories of some possible past mistake caused her to often shudder, to avoid the present, and to fear the future which must be shaped by the impress of that possible wrong-doing. Still she could not find the heart to blame herself: she could only not understand.

As it fared with her, so fared it with Chandler. He also found himself involved in a sea of seeming self-inconsistency. But he behaved differently from Maud—she was a woman. His masculinity and choleric disposition asserted itself, and not only did he clearly see his past mistake, but he grew enraged and waxed indignant at himself, often cursing the son of his father with such sublime abstraction from self as to be truly startling. Still, in the obscurity of his mental vision, he could see so far and no farther. If he could have seen beyond, doubtless he would not have figuratively kicked himself so often, nor would his life had been tinged with the savage melancholy which now gnawed at his heart-strings so unceasingly.

With these inward ills tormenting them, their intercourse with each other was not exactly that of fond lovers; and their very cognizance of this but increased the pitch of their misery. They constantly upbraided themselves after the many such unsatisfactory meetings, as being the causes of the same—nor was this the less severe, for each unselfishly and ignorantly pocketed all the blame, deeming the other to have the person injured. Under such circumstances, he became gloomy and irritable, while she well hid hers beneath a mask of gaiety and enthusiasm in all the little social events on shipboard. Very naturally, this diversity of mood drew them the farther apart.

And so, while the collective prospects of the little community went from good to better, their individual affairs traveled with unseemly haste from bad to worse. Logically, this stretching out to the extremes must reach an end sometime, and both, intuitively recognizing this, pondered expectantly over the outcome. To make matters worse, they no longer quarreled: this new state of affairs was maintained with the stiff awkwardness of self-consciousness, from which each suffered the more acutely, never suspecting the other to be in the same dilemma. So affairs rapidly approached a crisis, and one night, when the situation had become almost absolutely unbearable to both parties, the electric search-light of a man of war, sent out in quest of them vaguely foreshadowed to each a cessation of their troubles.

The passengers were crowding the weather rail of the

Caspar, devouring the lights of the vessel in the offing and feasting their eyes upon its dim, bulky loom. Amid this scene of boisterous rejoicing, Maud felt strangely out of place. It jarred upon her—this gregarious mass which clustered like bees on every hand. She became aware of a longing for solitude. Yielding to the mood, she slipped away and climbed to the deserted bridge.

Similar had been the feeling of Chandler, and similar the action. He burned from one side as she did from the other. Face to face, with the glare of the search-light shining full upon them, they met, midway on the bridge. The next instant and they were in darkness. He had taken her hand, yet they spoke not as they gazed on the dancing lights, heard the merry scream of the boatswain's whistles upon the battleship, and dimly discerned a boat as it sprang to the man of war's stroke. Nearer and nearer it came; but it was with a strange apathy that they watched it. The next moment and it would be alongside. Seemingly, they both resolved and spoke at the same time. What each said seemed to startle the other. Surprise, doubt, assurance, gratification, happiness, in turn were mutually delineated upon their countenances. What was said they only knew, but it was with light steps and joyous faces, all wreathed in smiles, that they joined their companions of the now-to-be-abandoned plague ship.

Extract from the *San Francisco Daily Herald* of six weeks later —

At the Palace Hotel, the consummation of a
happy romance, strangely connected with the

ill-fated Caspar, *is about to be attained. Miss Maud Appleton—an M.D. by the way—of New Orleans, and Doctor Chandler of Boston—the two that rendered such effective service in overcoming the plague on the* Caspar—*are to marry respectively, Mr. Charles Waldworth, Stanford '93, and his sister, the charming Miss Waldworth, of local social note. It is whispered that Mr. and Miss Waldworth, while ill with the fever, were made test cases for a professional contest between the two M.D.s, and so strenuous and successful were their efforts, that the fruition is the happy dual marriage to be celebrated shortly. But more of this anon.*

THE HANDSOME
CABIN BOY

THE HANDSOME CABIN BOY (1899)

"AND THE DAPPER YOUNG FELLOW was—"

"None other than the veiled woman, of course."

"O, pshaw!" I cried. "That's well enough for a Sunday newspaper, but in real life people are not so easily misled."

"Look at the authentic instances—women serving as soldiers, sailors, scouts—"

"Bosh!"

"Why, there's my little brother Bob, as clever an impersonator—"

"Bosh!"

"People are fooled every day and—"

"Stuff and nonsense," I said. "Anyone but a ninny should penetrate such a make-up at a glance. I don't think much of a fellow who can't tell a man from a woman. Catch me napping that way."

"I'll catch you," cried Jack.

"I like that," was my reply. "I'll wager I fool you within six months."

"Done! For how much?"

"The loser to foot a supper; the setting, ordering, and inviting of the same to be at the winner's discretion."

"Done!" We shook hands, and the fellows crowded round with all sorts of advice and persiflage. Thus was the seed sown, out of which was to spring the never-to-be-forgotten romance of "The Handsome Cabin Boy."

The succeeding fortnight found me in solitary grandeur aboard my schooner yacht *Falcon*, bound for a short cruise to Honolulu. We had hardly sunk the Farralone Light when my suspicions were aroused. From the cook to the sailing-master complaints began to pour in about the new cabin boy. They held he was willing enough, but worthless. At the last moment, Billy, the old boy, had left us in the lurch, and my agent, to whom all such matters were entrusted, had hastily procured the present incumbent.

As they said, he was willing enough, but—in short, he was ignorant of his duties and totally unfit for such a position. Yet he tried so hard that everybody was drawn toward him. And he was such a handsome lad. Dark-eyed, rosy-cheeked, with a delicate olive complexion and an exquisite oval—small wonder that he recalled to my mind the bet with Jack Haliday. And then, for the slender lad of fifteen or sixteen that he appeared, there was a vague, insinuating fullness about the figure, which did not fail to corroborate my suspicions.

But I held my hush and awaited confirmation. This came sooner than I expected. The sailing-master and myself were on the poop, one noon, with our sextants, bent on shooting the sun. The lad came up the companionway with a pan of soot and ashes; he had just cleaned the cabin stove.

Instead of going to the lee, he stepped to the weather rail and let fly the refuse. And fly it did—backwards, of course, and all over us.

Digging a handful out of his eyes, the sailing-master grabbed the young rascal by the arm. Now Nelson was a rough son of the sea and had a mellifluous command of the vernacular which serves for emphasis to those who sail the same. He shook him up and down and cursed him with as virile a combination of English and Scandinavian oaths as was ever my luck to hear.

The boy lost his wits and began to cry. Picking up the pan, he started for the cabin, but just opposite me, reeled and toppled over. I caught him before he could fall, and—well, my arm had strayed in forbidden pastures too often to be mistaken now.

"Why, you're a girl!" I cried.

The man at the wheel began to snicker, so I hurried her below to save her from confusion before the men. There she cried, and sobbed, and carried on, till I was almost as distracted myself, in my efforts to soothe her. At last she calmed down.

"O, sir," she began, "I hope you won't be angry with me. I—he—Mr.—"

"It's Jack Haliday's doing, isn't it?" I interrupted.

"Yes, sir."

"Then you know all about the bet, and you'll have to testify that I discovered your—er—identity."

"Yes, sir, and he'll be angry because I lost. Boo—hoo—oo—"

"O, you did very well." I thought she needed a little

cheering. "The cook would never have discovered—say! how the deuce—you'll have to change your—"

It was indeed embarrassing for both of us. And that blundering cook had never tumbled! I called him into the cabin.

"Tell off that German deck boy to help you," I ordered. "And go to your room and pack up Miss—er—"

"E—E—Eastman," sobbed the disconsolate bundle on the floor.

"And pack up Miss Eastman's belongings. Take them to the spare state-room and make everything comfortable. I'll see you get extra pay for this trip. Go! Don't stand there all day!" I could not help laughing at his round-eyed wonder.

"I don't know what to do in the way of suitable clothes," I said, as she entered her new berth in the wake of a trim little sea-chest.

"That's all right, sir," she replied, between her sobs. "I b—brought some dresses along."

"Strike me blind!" cried the cook, as the door shut. "O, I beg your pardon, sir; but do you mean to tell me, sir, that he's a—a she? Think of it!—and me a married man! What'll my wife say?"

Though I tried to explain that there was no necessity of his wife knowing, he wandered away to the galley, more woe-begone, if anything, than the poor creature who had caused his distress. Still, I could sympathize with him, realizing as I did, my own false position, and knowing how the sailors must be haw-hawing among themselves.

Dinner was sent into her, and it was not till next morning that she showed herself. And then it was a demure little maid, for all her short brown locks. It seemed a pity they had been clipped for the sake of a paltry bet.

"What will your people say?" I asked, in the course of explanations. "Do they know?"

"My brother does. I came with his consent."

"Your brother's a scoundrel and ought to be horse-whipped. It's disgraceful, to say the least."

"How?"

This was a poser. How? I began to comprehend the mess Jack Haliday had got me into. How? What innocence!

"You must have been brought up in a convent," I said bluntly.

"Yes, sir; I went to the Sacred Heart until a year ago."

Worse and worse—it was no light responsibility thus thrust upon me. I finally wormed her story from her. She had lost her mother during her childhood, and her father, a small tradesman, had educated her at the Convent of the Sacred Heart. Things had gone from bad to worse with him, and when he died, she and her brother were left penniless. To curtail the story: they had become protégés of Haliday's. She had shown an aptitude for the stage, and Haliday encouraged her, prophesying that someday the metropolitan vaudeville would open its arms to a soubrette of no mean ability.

"And when he asked this favor of me," she concluded, "what could I do? Refuse, after all he had done for me?"

Well, the yacht took on new life. Strange how this chit of a child, this girl of sixteen, brightened things up! She became the idol of all hands and even Nelson apologized—first time the stubborn dog ever did such a thing, I'll wager.

She could play the piano fairly well, and though her voice was not strong and had no register, her singing was sweet indeed.

When we arrived at Honolulu, I was for making arrangements to send her back by steamer; but the guiless creature would not hear of it, and looked so miserable when I insisted, that I gave in. Besides, nobody knew us. And she—why, she had no conception of evil, and to undeceive her was a task beyond my power. I supplied her with funds, and she soon had a stunning array of gowns and other female fripperies. Then we took in the concerts of the Hawaiian Band, made long drives into the country, and visited many places of interest and recreation. We had a delightful time; but the best of good things must end, and a month later found us off the Golden Gate. Tomorrow we should be in San-Francisco.

Tomorrow—I half sighed as I lighted a cigar, and glanced at her state-room door. What were her dreams, I wondered. Then I thought of my long, lonely cruises. How bright this one had been! Life took on new possibilities, as I began to realize some of its hitherto unknown charms—charms which my benedict friends never ceased to dwell upon. How she had changed things! A neatly turned ankle on the cabin stairs, a twinkling slipper along the deck, a girl's light laughter, a song at twilight, a—in short, the ineffable something of a woman's presence. I was startled at the thought. Let me see: sixteen—twenty-six; nineteen—twenty-nine; no, that would be too long to wait, eighteen—twenty-eight—that's it. And not such a disparity after all. Two years! What would not two years do?

Development, the rounding of that mind—aye, and that form, already so rich of promise. Two years, and then—

"Eight bells!"

The clamor of changing watch had destroyed the fairy pictures; so I tossed away my cigar and went to bed.

Jack Haliday and the whole crowd were at the club-house pier to meet us. Evidently, the lookout of the Merchants' Exchange had telegraphed our arrival off the Heads the previous night. They trooped aboard in a body, and I trembled for Miss Eastman. However, Clara, as I had come to call her, faced the ordeal bravely. The subdued expectancy and smothered giggles angered me. Jack Haliday opened the ball at once.

"I say, you know, about that supper—"

"What about it?" I asked sharply.

"Well, I've made all the plans, but I thought it better to submit them to you. You might make a few suggestions, you know."

"You've made all the plans!" I shouted. "I have an idea that the ordering of this supper belongs to me."

"Ha! ha! ha!" Everybody began to laugh.

"Hope you had a pleasant trip, Miss Eastman," he said, turning to her.

"O, I did," she assured him, though I could see her lips were trembling.

"How did you discover it?" he asked, addressing me.

"Why she fainted in my arms, and—"

"Ho! ho! He! he! he!" the crowd fairly roared, and I beamed triumphantly on my discomfited opponent.

"Was he angry?" continued the imperturbable Haliday.

"No," Clara replied, "he was real nice. And when we got to Honolulu he wanted to send me home on the steamer, but I wouldn't let him. Then we had a gorgeous time— bought me candy and gloves, took me buggy riding, and—"

With this the crowd went mad. They slapped Jack on the shoulder, poked him in the ribs, and hugged each other in ecstasies of glee.

"Why, you ninny!" Jack cried. "That's my brother Bob."

"Impossible," I rejoined. "Why, when she fainted in my arms, I—"

At this juncture speech failed me, for the modest Miss Eastman turned a couple of back-flips, came up smiling, thrust a hand into her maidenly bosom and drew forth— heavens!—a couple of pneumatic cushions, the kind used by football players.

It were needless for me to tell how I led the stampede to the club-house; how the supper came off, with Bob Haliday at the head of the table; or how, to this day, the mere mention of "The Handsome Cabin Boy" arouses a certain choler which I can never hope to overcome.

THE LOST
POACHER

THE LOST
POACHER
(1901)

"BUT THEY WON'T TAKE excuses. You're across the line, and that's enough. They'll take you. In you go, Siberia and the salt-mines. And as for Uncle Sam, why, what's he to know about it? Never a word will get back to the States. 'The *Mary Thomas*,' the papers will say, 'the *Mary Thomas* lost with all hands. Probably in a typhoon in the Japanese seas.' That's what the papers will say, and people, too. In you go, Siberia and the salt-mines. Dead to the world and kith and kin, though you live fifty years."

In such manner John Lewis, commonly known as the "sea-lawyer," settled the matter out of hand.

It was a serious moment in the forecastle of the *Mary Thomas*. No sooner had the watch below begun to talk the trouble over, than the watch on deck came down and joined them. As there was no wind, every hand could be spared with the exception of the man at the wheel, and he remained only for the sake of discipline. Even "Bub" Russell, the cabin-boy, had crept forward to hear what was going on.

However, it was a serious moment, as the grave faces of the sailors bore witness. For the three preceding months, the *Mary Thomas* sealing schooner had hunted the seal pack along the coast of Japan and north to Bering Sea. Here, on the Asiatic side of the sea, they were forced to give over the chase, or rather, to go no farther; for beyond, the Russian cruisers patrolled forbidden ground, where the seals might breed in peace.

A week before she had fallen into a heavy fog accompanied by calm. Since then, the fog-bank had not lifted, and the only wind had been light airs and catspaws. This in itself was not so bad, for the sealing schooners are never in a hurry so long as they are in the midst of the seals; but the trouble lay in the fact that the current at this point bore heavily to the north. Thus the *Mary Thomas* had unwittingly drifted across the line, and every hour she was penetrating, unwillingly, farther and farther into the dangerous waters where the Russian bear kept guard.

How far she had drifted no man knew. The sun had not been visible for a week, nor the stars, and the captain had been unable to take observations in order to determine his position. At any moment a cruiser might swoop down and hale the crew away to Siberia. The fate of other poaching seal-hunters was too well known to the men of the *Mary Thomas*, and there was cause for grave faces.

"Mine friends," spoke up a German boat-steerer, "it vas a pad piziness. Shust as ve make a big catch, und all honest, somedings go wrong, und der Russians nab us, dake our skins and our schooner, und send us mit der anarchists to Siberia. Ach! a pretty pad piziness!"

"Yes, that's where it hurts," the sea lawyer went on. "Fifteen hundred skins in the salt piles, and all honest, a big pay-day coming to every man Jack of us, and then to be captured and lose it all! It'd be different if we'd been poaching, but it's all honest work in open water."

"But if we haven't done anything wrong, they can't do anything to us, can they?" Bub queried.

"It strikes me as 'ow it ain't the proper thing for a boy o' your age shovin' in when 'is elders is talkin'," protested an English sailor, from over the edge of his bunk.

"Oh, that's all right, Jack," answered the sea-lawyer. "He's a perfect right to. Ain't he just as liable to lose his wages as the rest of us?"

"Wouldn't give thruppence for them!" Jack sniffed back. He had been planning to go home and see his family in Chelsea when he was paid off, and he was now feeling rather blue over the highly possible loss, not only of his pay, but of his liberty.

"How are they to know?" the sea-lawyer asked in answer to Bub's previous question. "Here we are in forbidden water. How do they know but what we came here of our own accord? Here we are, fifteen hundred skins in the hold. How do they, know whether we got them in open water or in the closed sea? Don't you see, Bub, the evidence is all against us. If you caught a man with his pockets full of apples like those which grow on your tree, and if you caught him in your tree besides, what'd you think if he told you he couldn't help it, and had just been sort of blown there, and that anyway those apples came from some other tree—what'd you think, eh?"

Bub saw it clearly when put in that light and shook his head despondently.

"You'd rather be dead than go to Siberia," one of the boat-pullers said. "They put you into the salt-mines and work you till you die. Never see daylight again. Why, I've heard tell of one fellow that was chained to his mate, and that mate died. And they were both chained together! And if they send you to the quicksilver mines you get salivated. I'd rather be hung than salivated."

"Wot's salivated?" Jack asked, suddenly sitting up in his bunk at the hint of fresh misfortunes.

"Why, the quicksilver gets into your blood; I think that's the way. And your gums all swell like you had the scurvy, only worse, and your teeth get loose in your jaws. And big ulcers form, and then you die horrible. The strongest man can't last long a-mining quicksilver."

"A pad piziness," the boat-steerer reiterated, dolorously, in the silence which followed. "A pad piziness. I vish I was in Yokohama. Eh? Vot vas dot?"

The vessel had suddenly heeled over. The decks were aslant. A tin pannikin rolled down the inclined plane, rattling and banging. From above came the slapping of canvas and the quivering rat-tat-tat of the after leech of the loosely stretched foresail. Then the mate's voice sang down the hatch, "All hands on deck and make sail!"

Never had such summons been answered with more enthusiasm. The calm had broken. The wind had come which was to carry them south into safety. With a wild cheer all sprang on deck. Working with mad haste, they flung out topsails, flying jibs and staysails. As they worked, the fog-bank lifted and the black vault of heaven, bespangled with the old familiar stars, rushed into view. When all was ship-shape, the *Mary Thomas* was lying gallantly over on her side to a beam wind and plunging ahead due south.

"Steamer's lights ahead on the port bow, sir!" cried the lookout from his station on the forecastle-head. There was excitement in the man's voice.

The captain sent Bub below for his night-glasses. Everybody crowded to the lee-rail to gaze at the suspicious stranger, which already began to loom up vague and indistinct. In those unfrequented waters the chance was one in a thousand that it could be anything else than a Russian patrol. The captain was still anxiously gazing through the glasses, when a flash of flame left the stranger's side, followed by the loud report of a cannon. The worst fears were confirmed. It was a patrol, evidently firing across the bows of the *Mary Thomas* in order to make her heave to.

"Hard down with your helm!" the captain commanded the steers-man, all the life gone out of his voice. Then to the crew, "Back over the jib and foresail! Run down the flying jib! Clew up the foretopsail! And aft here and swing on to the main-sheet!"

The *Mary Thomas* ran into the eye of the wind, lost headway, and fell to courtsying gravely to the long seas rolling up from the west.

The cruiser steamed a little nearer and lowered a boat. The sealers watched in heartbroken silence. They could see the white bulk of the boat as it was slacked away to the water, and its crew sliding aboard. They could hear the creaking of the davits and the commands of the officers.

Then the boat sprang away under the impulse of the oars and came toward them. The wind had been rising, and already the sea was too rough to permit the frail craft to lie alongside the tossing schooner; but watching their chance and taking advantage of the boarding ropes thrown to them, an officer and a couple of men clambered aboard. The boat then sheered off into safety and lay to its oars, a young midshipman, sitting in the stern and holding the yoke-lines, in charge.

The officer, whose uniform disclosed his rank as that of second lieutenant in the Russian navy, went below with the captain of the *Mary Thomas* to look at the ship's papers. A few minutes later he emerged, and upon his sailors removing the hatch-covers, passed down into the hold with a lantern to inspect the salt piles. It was a goodly heap which confronted him—fifteen hundred fresh skins, the season's catch; and under the circumstances he could have had but one conclusion.

"I am very sorry," he said, in broken English to the sealing captain, when he again came on deck, "but it is my duty, in the name of the tsar, to seize your vessel as a poacher caught with fresh skins in the closed sea. The penalty, as you may know, is confiscation and imprisonment."

The captain of the *Mary Thomas* shrugged his shoulders in seeming indifference and turned away. Although they may restrain all outward show, strong men, under unmerited misfortune, are sometimes very close to tears. Just then the vision of his little California home, and of the wife and two yellow-haired boys, was strong upon him, and there was a strange, choking sensation in his throat, which made him afraid that if he attempted to speak, he would sob instead.

And also there was upon him the duty he owed his men. No weakness before them, for he must be a tower of strength to sustain them in misfortune. He had already explained to the second lieutenant and knew the hopelessness of the situation. As the sea-lawyer had said, the evidence was all against him. So he turned aft, and fell to pacing up and down the poop of the vessel over which he was no longer commander.

The Russian officer now took temporary charge. He ordered more of his men aboard and had all the canvas clewed up and furled snugly away. While this was being done, the boat plied back and forth between the two vessels, passing a heavy hawser, which was made fast to the great towing-bitts on the schooner's forecastle-head. During all this work the sealers stood about in sullen groups. It was madness to think of resisting, with the guns of a man-of-war not a biscuit-toss away; but they refused to lend a hand, preferring instead to maintain a gloomy silence.

Having accomplished his task, the lieutenant ordered all but four of his men back into the boat. Then the midshipman, a lad of sixteen, looking strangely mature and dignified in his uniform and sword, came aboard to take command of the captured sealer. Just as the lieutenant prepared to depart, his eyes chanced to alight upon Bub. Without a word of warning, he seized him by the arm and dropped him over the rail into the waiting boat; and then, with a parting wave of his hand, he followed him.

It was only natural that Bub should be frightened at this unexpected happening. All the terrible stories he had heard of the Russians served to make him fear them, and now returned to his mind with double force. To be captured by them was bad enough, but to be carried off by them, away from his comrades, was a fate of which he had not dreamed.

"Be a good boy, Bub," the captain called to him, as the boat drew away from the *Mary Thomas*'s side, "and tell the truth!"

"Aye, aye, sir!" he answered, bravely enough, by all outward appearance. He felt a certain pride of race and was ashamed to be a coward before these strange enemies, these wild Russian bears.

"Und be politeful!" the German boat-steerer added, his rough voice lifting across the water like a fog-horn.

Bub waved his hand in farewell, and his mates clustered along the rail as they answered with a cheering shout. He found room in the stern-sheets, where he fell to regarding the lieutenant. He didn't look so wild or bearish, after all—very much like other men, Bub concluded, and the sailors were much the same as all other man-of-war's men he had ever known. Nevertheless, as his feet struck the steel deck of the cruiser, he felt as if he had entered the portals of a prison.

For a few minutes he was left unheeded. The sailors hoisted the boat up and swung it in on the davits. Then great clouds of black smoke poured out of the funnels, and they were under way—to Siberia, Bub could not help but think. He saw the *Mary Thomas* swing abruptly into line as she took the pressure from the hawser, and her side-lights, red and green, rose and fell as she was towed through the sea.

Bub's eyes dimmed at the melancholy sight, but just then the lieutenant came to take him down to the commander, and he straightened up and set his lips firmly, as if this were a very commonplace affair and he were used to being sent to Siberia every day in the week. The cabin in which the commander sat was like a palace compared to the humble fittings of the *Mary Thomas*, and the commander himself, in gold lace and dignity, was a most august personage, quite unlike the simple man who navigated his schooner on the trail of the seal pack.

Bub now quickly learned why he had been brought aboard, and in the prolonged questioning which followed, told nothing but the plain truth. The truth was harmless; only a lie could have injured his cause. He did not know much, except that they had been sealing far to the south in open water, and that when the calm and fog came down upon them, being close to the line, they had drifted across. Again and again he insisted that they had not lowered a boat or shot a seal in the week they had been drifting about in the forbidden sea; but the commander chose to consider all that he said to be a tissue of falsehoods, and adopted a bullying tone in an effort to frighten the boy. He threatened and cajoled by turns, but failed in the slightest to shake Bub's statements, and at last ordered him out of his presence.

By some oversight, Bub was not put in anybody's charge, and wandered up on deck unobserved. Sometimes the sailors, in passing, bent curious glances upon him, but otherwise he was left strictly alone. Nor could he have attracted much attention, for he was small, the night dark, and the watch on deck intent on its own business. Stumbling over the strange decks, he made his way aft where he could look upon the side-lights of the *Mary Thomas*, following steadily in the rear.

For a long while he watched, and then lay down in the darkness close to where the hawser passed over the stern to the captured schooner. Once an officer came up and examined the straining rope to see if it were chafing, but Bub cowered away in the shadow undiscovered. This, however, gave him an idea which concerned the lives and liberties of twenty-two men, and which was to avert crushing sorrow from more than one happy home many thousand miles away.

In the first place, he reasoned, the crew were all guiltless of any crime, and yet were being carried relentlessly away to imprisonment in Siberia—a living death, he had heard, and he believed it implicitly. In the second place, he was a prisoner, hard and fast, with no chance of escape. In the third, it was possible for the twenty-two men on the *Mary Thomas* to escape. The only thing which bound them was a four-inch hawser. They dared not cut it at their end, for a watch was sure to be maintained upon it by their Russian captors; but at this end, ah! at his end...

Bub did not stop to reason further. Wriggling close to the hawser, he opened his jack-knife and went to work. The blade was not very sharp, and he sawed away, rope-yarn by rope-yarn, the awful picture of the solitary Siberian exile he must endure growing clearer and more terrible at every stroke. Such a fate was bad enough to undergo with one's comrades, but to face it alone seemed frightful. And besides, the very act he was performing was sure to bring greater punishment upon him.

In the midst of such somber thoughts, he heard footsteps approaching. He wriggled away into the shadow. An officer stopped where he had been working, half-stooped to examine the hawser, then changed his mind and straightened up. For a few minutes he stood there, gazing at the lights of the captured schooner, and then went forward again.

Now was the time! Bub crept back and went on sawing. Now two parts were severed. Now three. But one remained. The tension upon this was so great that it readily yielded. Splash! The freed end went overboard. He lay quietly, his heart in his mouth, listening. No one on the cruiser but himself had heard.

He saw the red and green lights of the *Mary Thomas* grow dimmer and dimmer. Then a faint hallo came over the water from the Russian prize crew. Still nobody heard. The smoke continued to pour out of the cruiser's funnels, and her propellers throbbed as mightily as ever.

What was happening on the *Mary Thomas*? Bub could only surmise; but of one thing he was certain: his comrades would assert themselves and overpower the four sailors and the midshipman. A few minutes later he saw a small flash, and straining his ears heard the very faint report of a pistol. Then, oh joy! both the red and green lights suddenly disappeared. The *Mary Thomas* was retaken!

Just as an officer came aft, Bub crept forward, and hid

away in one of the boats. Not an instant too soon. The alarm was given. Loud voices rose in command. The cruiser altered her course. An electric search-light began to throw its white rays across the sea, here, there, everywhere; but in its flashing path no tossing schooner was revealed.

Bub went to sleep soon after that, nor did he wake till the gray of dawn. The engines were pulsing monotonously, and the water, splashing noisily, told him the decks were being washed down. One sweeping glance, and he saw that they were alone on the expanse of ocean. The *Mary Thomas* had escaped. As he lifted his head, a roar of laughter went up from the sailors. Even the officer, who ordered him taken below and locked up, could not quite conceal the laughter in his eyes. Bub thought often in the days of confinement which followed, that they were not very angry with him for what he had done.

He was not far from right. There is a certain innate nobility deep down in the hearts of all men, which forces them to admire a brave act, even if it is performed by an enemy. The Russians were in nowise different from other men. True, a boy had outwitted them; but they could not blame him, and they were sore puzzled as to what to do with him. It would never do to take a little mite like him in to represent all that remained of the lost poacher.

So, two weeks later, a United States man-of-war, steaming out of the Russian port of Vladivostok, was signaled by a Russian cruiser. A boat passed between the two ships, and a small boy dropped over the rail upon the deck of the American vessel. A week later he was put ashore at Hakodate, and after some telegraphing, his fare was paid on the railroad to Yokohama.

From the depot, he hurried through the quaint Japanese streets to the harbor and hired a sampan boatman to put him aboard a certain vessel whose familiar rigging had quickly caught his eye. Her gaskets were off, her sails unfurled; she was just starting back to the United States. As he came closer, a crowd of sailors sprang upon the forecastle head, and the windlass-bars rose and fell as the anchor was torn from its muddy bottom.

"Yankee ship come down the ribber!" the sea-lawyer's voice rolled out as he led the anchor song.

"Pull, my bully boys, pull!" roared back the old familiar chorus, the men's bodies lifting and bending to the rhythm.

Bub Russell paid the boatman and stepped on deck. The anchor was forgotten. A mighty cheer went up from the men, and almost before he could catch his breath he was on the shoulders of the captain, surrounded by his mates, and endeavoring to answer twenty questions to the second.

The next day a schooner hove to off a Japanese fishing village, sent ashore four sailors and a little midshipman, and sailed away. These men did not talk English, but they had money and quickly made their way to Yokohama. From that day the Japanese village folk never heard anything more about them, and they are still a much-talked-of mystery. As the Russian government never said anything about the incident, the United States is still ignorant of the whereabouts of the lost poacher, nor has she ever heard, officially, of the way in which some of her citizens "shanghaied" five subjects of the tsar.

Even nations have secrets sometimes.

CHRIS FARRINGTON, ABLE SEAMAN

CHRIS FARRINGTON, ABLE SEAMAN (1901)

"IF YOU VAS IN der old country ships, a liddle shaver like you vood pe only der boy, und you vood wait on der able seamen. Und ven der able seaman sing out, 'Boy, der water-jug!' you vood jump quick, like a shot, und bring der water-jug. Und ven der able seaman sing out, 'Boy, my boots!' you vood get der boots. Und you vood pe politeful, und say 'Yessir' und 'No sir.' But you pe in der American ship, und you t'ink you are so good as der able seamen. Chris, mine boy, I haf ben a sailorman for twenty-two years, und do you t'ink you are so good as me? I vas a sailorman pefore you vas borned, und I knot und reef und splice ven you play mit topstrings und fly kites."

"But you are unfair, Emil!" cried Chris Farrington, his sensitive face flushed and hurt. He was a slender though strongly built young fellow of seventeen, with Yankee ancestry writ large all over him.

"Dere you go vonce again!" the Swedish sailor exploded. "My name is Mister Johansen, und a kid of a boy like you call me 'Emil!' It vas insulting, und comes pecause of der American ship!"

"But you call me 'Chris!'" the boy expostulated, reproachfully.

"But you vas a boy."

"Who does a man's work," Chris retorted. "And because I do a man's work I have as much right to call you by your first name as you me. We are all equals in this fo'castle, and you know it. When we signed for the voyage in San Francisco, we signed as sailors on the *Sophie Sutherland* and there was no difference made with any of us. Haven't I always done my work? Did I ever shirk? Did you or any other man ever have to take a wheel for me? Or a lookout? Or go aloft?"

"Chris is right," interrupted a young English sailor. "No man has had to do a tap of his work yet. He signed as good as any of us, and he's shown himself as good—"

"Better!" broke in a Nova Scotia man. "Better than some of us! When we struck the sealing-grounds he turned out to be next to the best boat-steerer aboard. Only French Louis, who'd been at it for years, could beat him. I'm only a boat-puller, and you're only a boat-puller, too, Emil Johansen, for all your twenty-two years at sea. Why don't you become a boat-steerer?"

"Too clumsy," laughed the Englishman, "and too slow."

"Little that counts, one way or the other," joined in Dane Jurgensen, coming to the aid of his Scandinavian brother. "Emil is a man grown and an able seaman; the boy is neither."

And so the argument raged back and forth, the Swedes, Norwegians and Danes, because of race kinship, taking the part of Johansen, and the English, Canadians and Americans taking the part of Chris. From an unprejudiced point of view, the right was on the side of Chris. As he had truly said, he did a man's work, and the same work that any of them did. But they were prejudiced, and badly so, and out of the words which passed rose a standing quarrel which divided the forecastle into two parties.

The *Sophie Sutherland* was a seal-hunter, registered out of San Francisco, and engaged in hunting the furry sea-animals along the Japanese coast north to Bering Sea. The other vessels were two-masted schooners, but she was a three-master and the largest in the fleet. In fact, she was a full-rigged, three-topmast schooner, newly built.

Although Chris Farrington knew that justice was with him, and that he performed all his work faithfully and well, many a time, in secret thought, he longed for some pressing emergency to arise whereby he could demonstrate to the Scandinavian seamen that he also was an able seaman.

But one stormy night, by an accident for which he was in nowise accountable, in overhauling a spare anchor-chain he had all the fingers of his left hand badly crushed. And his hopes were likewise crushed, for it was impossible for him to continue hunting with the boats, and he was forced to stay idly aboard until his fingers should heal. Yet, although he little dreamed it, this very accident was to give him the long-looked-for opportunity.

One afternoon in the latter part of May the *Sophie Sutherland* rolled sluggishly in a breathless calm. The seals were abundant, the hunting good, and the boats were all away and out of sight. And with them was almost every man of the crew. Besides Chris, there remained only the captain, the sailing-master and the Chinese cook.

The captain was captain only by courtesy. He was an old man, past eighty, and blissfully ignorant of the sea and its ways; but he was the owner of the vessel, and hence the honorable title. Of course the sailing-master, who was really captain, was a thorough-going seaman. The mate, whose post was aboard, was out with the boats, having temporarily taken Chris's place as boat-steerer.

When good weather and good sport came together, the boats were accustomed to range far and wide, and often did not return to the schooner until long after dark. But for all that it was a perfect hunting day, Chris noted a growing anxiety on the part of the sailing-master. He paced the deck nervously and was constantly sweeping the horizon with his marine glasses. Not a boat was in sight. As sunset arrived, he even sent Chris aloft to the mizzen-topmast-head, but with no better luck. The boats could not possibly be back before midnight.

Since noon the barometer had been falling with startling rapidity, and all the signs were ripe for a great storm—how great, not even the sailing-master anticipated. He and Chris set to work to prepare for it. They put storm gaskets on the furled topsails, lowered and stowed the foresail and spanker and took in the two inner jibs. In the one remaining jib they put a single reef, and a single reef in the mainsail.

Night had fallen before they finished, and with the darkness came the storm. A low moan swept over the sea, and the wind struck the *Sophie Sutherland* flat. But she righted quickly, and with the sailing-master at the wheel, sheered her bow into within five points of the wind. Working as well as he could with his bandaged hand, and with the feeble aid of the Chinese cook, Chris went forward and backed the jib over to the weather side. This with the flat mainsail, left the schooner hove to.

"God help the boats! It's no gale! It's a typhoon!" the sailing-master shouted to Chris at eleven o'clock. "Too much canvas! Got to get two more reefs into that mainsail and got to do it right away!" He glanced at the old captain, shivering in oilskins at the binnacle and holding on for dear life. "There's only you and I, Chris—and the cook; but he's next to worthless!"

In order to make the reef, it was necessary to lower the mainsail, and the removal of this after pressure was bound to make the schooner fall off before the wind and sea because of the forward pressure of the jib.

"Take the wheel!" the sailing-master directed. "And when I give the word, hard up with it! And when she's square before it, steady her! And keep her there! We'll heave to again as soon as I get the reefs in!"

Gripping the kicking spokes, Chris watched him, and the reluctant cook go forward into the howling darkness. The *Sophie Sutherland* was plunging into the huge head-seas and wallowing tremendously, the tense steel stays and taut rigging humming like harp-strings to the wind. A buffeted cry came to his ears, and he felt the schooner's bow paying off of its own accord. The mainsail was down!

He ran the wheel hard-over and kept anxious track of the changing direction of the wind on his face and of the heave of the vessel. This was the crucial moment. In performing the evolution she would have to pass broadside to the surge before she could get before it. The wind was blowing directly on his right cheek, when he felt the *Sophie Sutherland* lean over and begin to rise toward the sky—up—up—an infinite distance! Would she clear the crest of the gigantic wave?

Again by the feel of it, for he could see nothing, he knew that a wall of water was rearing and curving far above him along the whole weather side. There was an instant's calm as the liquid wall intervened and shut off the wind. The schooner righted, and for that instant seemed at perfect rest. Then she rolled to meet the descending rush.

Chris shouted to the captain to hold tight and prepared himself for the shock. But the man did not live who could face it. An ocean of water smote Chris's back and his clutch on the spokes was loosened as if it were a baby's. Stunned, powerless, like a straw on the face of a torrent, he was swept onward he knew not whither. Missing the corner of the cabin, he was dashed forward along the poop runway a hundred feet or more, striking violently against the foot of the foremast. A second wave, crushing inboard, hurled him back the way he had come, and left him half-drowned where the poop steps should have been.

Bruised and bleeding, dimly conscious, he felt for the rail and dragged himself to his feet. Unless something could be done, he knew the last moment had come. As he faced the poop, the wind drove into his mouth with suffocating force. This brought him back to his senses with a start. The wind was blowing from dead aft! The schooner was out of the trough and before it! But the send of the sea was bound to breach her to again. Crawling up the runway, he managed to get to the wheel just in time to prevent this. The binnacle light was still burning. They were safe!

That is, he and the schooner were safe. As to the welfare of his three companions he could not say. Nor did he dare leave the wheel in order to find out, for it took every second of his undivided attention to keep the vessel to her course. The least fraction of carelessness and the heave of the sea under the quarter was liable to thrust her into the trough. So, a boy of one hundred and forty pounds, he clung to his herculean task of guiding the two hundred straining tons of fabric amid the chaos of the great storm forces.

Half an hour later, groaning and sobbing, the captain crawled to Chris's feet. All was lost, he whimpered. He was smitten unto death. The galley had gone by the board, the mainsail and running-gear, the cook, everything!

"Where's the sailing-master?" Chris demanded when he had caught his breath after steadying a wild lurch of the schooner. It was no child's play to steer a vessel under single-reefed jib before a typhoon.

"Clean up for'ard," the old man replied. "Jammed under the fo'c'sle-head, but still breathing. Both his arms are broken, he says, and he doesn't know how many ribs. He's hurt bad."

"Well, he'll drown there the way she's shipping water

through the hawse-pipes. Go for'ard!" Chris commanded, taking charge of things as a matter of course. "Tell him not to worry; that I'm at the wheel. Help him as much as you can and make him help"—he stopped and ran the spokes to starboard as a tremendous billow rose under the stern and yawed the schooner to port—"and make him help himself for the rest. Unship the fo'castle hatch and get him down into a bunk. Then ship the hatch again."

The captain turned his aged face forward and wavered pitifully. The waist of the ship was full of water to the bulwarks. He had just come through it, and knew death lurked every inch of the way.

"Go!" Chris shouted, fiercely. And as the fear-stricken man started, "And take another look for the cook!"

Two hours later, almost dead from suffering, the captain returned. He had obeyed orders. The sailing-master was helpless, although safe in a bunk; the cook was gone. Chris sent the captain below to the cabin to change his clothes.

After interminable hours of toil, day broke cold and gray. Chris looked about him. The *Sophie Sutherland* was racing before the typhoon like a thing possessed. There was no rain, but the wind whipped the spray of the sea mast-high, obscuring everything except in the immediate neighborhood.

Two waves only could Chris see at a time—the one before and the one behind. So small and insignificant the schooner seemed on the long Pacific roll! Rushing up a maddening mountain, she would poise like a cockle-shell on the giddy summit, breathless and rolling, leap outward and down into the yawning chasm beneath, and bury herself in the smother of foam at the bottom. Then the recovery, another mountain, another sickening upward rush, another poise, and the downward crash. Abreast of him, to starboard, like a ghost of the storm, Chris saw the cook dashing apace with the schooner. Evidently, when washed overboard, he had grasped and become entangled in a trailing halyard.

For three hours more, alone with this gruesome companion, Chris held the *Sophie Sutherland* before the wind and sea. He had long since forgotten his mangled fingers. The bandages had been torn away, and the cold, salt spray had eaten into the half-healed wounds until they were numb and no longer pained. But he was not cold. The terrific labor of steering forced the perspiration from every pore. Yet he was faint and weak with hunger and exhaustion and hailed with delight the advent on deck of the captain, who fed him all of a pound of cake-chocolate. It strengthened him at once.

He ordered the captain to cut the halyard by which the cook's body was towing, and also to go forward and cut loose the jib-halyard and sheet. When he had done so, the jib fluttered a couple of moments like a handkerchief, then tore out of the bolt-ropes and vanished. The *Sophie Sutherland* was running under bare poles.

By noon, the storm had spent itself, and by six in the evening the waves had died down sufficiently to let Chris leave the helm. It was almost hopeless to dream of the small boats weathering the typhoon, but there is always the chance in saving human life, and Chris at once applied himself to going back over the course along which he had fled. He managed to get a reef in one of the inner jibs and two reefs in the spanker, and then, with the aid of the watch-tackle, to hoist them to the stiff breeze that yet blew. And all through the night, tacking back and forth on the back track, he shook out canvas as fast as the wind would permit.

The injured sailing-master had turned delirious and between tending him and lending a hand with the ship, Chris kept the captain busy. "Taught me more seamanship," as he afterward said, "than I'd learned on the whole voyage." But by daybreak the old man's feeble frame succumbed, and he fell off into exhausted sleep on the weather poop.

Chris, who could now lash the wheel, covered the tired man with blankets from below, and went fishing in the lazaretto for something to eat. But by the day following he found himself forced to give in, drowsing fitfully by the wheel and waking ever and anon to take a look at things.

On the afternoon of the third day, he picked up a schooner, dismasted and battered. As he approached, close-hauled on the wind, he saw her decks crowded by an unusually large crew, and on sailing in closer, made out among others the faces of his missing comrades. And he was just in the nick of time, for they were fighting a losing fight at the pumps. An hour later they, with the crew of the sinking craft, were aboard the *Sophie Sutherland*.

Having wandered so far from their own vessel, they had taken refuge on the strange schooner just before the storm broke. She was a Canadian sealer on her first voyage, and as was now apparent, her last.

The captain of the *Sophie Sutherland* had a story to tell,

also, and he told it well—so well, in fact, that when all hands were gathered together on deck during the dog-watch, Emil Johansen strode over to Chris and gripped him by the hand.

"Chris," he said, so loudly that all could hear, "Chris, I gif in. You vas yoost so good a sailorman as I. You vas a bully boy, und able seaman, und I pe proud for you!

"Und Chris!" He turned as if he had forgotten something, and called back, "From dis time always you call me 'Emil' mitout der 'Mister!'"

To Repel
Boarders

TO REPEL
BOARDERS
(1902)

"NO; HONEST, NOW, BOB, I'm sure I was born too late. The twentieth century's no place for me. If I'd had my way—"

"You'd have been born in the sixteenth," I broke in, laughing, "with Drake and Hawkins and Raleigh and the rest of the sea-kings."

"You're right!" Paul affirmed. He rolled over upon his back on the little after-deck, with a long sigh of dissatisfaction.

It was a little past midnight, and, with the wind nearly astern, we were running down Lower San Francisco Bay to Bay Farm Island. Paul Fairfax and I went to the same school, lived next door to each other, and "chummed it" together. By saving money, by earning more, and by each of us foregoing a bicycle on his birthday, we had collected the purchaseprice of the *Mist*, a beamy twenty-eight-footer, sloop-rigged, with baby topsail and centerboard. Paul's father was a yachtsman himself, and he had conducted the business for us, poking around, overhauling, sticking his penknife into the timbers, and testing the planks with the greatest care. In fact, it was on his schooner, the *Whim*, that Paul and I had picked up what we knew about boat-sailing, and now that the *Mist* was ours, we were hard at work adding to our knowledge.

The *Mist*, being broad of beam, was comfortable and roomy. A man could stand upright in the cabin, and what with the stove, cooking-utensils, and bunks, we were good for trips in her of a week at a time. And we were just starting out on the first of such trips, and it was because it was the first trip that we were sailing by night. Early in the evening we had beaten out from Oakland, and we were now off the mouth of Alameda Creek, a large salt-water estuary which fills and empties San Leandro Bay.

"Men lived in those days," Paul said, so suddenly as to startle me from my own thoughts. "In the days of the sea-kings, I mean," he explained.

I said "Oh!" sympathetically and began to whistle "Captain Kidd."

"Now, I've my ideas about things," Paul went on. "They talk about romance and adventure and all that, but I say romance and adventure are dead. We're too civilized. We don't have adventures in the twentieth century. We go to the circus—"

"But—" I strove to interrupt, though he would not listen to me.

"You look here, Bob," he said. "In all the time you and I've gone together what adventures have we had? True, we were out in the hills once, and didn't get back till late at night, and we were good and hungry, but we weren't even lost. We knew where we were all the time. It was only a case of walk. What I mean is, we've never had to fight for our lives. Understand? We've never had a pistol fired at us, or a cannon, or a sword waving over our heads, or—or anything.

"You'd better slack away three or four feet of that main-sheet," he said in a hopeless sort of way, as though it did not matter much anyway. "The wind's still veering around.

"Why, in the old times the sea was one constant glorious adventure," he continued. "A boy left school and became a midshipman, and in a few weeks was cruising after Spanish galleons or locking yard-arms with a French privateer, or—doing lots of things."

"Well—there are adventures today," I objected.

But Paul went on as though I had not spoken:

"And today we go from school to high school, and from high school to college, and then we go into the office or become doctors and things, and the only adventures we know about are the ones we read in books. Why, just as sure as I'm sitting here on the stern of the sloop *Mist*, just so sure am I that we wouldn't know what to do if a real adventure came along. Now, would we?"

"Oh, I don't know," I answered noncommittally.

"Well, you wouldn't be a coward, would you?" he demanded.

I was sure I wouldn't and said so.

"But you don't have to be a coward to lose your head, do you?"

I agreed that brave men might get excited.

"Well, then," Paul summed up, with a note of regret in his voice, "the chances are that we'd spoil the adventure. So it's a shame, and that's all I can say about it."

"The adventure hasn't come yet," I answered, not caring to see him down in the mouth over nothing. You see, Paul was a peculiar fellow in some things, and I knew him pretty well. He read a good deal, and had a quick imagination, and once in a while he'd get into moods like this one. So I said, "The adventure hasn't come yet, so there's no use worrying about its being spoiled. For all we know, it might turn out splendidly."

Paul didn't say anything for some time, and I was thinking he was out of the mood, when he spoke up suddenly:

"Just imagine, Bob Kellogg, as we're sailing along now, just as we are, and never mind what for, that a boat should bear down upon us with armed men in it, what would you do to repel boarders? Think you could rise to it?"

"What would you do?" I asked pointedly. "Remember, we haven't even a single shotgun aboard."

"You would surrender, then?" he demanded angrily. "But suppose they were going to kill you?"

"I'm not saying what I'd do," I answered stiffly, beginning to get a little angry myself. "I'm asking what you'd do, without weapons of any sort?"

"I'd find something," he replied—rather shortly, I thought.

I began to chuckle. "Then the adventure wouldn't be spoiled, would it? And you've been talking rubbish."

Paul struck a match, looked at his watch, and remarked that it was nearly one o'clock—a way he had when the argument went against him. Besides, this was the nearest we ever came to quarreling now, though our share of squabbles had fallen to us in the earlier days of our friendship. I had just seen a little white light ahead when Paul spoke again.

"Anchor-light," he said. "Funny place for people to drop the hook. It may be a scow-schooner with a dinky astern, so you'd better go wide."

I eased the *Mist* several points, and, the wind puffing up, we went plowing along at a pretty fair speed, passing the light so wide that we could not make out what manner of craft it marked. Suddenly the *Mist* slacked up in a slow and easy way, as though running upon soft mud. We were both startled. The wind was blowing stronger than ever, and yet we were almost at a standstill.

"Mud-flat out here? Never heard of such a thing!"

So Paul exclaimed with a snort of unbelief, and, seizing an oar, shoved it down over the side. And straight down it went till the water wet his hand. There was no bottom! Then we were dumbfounded. The wind was whistling by, and still the *Mist* was moving ahead at a snail's pace. There seemed something dead about her, and it was all I could do at the tiller to keep her from swinging up into the wind.

"Listen!" I laid my hand on Paul's arm. We could hear the sound of rowlocks, and saw the little white light bobbing up and down and now very close to us. "There's your armed boat," I whispered in fun. "Beat the crew to quarters and stand by to repel boarders!"

We both laughed and were still laughing when a wild scream of rage came out of the darkness, and the approaching boat shot under our stern. By the light of the lantern it carried, we could see the two men in it distinctly. They were foreign-looking fellows with sun-bronzed faces, and with knitted tam-o'-shanters perched seaman fashion on their heads. Bright-colored woolen sashes were around their waists, and long sea-boots covered their legs. I remember yet the cold chill which passed along my backbone as I noted the tiny gold earrings in the ears of one. For all the world they were like pirates stepped out of the pages of romance. And, to make the picture complete, their faces were distorted with anger, and each flourished a long knife. They were both shouting, in high-pitched voices, some foreign jargon we could not understand.

One of them, the smaller of the two, and if anything the more vicious-looking, put his hands on the rail of the *Mist* and started to come aboard. Quick as a flash Paul placed the end of the oar against the man's chest and shoved him back into his boat. He fell in a heap, but scrambled to his feet, waving the knife and shrieking:

"You break-a my net-a! You break-a my net-a!"

And he held forth in the jargon again, his companion joining him, and both preparing to make another dash to come aboard the *Mist*.

"They're Italian fishermen," I cried, the facts of the case breaking in upon me. "We've run over their smelt-net, and it's slipped along the keel and fouled our rudder. We're anchored to it."

"Yes, and they're murderous chaps, too," Paul said, sparring at them with the oar to make them keep their distance.

"Say, you fellows!" he called to them. "Give us a chance and we'll get it clear for you! We didn't know your net was there. We didn't mean to do it, you know!"

"You won't lose anything!" I added. "We'll pay the damages!"

But they could not understand what we were saying or did not care to understand.

"You break-a my net-a! You break-a my net-a!" the smaller man, the one with the earrings, screamed back, making furious gestures. "I fix-a you! You-a see, I fix-a you!"

This time, when Paul thrust him back, he seized the oar in his hands, and his companion jumped aboard. I put my back against the tiller, and no sooner had he landed, and before he had caught his balance, than I met him with another oar, and he fell heavily backward into the boat. It was getting serious, and when he arose and caught my oar, and I realized his strength, I confess that I felt a goodly tinge of fear. But though he was stronger than I, instead of dragging me overboard when he wrenched on the oar, he merely pulled his boat in closer; and when I shoved, the boat was forced away. Besides, the knife, still in his right hand, made him awkward and somewhat counterbalanced the advantage his superior strength gave him. Paul and his enemy were in the same situation—a sort of deadlock, which continued for several seconds, but which could not last. Several times I shouted that we would pay for whatever damage their net had suffered, but my words seemed to be without effect.

Then my man began to tuck the oar under his arm, and to come up along it, slowly, hand over hand. The small man did the same with Paul. Moment by moment they came closer, and closer, and we knew that the end was only a question of time.

"Hard up, Bob!" Paul called softly to me.

I gave him a quick glance and caught an instant's glimpse of what I took to be a very pale face and a very set jaw.

"Oh, Bob," he pleaded, "hard up your helm! Hard up your helm, Bob!"

And his meaning dawned upon me. Still holding to my end of the oar, I shoved the tiller over with my back, and even bent my body to keep it over. As it was the *Mist* was nearly dead before the wind, and this maneuver was bound to force her to jibe her mainsail from one side to the other. I could tell by the "feel" when the wind spilled out of the canvas and the boom tilted up. Paul's man had now gained a footing on the little deck, and my man was just scrambling up.

"Look out!" I shouted to Paul. "Here she comes!"

Both he and I let go the oars and tumbled into the cockpit. The next instant the big boom and the heavy blocks swept over our heads, the main-sheet whipping past like a great coiling snake and the *Mist* heeling over with a violent jar. Both men had jumped for it, but in some way the little man either got his knife-hand jammed or fell upon it, for the first sight we caught of him, he was standing in his boat, his bleeding fingers clasped close between his knees and his face all twisted with pain and helpless rage.

"Now's our chance!" Paul whispered. "Over with you!"

And on either side of the rudder, we lowered ourselves into the water, pressing the net down with our feet, till, with a jerk, it went clear. Then it was up and in, Paul at the mainsheet and I at the tiller, the *Mist* plunging ahead with freedom in her motion, and the little white light astern growing small and smaller.

"Now that you've had your adventure, do you feel any better?" I remember asking when we had changed our clothes and were sitting dry and comfortable again in the cockpit.

"Well, if I don't have the nightmare for a week to come"—Paul paused and puckered his brows in judicial fashion—"it will be because I can't sleep, that's one thing sure!"

THE CRUISE OF THE
DAZZLER

THE CRUISE OF THE DAZZLER (1902)

CHAPTER 1
BROTHER AND SISTER

THEY RAN ACROSS THE shining sand, the Pacific thundering its long surge at their backs, and when they gained the roadway leaped upon bicycles and dived at faster pace into the green avenues of the park. There were three of them, three boys, in as many bright-colored sweaters, and they "scorched" along the cycle-path as dangerously near the speed-limit as is the custom of boys in bright-colored sweaters to go. They may have exceeded the speed-limit. A mounted park policeman thought so, but was not sure, and contented himself with cautioning them as they flashed by. They acknowledged the warning promptly, and on the next turn of the path as promptly forgot it, which is also a custom of boys in bright-colored sweaters.

Shooting out through the entrance to Golden Gate Park, they turned into San Francisco, and took the long sweep of the descending hills at a rate that caused pedestrians to turn and watch them anxiously. Through the city streets the bright sweaters flew, turning and twisting to escape climbing the steeper hills, and, when the steep hills were unavoidable, doing stunts to see which would first gain the top.

The boy who more often hit up the pace, led the scorching, and instituted the stunts was called Joe by his companions. It was "follow the leader," and he led, the merriest and boldest in the bunch. But as they pedaled into the Western Addition, among the large and comfortable residences, his laughter became less loud and frequent, and he unconsciously lagged in the rear. At Laguna and Vallejo streets his companions turned off to the right.

"So long, Fred," he called as he turned his wheel to the left. "So long, Charley."

"See you to-night!" they called back.

"No—I can't come," he answered.

"Aw, come on," they begged.

"No, I've got to dig. So long!"

As he went on alone, his face grew grave and a vague worry came into his eyes. He began resolutely to whistle, but this dwindled away till it was a thin and very subdued little sound, which ceased altogether as he rode up the driveway to a large two-storied house.

"Oh, Joe!"

He hesitated before the door to the library. Bessie was there, he knew, studiously working up her lessons. She must be nearly through with them, too, for she was always done before dinner, and dinner could not be many minutes away. As for his lessons, they were as yet untouched. The thought made him angry. It was bad enough to have one's sister—and two years younger at that—in the same grade, but to have her continually head and shoulders above him in scholarship was a most intolerable thing. Not that he was dull. No one knew better than himself that he was not dull. But somehow—he did not quite know how—his mind was on other things and he was usually unprepared.

"Joe—please come here." There was the slightest possible plaintive note in her voice this time.

"Well?" he said, thrusting aside the portière with an impetuous movement.

He said it gruffly, but he was half sorry for it the next instant when he saw a slender little girl regarding him with wistful eyes across the big reading-table heaped with books. She was curled up, with pencil and pad, in an easy-chair of such generous dimensions that it made her seem more delicate and fragile than she really was.

"What is it, Sis?" he asked more gently, crossing over to her side.

She took his hand in hers and pressed it against her cheek, and as he stood beside her came closer to him with a nestling movement.

"What is the matter, Joe dear?" she asked softly. "Won't you tell me?"

He remained silent. It struck him as ridiculous to confess his troubles to a little sister, even if her reports were higher than his. And the little sister struck him as ridiculous to demand his troubles of him. "What a soft cheek she has!" he thought as she pressed her face gently against his hand. If he could but tear himself away—it was all so foolish! Only he might hurt her feelings, and, in his experience, girls' feelings were very easily hurt.

She opened his fingers and kissed the palm of his hand. It was like a rose-leaf falling; it was also her way of asking her question over again.

"Nothing's the matter," he said decisively. And then, quite inconsistently, he blurted out, "Father!"

His worry was now in her eyes. "But father is so good and kind, Joe," she began. "Why don't you try to please him? He doesn't ask much of you, and it's all for your own good. It's not as though you were a fool, like some boys. If you would only study a little bit—"

"That's it! Lecturing!" he exploded, tearing his hand roughly away. "Even you are beginning to lecture me now. I suppose the cook and the stable-boy will be at it next."

He shoved his hands into his pockets and looked forward into a melancholy and desolate future filled with interminable lectures and lecturers innumerable.

"Was that what you wanted me for?" he demanded, turning to go.

She caught at his hand again. "No, it wasn't; only you looked so worried that I thought—I—" Her voice broke, and she began again freshly. "What I wanted to tell you was that we're planning a trip across the bay to Oakland, next Saturday, for a tramp in the hills."

"Who's going?"

"Myrtle Hayes—"

"What! That little softy?" he interrupted.

"I don't think she is a softy," Bessie answered with spirit. "She's one of the sweetest girls I know."

"Which isn't saying much, considering the girls you know. But go on. Who are the others?"

"Pearl Sayther, and her sister Alice, and Jessie Hilborn, and Sadie French, and Edna Crothers. That's all the girls."

Joe sniffed disdainfully. "Who are the fellows, then?"

"Maurice and Felix Clement, Dick Schofield, Burt Layton, and—"

"That's enough. Milk-and-water chaps, all of them."

"I—I wanted to ask you and Fred and Charley," she said in a quavering voice. "That's what I called you in for—to ask you to come."

"And what are you going to do?" he asked.

"Walk, gather wild flowers—the poppies are all out now—eat luncheon at some nice place, and—and—"

"Come home," he finished for her.

Bessie nodded her head. Joe put his hands in his pockets again and walked up and down.

"A sissy outfit, that's what it is," he said abruptly; "and a sissy program. None of it in mine, please."

She tightened her trembling lips and struggled on bravely. "What would you rather do?" she asked.

"I'd sooner take Fred and Charley and go off somewhere and do something—well, anything."

He paused and looked at her. She was waiting patiently for him to proceed. He was aware of his inability to express in words what he felt and wanted, and all his trouble and general dissatisfaction rose up and gripped hold of him.

"Oh, you can't understand!" he burst out. "You can't understand. You're a girl. You like to be prim and neat, and to be good in deportment and ahead in your studies. You don't care for danger and adventure and such things, and you don't care for boys who are rough, and have life and go in them, and all that. You like good little boys in white collars, with clothes always clean and hair always combed, who like to stay in at recess and be petted by the teacher and told how they're always up in their studies; nice little boys who never get into scrapes—who are too busy walking around and picking flowers and eating lunches with girls, to get into scrapes. Oh, I know the kind—afraid of their own shadows, and no more spunk in them than in so many sheep. That's what they are—sheep. Well, I'm not a sheep, and there's no more to be said. And I don't want to go on your picnic, and, what's more, I'm not going."

The tears welled up in Bessie's brown eyes, and her lips were trembling. This angered him unreasonably. What were girls good for, anyway? Always blubbering, and interfering, and carrying on. There was no sense in them.

"A fellow can't say anything without making you cry," he began, trying to appease her. "Why, I didn't mean anything, Sis. I didn't, sure. I—"

He paused helplessly and looked down at her. She was sobbing, and at the same time shaking with the effort to control her sobs, while big tears were rolling down her cheeks.

"Oh, you—you girls!" he cried, and strode wrathfully out of the room.

Chapter 2
"The Draconian Reforms"

A FEW MINUTES LATER, and still wrathful, Joe went in to dinner. He ate silently, though his father and mother and Bessie kept up a genial flow of conversation. There she was, he communed savagely with his plate, crying one minute, and the next all smiles and laughter. Now that wasn't his way. If he had anything sufficiently important to cry about, rest assured he wouldn't get over it for days. Girls were hypocrites, that was all there was to it. They didn't feel one hundredth part of all that they said when they cried. It stood to reason that they didn't. It must be that they just carried on because they enjoyed it. It made them feel good to make other people miserable, especially boys. That was why they were always interfering.

Thus reflecting sagely, he kept his eyes on his plate and did justice to the fare; for one cannot scorch from the Cliff House to the Western Addition via the park without being guilty of a healthy appetite.

Now and then his father directed a glance at him in a certain mildly anxious way. Joe did not see these glances, but Bessie saw them, every one. Mr. Bronson was a middle-aged man, well developed and of heavy build, though not fat. His was a rugged face, square-jawed and stern-featured, though his eyes were kindly and there were lines about the mouth that betokened laughter rather than severity. A close examination was not required to discover the resemblance between him and Joe. The same broad forehead and strong jaw characterized them both, and the eyes, taking into consideration the difference of age, were as like as peas from one pod.

"How are you getting on, Joe?" Mr. Bronson asked finally. Dinner was over and they were about to leave the table.

"Oh, I don't know," Joe answered carelessly, and then added: "We have examinations tomorrow. I'll know then."

"Whither bound?" his mother questioned, as he turned to leave the room. She was a slender, willowy woman, whose brown eyes Bessie's were, and likewise her tender ways.

"To my room," Joe answered. "To work," he supplemented.

She rumpled his hair affectionately and bent and kissed him. Mr. Bronson smiled approval at him as he went out, and he hurried up the stairs, resolved to dig hard and pass the examinations of the coming day.

Entering his room, he locked the door and sat down at a desk most comfortably arranged for a boy's study. He ran his eye over his text-books. The history examination came the first thing in the morning, so he would begin on that. He opened the book where a page was turned down, and began to read:

Shortly after the Draconian reforms, a war

broke out between Athens and Megara
respecting the island of Salamis, to which both
cities laid claim.

That was easy; but what were the Draconian reforms? He must look them up. He felt quite studious as he ran over the back pages, till he chanced to raise his eyes above the top of the book and saw on a chair a baseball mask and a catcher's glove. They shouldn't have lost that game last Saturday, he thought, and they wouldn't have, either, if it hadn't been for Fred. He wished Fred wouldn't fumble so. He could hold a hundred difficult balls in succession, but when a critical point came, he'd let go of even a dewdrop. He'd have to send him out in the field and bring in Jones to first base. Only Jones was so excitable. He could hold any kind of a ball, no matter how critical the play was, but there was no telling what he would do with the ball after he got it.

Joe came to himself with a start. A pretty way of studying history! He buried his head in his book and began:

Shortly after the Draconian reforms—

He read the sentence through three times, and then recollected that he had not looked up the Draconian reforms.

A knock came at the door. He turned the pages over with a noisy flutter but made no answer.

The knock was repeated, and Bessie's "Joe, dear" came to his ears.

"What do you want?" he demanded. But before she

could answer he hurried on: "No admittance. I'm busy."

"I came to see if I could help you," she pleaded. "I'm all done, and I thought—"

"Of course you're all done!" he shouted. "You always are!"

He held his head in both his hands to keep his eyes on the book. But the baseball mask bothered him. The more he attempted to keep his mind on the history the more in his mind's eye he saw the mask resting on the chair and all the games in which it had played its part.

This would never do. He deliberately placed the book face downward on the desk and walked over to the chair. With a swift sweep he sent both mask and glove hurtling under the bed, and so violently that he heard the mask rebound from the wall.

Shortly after the Draconian reforms, a war broke out between Athens and Megara—

The mask had rolled back from the wall. He wondered if it had rolled back far enough for him to see it. No, he wouldn't look. What did it matter if it had rolled out? That wasn't history. He wondered.

He peered over the top of the book, and there was the mask peeping out at him from under the edge of the bed. This was not to be borne. There was no use attempting to study while that mask was around. He went over and fished it out, crossed the room to the closet, and tossed it inside, then locked the door. That was settled, thank goodness! Now he could do some work.

He sat down again.

Shortly after the Draconian reforms, a war broke out between Athens and Megara respecting the island of Salamis, to which, both cities laid claim.

Which was all very well, if he had only found out what the Draconian reforms were. A soft glow pervaded the room, and he suddenly became aware of it. What could cause it? He looked out of the window. The setting sun was slanting its long rays against low-hanging masses of summer clouds, turning them to warm scarlet and rosy red; and it was from them that the red light, mellow and glowing, was flung earthward.

His gaze dropped from the clouds to the bay beneath. The sea-breeze was dying down with the day, and off Fort Point a fishing-boat was creeping into port before the last light breeze. A little beyond, a tug was sending up a twisted pillar of smoke as it towed a three-masted schooner to sea. His eyes wandered over toward the Marin County shore. The line where land and water met was already in darkness, and long shadows were creeping up the hills toward Mount Tamalpais, which was sharply silhouetted against the western sky.

Oh, if he, Joe Bronson, were only on that fishing-boat and sailing in with a deep-sea catch! Or if he were on that schooner, heading out into the sunset, into the world! That was life, that was living, doing something and being something in the world. And, instead, here he was, pent up in a close room, racking his brains about people dead and gone thousands of years before he was born.

He jerked himself away from the window as though held there by some physical force, and resolutely carried his chair and history into the farthest corner of the room, where he sat down with his back to the window.

An instant later, so it seemed to him, he found himself again staring out of the window and dreaming. How he had got there he did not know. His last recollection was the finding of a subheading on a page on the right-hand side of the book which read: "The Laws and Constitution of Draco." And then, evidently like walking in one's sleep, he had come to the window. How long had he been there? he wondered. The fishing-boat which he had seen off Fort Point was now crawling into Meiggs's Wharf. This denoted nearly an hour's lapse of time. The sun had long since set; a solemn grayness was brooding over the water, and the first faint stars were beginning to twinkle over the crest of Mount Tamalpais.

He turned, with a sigh, to go back into his corner, when a long whistle, shrill and piercing, came to his ears. That was Fred. He sighed again. The whistle repeated itself. Then another whistle joined it. That was Charley. They were waiting on the corner—lucky fellows!

Well, they wouldn't see him this night. Both whistles arose in duet. He writhed in his chair and groaned. No, they wouldn't see him this night, he reiterated, at the same time rising to his feet. It was certainly impossible for him to join them when he had not yet learned about the Draconian reforms. The same force which had held him to the window now seemed drawing him across the room to the desk. It made him put the history on top of his school-books, and he had the door unlocked and was half-way into the hall before he realized it. He started to return, but the thought came to him that he could go out for a little while and then come back and do his work.

A very little while, he promised himself, as he went downstairs. He went down faster and faster, till at the bottom he was going three steps at a time. He popped his cap on his head and went out of the side entrance in a rush; and ere he reached the corner the reforms of Draco were as far away in the past as Draco himself, while the examinations on the morrow were equally far away in the future.

CHAPTER 3
"BRICK," "SORREL-TOP,"
AND "REDDY"

"WHAT'S UP?" JOE ASKED, as he joined Fred and Charley.

"Kites," Charley answered. "Come on. We're tired out waiting for you."

The three set off down the street to the brow of the hill, where they looked down upon Union Street, far below and almost under their feet. This they called the Pit, and it was well named. Themselves they called the Hill-dwellers, and a descent into the Pit by the Hill-dwellers was looked upon by them as a great adventure.

Scientific kite-flying was one of the keenest pleasures of these three particular Hill-dwellers, and six or eight kites strung out on a mile of twine and soaring into the clouds was an ordinary achievement for them. They were compelled to replenish their kite-supply often; for whenever an accident occurred, and the string broke, or a ducking kite dragged down the rest, or the wind suddenly died out, their kites fell into the Pit, from which place they were unrecoverable. The reason for this was the young people of the Pit were a piratical and robber race with peculiar ideas

100

of ownership and property rights.

On a day following an accident to a kite of one of the Hill-dwellers, the self-same kite could be seen riding the air attached to a string which led down into the Pit to the lairs of the Pit People. So it came about that the Pit People, who were a poor folk and unable to afford scientific kite-flying, developed great proficiency in the art when their neighbors the Hill-dwellers took it up.

There was also an old sailorman who profited by this recreation of the Hill-dwellers; for he was learned in sails and air-currents, and being deft of hand and cunning, he fashioned the best-flying kites that could be obtained. He lived in a rattletrap shanty close to the water, where he could still watch with dim eyes the ebb and flow of the tide, and the ships pass out and in, and where he could revive old memories of the days when he, too, went down to the sea in ships.

To reach his shanty from the Hill one had to pass through the Pit, and thither the three boys were bound. They had often gone for kites in the daytime, but this was their first trip after dark, and they felt it to be, as it indeed was, a hazardous adventure.

In simple words, the Pit was merely the cramped and narrow quarters of the poor, where many nationalities crowded together in cosmopolitan confusion, and lived as best they could, amid much dirt and squalor. It was still early evening when the boys passed through on their way to the sailorman's shanty, and no mishap befell them, though some of the Pit boys stared at them savagely and hurled a taunting remark after them, now and then.

The sailorman made kites which were not only splendid fliers but which folded up and were very convenient to carry. Each of the boys bought a few, and, with them wrapped in compact bundles and under their arms, started back on the return journey.

"Keep a sharp lookout for the b'ys," the kite-maker cautioned them. "They're like to be cruisin' round after dark."

"We're not afraid," Charley assured him; "and we know how to take care of ourselves."

Used to the broad and quiet streets of the Hill, the boys were shocked and stunned by the life that teemed in the close-packed quarter. It seemed some thick and monstrous growth of vegetation, and that they were wading through it. They shrank closely together in the tangle of narrow streets as though for protection, conscious of the strangeness of it all, and how unrelated they were to it.

Children and babies sprawled on the sidewalk and under their feet. Bareheaded and unkempt women gossiped in the doorways or passed back and forth with scant marketings in their arms. There was a general odor of decaying fruit and fish, a smell of staleness and putridity. Big hulking men slouched by, and ragged little girls walked gingerly through the confusion with foaming buckets of beer in their hands. There was a clatter and garble of foreign tongues and brogues, shrill cries, quarrels and wrangles, and the Pit pulsed with a great and steady murmur, like the hum of the human hive that it was.

"Phew! I'll be glad when we're out of it," Fred said.

He spoke in a whisper, and Joe and Charley nodded

grimly that they agreed with him. They were not inclined to speech, and they walked as rapidly as the crowd permitted, with much the same feelings as those of travelers in a dangerous and hostile jungle.

And danger and hostility stalked in the Pit. The inhabitants seemed to resent the presence of these strangers from the Hill. Dirty little urchins abused them as they passed, snarling with assumed bravery and prepared to run away at the first sign of attack. And still other little urchins formed a noisy parade at the heels of the boys and grew bolder with increasing numbers.

"Don't mind them," Joe cautioned. "Take no notice, but keep right on. We'll soon be out of it."

"No; we're in for it," said Fred, in an undertone. "Look there!"

On the corner they were approaching, four or five boys of about their own age were standing. The light from a street-lamp fell upon them and disclosed one with vivid red hair. It could be no other than "Brick" Simpson, the redoubtable leader of a redoubtable gang. Twice within their memory he had led his gang up the Hill and spread panic and terror among the Hill-dwelling young folk, who fled wildly to their homes, while their fathers and mothers hurriedly telephoned for the police.

At sight of the group on the corner, the rabble at the heels of the three boys melted away on the instant with like manifestations of fear. This but increased the anxiety of the boys, though they held boldly on their way.

The red-haired boy detached himself from the group, and stepped before them, blocking their path. They essayed to go around him, but he stretched out his arm.

"Wot yer doin' here?" he snarled. "Why don't yer stay where yer b'long?"

"We're just going home," Fred said mildly.

Brick looked at Joe. "Wot yer got under yer arm?" he demanded.

Joe contained himself and took no heed of him. "Come on," he said to Fred and Charley, at the same time starting to brush past the gang-leader.

But with a quick blow Brick Simpson struck him in the face, and with equal quickness snatched the bundle of kites from under his arm.

Joe uttered an inarticulate cry of rage, and, all caution flung to the winds, sprang at his assailant.

This was evidently a surprise to the gang-leader, who expected least of all to be attacked in his own territory. He retreated backward, still clutching the kites, and divided between desire to fight and desire to retain his capture.

The latter desire dominated him, and he turned and fled swiftly down the narrow side-street into a labyrinth of streets and alleys. Joe knew that he was plunging into the wilderness of the enemy's country, but his sense of both property and pride had been offended, and he took up the pursuit hot-footed.

Fred and Charley followed after, though he outdistanced them, and behind came the three other members of the gang, emitting a whistling call while they ran which was evidently intended for the assembling of the rest of the band. As the chase proceeded, these whistles were answered from many different directions, and soon a score of dark figures were tagging at the heels of Fred and Charley, who, in turn, were straining every muscle to keep the swifter-footed Joe in sight.

Brick Simpson darted into a vacant lot, aiming for a "slip," as such things are called which are prearranged passages through fences and over sheds and houses and around dark holes and corners, where the unfamiliar pursuer must go more carefully and where the chances are many that he will soon lose the track.

But Joe caught Brick before he could attain his end, and together they rolled over and over in the dirt, locked in each other's arms. By the time Fred and Charley and the gang had come up, they were on their feet, facing each other.

"Wot d' ye want, eh?" the red-headed gang-leader was saying in a bullying tone. "Wot d' ye want? That's wot I wanter know."

"I want my kites," Joe answered.

Brick Simpson's eyes sparkled at the intelligence. Kites were something he stood in need of himself.

"Then you 've got to fight fer 'em," he announced.

"Why should I fight for them?" Joe demanded indignantly. "They're mine." Which went to show how ignorant he was of the ideas of ownership and·property rights which obtained among the People of the Pit.

A chorus of jeers and catcalls went up from the gang, which clustered behind its leader like a pack of wolves.

"Why should I fight for them?" Joe reiterated.

"'Cos I say so," Simpson replied. "An' wot I say goes. Understand?"

But Joe did not understand. He refused to understand

that Brick Simpson's word was law in San Francisco, or any part of San Francisco. His love of honesty and right dealing was offended, and all his fighting blood was up.

"You give those kites to me, right here and now," he threatened, reaching out his hand for them.

But Simpson jerked them away. "D' ye know who I am?" he demanded. "I'm Brick Simpson, an' I don't 'low no one to talk to me in that tone of voice."

"Better leave him alone," Charley whispered in Joe's ear. "What are a few kites? Leave him alone and let's get out of this."

"They're my kites," Joe said slowly in a dogged manner. "They're my kites, and I'm going to have them."

"You can't fight the crowd," Fred interfered; "and if you do get the best of him they'll all pile on you."

The gang, observing this whispered colloquy, and mistaking it for hesitancy on the part of Joe, set up its wolf-like howling again.

"Afraid! afraid!" the young roughs jeered and taunted. "He's too high-toned, he is! Mebbe he'll spoil his nice clean shirt, and then what'll mama say?"

"Shut up!" their leader snapped authoritatively, and the noise obediently died away.

"Will you give me those kites?" Joe demanded, advancing determinedly.

"Will you fight for 'em?" was Simpson's counter-demand.

"Yes," Joe answered.

"Fight! fight!" the gang began to howl again.

"And it's me that'll see fair play," said a man's heavy

voice.

All eyes were instantly turned upon the man who had approached unseen and made this announcement. By the electric light, shining brightly on them from the corner, they made him out to be a big, muscular fellow, clad in a working-man's garments. His feet were incased in heavy brogans, a narrow strap of black leather held his overalls about his waist, and a black and greasy cap was on his head. His face was grimed with coal-dust, and a coarse blue shirt, open at the neck, revealed a wide throat and massive chest.

"An' who're you?" Simpson snarled, angry at the interruption.

"None of yer business," the newcomer retorted tartly. "But, if it'll do you any good, I'm a fireman on the China steamers, and, as I said, I'm goin' to see fair play. That's my business. Your business is to give fair play. So pitch in, and don't be all night about it."

The three boys were as pleased by the appearance of the fireman as Simpson and his followers were displeased. They conferred together for several minutes, when Simpson deposited the bundle of kites in the arms of one of his gang and stepped forward.

"Come on, then," he said, at the same time pulling off his coat.

Joe handed his to Fred and sprang toward Brick. They put up their fists and faced each other. Almost instantly Simpson drove in a fierce blow and ducked cleverly away and out of reach of the blow which Joe returned. Joe felt a sudden respect for the abilities of his antagonist, but the only effect upon him was to arouse all the doggedness of his nature and make him utterly determined to win.

Awed by the presence of the fireman, Simpson's followers confined themselves to cheering Brick and jeering Joe. The two boys circled round and round, attacking, feinting, and guarding, and now one and then the other getting in a telling blow. Their positions were in marked contrast. Joe stood erect, planted solidly on his feet, with legs wide apart and head up. On the other hand, Simpson crouched till his head was nearly lost between his shoulders, and all the while he was in constant motion, leaping and springing and maneuvering in the execution of a score or more of tricks quite new and strange to Joe.

At the end of a quarter of an hour, both were very tired, though Joe was much fresher. Tobacco, ill food, and unhealthy living were telling on the gang-leader, who was panting and sobbing for breath. Though at first (and because of superior skill) he had severely punished Joe, he was now weak and his blows were without force. Growing desperate, he adopted what might be called not an unfair but a mean method of attack: he would maneuver, leap in and strike swiftly, and then, ducking forward, fall to the ground at Joe's feet. Joe could not strike him while he was down, and so would step back until he could get on his feet again, when the thing would be repeated.

But Joe grew tired of this and prepared for him. Timing his blow with Simpson's attack, he delivered it just as Simpson was ducking forward to fall. Simpson fell, but he fell over on one side, whither he had been driven by the impact of Joe's fist upon his head. He rolled over and got half-way to his feet, where he remained, crying and gasping.

His followers called upon him to get up, and he tried once or twice, but was too exhausted and stunned.

"I give in," he said. "I'm licked."

The gang had become silent and depressed at its leader's defeat.

Joe stepped forward.

"I'll trouble you for those kites," he said to the boy who was holding them.

"Oh, I dunno," said another member of the gang, shoving in between Joe and his property. His hair was also a vivid red. "You've got to lick me before you kin have 'em."

"I don't see that," Joe said bluntly. "I've fought and I've won, and there's nothing more to it."

"Oh, yes, there is," said the other. "I'm 'sorrel-top' Simpson. Brick's my brother. See?"

And so, in this fashion, Joe learned another custom of the Pit People of which he had been ignorant.

"All right," he said, his fighting blood more fully aroused than ever by the unjustness of the proceeding. "Come on."

Sorrel-top Simpson, a year younger than his brother, proved to be a most unfair fighter, and the good-natured fireman was compelled to interfere several times before the second of the Simpson clan lay on the ground and acknowledged defeat.

This time Joe reached for his kites without the slightest doubt that he was to get them. But still another lad stepped in between him and his property. The telltale hair, vividly red, sprouted likewise on this lad's head, and Joe knew him at once for what he was, another member of the Simpson clan. He was a younger edition of his brothers, somewhat less heavily built, with a face covered with a vast quantity of freckles, which showed plainly under the electric light.

"You don't git them there kites till you git me," he challenged in a piping little voice. "I'm 'reddy' Simpson, an' you ain't licked the fambly till you 've licked me."

The gang cheered admiringly, and Reddy stripped a tattered jacket preparatory for the fray.

"Git ready," he said to Joe.

Joe's knuckles were torn, his nose was bleeding, his lip was cut and swollen, while his shirt had been ripped down from throat to waist. Further, he was tired, and breathing hard.

"How many more are there of you Simpsons?" he asked. "I've got to get home, and if your family's much larger this thing is liable to keep on all night."

"I'm the last an' the best," Reddy replied. "You gits me an' you gits the kites. Sure."

"All right," Joe sighed. "Come on."

While the youngest of the clan lacked the strength and skill of his elders, he made up for it by a wildcat manner of fighting that taxed Joe severely. Time and again it seemed to him that he must give in to the little whirlwind; but each time he pulled himself together and went doggedly on. For he felt that he was fighting for principle, as his forefathers had fought for principle; also, it seemed to him that the honor of the Hill was at stake, and that he, as its representative, could do nothing less than his very best.

So he held on and managed to endure his opponent's swift and continuous rushes till that young and less experienced person at last wore himself out with his own exertions, and from the ground confessed that, for the first time in its history, the "Simpson fambly was beat."

CHAPTER 4
THE BITER BITTEN

BUT LIFE IN THE PIT at best was a precarious affair, as the three Hill-dwellers were quickly to learn. Before Joe could even possess himself of his kites, his astonished eyes were greeted with the spectacle of all his enemies, the fireman included, taking to their heels in wild flight. As the little girls and urchins had melted away before the Simpson gang, so was melting away the Simpson gang before some new and correspondingly awe-inspiring group of predatory creatures.

Joe heard terrified cries of "Fish gang!" "Fish gang!" from those who fled, and he would have fled himself from this new danger, only he was breathless from his last encounter, and knew the impossibility of escaping whatever threatened. Fred and Charley felt mighty longings to run away from a danger great enough to frighten the redoubtable Simpson gang and the valorous fireman, but they could not desert their comrade.

Dark forms broke into the vacant lot, some surrounding the boys and others dashing after the fugitives. That the laggards were overtaken was evidenced by the cries of distress that went up, and when later the pursuers returned, they brought with them the luckless and snarling Brick, still clinging fast to the bundle of kites.

Joe looked curiously at this latest band of marauders. They were young men of from seventeen and eighteen to twenty-three and -four years of age, and bore the unmistakable stamp of the hoodlum class. There were vicious faces among them—faces so vicious as to make Joe's flesh creep as he looked at them. A couple grasped him tightly by the arms, and Fred and Charley were similarly held captive.

"Look here, you," said one who spoke with the authority of leader, "we've got to inquire into this. Wot's be'n goin' on here? Wot're you up to, Red-head? Wot you be'n doin'?"

"Ain't be'n doin' nothin'," Simpson whined.

"Looks like it." The leader turned up Brick's face to the electric light. "Who's been paintin' you up like that?" he demanded.

Brick pointed at Joe, who was forthwith dragged to the front.

"Wot was you scrappin' about?"

"Kites—my kites," Joe spoke up boldly. "That fellow tried to take them away from me. He's got them under his arm now."

"Oh, he has, has he? Look here, you Brick, we don't put up with stealin' in this territory. See? You never rightly owned nothin'. Come, fork over the kites. Last call."

The leader tightened his grasp threateningly, and Simpson, weeping tears of rage, surrendered the plunder.

"Wot yer got under yer arm?" the leader demanded abruptly of Fred, at the same time jerking out the bundle. "More kites, eh? Reg'lar kite-factory gone and got itself lost," he remarked finally, when he had appropriated Charley's bundle. "Now, wot I wants to know is wot we're goin' to do to you t'ree chaps?" he continued in a judicial tone.

"What for?" Joe demanded hotly. "For being robbed of our kites?"

"Not at all, not at all," the leader responded politely; "but for luggin' kites round these quarters an' causin' all this unseemly disturbance. It's disgraceful; that's wot it is—disgraceful."

At this juncture, when the Hill-dwellers were the center of attraction, Brick suddenly wormed out of his jacket, squirmed away from his captors, and dashed across the lot to the slip for which he had been originally headed when overtaken by Joe. Two or three of the gang shot over the fence after him in noisy pursuit. There was much barking and howling of backyard dogs and clattering of shoes over sheds and boxes. Then there came a splashing of water, as though a barrel of it had been precipitated to the ground. Several minutes later the pursuers returned, very sheepish and very wet from the deluge presented them by the wily Brick, whose voice, high up in the air from some friendly housetop, could be heard defiantly jeering them.

This event apparently disconcerted the leader of the gang, and just as he turned to Joe and Fred and Charley, a long and peculiar whistle came to their ears from the street—the warning signal, evidently, of a scout posted to keep a lookout. The next moment the scout himself came flying back to the main body, which was already beginning to retreat.

"Cops!" he panted.

Joe looked, and he saw two helmeted policemen approaching, with bright stars shining on their breasts.

"Let's get out of this," he whispered to Fred and Charley.

The gang had already taken to flight, and they blocked the boys' retreat in one quarter, and in another they saw the policemen advancing. So they took to their heels in the direction of Brick Simpson's slip, the policemen hot after them and yelling bravely for them to halt.

But young feet are nimble, and young feet when frightened become something more than nimble, and the boys were first over the fence and plunging wildly through a maze of backyards. They soon found that the policemen were discreet. Evidently, they had had experiences in slips, and they were satisfied to give over the chase at the first fence.

No streetlamps shed their light here, and the boys blundered along through the blackness with their hearts in their mouths. In one yard, filled with mountains of crates and fruit-boxes, they were lost for a quarter of an hour. Feel and quest about as they would, they encountered nothing but endless heaps of boxes. From this wilderness they finally emerged by way of a shed roof, only to fall into another yard, cumbered with countless empty chicken-coops.

Farther on they came upon the contrivance which had soaked Brick Simpson's pursuers with water. It was a cunning arrangement. Where the slip led through a fence with a board missing, a long slat was so arranged that the ignorant wayfarer could not fail to strike against it. This slat was the spring of the trap. A light touch upon it was sufficient to disconnect a heavy stone from a barrel perched overhead and nicely balanced. The disconnecting of the stone permitted the barrel to turn over and spill its contents on the one beneath who touched the slat.

The boys examined the arrangement with keen appreciation. Luckily for them, the barrel was overturned, or they too would have received a ducking, for Joe, who was in advance, had blundered against the slat.

"I wonder if this is Simpson's backyard?" he queried softly.

"It must be," Fred concluded, "or else the backyard of some member of his gang."

Charley put his hands warningly on both their arms.

"Hist! What's that?" he whispered.

They crouched down on the ground. Not far away was the sound of someone moving about. Then they heard a noise of falling water, as from a faucet into a bucket. This was followed by steps boldly approaching. They crouched lower, breathless with apprehension.

A dark form passed by within arm's reach and mounted on a box to the fence. It was Brick himself, resetting the trap. They heard him arrange the slat and stone, then right the barrel and empty into it a couple of buckets of water. As he came down from the box to go after more water, Joe sprang upon him, tripped him up, and held him to the ground.

"Don't make any noise," he said. "I want you to listen to me."

"Oh, it's you, is it?" Simpson replied, with such obvious

relief in his voice as to make them feel relieved also. "Wot d'
ye want here?"

"We want to get out of here," Joe said, "and the shortest
way's the best. There's three of us, and you're only one—"

"That's all right, that's all right," the gang-leader
interrupted. "I'd just as soon show you the way out as not. I
ain't got nothin' 'gainst you. Come on an' follow me, an'
don't step to the side, an' I'll have you out in no time."

Several minutes later they dropped from the top of a
high fence into a dark alley.

"Follow this to the street," Simpson directed; "turn to
the right two blocks, turn to the right again for three, an' yer
on Union. Tra-la-loo."

They said good-by, and as they started down the alley
received the following advice:

"Nex' time you bring kites along, you'd best leave 'em
to home."

CHAPTER 5
HOME AGAIN

FOLLOWING BRICK SIMPSON'S directions, they came into Union Street, and without further mishap gained the Hill. From the brow they looked down into the Pit, whence arose that steady, indefinable hum which comes from crowded human places.

"I'll never go down there again, not as long as I live," Fred said with a great deal of savagery in his voice. "I wonder what became of the fireman."

"We're lucky to get back with whole skins," Joe cheered them philosophically.

"I guess we left our share, and you more than yours," laughed Charley.

"Yes," Joe answered. "And I've got more trouble to face when I get home. Good night, fellows."

As he expected, the door on the side porch was locked, and he went around to the dining-room and entered like a burglar through a window. As he crossed the wide hall, walking softly toward the stairs, his father came out of the library. The surprise was mutual, and each halted aghast.

Joe felt a hysterical desire to laugh, for he thought that he knew precisely how he looked. In reality he looked far worse than he imagined. What Mr. Bronson saw was a boy with hat and coat covered with dirt, his whole face smeared with the stains of conflict, and, in particular, a badly swollen nose, a bruised eyebrow, a cut and swollen lip, a scratched cheek, knuckles still bleeding, and a shirt torn open from throat to waist.

"What does this mean, sir?" Mr. Bronson finally managed to articulate.

Joe stood speechless. How could he tell, in one brief sentence, all the whole night's happenings?—for all that must be included in the explanation of what his luckless disarray meant.

"Have you lost your tongue?" Mr. Bronson demanded with an appearance of impatience.

"I've—I've—"

"Yes, yes," his father encouraged.

"I've—well, I've been down in the Pit," Joe succeeded in blurting out.

"I must confess that you look like it—very much like it indeed." Mr. Bronson spoke severely, but if ever by great effort he conquered a smile, that was the time. "I presume," he went on, "that you do not refer to the abiding-place of sinners, but rather to some definite locality in San Francisco. Am I right?"

Joe swept his arm in a descending gesture toward Union Street, and said: "Down there, sir."

"And who gave it that name?"

"I did," Joe answered, as though confessing to a specified crime.

"It's most appropriate, I'm sure, and denotes imagination. It couldn't really be bettered. You must do well at school, sir, with your English."

This did not increase Joe's happiness, for English was the only study of which he did not have to feel ashamed.

And, while he stood thus a silent picture of misery and disgrace, Mr. Bronson looked upon him through the eyes of his own boyhood with an understanding which Joe could not have believed possible.

"However, what you need just now is not a discourse, but a bath and court-plaster and witch-hazel and cold-water bandages," Mr. Bronson said; "so to bed with you. You'll need all the sleep you can get, and you'll feel stiff and sore tomorrow morning, I promise you."

The clock struck one as Joe pulled the bedclothes around him; and the next he knew he was being worried by a soft, insistent rapping, which seemed to continue through several centuries, until at last, unable to endure it longer, he opened his eyes and sat up.

The day was streaming in through the window—bright and sunshiny day. He stretched his arms to yawn; but a shooting pain darted through all the muscles, and his arms came down more rapidly than they had gone up. He looked at them with a bewildered stare, till suddenly the events of the night rushed in upon him, and he groaned.

The rapping still persisted, and he cried: "Yes, I hear. What time is it?"

"Eight o'clock," Bessie's voice came to him through the door. "Eight o'clock, and you'll have to hurry if you don't want to be late for school."

"Goodness!" He sprang out of bed precipitately, groaned with the pain from all his stiff muscles, and collapsed slowly and carefully on a chair. "Why didn't you call me sooner?" he growled.

"Father said to let you sleep."

Joe groaned again, in another fashion Then his history-book caught his eye, and he groaned yet again and in still another fashion.

"All right," he called. "Go on. I'll be down in a jiffy."

He did come down in fairly brief order; but if Bessie had watched him descend the stairs she would have been astounded at the remarkable caution he observed and at the twinges of pain that every now and then contorted his face. As it was, when she came upon him in the dining-room she uttered a frightened cry and ran over to him.

"What's the matter, Joe?" she asked tremulously. "What has happened?"

"Nothing," he grunted, putting sugar on his porridge.

"But surely—" she began.

"Please don't bother me," he interrupted. "I'm late, and I want to eat my breakfast."

And just then Mrs. Bronson caught Bessie's eye, and that young lady, still mystified, made haste to withdraw herself.

Joe was thankful to his mother for that, and thankful that she refrained from remarking upon his appearance. Father had told her; that was one thing sure. He could trust her not to worry him; it was never her way.

And, meditating in this way, he hurried through with his solitary breakfast, vaguely conscious in an uncomfortable way that his mother was fluttering anxiously about him. Tender as she always was, he noticed that she kissed him with unusual tenderness as he started out with his books swinging at the end of a strap; and he also noticed, as he turned the corner, that she was still looking after him through the window.

But of more vital importance than that, to him, was his stiffness and soreness. As he walked along, each step was an effort and a torment. Severely as the reflected sunlight from the cement sidewalk hurt his bruised eye, and severely as his various wounds pained him, still more severely did he suffer from his muscles and joints. He had never imagined such stiffness. Each individual muscle in his whole body protested when called upon to move. His fingers were badly swollen, and it was agony to clasp and unclasp them; while his arms were sore from wrist to elbow. This, he said to himself, was caused by the many blows which he had warded off from his face and body. He wondered if Brick Simpson was in similar plight, and the thought of their mutual misery made him feel a certain kinship for that redoubtable young ruffian.

When he entered the school-yard he quickly became aware that he was the center of attraction for all eyes. The boys crowded around in an awe-stricken way, and even his classmates and those with whom he was well acquainted looked at him with a certain respect he had never seen before.

Chapter 6
Examination Day

IT WAS PLAIN THAT Fred and Charley had spread the news of their descent into the Pit, and of their battle with the Simpson clan and the Fishes. He heard the nine-o'clock bell with feelings of relief, and passed into the school, a mark for admiring glances from all the boys. The girls, too, looked at him in a timid and fearful way—as they might have looked at Daniel when he came out of the lions' den, Joe thought, or at David after his battle with Goliath. It made him uncomfortable and painfully self-conscious, this hero-worshiping, and he wished heartily that they would look in some other direction for a change.

Soon they did look in another direction. While big sheets of foolscap were being distributed to every desk, Miss Wilson, the teacher (an austere-looking young woman who went through the world as though it were a refrigerator, and who, even on the warmest days in the classroom, was to be found with a shawl or cape about her shoulders), arose, and on the blackboard where all could see wrote the Roman numeral "I." Every eye, and there were fifty pairs of them, hung with expectancy upon her hand, and in the pause that followed the room was quiet as the grave.

Underneath the Roman numeral "I" she wrote:

(a) What were the laws of Draco? (b) Why did an Athenian orator say that they were written 'not in ink, but in blood'?

Forty-nine heads bent down and forty-nine pens scratched lustily across as many sheets of foolscap. Joe's head alone remained up, and he regarded the blackboard with so blank a stare that Miss Wilson, glancing over her shoulder after having written "II," stopped to look at him. Then she wrote:

(a) How did the war between Athens and Megara, respecting the island of Salamis, bring about the reforms of Solon? (b) In what way did they differ from the laws of Draco?"

She turned to look at Joe again. He was staring as blankly as ever.

"What is the matter, Joe?" she asked. "Have you no paper?"

"Yes, I have, thank you," he answered, and began moodily to sharpen a lead-pencil.

He made a fine point to it. Then he made a very fine point. Then, and with infinite patience, he proceeded to make it very much finer. Several of his classmates raised their heads inquiringly at the noise. But he did not notice.

He was too absorbed in his pencil-sharpening and in thinking thoughts far away from both pencil-sharpening and Greek history.

"Of course, you all understand that the examination papers are to be written with ink."

Miss Wilson addressed the class in general, but her eyes rested on Joe.

Just as it was about as fine as it could possibly be the point broke, and Joe began over again.

"I am afraid, Joe, that you annoy the class," Miss Wilson said in final desperation.

He put the pencil down, closed the knife with a snap, and returned to his blank staring at the blackboard. What did he know about Draco? or Solon? or the rest of the Greeks? It was a flunk, and that was all there was to it. No need for him to look at the rest of the questions, and even if he did know the answers to two or three, there was no use in writing them down. It would not prevent the flunk. Besides, his arm hurt him too much to write. It hurt his eyes to look at the blackboard, and his eyes hurt even when they were closed; and it seemed positively to hurt him to think.

So the forty-nine pens scratched on in a race after Miss Wilson, who was covering the blackboard with question after question; and he listened to the scratching, and watched the questions growing under her chalk, and was very miserable indeed. His head seemed whirling around. It ached inside and was sore outside, and he did not seem to have any control of it at all.

He was beset with memories of the Pit, like scenes from some monstrous nightmare, and, try as he would, he could not dispel them. He would fix his mind and eyes on Miss Wilson's face, who was now sitting at her desk, and even as he looked at her the face of Brick Simpson, impudent and pugnacious, would arise before him. It was of no use. He felt sick and sore and tired and worthless. There was nothing to be done but flunk. And when, after an age of waiting, the papers were collected, his went in a blank, save for his name, the name of the examination, and the date, which were written across the top.

After a brief interval, more papers were given out, and the examination in arithmetic began. He did not trouble himself to look at the questions. Ordinarily he might have pulled through such an examination, but in his present state of mind and body he knew it was impossible. He contented himself with burying his face in his hands and hoping for the noon hour. Once, lifting his eyes to the clock, he caught Bessie looking anxiously at him across the room from the girls' side. This but added to his discomfort. Why was she bothering him? No need for her to trouble. She was bound to pass. Then why couldn't she leave him alone? So he gave her a particularly glowering look and buried his face in his hands again. Nor did he lift it till the twelve-o'clock gong rang, when he handed in a second blank paper and passed out with the boys.

Fred and Charley and he usually ate lunch in a corner of the yard which they had arrogated to themselves; but this day, by some remarkable coincidence, a score of other boys had elected to eat their lunches on the same spot. Joe surveyed them with disgust. In his present condition he did not feel inclined to receive hero-worship. His head ached too much, and he was troubled over his failure in the examinations; and there were more to come in the afternoon.

He was angry with Fred and Charley. They were chattering like magpies over the adventures of the night (in which, however, they did not fail to give him chief credit), and they conducted themselves in quite a patronizing fashion toward their awed and admiring schoolmates. But every attempt to make Joe talk was a failure. He grunted and gave short answers and said "yes" and "no" to questions asked with the intention of drawing him out.

He was longing to get away somewhere by himself, to throw himself down some place on the green grass and forget his aches and pains and troubles. He got up to go and find such a place and found half a dozen of his following tagging after him. He wanted to turn around and scream at them to leave him alone, but his pride restrained him. A great wave of disgust and despair swept over him, and then an idea flashed through his mind. Since he was sure to flunk in his examinations, why endure the afternoon's torture, which could not but be worse than the morning's? And on the impulse of the moment he made up his mind.

He walked straight on to the schoolyard gate and passed out. Here his worshipers halted in wonderment, but he kept on to the corner and out of sight. For some time, he wandered along aimlessly, till he came to the tracks of a cable road. A down-town car happening to stop to let off passengers, he stepped aboard and ensconced himself in an outside corner seat. The next thing he was aware of, the car was swinging around on its turn-table and he was hastily scrambling off. The big ferry building stood before him. Seeing and hearing nothing, he had been carried through the heart of the business section of San Francisco.

He glanced up at the tower clock on top of the ferry building. It was ten minutes after one—time enough to catch the quarter-past-one boat. That decided him, and without the least idea in the world as to where he was going, he paid ten cents for a ticket, passed through the gate, and was soon speeding across the bay to the pretty city of Oakland.

In the same aimless and unwitting fashion, he found himself, an hour later, sitting on the string-piece of the Oakland city wharf and leaning his aching head against a friendly timber. From where he sat he could look down upon the decks of a number of small sailing-craft. Quite a crowd of curious idlers had collected to look at them, and Joe found himself growing interested.

There were four boats, and from where he sat, he could make out their names. The one directly beneath him had the name *Ghost* painted in large green letters on its stern. The other three, which lay beyond, were called respectively *La Caprice*, the *Oyster Queen*, and the *Flying Dutchman*.

Each of these boats had cabins built amidships, with short stovepipes projecting through the roofs, and from the pipe of the *Ghost* smoke was ascending. The cabin doors were open, and the roof-slide pulled back, so that Joe could look inside and observe the inmate, a young fellow of nineteen or twenty who was engaged just then in cooking. He was clad in long sea-boots which reached the hips, blue overalls, and dark woolen shirt. The sleeves, rolled back to the elbows, disclosed sturdy, sun-bronzed arms, and when the young fellow looked up his face proved to be equally bronzed and tanned.

The aroma of coffee arose to Joe's nose, and from a light iron pot came the unmistakable smell of beans nearly done. The cook placed a frying-pan on the stove, wiped it around with a piece of suet when it had heated, and tossed in a thick chunk of beefsteak. While he worked he talked with a companion on deck, who was busily engaged in filling a bucket overside and flinging the salt water over heaps of oysters that lay on the deck. This completed, he covered the oysters with wet sacks, and went into the cabin, where a place was set for him on a tiny table, and where the cook served the dinner and joined him in eating it.

All the romance of Joe's nature stirred at the sight. That was life. They were living, and gaining their living, out in the free open, under the sun and sky, with the sea rocking beneath them, and the wind blowing on them, or the rain falling on them, as the chance might be. Each day and every day he sat in a room, pent up with fifty more of his kind, racking his brains and cramming dry husks of knowledge, while they were doing all this, living glad and careless and happy, rowing boats and sailing, and cooking their own food, and certainly meeting with adventures such as one only dreams of in the crowded school-room.

Joe sighed. He felt that he was made for this sort of life and not for the life of a scholar. As a scholar he was undeniably a failure. He had flunked in his examinations, while at that very moment, he knew, Bessie was going triumphantly home, her last examination over and done, and with credit. Oh, it was not to be borne! His father was wrong in sending him to school. That might be well enough for boys who were inclined to study, but it was manifest that he was not so inclined. There were more careers in life than that of the schools. Men had gone down to the sea in the lowest capacity, and risen in greatness, and owned great fleets, and done great deeds, and left their names on the pages of time. And why not he, Joe Bronson?

He closed his eyes and felt immensely sorry for himself; and when he opened his eyes again, he found that he had been asleep, and that the sun was sinking fast.

It was after dark when he arrived home, and he went straight to his room and to bed without meeting anyone. He sank down between the cool sheets with a sigh of satisfaction at the thought that, come what would, he need no longer worry about his history. Then another and unwelcome thought obtruded itself, and he knew that the next school term would come, and that six months thereafter, another examination in the same history awaited him.

CHAPTER 7
FATHER AND SON

ON THE FOLLOWING morning, after breakfast, Joe was summoned to the library by his father, and he went in almost with a feeling of gladness that the suspense of waiting was over. Mr. Bronson was standing by the window. A great chattering of sparrows outside seemed to have attracted his attention. Joe joined him in looking out, and saw a fledgling sparrow on the grass, tumbling ridiculously about in its efforts to stand on its feeble baby legs. It had fallen from the nest in the rose-bush that climbed over the window, and the two parent sparrows were wild with anxiety over its plight.

"It's a way young birds have," Mr. Bronson remarked, turning to Joe with a serious smile, "and I dare say you are on the verge of a somewhat similar predicament, my boy," he went on. "I am afraid things have reached a crisis, Joe. I have watched it coming on for a year now—your poor scholarship, your carelessness and inattention, your constant desire to be out of the house and away in search of adventures of one sort or another."

He paused, as though expecting a reply; but Joe remained silent.

"I have given you plenty of liberty. I believe in liberty. The finest souls grow in such soil. So I have not hedged you in with endless rules and irksome restrictions. I have asked little of you, and you have come and gone pretty much as you pleased. In a way, I have put you on your honor, made you largely your own master, trusting to your sense of right to restrain you from going wrong and at least to keep you up in your studies. And you have failed me. What do you want me to do? Set you certain bounds and time-limits? Keep a watch over you? Compel you by main strength to go through your books?

"I have here a note," Mr. Bronson said after another pause, in which he picked up an envelope from the table and drew forth a written sheet.

Joe recognized the stiff and uncompromising scrawl of Miss Wilson, and his heart sank.

His father began to read:

"Listlessness and carelessness have characterized his term's work, so that when the examinations came, he was wholly unprepared. In neither history nor arithmetic did he attempt to answer a question, passing in his papers perfectly blank. These examinations took place in the morning. In the afternoon he did not take the trouble even to appear for the remainder."

Mr. Bronson ceased reading and looked up.

"Where were you in the afternoon?" he asked.

"I went across on the ferry to Oakland," Joe answered, not caring to offer his aching head and body in extenuation.

"That is what is called 'playing hooky,' is it not?"

"Yes, sir," Joe answered.

"The night before the examinations, instead of studying, you saw fit to wander away and involve yourself in a disgraceful fight with hoodlums. I did not say anything at the time. In my heart I think I might almost have forgiven you that, if you had done well in your school-work."

Joe had nothing to say. He knew that there was his side to the story, but he felt that his father did not understand, and that there was little use of telling him.

"The trouble with you, Joe, is carelessness and lack of concentration. What you need is what I have not given you, and that is rigid discipline. I have been debating for some time upon the advisability of sending you to some military school, where your tasks will be set for you, and what you do every moment in the twenty-four hours will be determined for you—"

"Oh, father, you don't understand, you can't understand!" Joe broke forth at last. "I try to study—I honestly try to study; but somehow—I don't know how—I can't study. Perhaps I am a failure. Perhaps I am not made for study. I want to go out into the world. I want to see life—to live. I don't want any military academy; I'd sooner go to sea—anywhere where I can do something and be something."

Mr. Bronson looked at him kindly. "It is only through study that you can hope to do something and be something in the world," he said.

Joe threw up his hand with a gesture of despair.

"I know how you feel about it," Mr. Bronson went on; "but you are only a boy, very much like that young sparrow we were watching. If at home you have not sufficient control over yourself to study, then away from home, out in the world which you think is calling to you, you will likewise not have sufficient control over yourself to do the work of that world.

"But I am willing, Joe, I am willing, after you have finished high school and before you go into the university, to let you out into the world for a time."

"Let me go now?" Joe asked impulsively.

"No; it is too early. You haven't your wings yet. You are too unformed, and your ideals and standards are not yet thoroughly fixed."

"But I shall not be able to study," Joe threatened. "I know I shall not be able to study."

Mr. Bronson consulted his watch and arose to go. "I have not made up my mind yet," he said. "I do not know what I shall do—whether I shall give you another trial at the public school or send you to a military academy."

He stopped a moment at the door and looked back. "But remember this, Joe," he said. "I am not angry with you; I am more grieved and hurt. Think it over, and tell me this evening what you intend to do."

His father passed out, and Joe heard the front door close after him. He leaned back in the big easy-chair and closed his eyes. A military school! He feared such an institution as the animal fears a trap. No, he would certainly never go to such a place. And as for public school—He sighed deeply at the thought of it. He was given till evening to make up his mind as to what he intended to do. Well, he knew what he would do, and he did not have to wait till evening to find it out.

He got up with a determined look on his face, put on his hat, and went out the front door. He would show his father that he could do his share of the world's work, he thought as he walked along—he would show him.

By the time he reached the school he had his whole plan worked out definitely. Nothing remained but to put it through. It was the noon hour, and he passed in to his room and packed up his books unnoticed. Coming out through the yard, he encountered Fred and Charley.

"What's up?" Charley asked.

"Nothing," Joe grunted.

"What are you doing there?"

"Taking my books home, of course. What did you suppose I was doing?"

"Come, come," Fred interposed. "Don't be so mysterious. I don't see why you can't tell us what has happened."

"You'll find out soon enough," Joe said significantly—more significantly than he had intended.

And, for fear that he might say more, he turned his back on his astonished chums and hurried away. He went straight home and to his room, where he busied himself at once with putting everything in order. His clothes he hung carefully away, changing the suit he had on for an older one. From his bureau he selected a couple of changes of underclothing, a couple of cotton shirts, and half a dozen pairs of socks. To these he added as many handkerchiefs, a comb, and a tooth-brush.

When he had bound the bundle in stout wrapping-paper he contemplated it with satisfaction. Then he went over to his desk and took from a small inner compartment his savings for some months, which amounted to several dollars. This sum he had been keeping for the Fourth of July, but he thrust it into his pocket with hardly a regret. Then he pulled a writing-pad over to him, sat down and wrote:

> *Don't look for me. I am a failure and I am going away to sea. Don't worry about me. I am all right and able to take care of myself. I shall come back someday, and then you will all be proud of me. Good-by, papa, and mama, and Bessie.*
>
> *Joe*

This he left lying on his desk where it could easily be seen. He tucked the bundle under his arm, and, with a last farewell look at the room, stole out.

CHAPTER 8
'FRISCO KID AND THE NEW BOY

'FRISCO KID WAS discontented—discontented and disgusted. This would have seemed impossible to the boys who fished from the dock above and envied him greatly. True, they wore cleaner and better clothes, and were blessed with fathers and mothers; but his was the free-floating life of the bay, the domain of moving adventure, and the companionship of men—theirs the rigid discipline and dreary sameness of home life. They did not dream that 'Frisco Kid ever looked up at them from the cockpit of the *Dazzler* and in turn envied them just those things which sometimes were the most distasteful to them and from which they suffered to repletion. Just as the romance of adventure sang its siren song in their ears and whispered vague messages of strange lands and lusty deeds, so the delicious mysteries of home enticed 'Frisco Kid's roving fancies, and his brightest day-dreams were of the things he knew not—brothers, sisters, a father's counsel, a mother's kiss.

He frowned, got up from where he had been sunning himself on top of the *Dazzler*'s cabin, and kicked off his heavy rubber boots. Then he stretched himself on the narrow side-deck and dangled his feet in the cool salt water.

"Now that's freedom," thought the boys who watched him. Besides, those long sea-boots, reaching to the hips and buckled to the leather strap about the waist, held a strange and wonderful fascination for them. They did not know that 'Frisco Kid did not possess such things as shoes—that the boots were an old pair of Pete Le Maire's and were three sizes too large for him. Nor could they guess how uncomfortable they were to wear on a hot summer day.

The cause of 'Frisco Kid's discontent was those very boys who sat on the string-piece and admired him; but his disgust was the result of quite another event. The *Dazzler* was short one in its crew, and he had to do more work than was justly his share. He did not mind the cooking, nor the washing down of the decks and the pumping; but when it came to the paint-scrubbing and dishwashing he rebelled. He felt that he had earned the right to be exempt from such scullion work. That was all the green boys were fit for, while he could make or take in sail, lift anchor, steer, and make landings.

"Stan' from un'er!" Pete Le Maire or "French Pete," captain of the *Dazzler* and lord and master of 'Frisco Kid, threw a bundle into the cockpit and came aboard by the starboard rigging.

"Come! Queeck!" he shouted to the boy who owned the bundle and who now hesitated on the dock. It was a good fifteen feet to the deck of the sloop, and he could not reach the steel stay by which he must descend.

"Now! One, two, three!" the Frenchman counted good-naturedly, after the manner of captains when their crews are short-handed.

The boy swung his body into space and gripped the rigging. A moment later he struck the deck, his hands tingling warmly from the friction.

"Kid, dis is ze new sailor. I make your acquaintance." French Pete smirked and bowed and stood aside. "Mistaire Sho Bronson," he added as an afterthought.

The two boys regarded each other silently for a moment. They were evidently about the same age, though the stranger looked the heartier and stronger of the two. 'Frisco Kid put out his hand, and they shook.

"So you're thinking of tackling the water, eh?" he said.

Joe Bronson nodded and glanced curiously about him before answering: "Yes; I think the bay life will suit me for a while, and then, when I've got used to it, I'm going to sea in the forecastle."

"In the what?"

"In the forecastle—the place where the sailors live," he explained, flushing and feeling doubtful of his pronunciation.

"Oh, the fo'c'sle. Know anything about going to sea?"

"Yes—no; that is, except what I've read."

'Frisco Kid whistled, turned on his heel in a lordly manner, and went into the cabin.

"Going to sea," he chuckled to himself as he built the fire and set about cooking supper; "in the 'forecastle,' too; and thinks he'll like it."

In the meanwhile, French Pete was showing the newcomer about the sloop as though he were a guest. Such affability and charm did he display that 'Frisco Kid, popping his head up through the scuttle to call them to supper, nearly choked in his effort to suppress a grin.

Joe Bronson enjoyed that supper. The food was rough but good, and the smack of the salt air and the sea-fittings around him gave zest to his appetite. The cabin was clean and snug, and, though not large, the accommodations surprised him. Every bit of space was utilized. The table swung to the centerboard-case on hinges, so that when not in use it actually occupied no room at all. On either side and partly under the deck were two bunks. The blankets were rolled back, and the boys sat on the well-scrubbed bunk boards while they ate. A swinging sea-lamp of brightly polished brass gave them light, which in the daytime could be obtained through the four deadeyes, or small round panes of heavy glass which were fitted into the walls of the cabin. On one side of the door was the stove and wood-box, on the other the cupboard. The front end of the cabin was ornamented with a couple of rifles and a shotgun, while exposed by the rolled-back blankets of French Pete's bunk was a cartridge-lined belt carrying a brace of revolvers.

It all seemed like a dream to Joe. Countless times he had imagined scenes somewhat similar to this; but here he was right in the midst of it, and already it seemed as though he had known his two companions for years. French Pete was smiling genially at him across the board. It really was a villainous countenance, but to Joe it seemed only weather-beaten. 'Frisco Kid was describing to him, between mouthfuls, the last sou'easter the *Dazzler* had weathered, and Joe experienced an increasing awe for this boy who had lived so long upon the water and knew so much about it.

The captain, however, drank a glass of wine, and topped it off with a second and a third, and then, a vicious flush lighting his swarthy face, stretched out on top of his blankets, where he soon was snoring loudly.

"Better turn in and get a couple of hours' sleep," 'Frisco Kid said kindly, pointing Joe's bunk out to him. "We'll most likely be up the rest of the night."

Joe obeyed, but he could not fall asleep so readily as the others. He lay with his eyes wide open, watching the hands of the alarm-clock that hung in the cabin, and thinking how quickly event had followed event in the last twelve hours. Only that very morning he had been a school-boy, and now he was a sailor, shipped on the *Dazzler* and bound he knew not whither. His fifteen years increased to twenty at the thought of it, and he felt every inch a man—a sailorman at that. He wished Charley and Fred could see him now. Well, they would hear of it soon enough. He could see them talking it over, and the other boys crowding around. "Who?" "Oh, Joe Bronson; he's gone to sea. Used to chum with us."

Joe pictured the scene proudly. Then he softened at the thought of his mother worrying but hardened again at the recollection of his father. Not that his father was not good and kind; but he did not understand boys, Joe thought. That was where the trouble lay. Only that morning he had said that the world wasn't a playground, and that the boys who thought it was were liable to make sore mistakes and be glad to get home again. Well, he knew that there was plenty of hard work and rough experience in the world; but he also thought boys had some rights. He'd show him he could take care of himself; and, anyway, he could write home after he got settled down to his new life.

CHAPTER 9
ABOARD THE
"DAZZLER"

A SKIFF GRAZED THE side of the *Dazzler* softly and interrupted Joe's reveries. He wondered why he had not heard the sound of the oars in the rowlocks. Then two men jumped over the cockpit-rail and came into the cabin.

"Bli' me, if 'ere they ain't snoozin'," said the first of the newcomers, deftly rolling 'Frisco Kid out of his blankets with one hand and reaching for the wine-bottle with the other.

French Pete put his head up on the other side of the centerboard, his eyes heavy with sleep, and made them welcome.

"'Oo's this?" asked the Cockney, as he was called, smacking his lips over the wine and rolling Joe out upon the floor. "Passenger?"

"No, no," French Pete made haste to answer. "Ze new

sailorman. Vaire good boy."

"Good boy or not, he's got to keep his tongue atween his teeth," growled the second newcomer, who had not yet spoken, glaring fiercely at Joe.

"I say," queried the other man, "'ow does 'e whack up on the loot? I'ope as me and Bill 'ave a square deal."

"Ze *Dazzler* she take one share—what you call—one third; den we split ze rest in five shares. Five men, five shares. Vaire good."

French Pete insisted in excited gibberish that the *Dazzler* had the right to have three men in its crew and appealed to 'Frisco Kid to bear him out. But the latter left them to fight it over by themselves and proceeded to make hot coffee.

It was all Greek to Joe, except he knew that he was in some way the cause of the quarrel. In the end French Pete had his way, and the newcomers gave in after much grumbling. After they had drunk their coffee, all hands went on deck.

"Just stay in the cockpit and keep out of their way," 'Frisco Kid whispered to Joe. "I'll teach you about the ropes and everything when we ain't in a hurry."

Joe's heart went out to him in sudden gratitude, for the strange feeling came to him that of those on board, to 'Frisco Kid, and to 'Frisco Kid only, could he look for help in time of need. Already a dislike for French Pete was growing up within him. Why, he could not say; he just simply felt it.

A creaking of blocks for'ard, and the huge mainsail loomed above him in the night. Bill cast off the bowline, the Cockney followed suit with the stern, 'Frisco Kid gave her the jib as French Pete jammed up the tiller, and the *Dazzler* caught the breeze, heeling over for mid-channel. Joe heard talk of not putting up the side-lights, and of keeping a sharp lookout, though all he could comprehend was that some law of navigation was being violated.

The waterfront lights of Oakland began to slip past. Soon the stretches of docks and the shadowy ships began to be broken by dim sweeps of marshland, and Joe knew that they were heading out for San Francisco Bay. The wind was blowing from the north in mild squalls, and the *Dazzler* cut noiselessly through the landlocked water.

"Where are we going?" Joe asked the Cockney, in an endeavor to be friendly and at the same time satisfy his curiosity.

"Oh, my pardner 'ere, Bill, we're goin' to take a cargo from 'is factory," that worthy airily replied.

Joe thought he was rather a funny-looking individual to own a factory; but, conscious that even stranger things might be found in this new world he was entering, he said nothing. He had already exposed himself to 'Frisco Kid in the matter of his pronunciation of "fo'c'sle," and he had no desire further to advertise his ignorance.

A little after that he was sent in to blow out the cabin lamp. The *Dazzler* tacked about and began to work in toward the north shore. Everybody kept silent, save for occasional whispered questions and answers which passed between Bill and the captain. Finally, the sloop was run into the wind, and the jib and mainsail lowered cautiously.

"Short hawse," French Pete whispered to 'Frisco Kid, who went for'ard and dropped the anchor, paying out the slightest quantity of slack.

The *Dazzler's* skiff was brought alongside, as was also the small boat in which the two strangers had come aboard.

"See that that cub don't make a fuss," Bill commanded in an undertone, as he joined his partner in his own boat.

"Can you row?" 'Frisco Kid asked as they got into the other boat.

Joe nodded his head.

"Then take these oars, and don't make a racket."

'Frisco Kid took the second pair, while French Pete steered. Joe noticed that the oars were muffled with sennit, and that even the rowlock sockets were protected with leather. It was impossible to make a noise except by a misstroke, and Joe had learned to row on Lake Merrit well enough to avoid that. They followed in the wake of the first boat, and, glancing aside, he saw they were running along the length of a pier which jutted out from the land. A couple of ships, with riding-lanterns burning brightly, were moored to it, but they kept just beyond the edge of the light. He stopped rowing at the whispered command of 'Frisco Kid. Then the boats grounded like ghosts on a tiny beach, and they clambered out.

Joe followed the men, who picked their way carefully up a twenty-foot bank. At the top he found himself on a narrow railway track which ran between huge piles of rusty scrap-iron. These piles, separated by tracks, extended in every direction he could not tell how far, though in the distance he could see the vague outlines of some great factory-like building. The men began to carry loads of the iron down to the beach, and French Pete, gripping him by the arm and again warning him not to make any noise, told him to do likewise. At the beach they turned their burdens over to 'Frisco Kid, who loaded them, first in the one skiff and then in the other. As the boats settled under the weight, he kept pushing them farther and farther out, in order that they should keep clear of the bottom.

Joe worked away steadily, though he could not help marveling at the queerness of the whole business. Why should there be such a mystery about it? and why such care taken to maintain silence? He had just begun to ask himself these questions, and a horrible suspicion was forming itself in his mind, when he heard the hoot of an owl from the direction of the beach. Wondering at an owl being in so unlikely a place, he stooped to gather a fresh load of iron. But suddenly a man sprang out of the gloom, flashing a dark lantern full upon him. Blinded by the light, he staggered back. Then a revolver in the man's hand went off like the roar of a cannon. All Joe realized was that he was being shot at, while his legs manifested an overwhelming desire to get away. Even if he had so wished, he could not very well have stayed to explain to the excited man with the smoking revolver. So he took to his heels for the beach, colliding with another man with a dark lantern who came running around the end of one of the piles of iron. This second man quickly regained his feet and peppered away at Joe as he flew down the bank.

He dashed out into the water for the boat. French Pete at the bow-oars and 'Frisco Kid at the stroke had the skiff's nose pointed seaward and were calmly awaiting his arrival. They had their oars ready for the start, but they held them quietly at rest, for all that both men on the bank had begun to fire at them. The other skiff lay closer inshore, partially aground. Bill was trying to shove it off and was calling on the Cockney to lend a hand; but that gentleman had lost his head completely and came floundering through the water hard after Joe. No sooner had Joe climbed in over the stern than he followed him. This extra weight on the stern of the heavily loaded craft nearly swamped them. As it was, a dangerous quantity of water was shipped. In the meantime, the men on the bank had reloaded their pistols and opened fire again, this time with better aim. The alarm had spread. Voices and cries could be heard from the ships on the pier, along which men were running. In the distance a police whistle was being frantically blown.

"Get out!" 'Frisco Kid shouted. "You ain't a-going to sink us if I know it. Go and help your pardner."

But the Cockney's teeth were chattering with fright, and he was too unnerved to move or speak.

"T'row ze crazy man out!" French Pete ordered from the bow. At this moment, a bullet shattered an oar in his hand, and he coolly proceeded to ship a spare one.

"Give us a hand, Joe," 'Frisco Kid commanded.

Joe understood, and together they seized the terror-stricken creature and flung him overboard. Two or three bullets splashed about him as he came to the surface, just in time to be picked up by Bill, who had at last succeeded in getting clear.

"Now!" French Pete called, and a few strokes into the darkness quickly took them out of the zone of fire.

So much water had been shipped that the light skiff

was in danger of sinking at any moment. While the other two rowed, and by the Frenchman's orders, Joe began to throw out the iron. This saved them for the time being. But just as they swept alongside the *Dazzler*, the skiff lurched, shoved a side under, and turned turtle, sending the remainder of the iron to bottom. Joe and 'Frisco Kid came up side-by-side, and together they clambered aboard with the skiff's painter in tow. French Pete had already arrived, and now helped them out.

By the time they had canted the water out of the swamped boat, Bill and his partner appeared on the scene. All hands worked rapidly, and, almost before Joe could realize, the mainsail and jib had been hoisted, the anchor broken out, and the *Dazzler* was leaping down the channel. Off a bleak piece of marshland Bill and the Cockney said good-by and cast loose in their skiff. French Pete, in the cabin, bewailed their bad luck in various languages, and sought consolation in the wine-bottle.

Chapter 10
With the Bay
Pirates

THE WIND FRESHENED as they got clear of the land, and soon the *Dazzler* was heeling it with her lee deck buried and the water churning by, half-way up the cockpit-rail. Side-lights had been hung out. 'Frisco Kid was steering, and by his side sat Joe, pondering over the events of the night.

He could no longer blind himself to the facts. His mind was in a whirl of apprehension. If he had done wrong, he reasoned, he had done it through ignorance; and he did not feel shame for the past so much as he did fear for the future. His companions were thieves and robbers—the bay pirates, of whose wild deeds he had heard vague tales. And here he was, right in the midst of them, already possessing information which could send them to State's prison. This very fact, he knew, would force them to keep a sharp watch upon him and so lessen his chances of escape. But escape he would, at the very first opportunity.

At this point his thoughts were interrupted by a sharp squall, which hurled the *Dazzler* over till the sea rushed inboard. 'Frisco Kid luffed quickly, at the same time slacking off the main-sheet. Then, single-handed—for French Pete remained below—and with Joe looking idly on, he proceeded to reef down.

The squall which had so nearly capsized the *Dazzler* was of short duration, but it marked the rising of the wind, and soon puff after puff was shrieking down upon them out of the north. The mainsail was spilling the wind and slapping and thrashing about till it seemed it would tear itself to pieces. The sloop was rolling wildly in the quick sea which had come up. Everything was in confusion; but even Joe's untrained eye showed him that it was an orderly confusion. He could see that 'Frisco Kid knew just what to do and just how to do it. As he watched him, he learned a lesson, the lack of which has made failures of the lives of many men—the value of knowledge of one's own capacities. 'Frisco Kid knew what he was able to do, and because of this he had confidence in himself. He was cool and self-possessed, working hurriedly but not carelessly. There was no bungling. Every reef-point was drawn down to stay. Other accidents might occur, but the next squall, or the next forty squalls, would not carry one of those reef-knots away.

He called Joe for'ard to help stretch the mainsail by means of swinging on the peak and throat-halyards. To lay out on the long bowsprit and put a single reef in the jib was a slight task compared with what had been already accomplished; so a few moments later they were again in the cockpit. Under the other lad's directions, Joe flattened down the jib-sheet, and, going into the cabin, let down a foot or so of centerboard. The excitement of the struggle had chased all unpleasant thoughts from his mind. Patterning after the other boy, he had retained his coolness. He had executed his orders without fumbling, and at the same time without undue slowness. Together they had exerted their puny strength in the face of violent nature, and together they had outwitted her.

He came back to where his companion stood at the tiller steering, and he felt proud of him and of himself; and when he read the unspoken praise in 'Frisco Kid's eyes he blushed like a girl at her first compliment. But the next instant the thought flashed across him that this boy was a thief, a common thief; and he instinctively recoiled. His whole life had been sheltered from the harsher things of the world. His reading, which had been of the best, had laid a premium upon honesty and uprightness, and he had learned to look with abhorrence upon the criminal classes. So he drew a little away from 'Frisco Kid and remained silent. But 'Frisco Kid, devoting all his energies to the handling of the sloop, had no time in which to remark this sudden change of feeling on the part of his companion.

But there was one thing Joe found in himself that surprised him. While the thought of 'Frisco Kid being a thief was repulsive to him, 'Frisco Kid himself was not. Instead of feeling an honest desire to shun him, he felt drawn toward him. He could not help liking him, though he knew not why. Had he been a little older he would have understood that it was the lad's good qualities which appealed to him—his coolness and self-reliance, his manliness and bravery, and a certain kindliness and sympathy in his nature. As it was, he thought it his own natural badness which prevented him from disliking 'Frisco Kid; but, while he felt shame at his own weakness, he could not smother the warm regard which he felt growing up for this particular bay pirate.

"Take in two or three feet on the skiff's painter," commanded 'Frisco Kid, who had an eye for everything.

The skiff was towing with too long a painter and was behaving very badly. Every once in a while, it would hold back till the tow-rope tautened, then come leaping ahead and sheering and dropping slack till it threatened to shove its nose under the huge whitecaps which roared so hungrily on every hand. Joe climbed over the cockpit-rail to the slippery after-deck and made his way to the bitt to which the skiff was fastened.

"Be careful," 'Frisco Kid warned, as a heavy puff struck the *Dazzler* and careened her dangerously over on her side. "Keep one turn round the bitt and heave in on it when the painter slacks."

It was ticklish work for a greenhorn. Joe threw off all the turns save the last, which he held with one hand, while with the other he attempted to bring in on the painter. But at that instant it tightened with a tremendous jerk, the boat sheering sharply into the crest of a heavy sea. The rope slipped from his hands and began to fly out over the stern. He clutched it frantically and was dragged after it over the sloping deck.

"Let her go! Let her go!" 'Frisco Kid shouted.

Joe let go just as he was on the verge of going overboard, and the skiff dropped rapidly astern. He glanced in a shamefaced way at his companion, expecting to be sharply reprimanded for his awkwardness. But 'Frisco Kid smiled good-naturedly.

"That's all right," he said. "No bones broke and nobody overboard. Better to lose a boat than a man any day; that's what I say. Besides, I shouldn't have sent you out there. And there's no harm done. We can pick it up all right. Go in and drop some more centerboard—a couple of feet—and then come out and do what I tell you. But don't be in a hurry. Take it easy and sure."

Joe dropped the centerboard and returned, to be stationed at the jib-sheet.

"Hard a-lee!" 'Frisco Kid cried, throwing the tiller down, and following it with his body. "Cast off! That's right. Now lend a hand on the main-sheet!"

Together, hand over hand, they came in on the reefed mainsail. Joe began to warm up with the work. The *Dazzler* turned on her heel like a race-horse, and swept into the wind, her canvas snarling and her sheets slatting like hail.

"Draw down the jib-sheet!"

Joe obeyed, and, the head-sail filling, forced her off on the other tack. This maneuver had turned French Pete's bunk from the lee to the weather side, and rolled him out on the cabin floor, where he lay in a drunken stupor.

'Frisco Kid, with his back against the tiller and holding the sloop off that it might cover their previous course, looked at him with an expression of disgust, and muttered: "The dog! We could well go to the bottom, for all he'd care or do!"

Twice they tacked, trying to go over the same ground; and then Joe discovered the skiff bobbing to windward in the star-lit darkness.

"Plenty of time," 'Frisco Kid cautioned, shooting the *Dazzler* into the wind toward it and gradually losing headway. "Now!"

Joe leaned over the side, grasped the trailing painter, and made it fast to the bitt. Then they tacked ship again and started on their way. Joe still felt ashamed for the trouble he had caused; but 'Frisco Kid quickly put him at ease.

"Oh, that's nothing," he said. "Everybody does that when they're beginning. Now some men forget all about the trouble they had in learning and get mad when a greeny makes a mistake. I never do. Why, I remember—"

And then he told Joe of many of the mishaps which fell to him when, as a little lad, he first went on the water, and of some of the severe punishments for the same which were measured out to him. He had passed the running end of a lanyard over the tiller-neck, and as they talked, they sat side-by-side and close against each other in the shelter of the cockpit.

"What place is that?" Joe asked, as they flew by a lighthouse blinking from a rocky headland.

"Goat Island. They've got a naval training station for boys over on the other side, and a torpedo-magazine. There's jolly good fishing, too—rock-cod. We'll pass to the lee of it, and make across, and anchor in the shelter of Angel Island. There's a quarantine station there. Then when French Pete gets sober, we'll know where he wants to go. You can turn in now and get some sleep. I can manage all right."

Joe shook his head. There had been too much excitement for him to feel in the least like sleeping. He could not bear to think of it with the *Dazzler* leaping and surging along and shattering the seas into clouds of spray on her weather bow. His clothes had half dried already, and he preferred to stay on deck and enjoy it.

The lights of Oakland had dwindled till they made only a hazy flare against the sky; but to the south the San Francisco lights, topping hills and sinking into valleys, stretched miles upon miles. Starting from the great ferry building, and passing on to Telegraph Hill, Joe was soon able to locate the principal places of the city. Somewhere over in that maze of light and shadow was the home of his father, and perhaps even now they were thinking and worrying about him; and over there Bessie was sleeping cozily, to wake up in the morning and wonder why her brother Joe did not come down to breakfast. Joe shivered. It was almost morning. Then slowly his head dropped over on 'Frisco Kid's shoulder and he was fast asleep.

CHAPTER 11
CAPTAIN AND CREW

"COME! WAKE UP! WE'RE going into anchor."

Joe roused with a start, bewildered at the unusual scene; for sleep had banished his troubles for the time being, and he knew not where he was. Then he remembered. The wind had dropped with the night. Beyond, the heavy after-sea was still rolling; but the *Dazzler* was creeping up in the shelter of a rocky island. The sky was clear, and the air had the snap and vigor of early morning about it. The rippling water was laughing in the rays of the sun just shouldering above the eastern skyline. To the south lay Alcatraz Island, and from its gun-crowned heights a flourish of trumpets saluted the day. In the west the Golden Gate yawned between the Pacific Ocean and San Francisco Bay. A full-rigged ship, with her lightest canvas, even to the skysails, set, was coming slowly in on the flood-tide.

It was a pretty sight. Joe rubbed the sleep from his eyes and drank in the glory of it till 'Frisco Kid told him to go for'ard and make ready for dropping the anchor.

"Overhaul about fifty fathoms of chain," he ordered, "and then stand by." He eased the sloop gently into the wind, at the same time casting off the jib-sheet. "Let go the jib-halyards and come in on the downhaul!"

Joe had seen the maneuver performed the previous night, and so was able to carry it out with fair success.

"Now! Over with the mud-hook! Watch out for turns! Lively, now!"

The chain flew out with startling rapidity and brought the *Dazzler* to rest. 'Frisco Kid went for'ard to help, and together they lowered the mainsail, furled it in shipshape manner and made all fast with the gaskets, and put the crutches under the main-boom.

"Here's a bucket," said 'Frisco Kid, as he passed him the article in question. "Wash down the decks, and don't be afraid of the water, nor of the dirt either. Here's a broom. Give it what for and have everything shining. When you get that done bail out the skiff. She opened her seams a little last night. I'm going below to cook breakfast."

The water was soon slushing merrily over the deck, while the smoke pouring from the cabin stove carried a promise of good things to come. Time and again Joe lifted his head from his task to take in the scene. It was one to appeal to any healthy boy, and he was no exception. The romance of it stirred him strangely, and his happiness would have been complete could he have escaped remembering who and what his companions were. The thought of this, and of French Pete in his bleary sleep below, marred the beauty of the day. He had been unused to such things and was shocked at the harsh reality of life. But instead of hurting him, as it might a lad of weaker nature, it had the opposite effect. It strengthened his desire to be clean and strong, and to not be ashamed of himself in his own eyes. He glanced about him and sighed. Why could not men be honest and true? It seemed too bad that he must go away and leave all this; but the events of the night were strong upon him, and he knew that in order to be true to himself he must escape.

At this juncture he was called to breakfast. He discovered that 'Frisco Kid was as good a cook as he was a sailor and made haste to do justice to the fare. There were mush and condensed milk, beefsteak and fried potatoes, and all topped off with good French bread, butter, and coffee. French Pete did not join them, though 'Frisco Kid attempted a couple of times to rouse him. He mumbled and grunted, half opened his bleared eyes, then fell to snoring again.

"Can't tell when he's going to get those spells," 'Frisco Kid explained, when Joe, having finished washing dishes, came on deck. "Sometimes he won't get that way for a month, and others he won't be decent for a week at a stretch. Sometimes he's good-natured, and sometimes he's dangerous; so the best thing to do is to let him alone and keep out of his way; and don't cross him, for if you do there's liable to be trouble.

"Come on; let's take a swim," he added, abruptly changing the subject to one more agreeable. "Can you swim?"

Joe nodded.

"What's that place?" he asked, as he poised before diving, pointing toward a sheltered beach on the island where there were several buildings and a large number of tents.

"Quarantine station. Lots of smallpox coming in now on the China steamers, and they make them go there till the doctors say they're safe to land. I tell you, they're strict about it, too. Why—"

Splash! Had 'Frisco Kid finished his sentence just then, instead of diving overboard, much trouble might have been saved to Joe. But he did not finish it, and Joe dived after him.

"I'll tell you what," 'Frisco Kid suggested half an hour later, while they clung to the bobstay preparatory to climbing out. "Let's catch a mess of fish for dinner, and then turn in and make up for the sleep we lost last night. What d' you say?"

They made a race to clamber aboard, but Joe was shoved over the side again. When he finally did arrive, the other lad had brought to light a pair of heavily leaded, large-hooked lines and a mackerel-keg of salt sardines.

"Bait," he said. "Just shove a whole one on. They're not a bit partic'lar. Swallow the bait, hook and all, and go—that's their caper. The fellow that doesn't catch the first fish has to clean 'em."

Both sinkers started on their long descent together, and seventy feet of line whizzed out before they came to rest. But at the instant his sinker touched the bottom Joe felt the struggling jerks of a hooked fish. As he began to haul in he glanced at 'Frisco Kid and saw that he too had evidently captured a finny prize. The race between them was exciting. Hand over hand the wet lines flashed inboard. But 'Frisco Kid was more expert, and his fish tumbled into the cockpit first. Joe's followed an instant later—a three-pound rock-cod. He was wild with joy. It was magnificent—the largest fish he had ever landed or ever seen landed. Over went the lines again, and up they came with two mates of the ones already captured. It was sport royal. Joe would certainly have continued till he had fished the bay empty, had not 'Frisco Kid persuaded him to stop.

"We've got enough for three meals now," he said, "so there's no use in having them spoil. Besides, the more you catch the more you clean, and you'd better start in right away. I'm going to bed."

CHAPTER 12
JOE TRIES TO TAKE
THE FRENCH LEAVE

JOE DID NOT MIND. In fact, he was glad he had not caught the first fish, for it helped out a little plan which had come to him while swimming. He threw the last cleaned fish into a bucket of water and glanced about him. The quarantine station was a bare half-mile away, and he could make out a soldier pacing up and down at sentry duty on the beach. Going into the cabin, he listened to the heavy breathing of the sleepers. He had to pass so close to 'Frisco Kid to get his bundle of clothes that he decided not to take it. Returning outside, he carefully pulled the skiff alongside, got aboard with a pair of oars, and cast off.

At first he rowed very gently in the direction of the station, fearing the chance of noise if he made undue haste. But gradually he increased the strength of his strokes till he had settled down to the regular stride. When he had covered half the distance he glanced about. Escape was sure now, for he knew, even if he were discovered, that it would be impossible for the *Dazzler* to get under way and head him off before he made the land and the protection of that man who wore the uniform of Uncle Sam's soldiers.

The report of a gun came to him from the shore, but

his back was in that direction and he did not bother to turn around. A second report followed, and a bullet cut the water within a couple of feet of his oar-blade. This time he did turn around. The soldier on the beach was leveling his rifle at him for a third shot.

Joe was in a predicament, and a very tantalizing one at that. A few minutes of hard rowing would bring him to the beach and to safety; but on that beach, for some unaccountable reason, stood a United States soldier who persisted in firing at him. When Joe saw the gun aimed at him for the third time, he backed water hastily. As a result, the skiff came to a standstill, and the soldier, lowering his rifle, regarded him intently.

"I want to come ashore! Important!" Joe shouted out to him.

The man in uniform shook his head.

"But it's important, I tell you! Won't you let me come ashore?"

He took a hurried look in the direction of the *Dazzler*. The shots had evidently awakened French Pete, for the mainsail had been hoisted, and as he looked he saw the anchor broken out and the jib flung to the breeze.

"Can't land here!" the soldier shouted back. "Smallpox!"

"But I must!" he cried, choking down a half-sob and preparing to row.

"Then I'll shoot you," was the cheering response, and the rifle came to shoulder again.

Joe thought rapidly. The island was large. Perhaps there were no soldiers farther on, and if he only once got ashore, he did not care how quickly they captured him. He might catch the smallpox, but even that was better than going back to the bay pirates. He whirled the skiff half about to the right and threw all his strength against the oars. The cove was quite wide, and the nearest point which he must go around a good distance away. Had he been more of a sailor, he would have gone in the other direction for the opposite point, and thus had the wind on his pursuers. As it was, the *Dazzler* had a beam wind in which to overtake him.

It was nip and tuck for a while. The breeze was light and not very steady, so sometimes he gained and sometimes they. Once it freshened till the sloop was within a hundred yards of him, and then it dropped suddenly flat, the *Dazzler*'s big mainsail flapping idly from side to side.

"Ah! you steal ze skiff, eh?" French Pete howled at him, running into the cabin for his rifle. "I fix you! You come back queeck, or I kill you!" But he knew the soldier was watching them from the shore, and did not dare to fire, even over the lad's head.

Joe did not think of this, for he, who had never been shot at in all his previous life, had been under fire twice in the last twenty-four hours. Once more or less couldn't amount to much. So he pulled steadily away, while French Pete raved like a wild man, threatening him with all manner of punishments once he laid hands upon him again. To complicate matters, 'Frisco Kid waxed mutinous.

"Just you shoot him, and I'll see you hung for it—see if I don't," he threatened. "You'd better let him go. He's a good boy and all right, and not raised for the dirty life you and I are leading."

"You too, eh!" the Frenchman shrieked, beside himself with rage. "Den I fix you, you rat!"

He made a rush for the boy, but 'Frisco Kid led him a lively chase from cockpit to bowsprit and back again. A sharp capful of wind arriving just then, French Pete abandoned the one chase for the other. Springing to the tiller and slacking away on the main-sheet—for the wind favored—he headed the sloop down upon Joe. The latter made one tremendous spurt, then gave up in despair and hauled in his oars. French Pete let go the main-sheet, lost steerageway as he rounded up alongside the motionless skiff and dragged Joe out.

"Keep mum," 'Frisco Kid whispered to him while the irate Frenchman was busy fastening the painter. "Don't talk back. Let him say all he wants to and keep quiet. It'll be better for you."

But Joe's Anglo-Saxon blood was up, and he did not heed.

"Look here, Mr. French Pete, or whatever your name is," he commenced; "I give you to understand that I want to quit, and that I'm going to quit. So you'd better put me ashore at once. If you don't, I'll put you in prison, or my name's not Joe Bronson."

'Frisco Kid waited the outcome fearfully. French Pete was aghast. He was being defied aboard his own vessel—and by a boy! Never had such a thing been heard of. He knew he was committing an unlawful act in detaining him, but at the same time he was afraid to let him go with the information he had gathered concerning the sloop and its occupation. The boy had spoken the unpleasant truth when he said he could send him to prison. The only thing for him to do was to bully him.

"You will, eh?" His shrill voice rose wrathfully. "Den you come too. You row ze boat last-a night—answer me dat! You steal ze iron—answer me dat! You run away—answer me dat! And den you say you put me in jail? Bah!"

"But I didn't know," Joe protested.

"Ha, ha! Dat is funny. You tell dat to ze judge; mebbe him laugh, eh?"

"I say I didn't," he reiterated manfully. "I didn't know I'd shipped along with a lot of thieves."

'Frisco Kid winced at this epithet, and had Joe been looking at him he would have seen a red flush mount to his face.

"And now that I do know," he continued, "I wish to be put ashore. I don't know anything about the law, but I do know something of right and wrong; and I'm willing to take my chance with any judge for whatever wrong I have done—with all the judges in the United States, for that matter. And that's more than you can say, Mr. Pete."

"You say dat, eh? Vaire good. But you are one big t'ief—"

"I'm not—don't you dare call me that again!" Joe's face was pale, and he was trembling—but not with fear.

"T'ief!" the Frenchman taunted back.

"You lie!"

Joe had not been a boy among boys for nothing. He knew the penalty which attached itself to the words he had just spoken, and he expected to receive it. So he was not overmuch surprised when he picked himself up from the floor of the cockpit an instant later, his head still ringing from a stiff blow between the eyes.

"Say dat one time more," French Pete bullied, his fist raised and prepared to strike.

Tears of anger stood in Joe's eyes, but he was calm and in deadly earnest. "When you say I am a thief, Pete, you lie. You can kill me, but still I will say you lie."

"No, you don't!" 'Frisco Kid had darted in like a cat, preventing a second blow, and shoving the Frenchman back across the cockpit.

"You leave the boy alone!" he continued, suddenly unshipping and arming himself with the heavy iron tiller and standing between them. "This thing's gone just about as far as it's going to go. You big fool, can't you see the stuff the boy's made of? He speaks true. He's right, and he knows it, and you could kill him, and he wouldn't give in. There's my hand on it, Joe." He turned and extended his hand to Joe, who returned the grip. "You 've got spunk and you're not afraid to show it."

French Pete's mouth twisted itself in a sickly smile, but the evil gleam in his eyes gave it the lie. He shrugged his shoulders and said, "Ah! So? He does not dee-sire dat I call him pet names. Ha, ha! It is only ze sailorman play. Let us—what you call—forgive and forget, eh? Vaire good; forgive and forget."

He reached out his hand, but Joe refused to take it. 'Frisco Kid nodded approval, while French Pete, still shrugging his shoulders and smiling, passed into the cabin.

"Slack off ze main-sheet," he called out, "and run down for Hunter's Point. For one time I will cook ze dinner, and den you will say dat it is ze vaire good dinner. Ah! French Pete is ze great cook!"

"That's the way he always does—gets real good and cooks when he wants to make up," 'Frisco Kid hazarded, slipping the tiller into the rudder-head and obeying the order. "But even then you can't trust him."

Joe nodded his head, but did not speak. He was in no mood for conversation. He was still trembling from the excitement of the last few moments, while deep down he questioned himself on how he had behaved and found nothing to be ashamed of.

CHAPTER 13
BEFRIENDING EACH
OTHER

THE AFTERNOON SEA-BREEZE had sprung up and was now rioting in from the Pacific. Angel Island was fast dropping astern, and the waterfront of San Francisco showing up, as the *Dazzler* plowed along before it. Soon they were in the midst of the shipping, passing in and out among the vessels which had come from the ends of the earth. Later they crossed the fairway, where the ferry steamers, crowded with passengers, passed to and fro between San Francisco and Oakland. One came so close that the passengers crowded to the side to see the gallant little sloop and the two boys in the cockpit. Joe gazed enviously at the row of down-turned faces. They were all going to their homes, while he—he was going he knew not whither, at the will of French Pete. He was half tempted to cry out for help; but the foolishness of such an act struck him, and he held his tongue. Turning his head, his eyes wandered along the smoky heights of the city, and he fell to musing on the strange way of men and ships on the sea.

'Frisco Kid watched him from the corner of his eye, following his thoughts as accurately as though he spoke them aloud.

"Got a home over there somewheres?" he queried suddenly, waving his hand in the direction of the city.

Joe started, so correctly had his thought been guessed. "Yes," he said simply.

"Tell us about it."

Joe rapidly described his home, though forced to go into greater detail because of the curious questions of his companion. 'Frisco Kid was interested in everything, especially in Mrs. Bronson and Bessie. Of the latter he could not seem to tire and poured forth question after question concerning her. So peculiar and artless were some of them that Joe could hardly forbear to smile.

"Now tell me about yours," he said when he at last had finished.

'Frisco Kid seemed suddenly to harden, and his face took on a stern look which the other had never seen there before. He swung his foot idly to and fro, and lifted a dull eye aloft to the main-peak blocks, with which, by the way, there was nothing the matter.

"Go ahead," the other encouraged.

"I haven't no home."

The four words left his mouth as though they had been forcibly ejected, and his lips came together after them almost with a snap.

Joe saw he had touched a tender spot and strove to ease the way out of it again. "Then the home you did have." He did not dream that there were lads in the world who never had known homes, or that he had only succeeded in probing deeper.

"Never had none."

"Oh!" His interest was aroused, and he now threw solicitude to the winds. "Any sisters?"

"Nope."

"Mother?"

"I was so young when she died that I don't remember her."

"Father?"

"I never saw much of him. He went to sea—anyhow, he disappeared."

"Oh!" Joe did not know what to say, and an oppressive silence, broken only by the churn of the *Dazzler's* forefoot, fell upon them.

Just then Pete came out to relieve at the tiller while they went in to eat. Both lads hailed his advent with feelings of relief, and the awkwardness vanished over the dinner, which was all their skipper had claimed it to be. Afterward 'Frisco Kid relieved Pete, and while he was eating Joe washed up the dishes and put the cabin shipshape. Then they all gathered in the stern, where the captain strove to increase the general cordiality by entertaining them with descriptions of life among the pearl-divers of the South Seas.

In this fashion the afternoon wore away. They had long since left San Francisco behind, rounded Hunter's Point, and were now skirting the San Mateo shore. Joe caught a glimpse, once, of a party of cyclists rounding a cliff on the San Bruno Road and remembered the time when he had gone over the same ground on his own wheel. It was only a month or two before, but it seemed an age to him now, so much had there been to come between.

By the time supper had been eaten and the things cleared away, they were well down the bay, off the marshes behind which Redwood City clustered. The wind had gone down with the sun, and the *Dazzler* was making but little headway, when they sighted a sloop bearing down upon them on the dying wind. 'Frisco Kid instantly named it as the *Reindeer*, to which French Pete, after a deep scrutiny, agreed. He seemed very much pleased at the meeting.

"Red Nelson runs her," 'Frisco Kid informed Joe. "And he's a terror and no mistake. I'm always afraid of him when he comes near. They've got something big down here, and they're always after French Pete to tackle it with them. He knows more about it, whatever it is."

Joe nodded and looked at the approaching craft curiously. Though somewhat larger, it was built on about the same lines as the *Dazzler* which meant, above everything else, that it was built for speed. The mainsail was so large that it was more like that of a racing-yacht, and it carried the points for no less than three reefs in case of rough weather. Aloft and on deck everything was in place—nothing was untidy or useless. From running-gear to standing rigging, everything bore evidence of thorough order and smart seamanship.

The *Reindeer* came up slowly in the gathering twilight and went to anchor a biscuit-toss away. French Pete followed suit with the *Dazzler*, and then went in the skiff to pay them a visit. The two lads stretched themselves out on top the cabin and awaited his return.

"Do you like the life?" Joe broke silence.

The other turned on his elbow. "Well—I do, and then

again I don't. The fresh air, and the salt water, and all that, and the freedom—that's all right; but I don't like the—the—" He paused a moment, as though his tongue had failed in its duty, and then blurted out: "the stealing."

"Then why don't you quit it?" Joe liked the lad more than he dared confess to himself, and he felt a sudden missionary zeal come upon him.

"I will just as soon as I can turn my hand to something else."

"But why not now?"

Now is the accepted time was ringing in Joe's ears, and if the other wished to leave, it seemed a pity that he did not, and at once.

"Where can I go? What can I do? There's nobody in all the world to lend me a hand, just as there never has been. I tried it once and learned my lesson too well to do it again in a hurry."

"Well, when I get out of this I'm going home. Guess my father was right, after all. And I don't see, maybe—what's the matter with you going with me?" He said this last without thinking, impulsively, and 'Frisco Kid knew it.

"You don't know what you're talking about," he answered. "Fancy me going off with you! What'd your father say? and—and the rest? How would he think of me? And what'd he do?"

Joe felt sick at heart. He realized that in the spirit of the moment he had given an invitation which, on sober thought, he knew would be impossible to carry out. He tried to imagine his father receiving in his own house a stranger like 'Frisco Kid—no, that was not to be thought of. Then, forgetting his own plight, he fell to racking his brains for some other method by which 'Frisco Kid could get away from his present surroundings.

"He might turn me over to the police," the other went on, "and send me to a refuge. I'd die first, before I'd let that happen to me. And besides, Joe, I'm not of your kind, and you know it. Why, I'd be like a fish out of water, what with all the things I didn't know. Nope; I guess I'll have to wait a little before I strike out. But there's only one thing for you to do, and that's to go straight home. First chance I get I'll land you, and then I'll deal with French Pete—"

"No, you don't," Joe interrupted hotly. "When I leave, I'm not going to leave you in trouble on my account. So don't you try anything like that. I'll get away, never fear, and if I can figure it out, I want you to come along too; come along anyway, and figure it out afterward. What d' you say?"

'Frisco Kid shook his head, and, gazing up at the starlit heavens, wandered off into dreams of the life he would like to lead but from which he seemed inexorably shut out. The seriousness of life was striking deeper than ever into Joe's heart, and he lay silent, thinking hard. A mumble of heavy voices came to them from the *Reindeer*; and from the land the solemn notes of a church bell floated across the water, while the summer night wrapped them slowly in its warm darkness.

CHAPTER 14
AMONG THE OYSTER
BEDS

TIME AND THE WORLD slipped away, and both boys were aroused by the harsh voice of French Pete from the sleep into which they had fallen.

"Get under way!" he was bawling. "Here, you Sho! Cast off ze gaskets! Queeck! Lively! You Kid, ze jib!"

Joe was clumsy in the darkness, not knowing the names of things and the places where they were to be found; but he made fair progress, and when he had tossed the gaskets into the cockpit was ordered forward to help hoist the mainsail. After that the anchor was hove in and the jib set. Then they coiled down the halyards and put everything in order before they returned aft.

"Vaire good, vaire good," the Frenchman praised, as Joe dropped in over the rail. "Splendeed! You make ze good sailorman, I know for sure."

'Frisco Kid lifted the cover of one of the cockpit lockers and glanced questioningly at French Pete.

"For sure," that mariner replied. "Put up ze side-lights."

'Frisco Kid took the red and green lanterns into the cabin to light them, and then went forward with Joe to hang them in the rigging.

"They're not goin' to tackle it," 'Frisco Kid said in an undertone.

"What?" Joe asked.

"That big thing I was tellin' you was down here somewhere. It's so big, I guess, that French Pete's 'most afraid to go in for it. Red Nelson'd go in quicker 'n a wink, but he don't know enough about it. Can't go in, you see, till Pete gives the word."

"Where are we going now?" Joe questioned.

"Don't know; oyster-beds most likely, from the way we're heading."

It was an uneventful trip. A breeze sprang up out of the night behind them and held steady for an hour or more. Then it dropped and became aimless and erratic, puffing gently first from one quarter and then another. French Pete remained at the tiller, while occasionally Joe or 'Frisco Kid took in or slacked off a sheet.

Joe sat and marveled that the Frenchman should know where he was going. To Joe it seemed that they were lost in the impenetrable darkness which shrouded them. A high fog had rolled in from the Pacific, and though they were beneath, it came between them and the stars, depriving them of the little light from that source.

But French Pete seemed to know instinctively the direction he should go, and once, in reply to a query from Joe, bragged of his ability to go by the "feel" of things.

"I feel ze tide, ze wind, ze speed," he explained. "Even do I feel ze land. Dat I tell you for sure. How? I do not know. Only do I know dat I feel ze land, just like my arm grow long, miles and miles long, and I put my hand upon ze land and feel it and know dat it is there."

Joe looked incredulously at 'Frisco Kid.

"That's right," he affirmed. "After you 've been on the water a good while you come to feel the land. And if your nose is any account, you can usually smell it."

An hour or so later, Joe surmised from the Frenchman's actions that they were approaching their destination. He seemed on the alert, and was constantly peering into the darkness ahead as though he expected to see something at any moment. Joe looked very hard but saw only the darkness.

"Try ze stick, Kid," French Pete ordered. "I t'ink it is about ze time."

'Frisco Kid unlashed a long and slender pole from the top of the cabin, and, standing on the narrow deck amidships, plunged one end of it into the water and drove it straight down.

"About fifteen feet," he said.

"What ze bottom?"

"Mud," was the answer.

"Wait one while, den we try some more."

Five minutes afterward the pole was plunged overside again.

"Two fathoms," Joe answered. "Shells."

French Pete rubbed his hands with satisfaction. "Vaire good, vaire well," he said. "I hit ze ground every time. You can't fool-a ze old man; I tell you dat for sure."

'Frisco Kid continued operating the pole and announcing the results, to the mystification of Joe, who could not comprehend their intimate knowledge of the bottom of the bay.

"Ten feet—shells," 'Frisco Kid went on in a monotonous voice. "'Leven feet—shells. Fourteen feet—soft. Sixteen feet—mud. No bottom."

"Ah, ze channel," said French Pete at this.

For a few minutes it was "No bottom"; and then, suddenly, came 'Frisco Kid's cry: "Eight feet—hard!"

"Dat'll do," French Pete commanded. "Run for'ard, you Sho, an' let go ze jib. You, Kid, get all ready ze hook."

Joe found the jib-halyard and cast it off the pin, and, as the canvas fluttered down, came in hand over hand on the downhaul.

"Let 'er go!" came the command, and the anchor dropped into the water, carrying but little chain after it.

'Frisco Kid threw over plenty of slack and made fast. Then they furled the sails, made things tidy, and went below and to bed.

It was six o'clock when Joe awoke and went out into the cockpit to look about. Wind and sea had sprung up, and the *Dazzler* was rolling and tossing and now and again fetching up on her anchor-chain with a savage jerk. He was forced to hold on to the boom overhead to steady himself. It was a gray and leaden day, with no signs of the rising sun, while the sky was obscured by great masses of flying clouds.

Joe sought for the land. A mile and a half away it lay—a long, low stretch of sandy beach with a heavy surf thundering upon it. Behind appeared desolate marshlands, while far beyond towered the Contra Costa Hills.

Changing the direction of his gaze, Joe was startled by the sight of a small sloop rolling and plunging at her anchor not a hundred yards away. She was nearly to windward, and as she swung off slightly, he read her name on the stern, the *Flying Dutchman*, one of the boats he had seen lying at the city wharf in Oakland. A little to the left of her he discovered the *Ghost*, and beyond were half a dozen other sloops at anchor.

"What I tell you?"

Joe looked quickly over his shoulder. French Pete had come out of the cabin and was triumphantly regarding the spectacle.

"What I tell you? Can't fool-a ze old man, dat's what. I hit it in ze dark just so well as in ze sunshine. I know—I know."

"Is she goin' to howl?" 'Frisco Kid asked from the cabin, where he was starting the fire.

The Frenchman gravely studied sea and sky for a couple of minutes.

"Mebbe blow over—mebbe blow up," was his doubtful verdict. "Get breakfast queeck, and we try ze dredging."

Smoke was rising from the cabins of the different sloops, denoting that they were all bent on getting the first meal of the day. So far as the *Dazzler* was concerned, it was a simple matter, and soon they were putting a single reef in the mainsail and getting ready to weigh anchor.

Joe was curious. These were undoubtedly the oyster-beds; but how under the sun, in that wild sea, were they to get oysters? He was quickly to learn the way. Lifting a section of the cockpit flooring, French Pete brought out two triangular frames of steel. At the apex of one of these triangles; in a ring for the purpose, he made fast a piece of stout rope. From this the sides (inch rods) diverged at almost right angles and extended down for a distance of four feet or more, where they were connected by the third side of the triangle, which was the bottom of the dredge. This was a flat plate of steel over a yard in length, to which was bolted a row of long, sharp teeth, likewise of steel. Attached to the toothed plate, and to the sides of the frame was a net of very coarse fishing-twine, which Joe correctly surmised was there to catch the oysters raked loose by the teeth from the bottom of the bay.

A rope being made fast to each of the dredges, they were dropped overboard from either side of the *Dazzler*. When they had reached the bottom and were dragging with the proper length of line out, they checked her speed quite noticeably. Joe touched one of the lines with his hands and could feel plainly the shock and jar and grind as it tore over the bottom.

"All in!" French Pete shouted.

The boys laid hold of the line and hove in the dredge. The net was full of mud and slime and small oysters, with here and there a large one. This mess they dumped on the deck and picked over while the dredge was dragging again. The large oysters they threw into the cockpit and shoveled the rubbish overboard. There was no rest, for by this time the other dredge required emptying. And when this was done and the oysters sorted, both dredges had to be hauled aboard, so that French Pete could put the *Dazzler* about on the other tack.

The rest of the fleet was under way and dredging back in similar fashion. Sometimes the different sloops came quite close to them, and they hailed them and exchanged snatches of conversation and rough jokes. But in the main it was hard work, and at the end of an hour Joe's back was aching from the unaccustomed strain, and his fingers were cut and bleeding from his clumsy handling of the sharp-edged oysters.

"Dat's right," French Pete said approvingly. "You learn queeck. Vaire soon you know how."

Joe grinned ruefully and wished it was dinner-time. Now and then, when a light dredge was hauled, the boys managed to catch breath and say a couple of words.

"That's Asparagus Island," 'Frisco Kid said, indicating the shore. "At least, that's what the fishermen and scow-sailors call it. The people who live there call it Bay Farm Island." He pointed more to the right. "And over there is San Leandro. You can't see it, but it's there."

"Ever been there?" Joe asked.

'Frisco Kid nodded his head and signed to him to help heave in the starboard dredge.

"These are what they call the deserted beds," he said again. "Nobody owns them, so the oyster pirates come down and make a bluff at working them."

"Why a bluff?"

"'Cause they're pirates, that's why, and because there's more money in raiding the private beds."

He made a sweeping gesture toward the east and southeast. "The private beds are over yonder, and if it don't storm the whole fleet'll be raidin' 'em to-night."

"And if it does storm?" Joe asked.

"Why, we won't raid them, and French Pete'll be mad,

that's all. He always hates being put out by the weather. But it don't look like lettin' up, and this is the worst possible shore in a sou'wester. Pete may try to hang on, but it's best to get out before she howls."

At first it did seem as though the weather were growing better. The stiff southwest wind dropped perceptibly, and by noon, when they went to anchor for dinner, the sun was breaking fitfully through the clouds.

"That's all right," 'Frisco Kid said prophetically. "But I ain't been on the bay for nothing. She's just gettin' ready to let us have it good an' hard."

"I t'ink you're right, Kid," French Pete agreed; "but ze *Dazzler* hang on all ze same. Last-a time she run away, an' fine night come. Dis time she run not away. Eh? Vaire good."

CHAPTER 15
GOOD SAILORS IN A
WILD ANCHORAGE

ALL AFTERNOON, THE DAZZLER pitched and rolled at her anchorage, and as evening drew on the wind deceitfully eased down. This, and the example set by French Pete, encouraged the rest of the oyster-boats to attempt to ride out the night; but they looked carefully to their moorings and put out spare anchors.

French Pete ordered the two boys into the skiff, and, at the imminent risk of swamping, they carried out a second anchor, at nearly right angles to the first one, and dropped it over. French Pete then ran out a great quantity of chain and rope, so that the *Dazzler* dropped back a hundred feet or more, where she rode more easily.

It was a wild stretch of water which Joe looked upon from the shelter of the cockpit. The oyster-beds were out in the open bay, utterly unprotected, and the wind, sweeping the water for a clean twelve miles, kicked up so tremendous a sea that at every moment it seemed as though the wallowing sloops would roll their masts overside. Just before twilight a patch of sail sprang up to windward and grew and grew until it resolved itself into the huge mainsail of the *Reindeer*.

"Ze beeg fool!" French Pete cried, running out of the cabin to see. "Sometime—ah, sometime, I tell you—he crack on like dat, an' he go, pouf! just like dat, pouf!—an' no more Nelson, no more *Reindeer*, no more nothing."

Joe looked inquiringly at 'Frisco Kid.

"That's right," he answered. "Nelson ought to have at least one reef in. Two'd be better. But there he goes, every inch spread, as though some fiend was after 'im. He drives too hard; he's too reckless, when there ain't the smallest need for it. I've sailed with him, and I know his ways."

Like some huge bird of the air, the *Reindeer* lifted and soared down on them on the foaming crest of a wave.

"Don't mind," 'Frisco Kid warned. "He's only tryin' to see how close he can come to us without hittin' us."

Joe nodded and stared with wide eyes at the thrilling sight. The *Reindeer* leaped up in the air, pointing her nose to the sky till they could see her whole churning forefoot; then she plunged downward till her for'ard deck was flush with the foam, and with a dizzying rush she drove past them, her main-boom missing the *Dazzler*'s rigging by scarcely a foot.

Nelson, at the wheel, waved his hand to them as he hurtled past, and laughed joyously in French Pete's face, who was angered by the dangerous trick.

When to leeward, the splendid craft rounded to the wind, rolling once till her brown bottom showed to the centerboard and they thought she was over, then righting and dashing ahead again like a thing possessed. She passed abreast of them on the starboard side. They saw the jib run down with a rush and an anchor go overboard as she shot into the wind; and as she fell off and back and off and back with a spilling mainsail, they saw a second anchor go overboard, wide apart from the first. Then the mainsail came down on the run and was furled and fastened by the time she had tightened to her double hawsers.

"Ah, ah! Never was there such a man!"

The Frenchman's eyes were glistening with admiration for such perfect seamanship, and 'Frisco Kid's were likewise moist.

"Just like a yacht," he said as he went back into the cabin. "Just like a yacht, only better."

As night came on the wind began to rise again, and by eleven o'clock had reached the stage which 'Frisco Kid described as "howlin'." There was little sleep on the *Dazzler*. He alone closed his eyes. French Pete was up and down every few minutes. Twice, when he went on deck, he paid out more chain and rope. Joe lay in his blankets and listened, the while vainly courting sleep. He was not frightened, but he was untrained in the art of sleeping in the midst of such turmoil and uproar and violent commotion. Nor had he imagined a boat could play as wild antics as did the *Dazzler* and still survive. Often, she wallowed over on her beam till he thought she would surely capsize. At other times she leaped and plunged in the air and fell upon the seas with thunderous crashes as though her bottom were shattered to fragments. Again, she would fetch up taut on her hawsers so suddenly and so fiercely as to reel from the shock and to groan and protest through every timber.

'Frisco Kid awoke once, and smiled at him, saying:

"This is what they call hangin' on. But just you wait till daylight comes and watch us clawin' off. If some of the sloops don't go ashore, I'm not me, that's all."

And thereat he rolled over on his side and was off to sleep. Joe envied him. About three in the morning, he heard French Pete crawl up for'ard and rummage around in the eyes of the boat. Joe looked on curiously, and by the dim light of the wildly swinging sea-lamp saw him drag out two spare coils of line. These he took up on deck, and Joe knew he was bending them on to the hawsers to make them still longer.

At half-past four French Pete had the fire going, and at five he called the boys for coffee. This over, they crept into the cockpit to gaze on the terrible scene. The dawn was breaking bleak and gray over a wild waste of tumbling water. They could faintly see the beach-line of Asparagus Island, but they could distinctly hear the thunder of the surf upon it; and as the day grew stronger they made out that they had dragged fully half a mile during the night.

The rest of the fleet had likewise dragged. The *Reindeer* was almost abreast of them; *La Caprice* lay a few hundred yards away; and to leeward, straggling between them and shore, were five more of the struggling oyster-boats.

"Two missing," 'Frisco Kid announced, putting the glasses to his eyes and searching the beach.

"And there's one!" he cried. And after studying it carefully he added: "The *Go Ask Her*. She'll be in pieces in no time. I hope they got ashore."

French Pete looked through the glasses, and then Joe. He could clearly see the unfortunate sloop lifting and pounding in the surf, and on the beach he spied the men who made up her crew.

"Where's ze *Ghost*?" French Pete queried.

'Frisco Kid looked for her in vain along the beach; but when he turned the glass seaward he quickly discovered her riding safely in the growing light, half a mile or more to windward.

"I'll bet she didn't drag a hundred feet all night," he said. "Must've struck good holding-ground."

"Mud," was French Pete's verdict. "Just one vaire small patch of mud right there. If she get t'rough it she's a sure-enough goner, I tell you dat. Her anchors vaire light, only good for mud. I tell ze boys get more heavy anchors, but dey laugh. Someday be sorry, for sure."

One of the sloops to leeward raised a patch of sail and began the terrible struggle out of the jaws of destruction and death. They watched her for a space, rolling and plunging fearfully, and making very little headway.

French Pete put a stop to their gazing. "Come on!" he shouted. "Put two reef in ze mainsail! We get out queeck!"

While occupied with this a shout aroused them. Looking up, they saw the *Ghost* dead ahead and right on top of them, dragging down upon them at a furious rate.

French Pete scrambled forward like a cat, at the same time drawing his knife, with one stroke of which he severed the rope that held them to the spare anchor. This threw the whole weight of the *Dazzler* on the chain-anchor. In consequence she swung off to the left, and just in time; for the next instant, drifting stern foremost, the *Ghost* passed over the spot she had vacated.

"Why, she's got four anchors out!" Joe exclaimed, at sight of four taut ropes entering the water almost horizontally from her bow.

"Two of 'em's dredges," 'Frisco Kid grinned; "and there goes the stove."

As he spoke, two young fellows appeared on deck and dropped the cooking-stove overside with a line attached.

"Phew!" 'Frisco Kid cried. "Look at Nelson. He's got one reef in, and you can just bet that's a sign she's howlin'!"

The *Reindeer* came foaming toward them, breasting the storm like some magnificent sea-animal. Red Nelson waved to them as he passed astern, and fifteen minutes later, when they were breaking out the one anchor that remained to them, he passed well to windward on the other tack.

French Pete followed her admiringly, though he said ominously: "Someday, pouf! he go just like dat, I tell you, sure."

A moment later the *Dazzler*'s reefed jib was flung out, and she was straining and struggling in the thick of the fight. It was slow work, and hard and dangerous, clawing off that lee shore, and Joe found himself marveling often that so small a craft could possibly endure a minute in such elemental fury. But little by little she worked off the shore and out of the ground-swell into the deeper waters of the bay, where the main-sheet was slacked away a bit, and she ran for shelter behind the rock wall of the Alameda Mole a few miles away. Here they found the *Reindeer* calmly at anchor; and here, during the next several hours, straggled in the remainder of the fleet, with the exception of the *Ghost*, which had evidently gone ashore to keep the *Go Ask Her* company.

By afternoon, the wind had dropped away with

surprising suddenness, and the weather had turned almost summer-like.

"It doesn't look right," 'Frisco Kid said in the evening, after French Pete had rowed over in the skiff to visit Nelson.

"What doesn't look right?" Joe asked.

"Why, the weather. It went down too sudden. It didn't have a chance to blow itself out, and it ain't going to quit till does blow itself out. It's likely to puff up and howl at any moment, if I know anything about it."

"Where will we go from here?" Joe asked. "Back to the oyster-beds?"

'Frisco Kid shook his head. "I can't say what French Pete'll do. He's been fooled on the iron, and fooled on the oysters, and he's that disgusted he's liable to do 'most anything desperate. I wouldn't be surprised to see him go off with Nelson towards Redwood City, where that big thing is that I was tellin' you about. It's somewhere over there."

"Well, I won't have anything to do with it," Joe announced decisively.

"Of course not," 'Frisco Kid answered. "And with Nelson and his two men an' French Pete, I don't think there'll be any need for you anyway."

Chapter 16
'Frisco Kid's Ditty-Box

AFTER THE CONVERSATION DIED away, the two lads lay upon the cabin for perhaps an hour. Then, without saying a word, 'Frisco Kid went below and struck a light. Joe could hear him fumbling about, and a little later heard his own name called softly. On going into the cabin, he saw 'Frisco Kid sitting on the edge of the bunk, a sailor's ditty-box on his knees, and in his hand a carefully folded page from a magazine.

"Does she look like this?" he asked, smoothing it out and turning it that the other might see.

It was a half-page illustration of two girls and a boy, grouped, evidently, in an old-fashioned roomy attic, and holding a council of some sort. The girl who was talking faced the onlooker, while the backs of the other two were turned.

"Who?" Joe queried, glancing in perplexity from the picture to 'Frisco Kid's face.

"Your—your sister—Bessie."

The word seemed reluctant in coming to his lips, and he expressed himself with a certain shy reverence, as though it were something unspeakably sacred.

Joe was nonplussed for the moment. He could see no bearing between the two in point, and, anyway, girls were rather silly creatures to waste one's time over. "He's actually blushing," he thought, regarding the soft glow on the other's cheeks. He felt an irresistible desire to laugh, and tried to smother it down.

"No, no; don't!" 'Frisco Kid cried, snatching the paper away and putting it back in the ditty-box with shaking fingers. Then he added more slowly: "I thought—I—I kind o' thought you would understand, and—and—"

His lips trembled and his eyes glistened with unwonted moistness as he turned hastily away.

The next instant Joe was by his side on the bunk, his arm around him. Prompted by some instinctive monitor, he had done it before he thought. A week before he could not have imagined himself in such an absurd situation—his arm around a boy; but now it seemed the most natural thing in the world. He did not comprehend, but he knew, whatever it was, that it was of deep importance to his companion.

"Go ahead and tell us," he urged. "I'll understand."

"No, you won't. You can't."

"Yes, sure. Go ahead."

'Frisco Kid choked and shook his head. "I don't think I could, anyway. It's more the things I feel, and I don't know how to put them in words." Joe's hand patted his shoulder reassuringly, and he went on: "Well, it's this way. You see, I don't know much about the land, and people, and things, and I never had any brothers or sisters or playmates. All the time I didn't know it, but I was lonely—sort of missed them down in here somewheres." He placed a hand over his breast.

"Did you ever feel downright hungry? Well, that's just the way I used to feel, only a different kind of hunger, and me not knowing what it was. But one day, oh, a long time back, I got ahold of a magazine and saw a picture—that picture, with the two girls and the boy talking together. I thought it must be fine to be like them, and I got to thinking about the things they said and did, till it came to me all-of-a-sudden-like, and I knew it was just loneliness was the matter with me.

"But, more than anything else, I got to wondering about the girl who looks out of the picture right at you. I was thinking about her all the time, and by and by she became real to me. You see, it was making believe, and I knew it all the time, and then again, I didn't. Whenever I'd think of the men, and the work, and the hard life, I'd know it was make-believe; but when I'd think of her, it wasn't. I don't know; I can't explain it."

Joe remembered all his own adventures which he had imagined on land and sea and nodded. He at least understood that much.

"Of course, it was all foolishness, but to have a girl like that for a comrade or friend seemed more like heaven to me than anything else I knew of. As I said, it was a long while back, and I was only a little kid—that was when Red Nelson gave me my name, and I've never been anything but 'Frisco Kid ever since. But the girl in the picture: I was always getting that picture out to look at her, and before long, if I wasn't square—why, I felt ashamed to look at her. Afterwards, when I was older, I came to look at it in another way. I thought, 'suppose, Kid, someday you were to meet a girl like that, what would she think of you? Could she like you? Could she be even the least bit of a friend to you?' And then I'd make up my mind to be better, to try and do something with myself so that she or any of her kind of people would not be ashamed to know me.

"That's why I learned to read. That's why I ran away. Nicky Perrata, a Greek boy, taught me my letters, and it wasn't till after I learned to read that I found out there was anything really wrong in bay-pirating. I'd been used to it ever since I could remember, and almost all the people I knew made their living that way. But when I did find out, I ran away, thinking to quit it for good. I'll tell you about it sometime, and how I'm back at it again.

"Of course, she seemed a real girl when I was a youngster, and even now she sometimes seems that way, I've thought so much about her. But while I'm talking to you it all clears up and she comes to me in this light: she stands just for a plain idea, a better, cleaner life than this, and one I'd like to live; and if I could live it, why, I'd come to know that kind of girls, and their kind of people—your kind, that's what I mean. So I was wondering about your sister and you, and that's why—I don't know; I guess I was just wondering. But I suppose you know lots of girls like that, don't you?"

Joe nodded his head.

"Then tell me about them—something, anything," he added as he noted the fleeting expression of doubt in the other's eyes.

"Oh, that's easy," Joe began valiantly. To a certain extent he did understand the lad's hunger, and it seemed a simple enough task to at least partially satisfy him. "To begin with, they're like—hem!—why, they're like—girls, just girls." He broke off with a miserable sense of failure.

'Frisco Kid waited patiently, his face a study in expectancy.

Joe struggled valiantly to marshal his forces. To his mind, in quick succession, came the girls with whom he had gone to school—the sisters of the boys he knew, and those who were his sister's friends: slim girls and plump girls, tall girls and short girls, blue-eyed and brown-eyed, curly-haired, black-haired, golden-haired; in short, a procession of girls of all sorts and descriptions. But, to save himself, he could say nothing about them. Anyway, he'd never been a "sissy," and why should he be expected to know anything about them? "All girls are alike," he concluded desperately. "They're just the same as the ones you know, Kid—sure they are."

"But I don't know any."

Joe whistled. "And never did?"

"Yes, one. Carlotta Gispardi. But she couldn't speak English, and I couldn't speak Dago; and she died. I don't care; though I never knew any, I seem to know as much about them as you do."

"And I guess I know more about adventures all over the world than you do," Joe retorted.

Both boys laughed. But a moment later, Joe fell into deep thought. It had come upon him quite swiftly that he had not been duly grateful for the good things of life he did possess. Already home, father, and mother had assumed a greater significance to him; but he now found himself placing a higher personal value upon his sister and his chums and friends. He had never appreciated them properly, he thought, but henceforth—well, there would be a different tale to tell.

The voice of French Pete hailing them put a finish to the conversation, for they both ran on deck.

Chapter 17
'Frisco Kid Tells His Story

"GET UP ZE MAINSAIL and break out ze hook!" the Frenchman shouted. "And den tail on to ze *Reindeer*! No side-lights!"

"Come! Cast off those gaskets—lively!" 'Frisco Kid ordered. "Now lay on to the peak-halyards—there, that rope—cast it off the pin. And don't hoist ahead of me. There! Make fast! We'll stretch it afterwards. Run aft and come in on the main-sheet! Shove the helm up!"

Under the sudden driving power of the mainsail, the *Dazzler* strained and tugged at her anchor like an impatient horse till the muddy iron left the bottom with a rush and she was free.

"Let go the sheet! Come for'ard again and lend a hand on the chain! Stand by to give her the jib!" 'Frisco Kid the boy who mooned over girls in pictorial magazines had vanished, and 'Frisco Kid the sailor, strong and dominant, was on deck. He ran aft and tacked about as the jib rattled aloft in the hands of Joe, who quickly joined him. Just then the *Reindeer*, like a monstrous bat, passed to leeward of them in the gloom.

"Ah, dose boys! Dey take all-a night!" they heard

196

French Pete exclaim, and then the gruff voice of Red Nelson, who said: "Never you mind, Frenchy. I taught the Kid his sailorizing, and I ain't never been ashamed of him yet."

The *Reindeer* was the faster boat, but by spilling the wind from her sails they managed so that the boys could keep them in sight. The breeze came steadily in from the west, with a promise of early increase. The stars were being blotted out by masses of driving clouds, which indicated a greater velocity in the upper strata. 'Frisco Kid surveyed the sky.

"Going to have it good and stiff before morning," he said, "just as I told you."

Several hours later, both boats stood in for the San Mateo shore, and dropped anchor not more than a cable's-length away. A little wharf ran out, the bare end of which was perceptible to them, though they could discern a small yacht lying moored to a buoy a short distance away.

According to their custom, everything was put in readiness for hasty departure. The anchors could be tripped and the sails flung out on a moment's notice. Both skiffs came over noiselessly from the *Reindeer*. Red Nelson had given one of his two men to French Pete, so that each skiff was doubly manned. They were not a very prepossessing group of men—at least, Joe did not think so—for their faces bore a savage seriousness which almost made him shiver. The captain of the *Dazzler* buckled on his pistol-belt and placed a rifle and a stout double-block tackle in the boat. Then he poured out wine all around, and, standing in the darkness of the little cabin, they pledged success to the expedition. Red Nelson was also armed, while his men wore at their hips the customary sailor's sheath-knife. They were very slow and careful to avoid noise in getting into the boats, French Pete pausing long enough to warn the boys to remain quietly aboard and not try any tricks.

"Now'd be your chance, Joe, if they hadn't taken the skiff," 'Frisco Kid whispered, when the boats had vanished into the loom of the land.

"What's the matter with the *Dazzler*?" was the unexpected answer. "We could up sail and away before you could say Jack Robinson."

'Frisco Kid hesitated. The spirit of comradeship was strong in the lad and deserting a companion in a pinch could not but be repulsive to him.

"I don't think it'd be exactly square to leave them in the lurch ashore," he said. "Of course," he went on hurriedly, "I know the whole thing's wrong; but you remember that first night, when you came running through the water for the skiff, and those fellows on the bank busy popping away? We didn't leave you in the lurch, did we?"

Joe assented reluctantly, and then a new thought flashed across his mind. "But they're pirates—and thieves—and criminals. They're breaking the law, and you and I are not willing to be lawbreakers. Besides, they'll not be left. There's the *Reindeer*. There's nothing to prevent them from getting away on her, and they'll never catch us in the dark."

"Come on, then." Though he had agreed, 'Frisco Kid did not quite like it, for it still seemed to savor of desertion.

They crawled forward and began to hoist the mainsail. The anchor they could slip, if necessary, and save the time of pulling it up. But at the first rattle of the halyards on the sheaves a warning "Hist!" came to them through the darkness, followed by a loudly whispered "Drop that!"

Glancing in the direction from which these sounds proceeded, they made out a white face peering at them from over the rail of the other sloop.

"Aw, it's only the *Reindeer*'s boy," 'Frisco Kid said. "Come on."

Again they were interrupted at the first rattling of the blocks.

"I say, you fellers, you'd better let go them halyards pretty quick, I'm a-tellin' you, or I'll give you what for!"

This threat being dramatically capped by the click of a cocking pistol, 'Frisco Kid obeyed and went grumblingly back to the cockpit. "Oh, there's plenty more chances to come," he whispered consolingly to Joe. "French Pete was cute, wasn't he? He thought you might be trying to make a break and put a guard on us."

Nothing came from the shore to indicate how the pirates were faring. Not a dog barked, not a light flared. Yet the air seemed quivering with an alarm about to burst forth. The night had taken on a strained feeling of intensity, as though it held in store all kinds of terrible things. The boys felt this keenly as they huddled against each other in the cockpit and waited.

"You were going to tell me about your running away," Joe ventured finally, "and why you came back again."

'Frisco Kid took up the tale at once, speaking in a muffled undertone close to the other's ear.

"You see, when I made up my mind to quit the life,

there wasn't a soul to lend me a hand; but I knew that the only thing for me to do was to get ashore and find some kind of work, so I could study. Then I figured there'd be more chance in the country than in the city; so I gave Red Nelson the slip—I was on the *Reindeer* then. One night on the Alameda oyster-beds, I got ashore and headed back from the bay as fast as I could sprint. Nelson didn't catch me. But they were all Portuguese farmers thereabouts, and none of them had work for me. Besides, it was in the wrong time of the year—winter. That shows how much I knew about the land.

"I'd saved up a couple of dollars, and I kept traveling back, deeper and deeper into the country, looking for work, and buying bread and cheese and such things from the storekeepers. I tell you, it was cold, nights, sleeping out without blankets, and I was always glad when morning came. But worse than that was the way everybody looked on me. They were all suspicious, and not a bit afraid to show it, and sometimes they'd set their dogs on me and tell me to get along. Seemed as though there wasn't any place for me on the land. Then my money gave out, and just about the time I was good and hungry I got captured."

"Captured! What for?"

"Nothing. Living, I suppose. I crawled into a haystack to sleep one night, because it was warmer, and along comes a village constable and arrests me for being a tramp. At first they thought I was a runaway, and telegraphed my description all over. I told them I didn't have any people, but they wouldn't believe me for a long while. And then, when nobody claimed me, the judge sent me to a boys' 'refuge' in

San Francisco."

He stopped and peered intently in the direction of the shore. The darkness and the silence in which the men had been swallowed up was profound. Nothing was stirring save the rising wind.

"I thought I'd die in that 'refuge.' It was just like being in jail. We were locked up and guarded like prisoners. Even then, if I could have liked the other boys it might have been all right. But they were mostly street-boys of the worst kind—lying, and sneaking, and cowardly, without one spark of manhood or one idea of square dealing and fair play. There was only one thing I did like, and that was the books. Oh, I did lots of reading, I tell you! But that couldn't make up for the rest. I wanted the freedom and the sunlight and the salt water. And what had I done to be kept in prison and herded with such a gang? Instead of doing wrong, I had tried to do right, to make myself better, and that's what I got for it. I wasn't old enough, you see, to reason anything out.

"Sometimes I'd see the sunshine dancing on the water and showing white on the sails, and the *Reindeer* cutting through it just as you please, and I'd get that sick I would know hardly what I did. And then the boys would come against me with some of their meannesses, and I'd start in to lick the whole kit of them. Then the men in charge would lock me up and punish me. Well, I couldn't stand it any longer; I watched my chance and ran for it. Seemed as though there wasn't any place on the land for me, so I picked up with French Pete and went back on the bay. That's about all there is to it, though I'm going to try it again when I get a little older—old enough to get a square deal for myself."

"You're going to go back on the land with me," Joe said authoritatively, laying a hand on his shoulder. "That's what you're going to do. As for—"

Bang! a revolver-shot rang out from the shore. Bang! bang! More guns were speaking sharply and hurriedly. A man's voice rose wildly on the air and died away. Somebody began to cry for help. Both boys were on their feet on the instant, hoisting the mainsail and getting everything ready to run. The *Reindeer* boy was doing likewise. A man, roused from his sleep on the yacht, thrust an excited head through the skylight, but withdrew it hastily at sight of the two stranger sloops. The intensity of waiting was broken, the time for action come.

CHAPTER 18
A NEW RESPONSIBILITY
FOR JOE

HEAVING IN ON THE anchor-chain till it was up and down, 'Frisco Kid and Joe ceased from their exertions. Everything was in readiness to give the *Dazzler* the jib and go. They strained their eyes in the direction of the shore. The clamor had died away, but here and there lights were beginning to flash. The creaking of a block and tackle came to their ears, and they heard Red Nelson's voice singing out: "Lower away!" and "Cast off!"

"French Pete forgot to oil it," 'Frisco Kid commented, referring to the tackle.

"Takin' their time about it, ain't they?" the boy on the *Reindeer* called over to them, sitting down on the cabin and mopping his face after the exertion of hoisting the mainsail single-handed.

"Guess they're all right," 'Frisco Kid rejoined. "All ready?"

"Yes—all right here."

"Say, you," the man on the yacht cried through the skylight, not venturing to show his head. "You'd better go away."

"And you'd better stay below and keep quiet," was the

response. "We'll take care of ourselves. You do the same."

"If I was only out of this, I'd show you!" he threatened.

"Lucky for you you're not," responded the boy on the *Reindeer*; and thereat the man kept quiet.

"Here they come!" said 'Frisco Kid suddenly to Joe.

The two skiffs shot out of the darkness and came alongside. Some kind of an altercation was going on, as French Pete's voice attested.

"No, no!" he cried. "Put it on ze *Dazzler*. Ze *Reindeer* she sail too fast-a, and run away, oh, so queeck, and never more I see it. Put it on ze *Dazzler*. Eh? Wot you say?"

"All right then," Red Nelson agreed. "We'll whack up afterwards. But, say, hurry up. Out with you, lads, and heave her up! My arm's broke."

The men tumbled out, ropes were cast inboard, and all hands, with the exception of Joe, tailed on. The shouting of men, the sound of oars, and the rattling and slapping of blocks and sails, told that the men on shore were getting under way for the pursuit.

"Now!" Red Nelson commanded. "All together! Don't let her come back or you'll smash the skiff. There she takes it! A long pull and a strong pull! Once again! And yet again! Get a turn there, somebody, and take a spell."

Though the task was but half accomplished, they were exhausted by the strenuous effort, and hailed the rest eagerly. Joe glanced over the side to discover what the heavy object might be and saw the vague outlines of a small office-safe.

"Now all together!" Red Nelson began again. "Take her on the run and don't let her stop! Yo, ho! heave, ho! Once again! And another! Over with her!"

Straining and gasping, with tense muscles and heaving chests, they brought the cumbersome weight over the side, rolled it on top of the rail, and lowered it into the cockpit on the run. The cabin doors were thrown apart, and it was moved along, end for end, till it lay on the cabin floor, snug against the end of the centerboard-case. Red Nelson had followed it aboard to superintend. His left arm hung helpless at his side, and from the finger-tips blood dripped with monotonous regularity. He did not seem to mind it, however, nor even the mutterings of the human storm he had raised ashore, and which, to judge by the sounds, was even then threatening to break upon them.

"Lay your course for the Golden Gate," he said to French Pete, as he turned to go. "I'll try to stand by you, but if you get lost in the dark I'll meet you outside, off the Farralones, in the morning." He sprang into the skiff after the men, and, with a wave of his uninjured arm, cried heartily: "And then it's for Mexico, my lads—Mexico and summer weather!"

Just as the *Dazzler*, freed from her anchor, paid off under the jib and filled away, a dark sail loomed under their stern, barely missing the skiff in tow. The cockpit of the stranger was crowded with men, who raised their voices angrily at sight of the pirates. Joe had half a mind to run forward and cut the halyards so that the *Dazzler* might be captured. As he had told French Pete the day before, he had done nothing to be ashamed of, and was not afraid to go before a court of justice. But the thought of 'Frisco Kid restrained him. He wanted to take him ashore with him, but in so doing he did not wish to take him to jail. So he, too, began to experience a keen interest in the escape of the *Dazzler*.

The pursuing sloop rounded up hurriedly to come about after them, and in the darkness fouled the yacht which lay at anchor. The man aboard of her, thinking that at last his time had come, gave one wild yell, ran on deck, and leaped overboard. In the confusion of the collision, and while they were endeavoring to save him, French Pete and the boys slipped away into the night.

The *Reindeer* had already disappeared, and by the time Joe and 'Frisco Kid had the running-gear coiled down and everything in shape, they were standing out in open water. The wind was freshening constantly, and the *Dazzler* heeled a lively clip through the comparatively smooth stretch. Before an hour had passed, the lights of Hunter's Point were well on her starboard beam. 'Frisco Kid went below to make coffee, but Joe remained on deck, watching the lights of South San Francisco grow, and speculating on their destination. Mexico! They were going to sea in such a frail craft! Impossible! At least, it seemed so to him, for his conceptions of ocean travel were limited to steamers and full-rigged ships. He was beginning to feel half sorry that he had not cut the halyards, and longed to ask French Pete a thousand questions; but just as the first was on his lips that worthy ordered him to go below and get some coffee and then to turn in. He was followed shortly afterward by 'Frisco Kid, French Pete remaining at his lonely task of beating down the bay and out to sea. Twice he heard the waves buffeted back from some flying forefoot, and once he saw a sail to leeward on the opposite tack, which luffed sharply and came about at sight of him. But the darkness favored, and he heard no more of it—perhaps because he worked into the wind closer by a point and held on his way with a shaking after-leech.

Shortly after dawn, the two boys were called and came sleepily on deck. The day had broken cold and gray, while the wind had attained half a gale. Joe noted with astonishment the white tents of the quarantine station on Angel Island. San Francisco lay a smoky blur on the southern horizon, while the night, still lingering on the western edge of the world, slowly withdrew before their eyes. French Pete was just finishing a long reach into the Raccoon Straits, and at the same time studiously regarding a plunging sloop-yacht half a mile astern.

"Dey t'ink to catch ze *Dazzler*, eh? Bah!" And he brought the craft in question about, laying a course straight for the Golden Gate.

The pursuing yacht followed suit. Joe watched her a few moments. She held an apparently parallel course to them and forged ahead much faster.

"Why, at this rate they'll have us in no time!" he cried.

French Pete laughed. "You t'ink so? Bah! Dey outfoot; we outpoint. Dey are scared of ze wind; we wipe ze eye of ze wind. Ah! you wait, you see."

"They're traveling ahead faster," 'Frisco Kid explained, "but we're sailing closer to the wind. In the end we'll beat them, even if they have the nerve to cross the bar—which I don't think they have. Look! See!"

Ahead could be seen the great ocean surges, flinging

themselves skyward and bursting into roaring caps of smother. In the midst of it, now rolling her dripping bottom clear, now sousing her deck-load of lumber far above the guards, a coasting steam-schooner was lumbering drunkenly into port. It was magnificent—this battle between man and the elements. Whatever timidity he had entertained fled away, and Joe's nostrils began to dilate and his eyes to flash at the nearness of the impending struggle.

French Pete called for his oilskins and sou'wester, and Joe also was equipped with a spare suit. Then he and 'Frisco Kid were sent below to lash and cleat the safe in place. In the midst of this task Joe glanced at the firm-name, gilt-lettered on the face of it, and read: "Bronson & Tate." Why, that was his father and his father's partner. That was their safe, their money! 'Frisco Kid, nailing the last cleat on the floor of the cabin, looked up and followed his fascinated gaze.

"That's rough, isn't it," he whispered. "Your father?"

Joe nodded. He could see it all now. They had run into San Andreas, where his father worked the big quarries, and most probably the safe contained the wages of the thousand men or more whom he employed. "Don't say anything," he cautioned.

'Frisco Kid agreed knowingly. "French Pete can't read, anyway," he muttered, "and the chances are that Red Nelson won't know what your name is. But, just the same, it's pretty rough. They'll break it open and divide up as soon as they can, so I don't see what you're going to do about it."

"Wait and see." Joe had made up his mind that he would do his best to stand by his father's property. At the worst, it could only be lost; and that would surely be the case were he not along, while, being along, he at least had a fighting chance to save it, or to be in position to recover it. Responsibilities were showering upon him thick and fast. But a few days back he had had but himself to consider; then, in some subtle way, he had felt a certain accountability for 'Frisco Kid's future welfare; and after that, and still more subtly, he had become aware of duties which he owed to his position, to his sister, to his chums and friends; and now, by a most unexpected chain of circumstances, came the pressing need of service for his father's sake. It was a call upon his deepest strength, and he responded bravely. While the future might be doubtful, he had no doubt of himself; and this very state of mind, this self-confidence, by a generous alchemy, gave him added resolution. Nor did he fail to be vaguely aware of it, and to grasp dimly at the truth that confidence breeds confidence—strength, strength.

Chapter 19
The Boys Plan an
Escape

"NOW SHE TAKES IT!" French Pete cried.

Both lads ran into the cockpit. They were on the edge of the breaking bar. A huge forty-footer reared a foam-crested head far above them, stealing their wind for the moment and threatening to crush the tiny craft like an eggshell. Joe held his breath. It was the supreme moment. French Pete luffed straight into it, and the *Dazzler* mounted the steep slope with a rush, poised a moment on the giddy summit, and fell into the yawning valley beyond. Keeping off in the intervals to fill the mainsail, and luffing into the combers, they worked their way across the dangerous stretch. Once they caught the tail-end of a whitecap and were well-nigh smothered in the froth, but otherwise the sloop bobbed and ducked with the happy facility of a cork.

To Joe it seemed as though he had been lifted out of himself—out of the world. Ah, this was life! this was action! Surely it could not be the old, commonplace world he had lived in so long! The sailors, grouped on the streaming deck-load of the steamer, waved their sou'westers, and, on the bridge, even the captain was expressing his admiration for the plucky craft.

"Ah, you see! you see!" French Pete pointed astern.

The sloop-yacht had been afraid to venture it and was skirting back and forth on the inner edge of the bar. The chase was over. A pilot-boat, running for shelter from the coming storm, flew by them like a frightened bird, passing the steamer as though the latter were standing still.

Half an hour later the *Dazzler* sped beyond the last smoking sea and was sliding up and down on the long Pacific swell. The wind had increased its velocity and necessitated a reefing down of jib and mainsail. Then they laid off again, full and free on the starboard tack, for the Farralones, thirty miles away. By the time breakfast was cooked and eaten they picked up the *Reindeer*, which was hove to and working offshore to the south and west. The wheel was lashed down, and there was not a soul on deck.

French Pete complained bitterly against such recklessness. "Dat is ze one fault of Red Nelson. He no care. He is afraid of not'ing. Someday he will die, oh, so vaire queeck! I know he will."

Three times they circled about the *Reindeer*, running under her weather quarter and shouting in chorus, before they brought anybody on deck. Sail was then made at once, and together the two cockle-shells plunged away into the vastness of the Pacific. This was necessary, as 'Frisco Kid informed Joe, in order to have an offing before the whole fury of the storm broke upon them. Otherwise, they would be driven on the lee shore of the California coast. Grub and water, he said, could be obtained by running into the land when fine weather came. He congratulated Joe upon the fact that he was not seasick, which circumstance likewise brought praise from French Pete and put him in better humor with his mutinous young sailor.

"I'll tell you what we'll do," 'Frisco Kid whispered, while cooking dinner. "To-night we'll drag French Pete down—"

"Drag French Pete down!"

"Yes, and tie him up good and snug, as soon as it gets dark; then put out the lights and make a run for land; get to port anyway, anywhere, just so long as we shake loose from Red Nelson."

"Yes," Joe deliberated; "that would be all right—if I could do it alone. But as for asking you to help me—why, that would be treason to French Pete."

"That's what I'm coming to. I'll help you if you promise me a few things. French Pete took me aboard when I ran away from the 'refuge,' when I was starving and had no place to go, and I just can't repay him for that by sending him to jail. 'T wouldn't be square. Your father wouldn't have you break your word, would he?"

"No; of course not." Joe knew how sacredly his father held his word of honor.

"Then you must promise, and your father must see it carried out, not to press any charge against French Pete."

"All right. And now, what about yourself? You can't very well expect to go away with him again on the *Dazzler*!"

"Oh, don't bother about me. There's nobody to miss me. I'm strong enough, and know enough about it, to ship to sea as ordinary seaman. I'll go away somewhere over on the other side of the world and begin all over again."

"Then we'll have to call it off, that's all."

"Call what off?"

"Tying French Pete up and running for it."

"No, sir. That's decided upon."

"Now listen here: I'll not have a thing to do with it. I'll go on to Mexico first, if you don't make me one promise."

"And what's the promise?"

"Just this: you place yourself in my hands from the moment we get ashore, and trust to me. You don't know anything about the land, anyway—you said so. And I'll fix it with my father—I know I can—so that you can get to know people of the right sort, and study and get an education, and be something else than a bay pirate or a sailor. That's what you'd like, isn't it?"

Though he said nothing, 'Frisco Kid showed how well he liked it by the expression of his face.

"And it'll be no more than your due, either," Joe continued. "You will have stood by me, and you'll have recovered my father's money. He'll owe it to you."

"But I don't do things that way. I don't think much of a man who does a favor just to be paid for it."

"Now you keep quiet. How much do you think it would cost my father for detectives and all that to recover that safe? Give me your promise, that's all, and when I've got things arranged, if you don't like them you can back out. Come on; that's fair."

They shook hands on the bargain and proceeded to map out their line of action for the night.

But the storm, yelling down out of the northwest, had something entirely different in store for the *Dazzler* and her crew. By the time dinner was over they were forced to put double reefs in mainsail and jib, and still the gale had not reached its height. The sea, also, had been kicked up till it was a continuous succession of water-mountains, frightful and withal grand to look upon from the low deck of the sloop. It was only when the sloops were tossed upon the crests of the waves at the same time that they caught sight of each other. Occasional fragments of seas swashed into the cockpit or dashed aft over the cabin, and Joe was stationed at the small pump to keep the well dry.

At three o'clock, watching his chance, French Pete motioned to the *Reindeer* that he was going to heave to and get out a sea-anchor. This latter was of the nature of a large shallow canvas bag, with the mouth held open by triangularly lashed spars. To this the towing-ropes were attached, on the kite principle, so that the greatest resisting surface was presented to the water. The sloop, drifting so much faster, would thus be held bow on to both wind and sea—the safest possible position in a storm. Red Nelson waved his hand in response that he understood and to go ahead.

French Pete went forward to launch the sea-anchor himself, leaving it to 'Frisco Kid to put the helm down at the proper moment and run into the wind. The Frenchman poised on the slippery fore-deck, waiting an opportunity. But at that moment the *Dazzler* lifted into an unusually large sea, and, as she cleared the summit, caught a heavy snort of the gale at the very instant she was righting herself to an even keel. Thus there was not the slightest yield to this sudden pressure on her sails and mast-gear.

There was a quick snap, followed by a crash. The steel weather-rigging carried away at the lanyards, and mast, jib,

mainsail,   blocks,   stays,   sea-anchor,   French
Pete—everything—went over the side. Almost by a miracle,
the captain clutched at the bobstay and managed to get one
hand up and over the bowsprit. The boys ran forward to drag
him into safety, and Red Nelson, observing the disaster, put
up his helm and ran down to the rescue.

CHAPTER 20
PERILOUS HOURS

FRENCH PETE WAS UNINJURED from the fall overboard with the *Dazzler*'s mast; but the sea-anchor, which had gone with him, had not escaped so easily. The gaff of the mainsail had been driven through it, and it refused to work. The wreckage, thumping alongside, held the sloop in a quartering slant to the seas—not so dangerous a position as it might be, nor so safe, either. "Good-by, old-a *Dazzler*. Never no more you wipe ze eye of ze wind. Never no more you kick your heels at ze crack gentlemen-yachts."

So the captain lamented, standing in the cockpit and surveying the ruin with wet eyes. Even Joe, who bore him great dislike, felt sorry for him at this moment. A heavier blast of the wind caught the jagged crest of a wave and hurled it upon the helpless craft.

"Can't we save her?" Joe spluttered.

'Frisco Kid shook his head.

"Nor the safe?"

"Impossible," he answered. "Couldn't lay another boat alongside for a United States mint. As it is, it'll keep us guessing to save ourselves."

Another sea swept over them, and the skiff, which had long since been swamped, dashed itself to pieces against the stern. Then the *Reindeer* towered above them on a mountain

216

of water. Joe caught himself half shrinking back, for it seemed she would fall down squarely on top of them; but the next instant she dropped into the gaping trough, and they were looking down upon her far below. It was a striking picture—one Joe was destined never to forget. The *Reindeer* was wallowing in the snow-white smother, her rails flush with the sea, the water scudding across her deck in foaming cataracts. The air was filled with flying spray, which made the scene appear hazy and unreal. One of the men was clinging to the perilous after-deck and striving to cast off the water-logged skiff. The boy, leaning far over the cockpit-rail and holding on for dear life, was passing him a knife. The second man stood at the wheel, putting it up with flying hands and forcing the sloop to pay off. Beside him, his injured arm in a sling, was Red Nelson, his sou'wester gone and his fair hair plastered in wet, wind-blown ringlets about his face. His whole attitude breathed indomitability, courage, strength. It seemed almost as though the divine were blazing forth from him. Joe looked upon him in sudden awe, and, realizing the enormous possibilities of the man, felt sorrow for the way in which they had been wasted. A thief and a robber! In that flashing moment Joe caught a glimpse of human truth, grasped at the mystery of success and failure. Life threw back its curtains that he might read it and understand. Of such stuff as Red Nelson were heroes made; but they possessed wherein he lacked—the power of choice, the careful poise of mind, the sober control of soul: in short, the very things his father had so often "preached" to him about.

These were the thoughts which came to Joe in the

flight of a second. Then the *Reindeer* swept skyward and hurtled across their bow to leeward on the breast of a mighty billow.

"Ze wild man! ze wild man!" French Pete shrieked, watching her in amazement. "He t'inks he can jibe! He will die! We will all die! He must come about. Oh, ze fool, ze fool!"

But time was precious, and Red Nelson ventured the chance. At the right moment he jibed the mainsail over and hauled back on the wind.

"Here she comes! Make ready to jump for it," 'Frisco Kid cried to Joe.

The *Reindeer* dashed by their stern, heeling over till the cabin windows were buried, and so close that it appeared she must run them down. But a freak of the waters lurched the two crafts apart. Red Nelson, seeing that the maneuver had miscarried, instantly instituted another. Throwing the helm hard up, the *Reindeer* whirled on her heel, thus swinging her overhanging main-boom closer to the *Dazzler*. French Pete was the nearest, and the opportunity could last no longer than a second. Like a cat he sprang, catching the foot-rope with both hands. Then the *Reindeer* forged ahead, dipping him into the sea at every plunge. But he clung on, working inboard every time he emerged, till he dropped into the cockpit as Red Nelson squared off to run down to leeward and repeat the maneuver.

"Your turn next," 'Frisco Kid said.

"No; yours," Joe replied.

"But I know more about the water," 'Frisco Kid insisted.

"And I can swim as well as you," the other retorted.

It would have been hard to forecast the outcome of this dispute; but, as it was, the swift rush of events made any settlement needless. The *Reindeer* had jibed over and was plowing back at breakneck speed, careening at such an angle that it seemed she must surely capsize. It was a gallant sight. Just then the storm burst in all its fury, the shouting wind flattening the ragged crests till they boiled. The *Reindeer* dipped from view behind an immense wave. The wave rolled on, but the next moment, where the sloop had been, the boys noted with startled eyes only the angry waters! Doubting, they looked a second time. There was no *Reindeer*. They were alone on the torn crest of the ocean!

"God have mercy on their souls!" 'Frisco Kid said solemnly.

Joe was too horrified at the suddenness of the catastrophe to utter a sound.

"Sailed her clean under, and, with the ballast she carried, went straight to bottom," 'Frisco Kid gasped. Then, turning to their own pressing need, he said: "Now we've got to look out for ourselves. The back of the storm broke in that puff, but the sea'll kick up worse yet as the wind eases down. Lend a hand and hang on with the other. We've got to get her head-on."

Together, knives in hand, they crawled forward to where the pounding wreckage hampered the boat sorely. 'Frisco Kid took the lead in the ticklish work, but Joe obeyed orders like a veteran. Every minute or two the bow was swept by the sea, and they were pounded and buffeted about like a pair of shuttlecocks. First the main portion of the wreckage was securely fastened to the forward bitts; then, breathless and gasping, more often under the water than out, they cut and hacked at the tangle of halyards, sheets, stays, and tackles. The cockpit was taking water rapidly, and it was a race between swamping and completing the task. At last, however, everything stood clear save the lee rigging. 'Frisco Kid slashed the lanyards. The storm did the rest. The *Dazzler* drifted swiftly to leeward of the wreckage till the strain on the line fast to the forward bitts jerked her bow into place and she ducked dead into the eye of the wind and sea.

Pausing only for a cheer at the success of their undertaking, the two lads raced aft, where the cockpit was half full and the dunnage of the cabin all afloat. With a couple of buckets procured from the stern lockers, they proceeded to fling the water overboard. It was heartbreaking work, for many a barrelful was flung back upon them again; but they persevered, and when night fell the *Dazzler*, bobbing merrily at her sea-anchor, could boast that her pumps sucked once more. As 'Frisco Kid had said, the backbone of the storm was broken, though the wind had veered to the west, where it still blew stiffly.

"If she holds," 'Frisco Kid said, referring to the breeze, "we'll drift to the California coast sometime tomorrow. Nothing to do now but wait."

They said little, oppressed by the loss of their comrades and overcome with exhaustion, preferring to huddle against each other for the sake of warmth and companionship. It was a miserable night, and they shivered constantly from the cold. Nothing dry was to be obtained aboard, food, blankets, everything being soaked with the salt water. Sometimes they dozed; but these intervals were short and harassing, for it seemed each took turn in waking with such sudden starts as to rouse the other.

At last day broke, and they looked about. Wind and sea had dropped considerably, and there was no question as to the safety of the *Dazzler*. The coast was nearer than they had expected, its cliffs showing dark and forbidding in the gray of dawn. But with the rising of the sun they could see the yellow beaches, flanked by the white surf, and beyond—it seemed too good to be true—the clustering houses and smoking chimneys of a town.

"Santa Cruz!" 'Frisco Kid cried, "and no chance of being wrecked in the surf!"

"Then the safe is safe?" Joe queried.

"Safe! I should say so. It ain't much of a sheltered harbor for large vessels, but with this breeze we'll run right up the mouth of the San Lorenzo River. Then there's a little lake like, and a boat-house. Water smooth as glass and hardly over your head. You see, I was down here once before, with Red Nelson. Come on. We'll be in in time for breakfast."

Bringing to light some spare coils of rope from the lockers, he put a clove-hitch on the standing part of the sea-anchor hawser, and carried the new running-line aft, making it fast to the stern bitts. Then he cast off from the forward bitts. The *Dazzler* swung off into the trough, completed the evolution, and pointed her nose toward shore. A couple of spare oars from below, and as many water-soaked blankets, sufficed to make a jury-mast and sail. When this was in place, Joe cast loose from the wreckage, which was now towing astern, while 'Frisco Kid took the tiller.

CHAPTER 21
JOE AND HIS FATHER

"HOW'S THAT?" CRIED 'Frisco Kid, as he finished making the *Dazzler* fast fore and aft and sat down on the stringpiece of the tiny wharf. "What'll we do next, captain?"

Joe looked up in quick surprise. "Why—I—what's the matter?"

"Well, ain't you captain now? Haven't we reached land? I'm crew from now on, ain't I? What's your orders?"

Joe caught the spirit of it. "Pipe all hands for breakfast—that is—wait a minute."

Diving below, he possessed himself of the money he had stowed away in his bundle when he came aboard. Then he locked the cabin door, and they went uptown in search of a restaurant. Over the breakfast Joe planned the next move, and, when they had done, communicated it to 'Frisco Kid.

In response to his inquiry, the cashier told him when the morning train started for San Francisco. He glanced at the clock.

"Just time to catch it," he said to 'Frisco Kid. "Keep the cabin doors locked, and don't let anybody come aboard. Here's money. Eat at the restaurants. Dry your blankets and sleep in the cockpit. I'll be back tomorrow. And don't let anybody into that cabin. Goodbye."

With a hasty hand-grip, he sped down the street to the

depot. The conductor looked at him with surprise when he punched his ticket. And well he might, for it was not the custom of his passengers to travel in sea-boots and sou'westers. But Joe did not mind. He did not even notice. He had bought a paper and was absorbed in its contents. Before long his eyes caught an interesting paragraph:

SUPPOSED TO HAVE BEEN LOST

The tug Sea Queen, chartered by Bronson & Tate, has returned from a fruitless cruise outside the Heads. No news of value could be obtained concerning the pirates who so daringly carried off their safe at San Andreas last Tuesday night. The lighthouse-keeper at the Farralones mentions having sighted the two sloops Wednesday morning, clawing offshore in the teeth of the gale. It is supposed by shipping men that they perished in the storm with, their ill-gotten treasure. Rumor has it that, in addition to the ten thousand dollars in gold, the safe contained papers of great importance.

When Joe had read this, he felt a great relief. It was evident no one had been killed at San Andreas the night of the robbery, else there would have been some comment on it in the paper. Nor, if they had had any clue to his own whereabouts, would they have omitted such a striking bit of information.

At the depot in San Francisco the curious onlookers were surprised to see a boy clad conspicuously in sea-boots and sou'wester hail a cab and dash away. But Joe was in a hurry. He knew his father's hours and was fearful lest he should not catch him before he went to lunch.

The office-boy scowled at him when he pushed open the door and asked to see Mr. Bronson; nor could the head clerk, when summoned by this disreputable intruder, recognize him.

"Don't you know me, Mr. Willis?"

Mr. Willis looked a second time. "Why, it's Joe Bronson! Of all things under the sun, where did you drop from? Go right in. Your father's in there."

Mr. Bronson stopped dictating to his stenographer and looked up. "Hello! Where have you been?" he said.

"To sea," Joe answered demurely, not sure of just what kind of a reception he was to get and fingering his sou'wester nervously.

"Short trip, eh? How did you make out?"

"Oh, so-so." He had caught the twinkle in his father's eye and knew that it was all clear sailing. "Not so bad—er—that is, considering."

"Considering?"

"Well, not exactly that; rather, it might have been worse, while it couldn't have been better."

"That's interesting. Sit down." Then, turning to the stenographer: "You may go, Mr. Brown, and—hum!—I won't need you any more today."

It was all Joe could do to keep from crying, so kindly and naturally had his father received him, making him feel at once as if not the slightest thing uncommon had occurred. It seemed as if he had just returned from a vacation, or, man-grown, had come back from some business trip.

"Now go ahead, Joe. You were speaking to me a moment ago in conundrums, and you have aroused my curiosity to a most uncomfortable degree."

Whereupon Joe sat down and told what had happened—all that had happened—from Monday night to that very moment. Each little incident he related—every detail—not forgetting his conversations with 'Frisco Kid nor his plans concerning him. His face flushed and he was carried away with the excitement of the narrative, while Mr. Bronson was almost as eager, urging him on whenever he slackened his pace, but otherwise remaining silent.

"So you see," Joe concluded, "it couldn't possibly have turned out any better."

"Ah, well," Mr. Bronson deliberated judiciously, "it may be so, and then again it may not."

"I don't see it." Joe felt sharp disappointment at his father's qualified approval. It seemed to him that the return of the safe merited something stronger.

That Mr. Bronson fully comprehended the way Joe felt about it was clearly in evidence, for he went on: "As to the matter of the safe, all hail to you, Joe! Credit, and plenty of it, is your due. Mr. Tate and myself have already spent five hundred dollars in attempting to recover it. So important was it that we have also offered five thousand dollars reward, and but this morning were considering the advisability of increasing the amount. But, my son,"—Mr.

Bronson stood up, resting a hand affectionately on his boy's shoulder—"there are certain things in this world which are of still greater importance than gold, or papers which represent what gold may buy. How about yourself? That's the point. Will you sell the best possibilities of your life right now for a million dollars?"

Joe shook his head.

"As I said, that's the point. A human life the money of the world cannot buy; nor can it redeem one which is misspent; nor can it make full and complete and beautiful a life which is dwarfed and warped and ugly. How about yourself? What is to be the effect of all these strange adventures on your life—your life, Joe? Are you going to pick yourself up tomorrow and try it over again? or the next day? or the day after? Do you understand? Why, Joe, do you think for one moment that I would place against the best value of my son's life the paltry value of a safe? And can I say, until time has told me, whether this trip of yours could not possibly have been better? Such an experience is as potent for evil as for good. One dollar is exactly like another—there are many in the world: but no Joe is like my Joe, nor can there be any others in the world to take his place. Don't you see, Joe? Don't you understand?"

Mr. Bronson's voice broke slightly, and the next instant Joe was sobbing as though his heart would break. He had never understood this father of his before, and he knew now the pain he must have caused him, to say nothing of his mother and sister. But the four stirring days he had lived had given him a clearer view of the world and humanity, and he had always possessed the power of putting his thoughts into speech; so he spoke of these things and the lessons he had learned—the conclusions he had drawn from his conversations with 'Frisco Kid, from his intercourse with French Pete, from the graphic picture he retained of the *Reindeer* and Red Nelson as they wallowed in the trough beneath him. And Mr. Bronson listened and, in turn, understood.

"But what of 'Frisco Kid, father?" Joe asked when he had finished.

"Hum! there seems to be a great deal of promise in the boy, from what you say of him." Mr. Bronson hid the twinkle in his eye this time. "And, I must confess, he seems perfectly capable of shifting for himself."

"Sir?" Joe could not believe his ears.

"Let us see, then. He is at present entitled to the half of five thousand dollars, the other half of which belongs to you. It was you two who preserved the safe from the bottom of the Pacific, and if you only had waited a little longer, Mr. Tate and myself would have increased the reward."

"Oh!" Joe caught a glimmering of the light. "Part of that is easily arranged. I simply refuse to take my half. As to the other—that isn't exactly what 'Frisco Kid desires. He wants friends—and—and—though you didn't say so, they are far higher than money, nor can money buy them. He wants friends and a chance for an education, not twenty-five hundred dollars."

"Don't you think it would be better for him to choose for himself?"

"Ah, no. That's all arranged."

"Arranged?"

"Yes, sir. He's captain on sea, and I'm captain on land. So he's under my charge now."

"Then you have the power of attorney for him in the present negotiations? Good. I'll make you a proposition. The twenty-five hundred dollars shall be held in trust by me, on his demand at any time. We'll settle about yours afterward. Then he shall be put on probation for, say, a year—in our office. You can either coach him in his studies, for I am confident now that you will be up in yours hereafter, or he can attend night-school. And after that, if he comes through his period of probation with flying colors, I'll give him the same opportunities for an education that you possess. It all depends on himself. And now, Mr. Attorney, what have you to say to my offer in the interests of your client?"

"That I close with it at once."

Father and son shook hands.

"And what are you going to do now, Joe?"

"Send a telegram to 'Frisco Kid first, and then hurry home."

"Then wait a minute till I call up San Andreas and tell Mr. Tate the good news, and then I'll go with you."

"Mr. Willis," Mr. Bronson said as they left the outer office, "the San Andreas safe is recovered, and we'll all take a holiday. Kindly tell the clerks that they are free for the rest of the day. And I say," he called back as they entered the elevator, "don't forget the office-boy."

WHITE AND YELLOW

WHITE AND YELLOW
(1905)

SAN FRANCISCO BAY IS so large that often its storms are
more disastrous to ocean-going craft than is the ocean itself
in its violent moments. The waters of the bay contain all
manner of fish, wherefore its surface is ploughed by the
keels of all manner of fishing boats manned by all manner of
fishermen. To protect the fish from this motley floating
population many wise laws have been passed, and there is a
fish patrol to see that these laws are enforced. Exciting
times are the lot of the fish patrol: in its history more than
one dead patrolman has marked defeat, and more often dead
fishermen across their illegal nets have marked success.

Wildest among the fisher-folk may be accounted the
Chinese shrimp-catchers. It is the habit of the shrimp to
crawl along the bottom in vast armies till it reaches fresh
water, when it turns about and crawls back again to the salt.
And where the tide ebbs and flows, the Chinese sink great
bag-nets to the bottom, with gaping mouths, into which the
shrimp crawls and from which it is transferred to the
boiling-pot. This in itself would not be bad, were it not for
the small mesh of the nets, so small that the tiniest fishes,
little new-hatched things not a quarter of an inch long,

cannot pass through. The beautiful beaches of Points Pedro and Pablo, where are the shrimp-catchers' villages, are made fearful by the stench from myriads of decaying fish, and against this wasteful destruction it has ever been the duty of the fish patrol to act.

When I was a youngster of sixteen, a good sloop-sailor and all-round bay-waterman, my sloop, the *Reindeer*, was chartered by the Fish Commission, and I became for the time being a deputy patrolman. After a deal of work among the Greek fishermen of the Upper Bay and rivers, where knives flashed at the beginning of trouble and men permitted themselves to be made prisoners only after a revolver was thrust in their faces, we hailed with delight an expedition to the Lower Bay against the Chinese shrimp-catchers.

There were six of us, in two boats, and to avoid suspicion we ran down after dark and dropped anchor under a projecting bluff of land known as Point Pinole. As the east paled with the first light of dawn we got under way again and hauled close on the land breeze as we slanted across the bay toward Point Pedro. The morning mists curled and clung to the water so that we could see nothing, but we busied ourselves driving the chill from our bodies with hot coffee. Also, we had to devote ourselves to the miserable task of bailing, for in some incomprehensible way the *Reindeer* had sprung a generous leak. Half the night had been spent in overhauling the ballast and exploring the seams, but the labor had been without avail. The water still poured in, and perforce we doubled up in the cockpit and tossed it out again.

After coffee, three of the men withdrew to the other boat, a Columbia River salmon boat, leaving three of us in the *Reindeer*. Then the two craft proceeded in company till the sun showed over the eastern skyline. Its fiery rays dispelled the clinging vapors, and there, before our eyes, like a picture, lay the shrimp fleet, spread out in a great half-moon, the tips of the crescent fully three miles apart, and each junk moored fast to the buoy of a shrimp-net. But there was no stir, no sign of life.

The situation dawned upon us. While waiting for slack water, in which to lift their heavy nets from the bed of the bay, the Chinese had all gone to sleep below. We were elated, and our plan of battle was swiftly formed.

"Throw each of your two men on to a junk," whispered Le Grant to me from the salmon boat. "And you make fast to a third yourself. We'll do the same, and there's no reason in the world why we shouldn't capture six junks at the least."

Then we separated. I put the *Reindeer* about on the other tack, ran up under the lee of a junk, shivered the mainsail into the wind and lost headway, and forged past the stern of the junk so slowly and so near that one of the patrolmen stepped lightly aboard. Then I kept off, filled the mainsail, and bore away for a second junk.

Up to this time there had been no noise, but from the first junk captured by the salmon boat an uproar now broke forth. There was shrill Oriental yelling, a pistol shot, and more yelling.

"It's all up. They're warning the others," said George, the remaining patrolman, as he stood beside me in the cockpit.

By this time, we were in the thick of the fleet, and the alarm was spreading with incredible swiftness. The decks were beginning to swarm with half-awakened and half-naked Chinese. Cries and yells of warning and anger were flying over the quiet water, and somewhere a conch shell was being blown with great success. To the right of us I saw the captain of a junk chop away his mooring line with an axe and spring to help his crew at the hoisting of the huge, outlandish lug-sail. But to the left the first heads were popping up from below on another junk, and I rounded up the *Reindeer* alongside long enough for George to spring aboard.

The whole fleet was now under way. In addition to the sails, they had gotten out long sweeps, and the bay was being ploughed in every direction by the fleeing junks. I was now alone in the *Reindeer*, seeking feverishly to capture a third prize. The first junk I took after was a clean miss, for it trimmed its sheets and shot away surprisingly into the wind. By fully half a point it outpointed the *Reindeer*, and I began to feel respect for the clumsy craft. Realizing the hopelessness of the pursuit, I filled away, threw out the main-sheet, and drove down before the wind upon the junks to leeward, where I had them at a disadvantage.

The one I had selected wavered indecisively before me, and, as I swung wide to make the boarding gentle, filled suddenly and darted away, the smart Mongols shouting a wild rhythm as they bent to the sweeps. But I had been ready for this. I luffed suddenly. Putting the tiller hard down, and holding it down with my body, I brought the main-sheet in, hand over hand, on the run, so as to retain all possible striking force. The two starboard sweeps of the junk were crumpled up, and then the two boats came together with a crash. The *Reindeer*'s bowsprit, like a monstrous hand, reached over and ripped out the junk's chunky mast and towering sail.

This was met by a curdling yell of rage. A big Chinaman, remarkably evil-looking, with his head swathed in a yellow silk handkerchief and face badly pock-marked, planted a pike-pole on the *Reindeer*'s bow and began to shove the entangled boats apart. Pausing long enough to let go the jib halyards, and just as the *Reindeer* cleared and began to drift astern, I leaped aboard the junk with a line and made fast. He of the yellow handkerchief and pock-marked face came toward me threateningly, but I put my hand into my hip pocket, and he hesitated. I was unarmed, but the Chinese have learned to be fastidiously careful of American hip pockets, and it was upon this that I depended to keep him and his savage crew at a distance.

I ordered him to drop the anchor at the junk's bow, to which he replied, "No sabbe." The crew responded in like fashion, and though I made my meaning plain by signs, they refused to understand. Realizing the inexpediency of discussing the matter, I went forward myself, overran the line, and let the anchor go.

"Now get aboard, four of you," I said in a loud voice, indicating with my fingers that four of them were to go with me and the fifth was to remain by the junk. The Yellow Handkerchief hesitated; but I repeated the order fiercely (much more fiercely than I felt), at the same time sending my hand to my hip. Again, the Yellow Handkerchief was overawed, and, with surly looks, he led three of his men aboard the *Reindeer*. I cast off at once, and, leaving the jib down, steered a course for George's junk. Here it was easier, for there were two of us, and George had a pistol to fall back on if it came to the worst. And here, as with my junk, four Chinese were transferred to the sloop and one left behind to take care of things.

Four more were added to our passenger list from the third junk. By this time the salmon boat had collected its twelve prisoners and came alongside, badly overloaded. To make matters worse, as it was a small boat, the patrolmen were so jammed in with their prisoners that they would have little chance in case of trouble.

"You'll have to help us out," said Le Grant.

I looked over my prisoners, who had crowded into the cabin and on top of it. "I can take three," I answered.

"Make it four," he suggested, "and I'll take Bill with me." (Bill was the third patrolman). "We haven't elbow room here, and in case of a scuffle one white to every two of them will be just about the right proportion."

The exchange was made, and the salmon boat got up its spritsail and headed down the bay toward the marshes off San Rafael. I ran up the jib and followed with the *Reindeer*. San Rafael, where we were to turn our catch over to the authorities, communicated with the bay by way of a long and tortuous slough, or marshland creek, which could be navigated only when the tide was in. Slack water had come, and, as the ebb was commencing, there was need for hurry if we cared to escape waiting half a day for the next tide.

But the land breeze had begun to die away with the rising sun, and now came only in failing puffs. The salmon boat got out its oars and soon left us far astern. Some of the Chinese stood in the forward part of the cockpit, near the cabin doors, and once, as I leaned over the cockpit rail to flatten down the jib-sheet a bit, I felt someone brush against my hip pocket. I made no sign, but out of the corner of my eye I saw that the Yellow Handkerchief had discovered the emptiness of the pocket which had hitherto overawed him.

To make matters serious, during all the excitement of boarding the junks the *Reindeer* had not been bailed, and the water was beginning to slush over the cockpit floor. The shrimp-catchers pointed at it and looked to me questioningly.

"Yes," I said. "Bime by, allee same dlown, velly quick, you no bail now. Sabbe?"

No, they did not "sabbe," or at least they shook their heads to that effect, though they chattered most comprehendingly to one another in their own lingo. I pulled up three or four of the bottom boards, got a couple of buckets from a locker, and by unmistakable sign-language invited them to fall to. But they laughed, and some crowded into the cabin and some climbed up on top.

Their laughter was not good laughter. There was a hint of menace in it, a maliciousness which their black looks verified. The Yellow Handkerchief, since his discovery of my empty pocket, had become most insolent in his bearing, and he wormed about among the other prisoners, talking to them with great earnestness.

Swallowing my chagrin, I stepped down into the

cockpit and began throwing out the water. But hardly had I begun, when the boom swung overhead, the mainsail filled with a jerk, and the *Reindeer* heeled over. The day wind was springing up. George was the veriest of landlubbers, so I was forced to give over bailing and take the tiller. The wind was blowing directly off Point Pedro and the high mountains behind, and because of this was squally and uncertain, half the time bellying the canvas out and the other half flapping it idly.

George was about the most all-round helpless man I had ever met. Among his other disabilities, he was a consumptive, and I knew that if he attempted to bail, it might bring on a hemorrhage. Yet the rising water warned me that something must be done. Again, I ordered the shrimp-catchers to lend a hand with the buckets. They laughed defiantly, and those inside the cabin, the water up to their ankles, shouted back and forth with those on top.

"You'd better get out your gun and make them bail," I said to George.

But he shook his head and showed all too plainly that he was afraid. The Chinese could see the funk he was in as well as I could, and their insolence became insufferable. Those in the cabin broke into the food lockers, and those above scrambled down and joined them in a feast on our crackers and canned goods.

"What do we care?" George said weakly.

I was fuming with helpless anger. "If they get out of hand, it will be too late to care. The best thing you can do is to get them in check right now."

The water was rising higher and higher, and the gusts,

forerunners of a steady breeze, were growing stiffer and stiffer. And between the gusts, the prisoners, having gotten away with a week's grub, took to crowding first to one side and then to the other till the *Reindeer* rocked like a cockle-shell. Yellow Handkerchief approached me, and, pointing out his village on the Point Pedro beach, gave me to understand that if I turned the *Reindeer* in that direction and put them ashore, they, in turn, would go to bailing. By now the water in the cabin was up to the bunks, and the bed- clothes were sopping. It was a foot deep on the cockpit floor. Nevertheless, I refused, and I could see by George's face that he was disappointed.

"If you don't show some nerve, they'll rush us and throw us overboard," I said to him. "Better give me your revolver, if you want to be safe."

"The safest thing to do," he chattered cravenly, "is to put them ashore. I, for one, don't want to be drowned for the sake of a handful of dirty Chinamen."

"And I, for another, don't care to give in to a handful of dirty Chinamen to escape drowning," I answered hotly.

"You'll sink the *Reindeer* under us all at this rate," he whined. "And what good that'll do I can't see."

"Every man to his taste," I retorted.

He made no reply, but I could see he was trembling pitifully. Between the threatening Chinese and the rising water, he was beside himself with fright; and, more than the Chinese and the water, I feared him and what his fright might impel him to do. I could see him casting longing glances at the small skiff towing astern, so in the next calm I hauled the skiff alongside. As I did so his eyes brightened with hope; but before he could guess my intention, I stove the frail bottom through with a hand-axe, and the skiff filled to its gunwales.

"It's sink or float together," I said. "And if you'll give me your revolver, I'll have the *Reindeer* bailed out in a jiffy."

"They're too many for us," he whimpered. "We can't fight them all."

I turned my back on him in disgust. The salmon boat had long since passed from sight behind a little archipelago known as the Marin Islands, so no help could be looked for from that quarter. Yellow Handkerchief came up to me in a familiar manner, the water in the cockpit slushing against his legs. I did not like his looks. I felt that beneath the pleasant smile he was trying to put on his face there was an ill purpose. I ordered him back, and so sharply that he obeyed.

"Now keep your distance," I commanded, "and don't you come closer!"

"Wha' fo'?" he demanded indignantly. "I t'ink-um talkee talkee heap good."

"Talkee talkee," I answered bitterly, for I knew now that he had understood all that passed between George and me. "What for talkee talkee? You no sabbe talkee talkee."

He grinned in a sickly fashion. "Yep, I sabbe velly much. I honest Chinaman."

"All right," I answered. "You sabbe talkee talkee, then you bail water plenty plenty. After that we talkee talkee."

He shook his head, at the same time pointing over his shoulder to his comrades. "No can do. Velly bad Chinamen, heap velly bad. I t'ink-um— "

"Stand back!" I shouted, for I had noticed his hand disappear beneath his blouse and his body prepare for a spring.

Disconcerted, he went back into the cabin, to hold a council, apparently, from the way the jabbering broke forth. The *Reindeer* was very deep in the water, and her movements had grown quite loggy. In a rough sea she would have inevitably swamped; but the wind, when it did blow, was off the land, and scarcely a ripple disturbed the surface of the bay.

"I think you'd better head for the beach," George said abruptly, in a manner that told me his fear had forced him to make up his mind to some course of action.

"I think not," I answered shortly.

"I command you," he said in a bullying tone.

"I was commanded to bring these prisoners into San Rafael," was my reply.

Our voices were raised, and the sound of the altercation brought the Chinese out of the cabin.

"Now will you head for the beach?"

This from George, and I found myself looking into the muzzle of his revolver—of the revolver he dared to use on me but was too cowardly to use on the prisoners.

My brain seemed smitten with a dazzling brightness. The whole situation, in all its bearings, was focused sharply before me—the shame of losing the prisoners, the worthlessness and cowardice of George, the meeting with Le Grant and the other patrol men and the lame explanation; and then there was the fight I had fought so hard, victory wrenched from me just as I thought I had it within my grasp.

And out of the tail of my eye I could see the Chinese crowding together by the cabin doors and leering triumphantly. It would never do.

I threw my hand up and my head down. The first act elevated the muzzle, and the second removed my head from the path of the bullet which went whistling past. One hand closed on George's wrist, the other on the revolver. Yellow Handkerchief and his gang sprang toward me. It was now or never. Putting all my strength into a sudden effort, I swung George's body forward to meet them. Then I pulled back with equal suddenness, ripping the revolver out of his fingers and jerking him off his feet. He fell against Yellow Handkerchief's knees, who stumbled over him, and the pair wallowed in the bailing hole where the cockpit floor was torn open. The next instant I was covering them with my revolver, and the wild shrimp-catchers were cowering and cringing away.

But I swiftly discovered that there was all the difference in the world between shooting men who are attacking and men who are doing nothing more than simply refusing to obey. For obey they would not when I ordered them into the bailing hole. I threatened them with the revolver, but they sat stolidly in the flooded cabin and on the roof and would not move.

Fifteen minutes passed, the *Reindeer* sinking deeper and deeper, her mainsail flapping in the calm. But from off the Point Pedro shore, I saw a dark line form on the water and travel toward us. It was the steady breeze I had been expecting so long. I called to the Chinese and pointed it out. They hailed it with exclamations. Then I pointed to the sail and to the water in the *Reindeer* and indicated by signs that when the wind reached the sail, what of the water aboard we would capsize. But they jeered defiantly, for they knew it was in my power to luff the helm and let go the main-sheet, so as to spill the wind and escape damage.

But my mind was made up. I hauled in the main-sheet a foot or two, took a turn with it, and bracing my feet, put my back against the tiller. This left me one hand for the sheet and one for the revolver. The dark line drew nearer, and I could see them looking from me to it and back again with an apprehension they could not successfully conceal. My brain and will and endurance were pitted against theirs, and the problem was which could stand the strain of imminent death the longer and not give in.

Then the wind struck us. The main-sheet tautened with a brisk rattling of the blocks, the boom uplifted, the sail bellied out, and the *Reindeer* heeled over—over, and over, till the lee-rail went under, the cabin windows went under, and the bay began to pour in over the cockpit rail. So violently had she heeled over, that the men in the cabin had been thrown on top of one another into the lee bunk, where they squirmed and twisted and were washed about, those underneath being perilously near to drowning.

The wind freshened a bit, and the *Reindeer* went over farther than ever. For the moment I thought she was gone, and I knew that another puff like that and she surely would go. While I pressed her under and debated whether I should give up or not, the Chinese cried for mercy. I think it was the sweetest sound I have ever heard. And then, and not until then, did I luff up and ease out the main-sheet. The *Reindeer* righted very slowly, and when she was on an even keel was so much awash that I doubted if she could be saved.

But the Chinese scrambled madly into the cockpit and fell to bailing with buckets, pots, pans, and everything they could lay hands on. It was a beautiful sight to see that water flying over the side! And when the *Reindeer* was high and proud on the water once more, we dashed away with the breeze on our quarter, and at the last possible moment crossed the mud flats and entered the slough.

The spirit of the Chinese was broken, and so docile did they become that ere we made San Rafael they were out with the tow-rope, Yellow Handkerchief at the head of the line. As for George, it was his last trip with the fish patrol. He did not care for that sort of thing, he explained, and he thought a clerkship ashore was good enough for him. And we thought so too.

THE KING OF THE GREEKS

THE KING OF THE GREEKS (1905)

BIG ALEC HAD NEVER been captured by the fish patrol. It was his boast that no man could take him alive, and it was his history that of the many men who had tried to take him dead none had succeeded. It was also history that at least two patrolmen who had tried to take him dead had died themselves. Further, no man violated the fish laws more systematically and deliberately than Big Alec.

He was called "Big Alec" because of his gigantic stature. His height was six feet three inches, and he was correspondingly broad- shouldered and deep-chested. He was splendidly muscled and hard as steel, and there were innumerable stories in circulation among the fisher-folk concerning his prodigious strength. He was as bold and dominant of spirit as he was strong of body, and because of this he was widely known by another name, that of "The King of the Greeks." The fishing population was largely composed of Greeks, and they looked up to him and obeyed him as their chief. And as their chief, he fought their fights for them, saw that they were protected, saved them from the law when they fell into its clutches, and made them stand by one another and himself in time of trouble.

In the old days, the fish patrol had attempted his capture many disastrous times and had finally given it over, so that when the word was out that he was coming to Benicia, I was most anxious to see him. But I did not have to hunt him up. In his usual bold way, the first thing he did on arriving was to hunt us up. Charley Le Grant and I at the time were under a patrolman named Carmintel, and the three of us were on the *Reindeer*, preparing for a trip, when Big Alec stepped aboard. Carmintel evidently knew him, for they shook hands in recognition. Big Alec took no notice of Charley or me.

"I've come down to fish sturgeon a couple of months," he said to Carmintel.

His eyes flashed with challenge as he spoke, and we noticed the patrolman's eyes drop before him.

"That's all right, Alec," Carmintel said in a low voice. "I'll not bother you. Come on into the cabin, and we'll talk things over," he added.

When they had gone inside and shut the doors after them, Charley winked with slow deliberation at me. But I was only a youngster, and new to men and the ways of some men, so I did not understand. Nor did Charley explain, though I felt there was something wrong about the business.

Leaving them to their conference, at Charley's suggestion we boarded our skiff and pulled over to the Old Steamboat Wharf, where Big Alec's ark was lying. An ark is a house-boat of small though comfortable dimensions, and is as necessary to the Upper Bay fisherman as are nets and boats. We were both curious to see Big Alec's ark, for history said that it had been the scene of more than one pitched battle, and that it was riddled with bullet-holes.

We found the holes (stopped with wooden plugs and painted over), but there were not so many as I had expected. Charley noted my look of disappointment and laughed; and then to comfort me he gave an authentic account of one expedition which had descended upon Big Alec's floating home to capture him, alive preferably, dead if necessary. At the end of half a day's fighting, the patrolmen had drawn off in wrecked boats, with one of their number killed and three wounded. And when they returned next morning with reinforcements, they found only the mooring-stakes of Big Alec's ark; the ark itself remained hidden for months in the fastnesses of the Suisun tules.

"But why was he not hanged for murder?" I demanded. "Surely the United States is powerful enough to bring such a man to justice."

"He gave himself up and stood trial," Charley answered. "It cost him fifty thousand dollars to win the case, which he did on technicalities and with the aid of the best lawyers in the state. Every Greek fisherman on the river contributed to the sum. Big Alec levied and collected the tax, for all the world like a king. The United States may be all-powerful, my lad, but the fact remains that Big Alec is a king inside the United States, with a country and subjects all his own."

"But what are you going to do about his fishing for sturgeon? He's bound to fish with a 'Chinese line.'"

Charley shrugged his shoulders. "We'll see what we will see," he said enigmatically.

Now a "Chinese line" is a cunning device invented by the people whose name it bears. By a simple system of floats, weights, and anchors, thousands of hooks, each on a separate leader, are suspended at a distance of from six inches to a foot above the bottom. The remarkable thing about such a line is the hook. It is barbless, and in place of the barb, the hook is filed long and tapering to a point as sharp as that of a needle. These hoods are only a few inches apart, and when several thousand of them are suspended just above the bottom, like a fringe, for a couple of hundred fathoms, they present a formidable obstacle to the fish that travel along the bottom.

Such a fish is the sturgeon, which goes rooting along like a pig, and indeed is often called "pig-fish." Pricked by the first hook it touches, the sturgeon gives a startled leap and comes into contact with half a dozen more hooks. Then it threshes about wildly, until it receives hook after hook in its soft flesh; and the hooks, straining from many different angles, hold the luckless fish fast until it is drowned. Because no sturgeon can pass through a Chinese line, the device is called a trap in the fish laws; and because it bids fair to exterminate the sturgeon, it is branded by the fish laws as illegal. And such a line, we were confident, Big Alec intended setting, in open and flagrant violation of the law.

Several days passed after the visit of Big Alec, during which Charley and I kept a sharp watch on him. He towed his ark around the Solano Wharf and into the big bight at Turner's Shipyard. The bight we knew to be good ground for sturgeon, and there we felt sure the King of the Greeks intended to begin operations. The tide circled like a mill-race in and out of this bight, and made it possible to raise, lower, or set a Chinese line only at slack water. So between the tides, Charley and I made it a point for one or the other of us to keep a lookout from the Solano Wharf.

On the fourth day, I was lying in the sun behind the stringer-piece of the wharf, when I saw a skiff leave the distant shore and pull out into the bight. In an instant the glasses were at my eyes and I was following every movement of the skiff. There were two men in it, and though it was a good mile away, I made out one of them to be Big Alec; and ere the skiff returned to shore I made out enough more to know that the Greek had set his line.

"Big Alec has a Chinese line out in the bight off Turner's Shipyard," Charley Le Grant said that afternoon to Carmintel.

A fleeting expression of annoyance passed over the patrolman's face, and then he said, "Yes?" in an absent way, and that was all.

Charley bit his lip with suppressed anger and turned on his heel.

"Are you game, my lad?" he said to me later on in the evening, just as we finished washing down the *Reindeer*'s decks and were preparing to turn in.

A lump came up in my throat, and I could only nod my head.

"Well, then," and Charley's eyes glittered in a determined way, "we've got to capture Big Alec between us, you and I, and we've got to do it in spite of Carmintel. Will you lend a hand?"

"It's a hard proposition, but we can do it," he added

after a pause.

"Of course we can," I supplemented enthusiastically.

And then he said, "Of course we can," and we shook hands on it and went to bed.

But it was no easy task we had set ourselves. In order to convict a man of illegal fishing, it was necessary to catch him in the act with all the evidence of the crime about him—the hooks, the lines, the fish, and the man himself. This meant that we must take Big Alec on the open water, where he could see us coming and prepare for us one of the warm receptions for which he was noted.

"There's no getting around it," Charley said one morning. "If we can only get alongside it's an even toss, and there's nothing left for us but to try and get alongside. Come on, lad."

We were in the Columbia River salmon boat, the one we had used against the Chinese shrimp-catchers. Slack water had come, and as we dropped around the end of the Solano Wharf we saw Big Alec at work, running his line and removing the fish.

"Change places," Charley commanded, "and steer just astern of him as though you're going into the shipyard."

I took the tiller, and Charley sat down on a thwart amidships, placing his revolver handily beside him.

"If he begins to shoot," he cautioned, "get down in the bottom and steer from there, so that nothing more than your hand will be exposed."

I nodded, and we kept silent after that, the boat slipping gently through the water and Big Alec growing nearer and nearer. We could see him quite plainly, gaffing the sturgeon and throwing them into the boat while his companion ran the line and cleared the hooks as he dropped them back into the water. Nevertheless, we were five hundred yards away when the big fisherman hailed us.

"Here! You! What do you want?" he shouted.

"Keep going," Charley whispered, "just as though you didn't hear him."

The next few moments were very anxious ones. The fisherman was studying us sharply, while we were gliding up on him every second.

"You keep off if you know what's good for you!" he called out suddenly, as though he had made up his mind as to who and what we were. "If you don't, I'll fix you!"

He brought a rifle to his shoulder and trained it on me.

"Now will you keep off?" he demanded.

I could hear Charley groan with disappointment. "Keep off," he whispered; "it's all up for this time."

I put up the tiller and eased the sheet, and the salmon boat ran off five or six points. Big Alec watched us till we were out of range, when he returned to his work.

"You'd better leave Big Alec alone," Carmintel said, rather sourly, to Charley that night.

"So he's been complaining to you, has he?" Charley said significantly.

Carmintel flushed painfully. "You'd better leave him alone, I tell you," he repeated. "He's a dangerous man, and it won't pay to fool with him."

"Yes," Charley answered softly; "I've heard that it pays better to leave him alone."

This was a direct thrust at Carmintel, and we could see

by the expression of his face that it sank home. For it was common knowledge that Big Alec was as willing to bribe as to fight, and that of late years more than one patrolman had handled the fisherman's money.

"Do you mean to say " Carmintel began, in a bullying tone.

But Charley cut him off shortly. "I mean to say nothing," he said. "You heard what I said, and if the cap fits, why—"

He shrugged his shoulders, and Carmintel glowered at him, speechless.

"What we want is imagination," Charley said to me one day, when we had attempted to creep upon Big Alec in the gray of dawn and had been shot at for our trouble.

And thereafter, and for many days, I cudgelled my brains trying to imagine some possible way by which two men, on an open stretch of water, could capture another who knew how to use a rifle and was never to be found without one. Regularly, every slack water, without slyness, boldly and openly in the broad day, Big Alec was to be seen running his line. And what made it particularly exasperating was the fact that every fisherman, from Benicia to Vallejo knew that he was successfully defying us. Carmintel also bothered us, for he kept us busy among the shad-fishers of San Pablo, so that we had little time to spare on the King of the Greeks. But Charley's wife and children lived at Benicia, and we had made the place our headquarters, so that we always returned to it.

"I'll tell you what we can do," I said, after several fruitless weeks had passed; "we can wait some slack water till Big Alec has run his line and gone ashore with the fish, and then we can go out and capture the line. It will put him to time and expense to make another, and then we'll figure to capture that too. If we can't capture him, we can discourage him, you see."

Charley saw, and said it wasn't a bad idea. We watched our chance, and the next low-water slack, after Big Alec had removed the fish from the line and returned ashore, we went out in the salmon boat. We had the bearings of the line from shore marks, and we knew we would have no difficulty in locating it. The first of the flood tide was setting in, when we ran below where we thought the line was stretched and dropped over a fishing-boat anchor. Keeping a short rope to the anchor, so that it barely touched the bottom, we dragged it slowly along until it stuck and the boat fetched up hard and fast.

"We've got it," Charley cried. "Come on and lend a hand to get it in."

Together we hove up the rope till the anchor I came in sight with the sturgeon line caught across one of the flukes. Scores of the murderous-looking hooks flashed into sight as we cleared the anchor, and we had just started to run along the line to the end where we could begin to lift it, when a sharp thud in the boat startled us. We looked about but saw nothing and returned to our work. An instant later there was a similar sharp thud and the gunwale splintered between Charley's body and mine.

"That's remarkably like a bullet, lad," he said reflectively. "And it's a long shot Big Alec's making."

"And he's using smokeless powder," he concluded, after

an examination of the mile-distant shore. "That's why we can't hear the report."

I looked at the shore, but could see no sign of Big Alec, who was undoubtedly hidden in some rocky nook with us at his mercy. A third bullet struck the water, glanced, passed singing over our heads, and struck the water again beyond.

"I guess we'd better get out of this," Charley remarked coolly. "What do you think, lad?"

I thought so, too, and said we didn't want the line anyway. Whereupon we cast off and hoisted the spritsail. The bullets ceased at once, and we sailed away, unpleasantly confident that Big Alec was laughing at our discomfiture.

And more than that, the next day on the fishing wharf, where we were inspecting nets, he saw fit to laugh and sneer at us, and this before all the fishermen. Charley's face went black with anger; but beyond promising Big Alec that in the end he would surely land him behind the bars, he controlled himself and said nothing. The King of the Greeks made his boast that no fish patrol had ever taken him or ever could take him, and the fishermen cheered him and said it was true. They grew excited, and it looked like trouble for a while; but Big Alec asserted his kingship and quelled them.

Carmintel also laughed at Charley, and dropped sarcastic remarks, and made it hard for him. But Charley refused to be angered, though he told me in confidence that he intended to capture Big Alec if it took all the rest of his life to accomplish it.

"I don't know how I'll do it," he said, "but do it I will, as sure as I am Charley Le Grant. The idea will come to me at the right and proper time, never fear."

And at the right time it came, and most unexpectedly. Fully a month had passed, and we were constantly up and down the river, and down and up the bay, with no spare moments to devote to the particular fisherman who ran a Chinese line in the bight of Turner's Shipyard. We had called in at Selby's Smelter one afternoon, while on patrol work, when all unknown to us our opportunity happened along. It appeared in the guise of a helpless yacht loaded with seasick people, so we could hardly be expected to recognize it as the opportunity. It was a large sloop-yacht, and it was helpless inasmuch as the trade-wind was blowing half a gale and there were no capable sailors aboard.

From the wharf at Selby's we watched with careless interest the lubberly maneuver performed of bringing the yacht to anchor, and the equally lubberly maneuver of sending the small boat ashore. A very miserable-looking man in draggled ducks, after nearly swamping the boat in the heavy seas, passed us the painter and climbed out. He staggered about as though the wharf were rolling, and told us his troubles, which were the troubles of the yacht. The only rough-weather sailor aboard, the man on whom they all depended, had been called back to San Francisco by a telegram, and they had attempted to continue the cruise alone. The high wind and big seas of San Pablo Bay had been too much for them; all hands were sick, nobody knew anything or could do anything; and so they had run in to the smelter either to desert the yacht or to get somebody to bring it to Benicia. In short, did we know of any sailors who would bring the yacht into Benicia?

Charley looked at me. The *Reindeer* was lying in a snug

place. We had nothing on hand in the way of patrol work till midnight. With the wind then blowing, we could sail the yacht into Benicia in a couple of hours, have several more hours ashore, and come back to the smelter on the evening train.

"All right, captain," Charley said to the disconsolate yachtsman, who smiled in sickly fashion at the title.

"I'm only the owner," he explained.

We rowed him aboard in much better style than he had come ashore and saw for ourselves the helplessness of the passengers. There were a dozen men and women, and all of them too sick even to appear grateful at our coming. The yacht was rolling savagely, broad on, and no sooner had the owner's feet touched the deck than he collapsed and joined, the others. Not one was able to bear a hand, so Charley and I between us cleared the badly tangled running gear, got up sail, and hoisted anchor.

It was a rough trip, though a swift one. The Carquinez Straits were a welter of foam and smother, and we came through them wildly before the wind, the big mainsail alternately dipping and flinging its boom skyward as we tore along. But the people did not mind. They did not mind anything. Two or three, including the owner, sprawled in the cockpit, shuddering when the yacht lifted and raced and sank dizzily into the trough, and between-whiles regarding the shore with yearning eyes. The rest were huddled on the cabin floor among the cushions. Now and again someone groaned, but for the most part they were as limp as so many dead persons.

As the bight at Turner's Shipyard opened out, Charley

edged into it to get the smoother water. Benicia was in view, and we were bowling along over comparatively easy water, when a speck of a boat danced up ahead of us, directly in our course. It was low-water slack. Charley and I looked at each other. No word was spoken, but at once the yacht began a most astonishing performance, veering and yawing as though the greenest of amateurs was at the wheel. It was a sight for sailormen to see. To all appearances, a runaway yacht was careering madly over the bight, and now and again yielding a little bit to control in a desperate effort to make Benicia.

The owner forgot his seasickness long enough to look anxious. The speck of a boat grew larger and larger, till we could see Big Alec and his partner, with a turn of the sturgeon line around a cleat, resting from their labor to laugh at us. Charley pulled his sou'wester over his eyes, and I followed his example, though I could not guess the idea he evidently had in mind and intended to carry into execution.

We came foaming down abreast of the skiff, so close that we could hear above the wind the voices of Big Alec and his mate as they shouted at us with all the scorn that professional watermen feel for amateurs, especially when amateurs are making fools of themselves.

We thundered on past the fishermen, and nothing had happened. Charley grinned at the disappointment he saw in my face, and then shouted:

"Stand by the main-sheet to jibe!"

He put the wheel hard over, and the yacht whirled around obediently. The main-sheet slacked and dipped, then shot over our heads after the boom and tautened with a crash on the traveller. The yacht heeled over almost on her beam ends, and a great wail went up from the seasick passengers as they swept across the cabin floor in a tangled mass and piled into a heap in the starboard bunks.

But we had no time for them. The yacht, completing the maneuver, headed into the wind with slatting canvas, and righted to an even keel. We were still plunging ahead, and directly in our path was the skiff. I saw Big Alec dive overboard and his mate leap for our bowsprit. Then came the crash as we struck the boat, and a series of grinding bumps as it passed under our bottom.

"That fixes his rifle," I heard Charley mutter, as he sprang upon the deck to look for Big Alec somewhere astern.

The wind and sea quickly stopped our forward movement, and we began to drift backward over the spot where the skiff had been. Big Alec's black head and swarthy face popped up within arm's reach; and all unsuspecting and very angry with what he took to be the clumsiness of amateur sailors, he was hauled aboard. Also he was out of breath, for he had dived deep and stayed down long to escape our keel.

The next instant, to the perplexity and consternation of the owner, Charley was on top of Big Alec in the cockpit, and I was helping bind him with gaskets. The owner was dancing excitedly about and demanding an explanation, but by that time Big Alec's partner had crawled aft from the bowsprit and was peering apprehensively over the rail into the cockpit. Charley's arm shot around his neck and the man landed on his back beside Big Alec.

"More gaskets!" Charley shouted, and I made haste to

supply them.

The wrecked skiff was rolling sluggishly a short distance to windward, and I trimmed the sheets while Charley took the wheel and steered for it.

"These two men are old offenders," he explained to the angry owner; "and they are most persistent violators of the fish and game laws. You have seen them caught in the act, and you may expect to be subpoenaed as witness for the state when the trial comes off."

As he spoke, he rounded alongside the skiff. It had been torn from the line, a section of which was dragging to it. He hauled in forty or fifty feet with a young sturgeon still fast in a tangle of barbless hooks, slashed that much of the line free with his knife, and tossed it into the cockpit beside the prisoners.

"And there's the evidence, Exhibit A, for the people," Charley continued. "Look it over carefully so that you may identify it in the court-room with the time and place of capture."

And then, in triumph, with no more veering and yawing, we sailed into Benicia, the King of the Greeks bound hard and fast in the cockpit, and for the first time in his life a prisoner of the fish patrol.

A Raid on the Oyster Pirates

A RAID ON THE
OYSTER PIRATES
(1905)

OF THE FISH PATROLMEN under whom we served at various times, Charley Le Grant and I were agreed, I think, that Neil Partington was the best. He was neither dishonest nor cowardly; and while he demanded strict obedience when we were under his orders, at the same time our relations were those of easy comradeship, and he permitted us a freedom to which we were ordinarily unaccustomed, as the present story will show.

Neil's family lived in Oakland, which is on the Lower Bay, not more than six miles across the water from San Francisco. One day, while scouting among the Chinese shrimp-catchers of Point Pedro, he received word that his wife was very ill; and within the hour the *Reindeer* was bowling along for Oakland, with a stiff northwest breeze astern. We ran up the Oakland Estuary and came to anchor, and in the days that followed, while Neil was ashore, we tightened up the *Reindeer*'s rigging, overhauled the ballast, scraped down, and put the sloop into thorough shape.

This done, time hung heavy on our hands. Neil's wife was dangerously ill, and the outlook was a week's lie-over, awaiting the crisis. Charley and I roamed the docks, wondering what we should do, and so came upon the oyster fleet lying at the Oakland City Wharf. In the main they were trim, natty boats, made for speed and bad weather, and we sat down on the stringer-piece of the dock to study them.

"A good catch, I guess," Charley said, pointing to the heaps of oysters, assorted in three sizes, which lay upon their decks.

Peddlers were backing their wagons to the edge of the wharf, and from the bargaining and chaffering that went on, I managed to learn the selling price of the oysters.

"That boat must have at least two hundred dollars' worth aboard," I calculated. "I wonder how long it took to get the load?"

"Three or four days," Charley answered. "Not bad wages for two men—twenty-five dollars a day apiece."

The boat we were discussing, the *Ghost*, lay directly beneath us. Two men composed its crew. One was a squat, broad-shouldered fellow with remarkably long and gorilla-like arms, while the other was tall and well proportioned, with clear blue eyes and a mat of straight black hair. So unusual and striking was this combination of hair and eyes that Charley and I remained somewhat longer than we intended.

And it was well that we did. A stout, elderly man, with

the dress and carriage of a successful merchant, came up and stood beside us, looking down upon the deck of the *Ghost*. He appeared angry, and the longer he looked the angrier he grew.

"Those are my oysters," he said at last. "I know they are my oysters. You raided my beds last night and robbed me of them."

The tall man and the short man on the *Ghost* looked up.

"Hello, Taft," the short man said, with insolent familiarity. (Among the bayfarers he had gained the nickname of "The Centipede" on account of his long arms.) "Hello, Taft," he repeated, with the same touch of insolence. "Wot 'r you growling about now?"

"Those are my oysters—that's what I said. You've stolen them from my beds."

"Yer mighty wise, ain't ye?" was the Centipede's sneering reply. "S'pose you can tell your oysters wherever you see 'em?"

"Now, in my experience," broke in the tall man, "oysters is oysters wherever you find 'em, an' they're pretty much alike all the Bay over, and the world over, too, for that matter. We're not wantin' to quarrel with you, Mr. Taft, but we jes' wish you wouldn't insinuate that them oysters is yours an' that we're thieves an' robbers till you can prove the goods."

"I know they're mine; I'd stake my life on it!" Mr. Taft snorted.

"Prove it," challenged the tall man, who we afterward learned was known as "The Porpoise" because of his wonderful swimming abilities.

Mr. Taft shrugged his shoulders helplessly. Of course he could not prove the oysters to be his, no matter how certain he might be.

"I'd give a thousand dollars to have you men behind the bars!" he cried. "I'll give fifty dollars a head for your arrest and conviction, all of you!"

A roar of laughter went up from the different boats, for the rest of the pirates had been listening to the discussion.

"There's more money in oysters," the Porpoise remarked dryly.

Mr. Taft turned impatiently on his heel and walked away. From out of the corner of his eye, Charley noted the way he went. Several minutes later, when he had disappeared around a corner, Charley rose lazily to his feet. I followed him, and we sauntered off in the opposite direction to that taken by Mr. Taft.

"Come on! Lively!" Charley whispered, when we passed from the view of the oyster fleet.

Our course was changed at once, and we dodged around corners and raced up and down side-streets till Mr. Taft's generous form loomed up ahead of us.

"I'm going to interview him about that reward," Charley explained, as we rapidly over-hauled the oyster-bed owner. "Neil will be delayed here for a week, and you and I might as well be doing something in the meantime. What do you say?"

"Of course, of course," Mr. Taft said, when Charley had introduced himself and explained his errand. "Those thieves are robbing me of thousands of dollars every year, and I shall be glad to break them up at any price—yes, sir, at any price. As I said, I'll give fifty dollars a head, and call it cheap at that. They've robbed my beds, torn down my signs, terrorized my watchmen, and last year killed one of them. Couldn't prove it. All done in the blackness of night. All I had was a dead watchman and no evidence. The detectives could do nothing. Nobody has been able to do anything with those men. We have never succeeded in arresting one of them. So I say, Mr.—What did you say your name was?"

"Le Grant," Charley answered.

"So I say, Mr. Le Grant, I am deeply obliged to you for the assistance you offer. And I shall be glad, most glad, sir, to co- operate with you in every way. My watchmen and boats are at your disposal. Come and see me at the San Francisco offices any time, or telephone at my expense. And don't be afraid of spending money. I'll foot your expenses, whatever they are, so long as they are within reason. The situation is growing desperate, and something must be done to determine whether I or that band of ruffians own those oyster beds."

"Now we'll see Neil," Charley said, when he had seen Mr. Taft upon his train to San Francisco.

Not only did Neil Partington interpose no obstacle to our adventure, but he proved to be of the greatest assistance. Charley and I knew nothing of the oyster industry, while his head was an encyclopedia of facts concerning it. Also, within an hour or so, he was able to bring to us a Greek boy of seventeen or eighteen who knew thoroughly well the ins and outs of oyster piracy.

At this point I may as well explain that we of the fish

patrol were free lances in a way. While Neil Partington, who was a patrolman proper, received a regular salary, Charley and I, being merely deputies, received only what we earned—that is to say, a certain percentage of the fines imposed on convicted violators of the fish laws. Also, any rewards that chanced our way were ours. We offered to share with Partington whatever we should get from Mr. Taft, but the patrolman would not hear of it. He was only too happy, he said, to do a good turn for us, who had done so many for him.

We held a long council of war and mapped out the following line of action. Our faces were unfamiliar on the Lower Bay, but as the *Reindeer* was well known as a fish-patrol sloop, the Greek boy, whose name was Nicholas, and I were to sail some innocent-looking craft down to Asparagus Island and join the oyster pirates' fleet. Here, according to Nicholas's description of the beds and the manner of raiding, it was possible for us to catch the pirates in the act of stealing oysters, and at the same time to get them in our power. Charley was to be on the shore, with Mr. Taft's watchmen and a posse of constables, to help us at the right time.

"I know just the boat," Neil said, at the conclusion of the discussion, "a crazy old sloop that's lying over at Tiburon. You and Nicholas can go over by the ferry, charter it for a song, and sail direct for the beds."

"Good luck be with you, boys," he said at parting, two days later. "Remember, they are dangerous men, so be careful."

Nicholas and I succeeded in chartering the sloop very

cheaply; and between laughs, while getting up sail, we agreed that she was even crazier and older than she had been described. She was a big, flat-bottomed, square-sterned craft, sloop-rigged, with a sprung mast, slack rigging, dilapidated sails, and rotten running-gear, clumsy to handle and uncertain in bringing about, and she smelled vilely of coal tar, with which strange stuff she had been smeared from stem to stern and from cabin-roof to centreboard. And to cap it all, *Coal Tar Maggie* was printed in great white letters the whole length of either side.

It was an uneventful though laughable run from Tiburon to Asparagus Island, where we arrived in the afternoon of the following day. The oyster pirates, a fleet of a dozen sloops, were lying at anchor on what was known as the "Deserted Beds." The *Coal Tar Maggie* came sloshing into their midst with a light breeze astern, and they crowded on deck to see us. Nicholas and I had caught the spirit of the crazy craft, and we handled her in most lubberly fashion.

"Wot is it?" someone called.

"Name it 'n' ye kin have it!" called another.

"I swan naow, ef it ain't the old Ark itself!" mimicked the Centipede from the deck of the *Ghost*.

"Hey! Ahoy there, clipper ship!" another wag shouted. "Wot's yer port?"

We took no notice of the joking, but acted, after the manner of greenhorns, as though the *Coal Tar Maggie* required our undivided attention. I rounded her well to windward of the *Ghost*, and Nicholas ran for'ard to drop the anchor. To all appearances it was a bungle, the way the chain tangled and kept the anchor from reaching the bottom. And to all appearances Nicholas and I were terribly excited as we strove to clear it. At any rate, we quite deceived the pirates, who took huge delight in our predicament.

But the chain remained tangled, and amid all kinds of mocking advice we drifted down upon and fouled the *Ghost*, whose bowsprit poked square through our mainsail and ripped a hole in it as big as a barn door. The Centipede and the Porpoise doubled up on the cabin in paroxysms of laughter and left us to get clear as best we could. This, with much unseaman-like performance, we succeeded in doing, and likewise in clearing the anchor-chain, of which we let out about three hundred feet. With only ten feet of water under us, this would permit the *Coal Tar Maggie* to swing in a circle six hundred feet in diameter, in which circle she would be able to foul at least half the fleet.

The oyster pirates lay snugly together at short hawsers, the weather being fine, and they protested loudly at our ignorance in putting out such an unwarranted length of anchor-chain. And not only did they protest, for they made us heave it in again, all but thirty feet.

Having sufficiently impressed them with our general lubberliness, Nicholas and I went below to congratulate ourselves and to cook supper. Hardly had we finished the meal and washed the dishes, when a skiff ground against the *Coal Tar Maggie*'s side, and heavy feet trampled on deck. Then the Centipede's brutal face appeared in the companionway, and he descended into the cabin, followed by the Porpoise. Before they could seat themselves on a bunk, another skiff came alongside, and another, and another, till the whole fleet was represented by the gathering in the cabin.

"Where'd you swipe the old tub?" asked a squat and hairy man, with cruel eyes and Mexican features.

"Didn't swipe it," Nicholas answered, meeting them on their own ground and encouraging the idea that we had stolen the *Coal Tar Maggie.* "And if we did, what of it?"

"Well, I don't admire your taste, that's all," sneered he of the Mexican features. "I'd rot on the beach first before I'd take a tub that couldn't get out of its own way."

"How were we to know till we tried her?" Nicholas asked, so innocently as to cause a laugh. "And how do you get the oysters?" he hurried on. "We want a load of them; that's what we came for, a load of oysters."

"What d'ye want 'em for?" demanded the Porpoise.

"Oh, to give away to our friends, of course," Nicholas retorted. "That's what you do with yours, I suppose."

This started another laugh, and as our visitors grew more genial, we could see that they had not the slightest suspicion of our identity or purpose.

"Didn't I see you on the dock in Oakland the other day?" the Centipede asked suddenly of me.

"Yep," I answered boldly, taking the bull by the horns. "I was watching you fellows and figuring out whether we'd go oystering or not. It's a pretty good business, I calculate, and so we're going in for it. That is," I hastened to add, "if you fellows don't mind."

"I'll tell you one thing, which ain't two things," he replied, "and that is you'll have to hump yerself an' get a better boat. We won't stand to be disgraced by any such box as this. Understand?"

"Sure," I said. "Soon as we sell some oysters we'll outfit in style."

"And if you show yerself square an' the right sort," he went on, "why, you kin run with us. But if you don't" (here his voice became stern and menacing), "why, it'll be the sickest day of yer life. Understand?"

"Sure," I said.

After that and more warning and advice of similar nature, the conversation became general, and we learned that the beds were to be raided that very night. As they got into their boats, after an hour's stay, we were invited to join them in the raid with the assurance of "the more the merrier."

"Did you notice that short, Mexican-looking chap?" Nicholas asked, when they had departed to their various sloops. "He's Barchi, of the Sporting Life Gang, and the fellow that came with him is Skilling. They're both out now on five thousand dollars' bail."

I had heard of the Sporting Life Gang before, a crowd of hoodlums and criminals that terrorized the lower quarters of Oakland, and two-thirds of which were usually to be found in state's prison for crimes that ranged from perjury and ballot-box stuffing to murder.

"They are not regular oyster pirates," Nicholas continued. "They've just come down for the lark and to make a few dollars. But we'll have to watch out for them."

We sat in the cockpit and discussed the details of our plan till eleven o'clock had passed, when we heard the rattle of an oar in a boat from the direction of the *Ghost*. We hauled up our own skiff, tossed in a few sacks, and rowed over. There we found all the skiffs assembling, it being the intention to raid the beds in a body.

To my surprise, I found barely a foot of water where we had dropped anchor in ten feet. It was the big June run-out of the full moon, and as the ebb had yet an hour and a half to run, I knew that our anchorage would be dry ground before slack water.

Mr. Taft's beds were three miles away, and for a long time we rowed silently in the wake of the other boats, once in a while grounding and our oar blades constantly striking bottom. At last we came upon soft mud covered with not more than two inches of water—not enough to float the boats. But the pirates at once were over the side, and by pushing and pulling on the flat-bottomed skiffs, we moved steadily along.

The full moon was partly obscured by high-flying clouds, but the pirates went their way with the familiarity born of long practice. After half a mile of the mud, we came upon a deep channel, up which we rowed, with dead oyster shoals looming high and dry on either side. At last we reached the picking grounds. Two men, on one of the shoals, hailed us and warned us off. But the Centipede, the Porpoise, Barchi, and Skilling took the lead, and followed by the rest of us, at least thirty men in half as many boats, rowed right up to the watchmen.

"You'd better slide outa this here," Barchi said threateningly, "or we'll fill you so full of holes you wouldn't float in molasses."

The watchmen wisely retreated before so

overwhelming a force, and rowed their boat along the channel toward where the shore should be. Besides, it was in the plan for them to retreat.

We hauled the noses of the boats up on the shore side of a big shoal, and all hands, with sacks, spread out and began picking. Every now and again the clouds thinned before the face of the moon, and we could see the big oysters quite distinctly. In almost no time sacks were filled and carried back to the boats, where fresh ones were obtained. Nicholas and I returned often and anxiously to the boats with our little loads, but always found someone of the pirates coming or going.

"Never mind," he said; "no hurry. As they pick farther and farther away, it will take too long to carry to the boats. Then they'll stand the full sacks on end and pick them up when the tide comes in and the skiffs will float to them."

Fully half an hour went by, and the tide had begun to flood, when this came to pass. Leaving the pirates at their work, we stole back to the boats. One by one, and noiselessly, we shoved them off and made them fast in an awkward flotilla. Just as we were shoving off the last skiff, our own, one of the men came upon us. It was Barchi. His quick eye took in the situation at a glance, and he sprang for us; but we went clear with a mighty shove, and he was left floundering in the water over his head. As soon as he got back to the shoal he raised his voice and gave the alarm.

We rowed with all our strength, but it was slow going with so many boats in tow. A pistol cracked from the shoal, a second, and a third; then a regular fusillade began. The bullets spat and spat all about us; but thick clouds had covered the moon, and in the dim darkness it was no more than random firing. It was only by chance that we could be hit.

"Wish we had a little steam launch," I panted.

"I'd just as soon the moon stayed hidden," Nicholas panted back.

It was slow work, but every stroke carried us farther away from the shoal and nearer the shore, till at last the shooting died down, and when the moon did come out we were too far away to be in danger. Not long afterward we answered a shoreward hail, and two Whitehall boats, each pulled by three pairs of oars, darted up to us. Charley's welcome face bent over to us, and he gripped us by the hands while he cried, "Oh, you joys! You joys! Both of you!"

When the flotilla had been landed, Nicholas and I and a watchman rowed out in one of the Whitehalls, with Charley in the stern- sheets. Two other Whitehalls followed us, and as the moon now shone brightly, we easily made out the oyster pirates on their lonely shoal. As we drew closer, they fired a rattling volley from their revolvers, and we promptly retreated beyond range.

"Lot of time," Charley said. "The flood is setting in fast, and by the time it's up to their necks there won't be any fight left in them."

So we lay on our oars and waited for the tide to do its work. This was the predicament of the pirates: because of the big run-out, the tide was now rushing back like a mill-race, and it was impossible for the strongest swimmer in the world to make against it the three miles to the sloops. Between the pirates and the shore were we, precluding escape in that direction. On the other hand, the water was rising rapidly over the shoals, and it was only a question of a few hours when it would be over their heads.

It was beautifully calm, and in the brilliant white moonlight we watched them through our night glasses and told Charley of the voyage of the *Coal Tar Maggie*. One o'clock came, and two o'clock, and the pirates were clustering on the highest shoal, waist-deep in water.

"Now this illustrates the value of imagination," Charley was saying. "Taft has been trying for years to get them, but he went at it with bull strength and failed. Now we used our heads..."

Just then I heard a scarcely audible gurgle of water, and holding up my hand for silence, I turned and pointed to a ripple slowly widening out in a growing circle. It was not more than fifty feet from us. We kept perfectly quiet and waited. After a minute the water broke six feet away, and a black head and white shoulder showed in the moonlight. With a snort of surprise and of suddenly expelled breath, the head and shoulder went down.

We pulled ahead several strokes and drifted with the current. Four pairs of eyes searched the surface of the water, but never another ripple showed, and never another glimpse did we catch of the black head and white shoulder.

"It's the Porpoise," Nicholas said. "It would take broad daylight for us to catch him."

At a quarter to three the pirates gave their first sign of weakening. We heard cries for help, in the unmistakable voice of the Centipede, and this time, on rowing closer, we were not fired upon. The Centipede was in a truly perilous plight. Only the heads and shoulders of his fellow-marauders showed above the water as they braced themselves against the current, while his feet were off the bottom and they were supporting him.

"Now, lads," Charley said briskly, "we have got you, and you can't get away. If you cut up rough, we'll have to leave you alone and the water will finish you. But if you're good we'll take you aboard, one man at a time, and you'll all be saved. What do you say?"

"Ay," they chorused hoarsely between their chattering teeth.

"Then one man at a time, and the short men first."

The Centipede was the first to be pulled aboard, and he came willingly, though he objected when the constable put the handcuffs on him. Barchi was next hauled in, quite meek and resigned from his soaking. When we had ten in, our boat we drew back, and the second Whitehall was loaded. The third Whitehall received nine prisoners only—a catch of twenty-nine in all.

"You didn't get the Porpoise," the Centipede said exultantly, as though his escape materially diminished our success.

Charley laughed. "But we saw him just the same, a-snorting for shore like a puffing pig."

It was a mild and shivering band of pirates that we marched up the beach to the oyster house. In answer to Charley's knock, the door was flung open, and a pleasant wave of warm air rushed out upon us.

"You can dry your clothes here, lads, and get some hot coffee," Charley announced, as they filed in.

And there, sitting ruefully by the fire, with a steaming mug in his hand, was the Porpoise. With one accord Nicholas and I looked at Charley. He laughed gleefully.

"That comes of imagination," he said. "When you see a thing, you've got to see it all around, or what's the good of seeing it at all? I saw the beach, so I left a couple of constables behind to keep an eye on it. That's all."

THE SIEGE OF THE "LANCASHIRE QUEEN"

THE SIEGE OF THE "LANCASHIRE QUEEN" (1905)

POSSIBLY OUR MOST exasperating experience on the fish patrol was when Charley Le Grant and I laid a two weeks' siege to a big four-masted English ship. Before we had finished with the affair, it became a pretty mathematical problem, and it was by the merest chance that we came into possession of the instrument that brought it to a successful termination.

After our raid on the oyster pirates we had returned to Oakland, where two more weeks passed before Neil Partington's wife was out of danger and on the highroad to recovery. So it was after an absence of a month, all told, that we turned the *Reindeer's* nose toward Benicia. When the cat's away the mice will play, and in these four weeks the fishermen had become very bold in violating the law. When we passed Point Pedro, we noticed many signs of activity among the shrimp-catchers, and, well into San Pablo Bay, we observed a widely scattered fleet of Upper Bay fishing-boats hastily pulling in their nets and getting up sail.

This was suspicious enough to warrant investigation, and the first and only boat we succeeded in boarding proved to have an illegal net. The law permitted no smaller mesh for catching shad than one that measured seven and one-half inches inside the knots, while the mesh of this particular net measured only three inches. It was a flagrant breach of the rules, and the two fishermen were forthwith put under arrest. Neil Partington took one of them with him to help manage the *Reindeer*, while Charley and I went on ahead with the other in the captured boat.

But the shad fleet had headed over toward the Petaluma shore in wild flight, and for the rest of the run through San Pablo Bay we saw no more fishermen at all. Our prisoner, a bronzed and bearded Greek, sat sullenly on his net while we sailed his craft. It was a new Columbia River salmon boat, evidently on its first trip, and it handled splendidly. Even when Charley praised it, our prisoner refused to speak or to notice us, and we soon gave him up as a most unsociable fellow.

We ran up the Carquinez Straits and edged into the bight at Turner's Shipyard for smoother water. Here were lying several English steel sailing ships, waiting for the wheat harvest; and here, most unexpectedly, in the precise place where we had captured Big Alec, we came upon two Italians in a skiff that was loaded with a complete "Chinese" sturgeon line. The surprise was mutual, and we were on top of them before either they or we were aware. Charley had barely time to luff into the wind and run up to them. I ran forward and tossed them a line with orders to make it fast. One of the Italians took a turn with it over a cleat, while I hastened to lower our big spritsail. This accomplished, the salmon boat dropped astern, dragging heavily on the skiff.

Charley came forward to board the prize, but when I proceeded to haul alongside by means of the line, the Italians cast it off. We at once began drifting to leeward, while they got out two pairs of oars and rowed their light craft directly into the wind. This maneuver for the moment disconcerted us, for in our large and heavily loaded boat we could not hope to catch them with the oars. But our prisoner came unexpectedly to our aid. His black eyes were flashing eagerly, and his face was flushed with suppressed excitement, as he dropped the centerboard, sprang forward with a single leap, and put up the sail.

"I've always heard that Greeks don't like Italians," Charley laughed, as he ran aft to the tiller.

And never in my experience have I seen a man so anxious for the capture of another as was our prisoner in the chase that followed. His eyes fairly snapped, and his nostrils quivered and dilated in a most extraordinary way. Charley steered while he tended the sheet; and though Charley was as quick and alert as a cat, the Greek could hardly control his impatience.

The Italians were cut off from the shore, which was fully a mile away at its nearest point. Did they attempt to make it, we could haul after them with the wind abeam, and overtake them before they had covered an eighth of the distance. But they were too wise to attempt it, contenting themselves with rowing lustily to windward along the starboard side of a big ship, the Lancashire Queen. But beyond the ship lay an open stretch of fully two miles to the shore in that direction. This, also, they dared not attempt, for we were bound to catch them before they could cover it. So, when they reached the bow of the Lancashire Queen, nothing remained but to pass around and row down her port side toward the stern, which meant rowing to leeward and giving us the advantage.

We in the salmon boat, sailing close on the wind, tacked about and crossed the ship's bow. Then Charley put up the tiller and headed down the port side of the ship, the Greek letting out the sheet and grinning with delight. The Italians were already half-way down the ship's length; but the stiff breeze at our back drove us after them far faster than they could row. Closer and closer we came, and I, lying down forward, was just reaching out to grasp the skiff, when it ducked under the great stern of the Lancashire Queen.

The chase was virtually where it had begun. The Italians were rowing up the starboard side of the ship, and we were hauled close on the wind and slowly edging out from the ship as we worked to windward. Then they darted around her bow and began the row down her port side, and we tacked about, crossed her bow, and went plunging down the wind hot after them. And again, just as I was reaching for the skiff, it ducked under the ship's stern and out of danger. And so it went, around and around, the skiff each time just barely ducking into safety.

By this time the ship's crew had become aware of what

was taking place, and we could see their heads in a long row as they looked at us over the bulwarks. Each time we missed the skiff at the stern, they set up a wild cheer and dashed across to the other side of the Lancashire Queen to see the chase to wind-ward. They showered us and the Italians with jokes and advice, and made our Greek so angry that at least once on each circuit he raised his fist and shook it at them in a rage. They came to look for this, and at each display greeted it with uproarious mirth.

"Wot a circus!" cried one.

"Tork about yer marine hippodromes—if this ain't one, I'd like to know!" affirmed another.

"Six-days-go-as-yer-please," announced a third. "Who says the dagoes won't win?"

On the next tack to windward the Greek offered to change places with Charley.

"Let-a me sail-a de boat," he demanded. "I fix-a them, I catch-a them, sure."

This was a stroke at Charley's professional pride, for pride himself he did upon his boat-sailing abilities; but he yielded the tiller to the prisoner and took his place at the sheet. Three times again we made the circuit, and the Greek found that he could get no more speed out of the salmon boat than Charley had.

"Better give it up," one of the sailors advised from above.

The Greek scowled ferociously and shook his fist in his customary fashion. In the meanwhile, my mind had not been idle, and I had finally evolved an idea.

"Keep going, Charley, one time more," I said.

And as we laid out on the next tack to wind-ward, I bent a piece of line to a small grappling hook I had seen lying in the bail-hole. The end of the line I made fast to the ring-bolt in the bow, and with the hook out of sight I waited for the next opportunity to use it. Once more they made their leeward pull down the port side of the Lancashire Queen, and once more we churned down after them before the wind. Nearer and nearer we drew, and I was making believe to reach for them as before. The stern of the skiff was not six feet away, and they were laughing at me derisively as they ducked under the ship's stern. At that instant I suddenly arose and threw the grappling iron. It caught fairly and squarely on the rail of the skiff, which was jerked backward out of safety as the rope tautened and the salmon boat ploughed on.

A groan went up from the row of sailors above, which quickly changed to a cheer as one of the Italians whipped out a long sheath-knife and cut the rope. But we had drawn them out of safety, and Charley, from his place in the stern-sheets, reached over and clutched the stern of the skiff. The whole thing happened in a second of time, for the first Italian was cutting the rope and Charley was clutching the skiff when the second Italian dealt him a rap over the head with an oar, Charley released his hold and collapsed, stunned, into the bottom of the salmon boat, and the Italians bent to their oars and escaped back under the ship's stern.

The Greek took both tiller and sheet and continued the chase around the Lancashire Queen, while I attended to Charley, on whose head a nasty lump was rapidly rising. Our sailor audience was wild with delight, and to a man encouraged the fleeing Italians. Charley sat up, with one hand on his head, and gazed about him sheepishly.

"It will never do to let them escape now," he said, at the same time drawing his revolver.

On our next circuit, he threatened the Italians with the weapon; but they rowed on stolidly, keeping splendid stroke and utterly disregarding him.

"If you don't stop, I'll shoot," Charley said menacingly.

But this had no effect, nor were they to be frightened into surrendering even when he fired several shots dangerously close to them. It was too much to expect him to shoot unarmed men, and this they knew as well as we did; so they continued to pull doggedly round and round the ship.

"We'll run them down, then!" Charley exclaimed. "We'll wear them out and wind them!"

So the chase continued. Twenty times more we ran them around the Lancashire Queen, and at last we could see that even their iron muscles were giving out. They were nearly exhausted, and it was only a matter of a few more circuits, when the game took on a new feature. On the row to windward they always gained on us, so that they were half-way down the ship's side on the row to leeward when we were passing the bow. But this last time, as we passed the bow, we saw them escaping up the ship's gangway, which had been suddenly lowered. It was an organized move on the part of the sailors, evidently countenanced by the captain; for by the time we arrived where the gangway had been, it was being hoisted up, and the skiff, slung in the ship's davits, was likewise flying aloft out of reach.

The parley that followed with the captain was short and snappy. He absolutely forbade us to board the Lancashire Queen, and as absolutely refused to give up the two men. By this time Charley was as enraged as the Greek. Not only had he been foiled in a long and ridiculous chase, but he had been knocked senseless into the bottom of his boat by the men who had escaped him.

"Knock off my head with little apples," he declared emphatically, striking the fist of one hand into the palm of the other, "if those two men ever escape me! I'll stay here to get them if it takes the rest of my natural life, and if I don't get them, then I promise you I'll live unnaturally long or until I do get them, or my name's not Charley Le Grant!"

And then began the siege of the Lancashire Queen, a siege memorable in the annals of both fishermen and fish patrol. When the *Reindeer* came along, after a fruitless pursuit of the shad fleet, Charley instructed Neil Partington to send out his own salmon boat, with blankets, provisions, and a fisherman's charcoal stove. By sunset this exchange of boats was made, and we said good-by to our Greek, who perforce had to go into Benicia and be locked up for his own violation of the law. After supper, Charley and I kept alternate four-hour watches till day-light. The fishermen made no attempt to escape that night, though the ship sent out a boat for scouting purposes to find if the coast were clear.

By the next day we saw that a steady siege was in order, and we perfected our plans with an eye to our own comfort. A dock, known as the Solano Wharf, which ran out from the Benicia shore, helped us in this. It happened that the

Lancashire Queen, the shore at Turner's Shipyard, and the Solano Wharf were the corners of a big equilateral triangle. From ship to shore, the side of the triangle along which the Italians had to escape, was a distance equal to that from the Solano Wharf to the shore, the side of the triangle along which we had to travel to get to the shore before the Italians. But as we could sail much faster than they could row, we could permit them to travel about half their side of the triangle before we darted out along our side. If we allowed them to get more than half-way, they were certain to beat us to shore; while if we started before they were half-way, they were equally certain to beat us back to the ship.

We found that an imaginary line, drawn from the end of the wharf to a windmill farther along the shore, cut precisely in half the line of the triangle along which the Italians must escape to reach the land. This line made it easy for us to determine how far to let them run away before we bestirred ourselves in pursuit. Day after day we would watch them through our glasses as they rowed leisurely along toward the half-way point; and as they drew close into line with the windmill, we would leap into the boat and get up sail. At sight of our preparation, they would turn and row slowly back to the Lancashire Queen, secure in the knowledge that we could not overtake them.

To guard against calms—when our salmon boat would be useless—we also had in readiness a light rowing skiff equipped with spoon- oars. But at such times, when the wind failed us, we were forced to row out from the wharf as soon as they rowed from the ship. In the night-time, on the other hand, we were compelled to patrol the immediate vicinity of the ship; which we did, Charley and I standing four-hour watches turn and turn about. The Italians, however, preferred the daytime in which to escape, and so our long night vigils were without result.

"What makes me mad," said Charley, "is our being kept from our honest beds while those rascally lawbreakers are sleeping soundly every night. But much good may it do them," he threatened. "I'll keep them on that ship till the captain charges them board, as sure as a sturgeon's not a catfish!"

It was a tantalizing problem that confronted us. As long as we were vigilant, they could not escape; and as long as they were careful, we would be unable to catch them. Charley cudgelled his brains continually, but for once his imagination failed him. It was a problem apparently without other solution than that of patience. It was a waiting game, and whichever waited the longer was bound to win. To add to our irritation, friends of the Italians established a code of signals with them from the shore, so that we never dared relax the siege for a moment. And besides this, there were always one or two suspicious-looking fishermen hanging around the Solano Wharf and keeping watch on our actions. We could do nothing but "grin and bear it," as Charley said, while it took up all our time and prevented us from doing other work.

The days went by, and there was no change in the situation. Not that no attempts were made to change it. One night, friends from the shore came out in a skiff and attempted to confuse us while the two Italians escaped. That they did not succeed was due to the lack of a little oil on the ship's davits. For we were drawn back from the pursuit of the strange boat by the creaking of the davits and arrived at the Lancashire Queen just as the Italians were lowering their skiff. Another night, fully half a dozen skiffs rowed around us in the darkness, but we held on like a leech to the side of the ship and frustrated their plan till they grew angry and showered us with abuse. Charley laughed to himself in the bottom of the boat.

"It's a good sign, lad," he said to me. "When men begin to abuse, make sure they're losing patience; and shortly after they lose patience, they lose their heads. Mark my words, if we only hold out, they'll get careless some fine day, and then we'll get them."

But they did not grow careless, and Charley confessed that this was one of the times when all signs failed. Their patience seemed equal to ours, and the second week of the siege dragged monotonously along. Then Charley's lagging imagination quickened sufficiently to suggest a ruse. Peter Boyelen, a new patrolman and one unknown to the fisher-folk, happened to arrive in Benicia and we took him into our plan. We were as secret as possible about it, but in some unfathomable way the friends ashore got word to the beleaguered Italians to keep their eyes open.

On the night we were to put our ruse into effect, Charley and I took up our usual station in our rowing skiff alongside the Lancashire Queen. After it was thoroughly dark, Peter Boyelen came out in a crazy duck boat, the kind you can pick up and carry away under one arm. When we heard him coming along, paddling noisily, we slipped away a short distance into the darkness, and rested on our oars.

Opposite the gangway, having jovially hailed the anchor-watch of the Lancashire Queen and asked the direction of the Scottish Chiefs, another wheat ship, he awkwardly capsized himself. The man who was standing the anchor-watch ran down the gangway and hauled him out of the water. This was what he wanted, to get aboard the ship; and the next thing he expected was to be taken on deck and then below to warm up and dry out. But the captain inhospitably kept him perched on the lowest gang-way step, shivering miserably and with his feet dangling in the water, till we, out of very pity, rowed in from the darkness and took him off. The jokes and gibes of the awakened crew sounded anything but sweet in our ears, and even the two Italians climbed up on the rail and laughed down at us long and maliciously.

"That's all right," Charley said in a low voice, which I only could hear. "I'm mighty glad it's not us that's laughing first. We'll save our laugh to the end, eh, lad?"

He clapped a hand on my shoulder as he finished, but it seemed to me that there was more determination than hope in his voice.

It would have been possible for us to secure the aid of United States marshals and board the English ship, backed by Government authority. But the instructions of the Fish Commission were to the effect that the patrolmen should avoid complications, and this one, did we call on the higher powers, might well end in a pretty international tangle.

The second week of the siege drew to its close, and there was no sign of change in the situation. On the morning of the fourteenth day the change came, and it came in a guise as unexpected and startling to us as it was to the men we were striving to capture.

Charley and I, after our customary night vigil by the side of the Lancashire Queen, rowed into the Solana Wharf.

"Hello!" cried Charley, in surprise. "In the name of reason and common sense, what is that? Of all unmannerly craft did you ever see the like?"

Well might he exclaim, for there, tied up to the dock, lay the strangest looking launch I had ever seen. Not that it could be called a launch, either, but it seemed to resemble a launch more than any other kind of boat. It was seventy feet long, but so narrow was it, and so bare of superstructure, that it appeared much smaller than it really was. It was built wholly of steel and was painted black. Three smokestacks, a good distance apart and raking well aft, arose in single file amidships; while the bow, long and lean and sharp as a knife, plainly advertised that the boat was made for speed. Passing under the stern, we read *Streak*, painted in small white letters.

Charley and I were consumed with curiosity. In a few minutes we were on board and talking with an engineer who was watching the sunrise from the deck. He was quite willing to satisfy our curiosity, and in a few minutes we learned that the *Streak* had come in after dark from San Francisco; that this was what might be called the trial trip; and that she was the property of Silas Tate, a young mining millionaire of California, whose fad was high-speed yachts. There was some talk about turbine engines, direct application of steam, and the absence of pistons, rods, and cranks—all of which was beyond me, for I was familiar only with sailing craft; but I did understand the last words of the engineer.

"Four thousand horse-power and forty-five miles an hour, though you wouldn't think it," he concluded proudly.

"Say it again, man! Say it again!" Charley exclaimed in an excited voice.

"Four thousand horse-power and forty-five miles an hour," the engineer repeated, grinning good-naturedly.

"Where's the owner?" was Charley's next question. "Is there any way I can speak to him?"

The engineer shook his head. "No, I'm afraid not. He's asleep, you see."

At that moment a young man in blue uniform came on deck farther aft and stood regarding the sunrise.

"There he is, that's him, that's Mr. Tate," said the engineer.

Charley walked aft and spoke to him, and while he talked earnestly the young man listened with an amused expression on his face. He must have inquired about the depth of water close in to the shore at Turner's Shipyard, for I could see Charley making gestures and explaining. A few minutes later he came back in high glee.

"Come on lad," he said. "On to the dock with you. We've got them!"

It was our good fortune to leave the *Streak* when we did, for a little later one of the spy fishermen appeared. Charley and I took up our accustomed places, on the stringer-piece, a little ahead of the *Streak* and over our own boat, where we could comfortably watch the Lancashire Queen. Nothing occurred till about nine o'clock, when we saw the two Italians leave the ship and pull along their side of the triangle toward the shore. Charley looked as unconcerned as could be, but before they had covered a quarter of the distance, he whispered to me:

"Forty-five miles an hour... nothing can save them... they are ours!"

Slowly the two men rowed along till they were nearly in line with the windmill. This was the point where we always jumped into our salmon boat and got up the sail, and the two men, evidently expecting it, seemed surprised when we gave no sign.

When they were directly in line with the windmill, as near to the shore as to the ship, and nearer the shore than we had ever allowed them before, they grew suspicious. We followed them through the glasses, and saw them standing up in the skiff and trying to find out what we were doing. The spy fisherman, sitting beside us on the stringer-piece was likewise puzzled. He could not understand our inactivity. The men in the skiff rowed nearer the shore, but stood up again and scanned it, as if they thought we might be in hiding there. But a man came out on the beach and waved a handkerchief to indicate that the coast was clear. That settled them. They bent to the oars to make a dash for it. Still Charley waited. Not until they had covered three-quarters of the distance from the Lancashire Queen, which left them hardly more than a quarter of a mile to gain the shore, did Charley slap me on the shoulder and cry:

"They're ours! They're ours!"

We ran the few steps to the side of the *Streak* and jumped aboard. Stern and bow lines were cast off in a jiffy. The *Streak* shot ahead and away from the wharf. The spy fisherman we had left behind on the stringer-piece pulled out a revolver and fired five shots into the air in rapid succession. The men in the skiff gave instant heed to the warning, for we could see them pulling away like mad.

But if they pulled like mad, I wonder how our progress can be described? We fairly flew. So frightful was the speed with which we displaced the water, that a wave rose up on either side our bow and foamed aft in a series of three stiff, up-standing waves, while astern a great crested billow pursued us hungrily, as though at each moment it would fall aboard and destroy us. The *Streak* was pulsing and vibrating and roaring like a thing alive. The wind of our progress was like a gale—a forty-five-mile gale. We could not face it and draw breath without choking and strangling. It blew the smoke straight back from the mouths of the smoke-stacks at a direct right angle to the perpendicular. In fact, we were travelling as fast as an express train. "We just streaked it," was the way Charley told it afterward, and I think his description comes nearer than any I can give.

As for the Italians in the skiff—hardly had we started, it seemed to me, when we were on top of them. Naturally, we had to slow down long before we got to them; but even then we shot past like a whirlwind and were compelled to circle back between them and the shore. They had rowed steadily, rising from the thwarts at every stroke, up to the moment we passed them, when they recognized Charley and me. That took the last bit of fight out of them. They hauled in their oars, and sullenly submitted to arrest.

"Well, Charley," Neil Partington said, as we discussed it on the wharf afterward, "I fail to see where your boasted imagination came into play this time."

But Charley was true to his hobby. "Imagination?" he demanded, pointing to the *Streak*. "Look at that! just look at it! If the invention of that isn't imagination, I should like to know what is."

"Of course," he added, "it's the other fellow's imagination, but it did the work all the same."

CHARLEY'S COUP

CHARLEY'S COUP
(1905)

PERHAPS OUR MOST LAUGHABLE exploit on the fish patrol, and at the same time our most dangerous one, was when we rounded in, at a single haul, an even score of wrathful fishermen. Charley called it a "coop," having heard Neil Partington use the term; but I think he misunderstood the word, and thought it meant "coop," to catch, to trap. The fishermen, however, coup or coop, must have called it a Waterloo, for it was the severest stroke ever dealt them by the fish patrol, while they had invited it by open and impudent defiance of the law.

During what is called the "open season" the fishermen might catch as many salmon as their luck allowed and their boats could hold. But there was one important restriction. From sun-down Saturday night to sun-up Monday morning, they were not permitted to set a net. This was a wise provision on the part of the Fish Commission, for it was necessary to give the spawning salmon some opportunity to ascend the river and lay their eggs. And this law, with only an occasional violation, had been obediently observed by the Greek fishermen who caught salmon for the canneries and the market.

One Sunday morning, Charley received a telephone call from a friend in Collinsville, who told him that the full force of fishermen was out with its nets. Charley and I jumped into our salmon boat and started for the scene of the trouble. With a light favoring wind at our back we went through the Carquinez Straits, crossed Suisun Bay, passed the Ship Island Light, and came upon the whole fleet at work.

But first let me describe the method by which they worked. The net used is what is known as a gill-net. It has a simple diamond- shaped mesh which measures at least seven and one-half inches between the knots. From five to seven and even eight hundred feet in length, these nets are only a few feet wide. They are not stationary, but float with the current, the upper edge supported on the surface by floats, the lower edge sunk by means of leaden weights,

This arrangement keeps the net upright in the current and effectually prevents all but the smaller fish from ascending the river. The salmon, swimming near the surface, as is their custom, run their heads through these meshes, and are prevented from going on through by their larger girth of body, and from going back because of their gills, which catch in the mesh. It requires two fishermen to set such a net—one to row the boat, while the other, standing in the stern, carefully pays out the net. When it is all out, stretching directly across the stream, the men make their boat fast to one end of the net and drift along with it.

As we came upon the fleet of law-breaking fishermen, each boat two or three hundred yards from its neighbors, and boats and nets dotting the river as far as we could see, Charley said:

"I've only one regret, lad, and that is that I have'nt a thousand arms so as to be able to catch them all. As it is, we'll only be able to catch one boat, for while we are tackling that one it will be up nets and away with the rest."

As we drew closer, we observed none of the usual flurry and excitement which our appearance invariably produced. Instead, each boat lay quietly by its net, while the fishermen favored us with not the slightest attention.

"It's curious," Charley muttered. "Can it be they don't recognize us?"

I said that it was impossible, and Charley agreed; yet there was a whole fleet, manned by men who knew us only too well, and who took no more notice of us than if we were a hay scow or a pleasure yacht.

This did not continue to be the case, however, for as we bore down upon the nearest net, the men to whom it belonged detached their boat and rowed slowly toward the shore. The rest of the boats showed no, sign of uneasiness.

"That's funny," was Charley's remark. "But we can confiscate the net, at any rate."

We lowered sail, picked up one end of the net, and began to heave it into the boat. But at the first heave we heard a bullet zip- zipping past us on the water, followed by the faint report of a rifle. The men who had rowed ashore were shooting at us. At the next heave a second bullet went zipping past, perilously near. Charley took a turn around a pin and sat down. There were no more shots. But as soon as he began to heave in, the shooting recommenced.

"That settles it," he said, flinging the end of the net overboard. "You fellows want it worse than we do, and you can have it."

We rowed over toward the next net, for Charley was intent on finding out whether or not we were face to face with an organized defiance. As we approached, the two fishermen proceeded to cast off from their net and row ashore, while the first two rowed back and made fast to the net we had abandoned. And at the second net we were greeted by rifle shots till we desisted and went on to the third, where the maneuver was again repeated.

Then we gave it up, completely routed, and hoisted sail and started on the long windward beat back to Benicia. A number of Sundays went by, on each of which the law was persistently violated. Yet, short of an armed force of soldiers, we could do nothing. The fishermen had hit upon a new idea and were using it for all it was worth, while there seemed no way by which we could get the better of them.

About this time Neil Partington happened along from the Lower Bay, where he had been for a number of weeks. With him was Nicholas, the Greek boy who had helped us in our raid on the oyster pirates, and the pair of them took a hand. We made our arrangements carefully. It was planned that while Charley and I tackled the nets, they were to be hidden ashore so as to ambush the fishermen who landed to shoot at us.

It was a pretty plan. Even Charley said it was. But we reckoned not half so well as the Greeks. They forestalled us by ambushing Neil and Nicholas and taking them prisoners, while, as of old, bullets whistled about our ears when Charley and I attempted to take possession of the nets. When we were again beaten off, Neil Partington and Nicholas were released. They were rather shamefaced when they put in an appearance, and Charley chaffed them unmercifully. But Neil chaffed back, demanding to know why Charley's imagination had not long since overcome the difficulty.

"Just you wait; the idea'll come all right," Charley promised.

"Most probably," Neil agreed. "But I'm afraid the salmon will be exterminated first, and then there will be no need for it when it does come."

Neil Partington, highly disgusted with his adventure, departed for the Lower Bay, taking Nicholas with him, and Charley and I were left to our own resources. This meant that the Sunday fishing would be left to itself, too, until such time as Charley's idea happened along. I puzzled my head a good deal to find out some way of checkmating the Greeks, as also did Charley, and we broached a thousand expedients which on discussion proved worthless.

The fishermen, on the other hand, were in high feather, and their boasts went up and down the river to add to our discomfiture. Among all classes of them we became aware of a growing insubordination. We were beaten, and they were losing respect for us. With the loss of respect, contempt began to arise. Charley began to be spoken of as the "olda woman," and I received my rating as the "pee-wee kid." The situation was fast becoming unbearable, and we knew that we should have to deliver a stunning stroke at the Greeks in order to regain the old-time respect in which we had stood.

Then one morning the idea came. We were down on Steamboat Wharf, where the river steamers made their landings, and where we found a group of amused long-shoremen and loafers listening to the hard- luck tale of a sleepy-eyed young fellow in long sea-boots. He was a sort of amateur fisherman, he said, fishing for the local market of Berkeley. Now Berkeley was on the Lower Bay, thirty miles away. On the previous night, he said, he had set his net and dozed off to sleep in the bottom of the boat.

The next he knew it was morning, and he opened his eyes to find his boat rubbing softly against the piles of Steamboat Wharf at Benicia. Also he saw the river steamer Apache lying ahead of him, and a couple of deck-hands disentangling the shreds of his net from the paddle-wheel. In short, after he had gone to sleep, his fisherman's riding light had gone out, and the Apache had run over his net. Though torn pretty well to pieces, the net in some way still remained foul, and he had had a thirty-mile tow out of his course.

Charley nudged me with his elbow. I grasped his thought on the instant, but objected:

"We can't charter a steamboat."

"Don't intend to," he rejoined. "But let's run over to Turner's Shipyard. I've something in my mind there that may be of use to us."

And over we went to the shipyard, where Charley led

the way to the *Mary Rebecca*, lying hauled out on the ways, where she was being cleaned and overhauled. She was a scow-schooner we both knew well, carrying a cargo of one hundred and forty tons and a spread of canvas greater than other schooner on the bay.

"How d'ye do, Ole," Charley greeted a big blue-shirted Swede who was greasing the jaws of the main gaff with a piece of pork rind.

Ole grunted, puffed away at his pipe, and went on greasing. The captain of a bay schooner is supposed to work with his hands just as well as the men.

Ole Ericsen verified Charley's conjecture that the *Mary Rebecca*, as soon as launched, would run up the San Joaquin River nearly to Stockton for a load of wheat. Then Charley made his proposition, and Ole Ericsen shook his head.

"Just a hook, one good-sized hook," Charley pleaded.

"No, Ay tank not," said Ole Ericsen. "Der *Mary Rebecca* yust hang up on efery mud-bank with that hook. Ay don't want to lose der *Mary Rebecca*. She's all Ay got."

"No, no," Charley hurried to explain. "We can put the end of the hook through the bottom from the outside and fasten it on the inside with a nut. After it's done its work, why, all we have to do is to go down into the hold, unscrew the nut, and out drops the hook. Then drive a wooden peg into the hole, and the *Mary Rebecca* will be all right again."

Ole Ericsen was obstinate for a long time; but in the end, after we had had dinner with him, he was brought round to consent.

"Ay do it, by Yupiter!" he said, striking one huge fist into the palm of the other hand. "But yust hurry you up wid der hook. Der *Mary Rebecca* slides into der water to-night."

It was Saturday, and Charley had need to hurry. We headed for the shipyard blacksmith shop, where, under Charley's directions, a most generously curved book of heavy steel was made. Back we hastened to the *Mary Rebecca*. Aft of the great centerboard case, through what was properly her keel, a hole was bored. The end of the hook was inserted from the outside, and Charley, on the inside, screwed the nut on tightly. As it stood complete, the hook projected over a foot beneath the bottom of the schooner. Its curve was something like the curve of a sickle, but deeper.

In the late afternoon, the *Mary Rebecca* was launched, and preparations were finished for the start up-river next morning. Charley and Ole intently studied the evening sky for signs of wind, for without a good breeze our project was doomed to failure. They agreed that there were all the signs of a stiff westerly wind—not the ordinary afternoon sea-breeze, but a half-gale, which even then was springing up.

Next morning found their predictions verified. The sun was shining brightly, but something more than a half-gale was shrieking up the Carquinez Straits, and the *Mary Rebecca* got under way with two reefs in her mainsail and one in her foresail. We found it quite rough in the Straits and in Suisun Bay; but as the water grew more land-locked it became calm, though without let-up in the wind.

Off Ship Island Light the reefs were shaken out, and at Charley's suggestion a big fisherman's staysail was made all ready for hoisting, and the maintopsail, bunched into a cap at the masthead, was overhauled so that it could be set on an instant's notice.

We were tearing along, wing-and-wing, before the wind, foresail to starboard and mainsail to port, as we came upon the salmon fleet. There they were, boats and nets, as on that first Sunday when they had bested us, strung out evenly over the river as far as we could see. A narrow space on the right-hand side of the channel was left clear for steamboats, but the rest of the river was covered with the wide-stretching nets. The narrow space was our logical course, but Charley, at the wheel, steered the *Mary Rebecca* straight for the nets. This did not cause any alarm among the fishermen, because up-river sailing craft are always provided with "shoes" on the ends of their keels, which permit them to slip over the nets without fouling them.

"Now she takes it!" Charley cried, as we dashed across the middle of a line of floats which marked a net. At one end of this line was a small barrel buoy, at the other the two fishermen in their boat. Buoy and boat at once began to draw together, and the fishermen to cry out, as they were jerked after us. A couple of minutes later we hooked a second net, and then a third, and in this fashion, we tore straight up through the center of the fleet.

The consternation we spread among the fishermen was tremendous. As fast as we hooked a net the two ends of it, buoy and boat, came together as they dragged out astern; and so many buoys and boats, coming together at such breakneck speed, kept the fishermen on the jump to avoid smashing into one another. Also, they shouted at us like mad to heave to into the wind, for they took it as some drunken prank on the part of scow-sailors, little dreaming that we were the fish patrol.

The drag of a single net is very heavy, and Charley and Ole Ericsen decided that even in such a wind ten nets were all the *Mary Rebecca* could take along with her. So when we had hooked ten nets, with ten boats containing twenty men streaming along behind us, we veered to the left out of the fleet and headed toward Collinsville.

We were all jubilant. Charley was handling the wheel as though he were steering the winning yacht home in a race. The two sailors who made up the crew of the *Mary Rebecca*, were grinning and joking. Ole Ericsen was rubbing his huge hands in child-like glee.

"Ay tank you fish patrol fallers never ban so lucky as when you sail with Ole Ericsen," he was saying, when a rifle cracked sharply astern, and a bullet gouged along the newly painted cabin, glanced on a nail, and sang shrilly onward into space.

This was too much for Ole Ericsen. At sight of his beloved paintwork thus defaced, he jumped up and shook his fist at the fishermen; but a second bullet smashed into the cabin not six inches from his head, and he dropped down to the deck under cover of the rail.

All the fishermen had rifles, and they now opened a general fusillade. We were all driven to cover—even Charley, who was compelled to desert the wheel. Had it not been for the heavy drag of the nets, we would inevitably have broached to at the mercy of the enraged fishermen. But the nets, fastened to the bottom of the *Mary Rebecca* well aft, held her stern into the wind, and she continued to plough on, though somewhat erratically.

Charley, lying on the deck, could just manage to reach the lower spokes of the wheel; but while he could steer after a fashion, it was very awkward. Ole Ericsen bethought himself of a large piece of sheet steel in the empty hold.

It was in fact a plate from the side of the *New Jersey*, a steamer which had recently been wrecked outside the Golden Gate, and in the salving of which the *Mary Rebecca* had taken part.

Crawling carefully along the deck, the two sailors, Ole, and myself got the heavy plate on deck and aft, where we reared it as a shield between the wheel and the fishermen. The bullets whanged and banged against it till it rang like a bull's-eye, but Charley grinned in its shelter, and coolly went on steering.

So we raced along, behind us a howling, screaming bedlam of wrathful Greeks, Collinsville ahead, and bullets spat-spatting all around us.

"Ole," Charley said in a faint voice, "I don't know what we're going to do."

Ole Ericsen, lying on his back close to the rail and grinning upward at the sky, turned over on his side and looked at him. "Ay tank we go into Collinsville yust der same," he said.

"But we can't stop," Charley groaned. "I never thought of it, but we can't stop."

A look of consternation slowly overspread Ole Ericsen's broad face. It was only too true. We had a hornet's nest on our hands, and to stop at Collinsville would be to have it about our ears.

"Every man Jack of them has a gun," one of the sailors

remarked cheerfully.

"Yes, and a knife, too," the other sailor added.

It was Ole Ericsen's turn to groan. "What for a Svaidish faller like me monkey with none of my biziness, I don't know," he soliloquized.

A bullet glanced on the stern and sang off to starboard like a spiteful bee. "There's nothing to do but plump the *Mary Rebecca* ashore and run for it," was the verdict of the first cheerful sailor.

"And leaf der *Mary Rebecca*?" Ole demanded, with unspeakable horror in his voice.

"Not unless you want to," was the response. "But I don't want to be within a thousand miles of her when those fellers come aboard"—indicating the bedlam of excited Greeks towing behind.

We were right in at Collinsville then, and went foaming by within biscuit-toss of the wharf.

"I only hope the wind holds out," Charley said, stealing a glance at our prisoners.

"What of der wind?" Ole demanded disconsolately. "Der river will not hold out, and then... and then..."

"It's head for tall timber, and the Greeks take the hindermost," adjudged the cheerful sailor, while Ole was stuttering over what would happen when we came to the end of the river.

We had now reached a dividing of the ways. To the left was the mouth of the Sacramento River, to the right the mouth of the San Joaquin. The cheerful sailor crept forward and jibed over the foresail as Charley put the helm to starboard and we swerved to the right into the San Joaquin.

The wind, from which we had been running away on an even keel, now caught us on our beam, and the *Mary Rebecca* was pressed down on her port side as if she were about to capsize.

Still we dashed on, and still the fishermen dashed on behind. The value of their nets was greater than the fines they would have to pay for violating the fish laws; so to cast off from their nets and escape, which they could easily do, would profit them nothing. Further, they remained by their nets instinctively, as a sailor remains by his ship. And still further, the desire for vengeance was roused, and we could depend upon it that they would follow us to the ends of the earth, if we undertook to tow them that far.

The rifle-firing had ceased, and we looked astern to see what our prisoners were doing. The boats were strung along at unequal distances apart, and we saw the four nearest ones bunching together. This was done by the boat ahead trailing a small rope astern to the one behind. When this was caught, they would cast off from their net and heave in on the line till they were brought up to the boat in front. So great was the speed at which we were travelling, however, that this was very slow work. Sometimes the men would strain to their utmost and fail to get in an inch of the rope; at other times they came ahead more rapidly.

When the four boats were near enough together for a man to pass from one to another, one Greek from each of three got into the nearest boat to us, taking his rifle with him. This made five in the foremost boat, and it was plain that their intention was to board us. This they undertook to do, by main strength and sweat, running hand over hand the float-line of a net. And though it was slow, and they stopped frequently to rest, they gradually drew nearer.

Charley smiled at their efforts, and said, "Give her the topsail, Ole."

The cap at the mainmast head was broken out, and sheet and downhaul pulled flat, amid a scattering rifle fire from the boats; and the *Mary Rebecca* lay over and sprang ahead faster than ever.

But the Greeks were undaunted. Unable, at the increased speed, to draw themselves nearer by means of their hands, they rigged from the blocks of their boat sail what sailors call a "watch-tackle." One of them, held by the legs by his mates, would lean far over the bow and make the tackle fast to the float-line. Then they would heave in on the tackle till the blocks were together, when the maneuver would be repeated.

"Have to give her the staysail," Charley said.

Ole Ericsen looked at the straining *Mary Rebecca* and shook his head. "It will take der masts out of her," he said.

"And we'll be taken out of her if you don't," Charley replied.

Ole shot an anxious glance at his masts, another at the boat load of armed Greeks, and consented.

The five men were in the bow of the boat—a bad place when a craft is towing. I was watching the behavior of their boat as the great fisherman's staysail, far, far larger than the top-sail and used only in light breezes, was broken out. As the *Mary Rebecca* lurched forward with a tremendous jerk, the nose of the boat ducked down into the water, and the men tumbled over one another in a wild rush into the stern to save the boat from being dragged sheer under water.

"That settles them!" Charley remarked, though he was anxiously studying the behavior of the *Mary Rebecca*, which was being driven under far more canvas than she was rightly able to carry.

"Next stop is Antioch!" announced the cheerful sailor, after the manner of a railway conductor. "And next comes Merryweather!"

"Come here, quick," Charley said to me.

I crawled across the deck and stood upright beside him in the shelter of the sheet steel.

"Feel in my inside pocket," he commanded, "and get my notebook. That's right. Tear out a blank page and write what I tell you."

And this is what I wrote:

> *Telephone to Merryweather, to the sheriff, the constable, or the judge. Tell them we are coming and to turn out the town. Arm everybody. Have them down on the wharf to meet us or we are gone gooses.*

"Now make it good and fast to that marlin-spike and stand by to toss it ashore."

I did as he directed. By then we were close to Antioch. The wind was shouting through our rigging, the *Mary Rebecca* was half over on her side and rushing ahead like an ocean greyhound. The seafaring folk of Antioch had seen us breaking out topsail and staysail, a most reckless performance in such weather, and had hurried to the wharf-ends in little groups to find out what was the matter.

Straight down the waterfront we boomed, Charley edging in till a man could almost leap ashore. When he gave the signal I tossed the marlinspike. It struck the planking of the wharf a resounding smash, bounced along fifteen or twenty feet, and was pounced upon by the amazed onlookers.

It all happened in a flash, for the next minute Antioch was behind and we were heeling it up the San Joaquin toward Merryweather, six miles away. The river straightened out here into its general easterly course, and we squared away before the wind, wing-and-wing once more, the foresail bellying out to starboard.

Ole Ericsen seemed sunk into a state of stolid despair. Charley and the two sailors were looking hopeful, as they had good reason to be. Merryweather was a coal-mining town, and, it being Sunday, it was reasonable to expect the men to be in town. Further, the coal-miners had never lost any love for the Greek fishermen, and were pretty certain to render us hearty assistance.

We strained our eyes for a glimpse of the town, and the first sight we caught of it gave us immense relief. The wharves were black with men. As we came closer, we could see them still arriving, stringing down the main street, guns in their hands and on the run. Charley glanced astern at the fishermen with a look of ownership in his eye which till then had been missing. The Greeks were plainly overawed by the display of armed strength and were putting their own rifles away.

We took in topsail and staysail, dropped the main peak,

and as we got abreast of the principal wharf jibed the mainsail. The *Mary Rebecca* shot around into the wind, the captive fishermen describing a great arc behind her, and forged ahead till she lost way, when lines we're flung ashore and she was made fast. This was accomplished under a hurricane of cheers from the delighted miners.

Ole Ericsen heaved a great sigh. "Ay never tank Ay see my wife never again," he confessed.

"Why, we were never in any danger," said Charley.

Ole looked at him incredulously.

"Sure, I mean it," Charley went on. "All we had to do, any time, was to let go our end—as I am going to do now, so that those Greeks can untangle their nets."

He went below with a monkey-wrench, unscrewed the nut, and let the hook drop off. When the Greeks had hauled their nets into their boats and made everything shipshape, a posse of citizens took them off our hands and led them away to jail.

"Ay tank Ay ban a great big fool," said Ole Ericsen. But he changed his mind when the admiring townspeople crowded aboard to shake hands with him, and a couple of enterprising newspaper men took photographs of the *Mary Rebecca* and her captain.

DEMETRIOS
CONTOS

DEMETRIOS CONTOS (1905)

IT MUST NOT BE THOUGHT, from what I have told of the Greek fishermen, that they were altogether bad. Far from it. But they were rough men, gathered together in isolated communities and fighting with the elements for a livelihood. They lived far away from the law and its workings, did not understand it, and thought it tyranny. Especially did the fish laws seem tyrannical. And because of this, they looked upon the men of the fish patrol as their natural enemies.

We menaced their lives, or their living, which is the same thing, in many ways. We confiscated illegal traps and nets, the materials of which had cost them considerable sums and the making of which required weeks of labor. We prevented them from catching fish at many times and seasons, which was equivalent to preventing them from making as good a living as they might have made had we not been in existence. And when we captured them, they were brought into the courts of law, where heavy cash fines were collected from them. As a result, they hated us vindictively. As the dog is the natural enemy of the cat, the snake of man, so were we of the fish patrol the natural enemies of the fishermen.

But it is to show that they could act generously as well as hate bitterly that this story of Demetrios Contos is told. Demetrios Contos lived in Vallejo. Next to Big Alec, he was the largest, bravest, and most influential man among the Greeks. He had given us no trouble, and I doubt if he would ever have clashed with us had he not invested in a new salmon boat. This boat was the cause of all the trouble. He had had it built upon his own model, in which the lines of the general salmon boat were somewhat modified.

To his high elation he found his new boat very fast—in fact, faster than any other boat on the bay or rivers. Forthwith he grew proud and boastful: and, our raid with the *Mary Rebecca* on the Sunday salmon fishers having wrought fear in their hearts, he sent a challenge up to Benicia. One of the local fishermen conveyed it to us; it was to the effect that Demetrios Contos would sail up from Vallejo on the following Sunday, and in the plain sight of Benicia set his net and catch salmon, and that Charley Le Grant, patrolman, might come and get him if he could. Of course Charley, and I had heard nothing of the new boat. Our own boat was pretty fast, and we were not afraid to have a brush with any other that happened along.

Sunday came. The challenge had been bruited abroad, and the fishermen and seafaring folk of Benicia turned out to a man, crowding Steamboat Wharf till it looked like the grand stand at a football match. Charley and I had been skeptical, but the fact of the crowd convinced us that there was something in Demetrios Contos's dare.

In the afternoon, when the sea-breeze had picked up in strength, his sail hove into view as he bowled along before the wind. He tacked a score of feet from the wharf, waved his hand theatrically, like a knight about to enter the lists, received a hearty cheer in return, and stood away into the Straits for a couple of hundred yards. Then he lowered sail, and, drifting the boat sidewise by means of the wind, proceeded to set his net. He did not set much of it, possibly fifty feet; yet Charley and I were thunderstruck at the man's effrontery. We did not know at the time, but we learned afterward, that the net he used was old and worthless. It could catch fish, true; but a catch of any size would have torn it to pieces.

Charley shook his head and said:

"I confess, it puzzles me. What if he has out only fifty feet? He could never get it in if we once started for him. And why does he come here anyway, flaunting his law-breaking in our faces? Right in our home town, too."

Charley's voice took on an aggrieved tone, and he continued for some minutes to inveigh against the brazenness of Demetrios Contos.

In the meantime, the man in question was lolling in the stern of his boat and watching the net floats. When a large fish is meshed in a gill-net, the floats by their agitation advertise the fact. And they evidently advertised it to Demetrios, for he pulled in about a dozen feet of net, and held aloft for a moment, before he flung it into the bottom of the boat, a big, glistening salmon. It was greeted by the audience on the wharf with round after round of cheers. This was more than Charley could stand.

"Come on, lad," he called to me; and we lost no time jumping into our salmon boat and getting up sail.

The crowd shouted warning to Demetrios, and as we darted out from the wharf we saw him slash his worthless net clear with a long knife. His sail was all ready to go up, and a moment later it fluttered in the sunshine. He ran aft, drew in the sheet, and filled on the long tack toward the Contra Costa Hills.

By this time we were not more than thirty feet astern. Charley was jubilant. He knew our boat was fast, and he knew, further, that in fine sailing few men were his equals. He was confident that we should surely catch Demetrios, and I shared his confidence. But somehow we did not seem to gain.

It was a pretty sailing breeze. We were gliding sleekly through the water, but Demetrios was slowly sliding away from us. And not only was he going faster, but he was eating into the wind a fraction of a point closer than we. This was sharply impressed upon us when he went about under the Contra Costa Hills and passed us on the other tack fully one hundred feet dead to windward.

"Whew!" Charley exclaimed. "Either that boat is a daisy, or we've got a five-gallon coal-oil can fast to our keel!"

It certainly looked it one way or the other. And by the time Demetrios made the Sonoma Hills, on the other side of the Straits, we were so hopelessly outdistanced that Charley told me to slack off the sheet, and we squared away for Benicia. The fishermen on Steamboat Wharf showered us with ridicule when we returned and tied up. Charley and I got out and walked away, feeling rather sheepish, for it is a sore stroke to one's pride when he thinks he has a good boat and knows how to sail it, and another man comes along and beats him.

Charley mooned over it for a couple of days; then word was brought to us, as before, that on the next Sunday Demetrios Contos would repeat his performance. Charley roused himself. He had our boat out of the water, cleaned and repainted its bottom, made a trifling alteration about the centerboard, overhauled the running gear, and sat up nearly all of Saturday night sewing on a new and much larger sail. So large did he make it, in fact, that additional ballast was imperative, and we stowed away nearly five hundred extra pounds of old railroad iron in the bottom of the boat.

Sunday came, and with it came Demetrios Contos, to break the law defiantly in open day. Again, we had the afternoon sea-breeze, and again Demetrios cut loose some forty or more feet of his rotten net, and got up sail and under way under our very noses. But he had anticipated Charley's move, and his own sail peaked higher than ever, while a whole extra cloth had been added to the after leech.

It was nip and tuck across to the Contra Costa Hills, neither of us seeming to gain or to lose. But by the time we had made the return tack to the Sonoma Hills, we could see that, while we footed it at about equal speed, Demetrios had eaten into the wind the least bit more than we. Yet Charley was sailing our boat as finely and delicately as it was possible to sail it and getting more out of it than he ever had before.

Of course, he could have drawn his revolver and fired at Demetrios; but we had long since found it contrary to our natures to shoot at a fleeing man guilty of only a petty offence. Also a sort of tacit agreement seemed to have been reached between the patrolmen and the fishermen. If we did not shoot while they ran away, they, in turn, did not fight if we once laid hands on them. Thus Demetrios Contos ran away from us, and we did no more than try our best to overtake him; and, in turn, if our boat proved faster than his, or was sailed better, he would, we knew, make no resistance when we caught up with him.

With our large sails and the healthy breeze romping up the Carquinez Straits, we found that our sailing was what is called "ticklish." We had to be constantly on the alert to avoid a capsize, and while Charley steered I held the mainsheet in my hand with but a single turn round a pin, ready to let go at any moment. Demetrios, we could see, sailing his boat alone, had his hands full.

But it was a vain undertaking for us to attempt to catch him. Out of his inner consciousness he had evolved a boat that was better than ours. And though Charley sailed fully as well, if not the least bit better, the boat he sailed was not so good as the Greek's.

"Slack away the sheet," Charley commanded; and as our boat fell off before the wind, Demetrios's mocking laugh floated down to us.

Charley shook his head, saying, "It's no use. Demetrios has the better boat. If he tries his performance again, we must meet it with some new scheme."

This time it was my imagination that came to the rescue.

"What's the matter," I suggested, on the Wednesday following, "with my chasing Demetrios in the boat next Sunday, while you wait for him on the wharf at Vallejo when he arrives?"

Charley considered it a moment and slapped his knee.

"A good idea! You're beginning to use that head of yours. A credit to your teacher, I must say."

"But you mustn't chase him too far," he went on, the next moment, "or he'll head out into San Pablo Bay instead of running home to Vallejo, and there I'll be, standing lonely on the wharf and waiting in vain for him to arrive."

On Thursday Charley registered an objection to my plan.

"Everybody'll know I've gone to Vallejo, and you can depend upon it that Demetrios will know, too. I'm afraid we'll have to give up the idea."

This objection was only too valid, and for the rest of the day I struggled under my disappointment. But that night a new way seemed to open to me, and in my eagerness I awoke Charley from a sound sleep.

"Well," he grunted, "what's the matter? House afire?"

"No," I replied, "but my head is. Listen to this. On Sunday you and I will be around Benicia up to the very moment Demetrios's sail heaves into sight. This will lull everybody's suspicions. Then, when Demetrios's sail does heave in sight, do you stroll leisurely away and up-town. All the fishermen will think you're beaten and that you know you're beaten."

"So far, so good," Charley commented, while I paused to catch breath.

"And very good indeed," I continued proudly. "You stroll carelessly up-town, but when you're once out of sight you leg it for all you're worth for Dan Maloney's. Take the little mare of his and strike out on the country road for Vallejo. The road's in fine condition, and you can make it in quicker time than Demetrios can beat all the way down against the wind."

"And I'll arrange right away for the mare, first thing in the morning," Charley said, accepting the modified plan without hesitation.

"But, I say," he said, a little later, this time waking me out of a sound sleep.

I could hear him chuckling in the dark.

"I say, lad, isn't it rather a novelty for the fish patrol to be taking to horseback?"

"Imagination," I answered. "It's what you're always preaching. 'Keep thinking one thought ahead of the other fellow, and you're bound to win out.'"

"He! he!" he chuckled. "And if one thought ahead, including a mare, doesn't take the other fellow's breath away this time, I'm not your humble servant, Charley Le Grant."

"But can you manage the boat alone?" he asked, on Friday. "Remember, we've a ripping big sail on her."

I argued my proficiency so well that he did not refer to the matter again till Saturday, when he suggested removing one whole cloth from the after leech. I guess it was the disappointment written on my face that made him desist; for I, also, had a pride in my boat-sailing abilities, and I was almost wild to get out alone with the big sail and go tearing down the Carquinez Straits in the wake of the flying Greek.

As usual, Sunday and Demetrios Contos arrived together. It had become the regular thing for the fishermen to assemble on Steamboat Wharf to greet his arrival and to laugh at our discomfiture. He lowered sail a couple of hundred yards out and set his customary fifty feet of rotten net.

"I suppose this nonsense will keep up as long as his old net holds out," Charley grumbled, with intention, in the hearing of several of the Greeks.

"Den I give-a heem my old-a net-a," one of them spoke up, promptly and maliciously,

"I don't care," Charley answered. "I've got some old net myself he can have—if he'll come around and ask for it."

They all laughed at this, for they could afford to be sweet-tempered with a man so badly outwitted as Charley was.

"Well, so long, lad," Charley called to me a moment later. "I think I'll go up-town to Maloney's."

"Let me take the boat out?" I asked.

"If you want to," was his answer, as he turned on his heel and walked slowly away.

Demetrios pulled two large salmon out of his net, and I jumped into the boat. The fishermen crowded around in a spirit of fun, and when I started to get up sail overwhelmed me with all sorts of jocular advice. They even offered extravagant bets to one another that I would surely catch Demetrios, and two of them, styling themselves the committee of judges, gravely asked permission to come along with me to see how I did it.

But I was in no hurry. I waited to give Charley all the time I could, and I pretended dissatisfaction with the stretch of the sail and slightly shifted the small tackle by which the huge sprit forces up the peak. It was not until I was sure that Charley had reached Dan Maloney's and was on the little mare's back, that I cast off from the wharf and gave the big sail to the wind. A stout puff filled it and suddenly pressed the lee gunwale down till a couple of buckets of water came inboard. A little thing like this will happen to the best small-boat sailors, and yet, though I instantly let go the sheet and righted, I was cheered sarcastically, as though I had been guilty of a very awkward blunder.

When Demetrios saw only one person in the fish patrol boat, and that one a boy, he proceeded to play with me. Making a short tack out, with me not thirty feet behind, he returned, with his sheet a little free, to Steamboat Wharf. And there he made short tacks, and turned and twisted and ducked around, to the great delight of his sympathetic audience. I was right behind him all the time, and I dared to do whatever he did, even when he squared away before the wind and jibed his big sail over—a most dangerous trick with such a sail in such a wind.

He depended upon the brisk sea breeze and the strong ebb-tide, which together kicked up a nasty sea, to bring me to grief. But I was on my mettle, and never in all my life did I sail a boat better than on that day. I was keyed up to concert pitch, my brain was working smoothly and quickly, my hands never fumbled once, and it seemed that I almost divined the thousand little things which a small-boat sailor must be taking into consideration every second.

It was Demetrios who came to grief instead. Something went wrong with his centerboard, so that it jammed in the case and would not go all the way down. In a moment's breathing space, which he had gained from me by a clever trick, I saw him working impatiently with the centerboard, trying to force it down. I gave him little time, and he was compelled quickly to return to the tiller and sheet.

The centerboard made him anxious. He gave over playing with me, and started on the long beat to Vallejo. To my joy, on the first long tack across, I found that I could eat into the wind just a little bit closer than he. Here was where another man in the boat would have been of value to him; for, with me but a few feet astern, he did not dare let go the tiller and run amidships to try to force down the centerboard.

Unable to hang on as close in the eye of the wind as formerly, he proceeded to slack his sheet a trifle and to ease off a bit, in order to outfoot me. This I permitted him to do till I had worked to windward, when I bore down upon him. As I drew close, he feinted at coming about. This led me to shoot into the wind to forestall him. But it was only a feint, cleverly executed, and he held back to his course while I hurried to make up lost ground.

He was undeniably smarter than I when it came to maneuvering. Time after time I all but had him, and each time he tricked me and escaped. Besides, the wind was freshening, constantly, and each of us had his hands full to avoid capsizing. As for my boat, it could not have been kept afloat but for the extra ballast. I sat cocked over the weather gunwale, tiller in one hand and sheet in the other; and the sheet, with a single turn around a pin, I was very often forced to let go in the severer puffs. This allowed the sail to spill the wind, which was equivalent to taking off so much driving power, and of course I lost ground. My consolation was that Demetrios was as often compelled to do the same thing.

The strong ebb-tide, racing down the Straits in the teeth of the wind, caused an unusually heavy and spiteful sea, which dashed aboard continually. I was dripping wet, and even the sail was wet half-way up the after leech. Once I did succeed in out-maneuvering Demetrios, so that my bow bumped into him amidships. Here was where I should have had another man. Before I could run forward and leap aboard, he shoved the boats apart with an oar, laughing mockingly in my face as he did so.

We were now at the mouth of the Straits, in a bad stretch of water. Here the Vallejo Straits and the Carquinez Straits rushed directly at each other. Through the first flowed all the water of Napa River and the great tide-lands; through the second flowed all the water of Suisun Bay and the Sacramento and San Joaquin rivers. And where such immense bodies of water, flowing swiftly, clashed together, a terrible tide-rip was produced. To make it worse, the wind howled up San Pablo Bay for fifteen miles and drove in a tremendous sea upon the tide-rip.

Conflicting currents tore about in all directions, colliding, forming whirlpools, sucks, and boils, and shooting up spitefully into hollow waves which fell aboard as often from leeward as from windward. And through it all, confused, driven into a madness of motion, thundered the great smoking seas from San Pablo Bay.

I was as wildly excited as the water. The boat was behaving splendidly, leaping and lurching through the welter like a race- horse. I could hardly contain myself with the joy of it. The huge sail, the howling wind, the driving seas, the plunging boat—I, a pygmy, a mere speck in the midst of it, was mastering the elemental strife, flying through it and over it, triumphant and victorious.

And just then, as I roared along like a conquering hero, the boat received a frightful smash and came instantly to a dead stop. I was flung forward and into the bottom. As I sprang up, I caught a fleeting glimpse of a greenish, barnacle-covered object, and knew it at once for what it was, that terror of navigation, a sunken pile. No man may guard against such a thing. Water-logged and floating just beneath the surface, it was impossible to sight it in the troubled water in time to escape.

The whole bow of the boat must have been crushed in, for in a few seconds the boat was half full. Then a couple of seas filled it, and it sank straight down, dragged to bottom by the heavy ballast. So quickly did it all happen that I was entangled in the sail and drawn under. When I fought my way to the surface, suffocating, my lungs almost bursting, I could see nothing of the oars. They must have been swept away by the chaotic currents. I saw Demetrios Contos looking back from his boat and heard the vindictive and mocking tones of his voice as he shouted exultantly. He held steadily on his course, leaving me to perish.

There was nothing to do but to swim for it, which, in

that wild confusion, was at the best a matter of but a few moments. Holding my breath and working with my hands, I managed to get off my heavy sea-boots and my jacket. Yet there was very little breath I could catch to hold, and I swiftly discovered that it was not so much a matter of swimming as of breathing.

I was beaten and buffeted, smashed under by the great San Pablo whitecaps, and strangled by the hollow tide-rip waves which flung themselves into my eyes, nose, and mouth. Then the strange sucks would grip my legs and drag me under, to spout me up in some fierce boiling, where, even as I tried to catch my breath, a great whitecap would crash down upon my head.

It was impossible to survive any length of time. I was breathing more water than air and drowning all the time. My senses began to leave me, my head to whirl around. I struggled on, spasmodically, instinctively, and was barely half conscious when I felt myself caught by the shoulders and hauled over the gunwale of a boat.

For some time I lay across a seat where I had been flung, face downward, and with the water running out of my mouth. After a while, still weak and faint, I turned around to see who was my rescuer. And there, in the stern, sheet in one hand and tiller in the other, grinning and nodding good-naturedly, sat Demetrios Contos. He had intended to leave me to drown—he said so afterward—but his better self had fought the battle, conquered, and sent him back to me.

"You all-a right?" he asked.

I managed to shape a "yes" on my lips, though I could not yet speak.

"You sail-a de boat verr-a good-a," he said. "So good-a as a man."

A compliment from Demetrios Contos was a compliment indeed, and I keenly appreciated it, though I could only nod my head in acknowledgment.

We held no more conversation, for I was busy recovering and he was busy with the boat. He ran in to the wharf at Vallejo, made the boat fast, and helped me out. Then it was, as we both stood on the wharf, that Charley stepped out from behind a net-rack and put his hand on Demetrios Contos's arm.

"He saved my life, Charley," I protested; "and I don't think he ought to be arrested."

A puzzled expression came into Charley's face, which cleared immediately after, in a way it had when he made up his mind.

"I can't help it, lad," he said kindly. "I can't go back on my duty, and it's plain duty to arrest him. To-day is Sunday; there are two salmon in his boat which he caught to-day. What else can I do?"

"But he saved my life," I persisted, unable to make any other argument.

Demetrios Contos's face went black with rage when he learned Charley's judgment. He had a sense of being unfairly treated. The better part of his nature had triumphed, he had performed a generous act and saved a helpless enemy, and in return the enemy was taking him to jail.

Charley and I were out of sorts with each other when we went back to Benicia. I stood for the spirit of the law and not the letter; but by the letter Charley made his stand. As far as he could see, there was nothing else for him to do. The law said distinctly that no salmon should be caught on Sunday. He was a patrolman, and it was his duty to enforce that law. That was all there was to it. He had done his duty, and his conscience was clear. Nevertheless, the whole thing seemed unjust to me, and I felt very sorry for Demetrios Contos.

Two days later we went down to Vallejo to the trial. I had to go along as a witness, and it was the most hateful task that I ever performed in my life when I testified on the witness stand to seeing Demetrios catch the two salmon Charley had captured him with.

Demetrios had engaged a lawyer, but his case was hopeless. The jury was out only fifteen minutes and returned a verdict of guilty. The judge sentenced Demetrios to pay a fine of one hundred dollars or go to jail for fifty days.

Charley stepped up to the clerk of the court. "I want to pay that fine," he said, at the same time placing five twenty dollar gold pieces on the desk. "It—it was the only way out of it, lad," he stammered, turning to me.

The moisture rushed into my eyes as I seized his hand. "I want to pay—" I began.

"To pay your half?" he interrupted. "I certainly shall expect you to pay it."

In the meantime, Demetrios had been informed by his lawyer that his fee likewise had been paid by Charley.

Demetrios came over to shake Charley's hand, and all his warm Southern blood flamed in his face. Then, not to be outdone in generosity, he insisted on paying his fine and lawyer's fee himself and flew half-way into a passion because Charley refused to let him.

More than anything else we ever did, I think, this action of Charley's impressed upon the fishermen the deeper significance of the law. Also Charley was raised high in their esteem, while I came in for a little share of praise as a boy who knew how to sail a boat. Demetrios Contos not only never broke the law again, but he became a very good friend of ours, and on more than one occasion he ran up to Benicia to have a gossip with us.

YELLOW
HANDKERCHIEF

Yellow
Handkerchief
(1905)

"I'M NOT WANTING TO dictate to you, lad," Charley said; "but I'm very much against your making a last raid. You've gone safely through rough times with rough men, and it would be a shame to have something happen to you at the very end."

"But how can I get out of making a last raid?" I demanded, with the cocksureness of youth. "There always has to be a last, you know, to anything."

Charley crossed his legs, leaned back, and considered the problem. "Very true. But why not call the capture of Demetrios Contos the last? You're back from it safe and sound and hearty, for all your good wetting, and—and—" His voice broke and he could not speak for a moment. "And I could never forgive myself if anything happened to you now."

I laughed at Charley's fears while I gave in to the claims of his affection and agreed to consider the last raid already performed. We had been together for two years, and now I was leaving the fish patrol in order to go back and finish my education. I had earned and saved money to put me through three years at the high school, and though the beginning of the term was several months away, I intended doing a lot of studying for the entrance examinations.

My belongings were packed snugly in a sea-chest, and I was all ready to buy my ticket and ride down on the train to Oakland, when Neil Partington arrived in Benicia. The *Reindeer* was needed immediately for work far down on the Lower Bay, and Neil said he intended to run straight for Oakland. As that was his home and as I was to live with his family while going to school, he saw no reason, he said, why I should not put my chest aboard and come along.

So the chest went aboard, and in the middle of the afternoon we hoisted the *Reindeer's* big mainsail and cast off. It was tantalizing fall weather. The sea-breeze, which had blown steadily all summer, was gone, and in its place were capricious winds and murky skies which made the time of arriving anywhere extremely problematical. We started on the first of the ebb, and as we slipped down the Carquinez Straits, I looked my last for some time upon Benicia and the bight at Turner's Shipyard, where we had besieged the Lancashire Queen, and had captured Big Alec, the King of the Greeks. And at the mouth of the Straits I looked with not a little interest upon the spot where a few days before I should have drowned but for the good that was in the nature of Demetrios Contos.

A great wall of fog advanced across San Pablo Bay to meet us, and in a few minutes the *Reindeer* was running blindly through the damp obscurity. Charley, who was steering, seemed to have an instinct for that kind of work. How he did it, he himself confessed that he did not know; but he had a way of calculating winds, currents, distance, time, drift, and sailing speed that was truly marvelous.

"It looks as though it were lifting," Neil Partington said, a couple of hours after we had entered the fog. "Where do you say we are, Charley?"

Charley looked at his watch, "Six o'clock, and three hours more of ebb," he remarked casually.

"But where do you say we are?" Neil insisted.

Charley pondered a moment, and then answered, "The tide has edged us over a bit out of our course, but if the fog lifts right now, as it is going to lift, you'll find we're not more than a thousand miles off McNear's Landing."

"You might be a little more definite by a few miles, anyway," Neil grumbled, showing by his tone that he disagreed.

"All right, then," Charley said, conclusively, "not less than a quarter of a mile, not more than a half."

The wind freshened with a couple of little puffs, and the fog thinned perceptibly.

"McNear's is right off there," Charley said, pointing directly into the fog on our weather beam.

The three of us were peering intently in that direction, when the *Reindeer* struck with a dull crash and came to a standstill. We ran forward, and found her bowsprit entangled in the tanned rigging of a short, chunky mast. She had collided, head on, with a Chinese junk lying at anchor.

At the moment we arrived forward, five Chinese, like so many bees, came swarming out of the little 'tween-decks cabin, the sleep still in their eyes.

Leading them came a big, muscular man, conspicuous for his pock-marked face and the yellow silk handkerchief swathed about his head. It was Yellow Handkerchief, the Chinaman whom we had arrested for illegal shrimp-fishing the year before, and who, at that time, had nearly sunk the *Reindeer*, as he had nearly sunk it now by violating the rules of navigation.

"What d'ye mean, you yellow-faced heathen, lying here in a fairway without a horn a-going?" Charley cried hotly.

"Mean?" Neil calmly answered. "Just take a look—that's what he means."

Our eyes followed the direction indicated by Neil's finger, and we saw the open amidships of the junk, half filled, as we found on closer examination, with fresh-caught shrimps. Mingled with the shrimps were myriads of small fish, from a quarter of an inch upward in size.

Yellow Handkerchief had lifted the trap-net at high-water slack, and, taking advantage of the concealment offered by the fog, had boldly been lying by, waiting to lift the net again at low-water slack.

"Well," Neil hummed and hawed, "in all my varied and extensive experience as a fish patrolman, I must say this is the easiest capture I ever made. What'll we do with them, Charley?"

"Tow the junk into San Rafael, of course," came the answer. Charley turned to me. "You stand by the junk, lad, and I'll pass you a towing line. If the wind doesn't fail us, we'll make the creek before the tide gets too low, sleep at San Rafael, and arrive in Oakland tomorrow by midday."

So saying, Charley and Neil returned to the *Reindeer* and got under way, the junk towing astern. I went aft and took charge of the prize, steering by means of an antiquated tiller and a rudder with large, diamond-shaped holes, through which the water rushed back and forth.

By now the last of the fog had vanished, and Charley's estimate of our position was confirmed by the sight of McNear's Landing a short half-mile away. Following along the west shore, we rounded Point Pedro in plain view of the Chinese shrimp villages, and a great to- do was raised when they saw one of their junks towing behind the familiar fish patrol sloop.

The wind, coming off the land, was rather puffy and uncertain, and it would have been more to our advantage had it been stronger. San Rafael Creek, up which we had to go to reach the town and turn over our prisoners to the authorities, ran through wide-stretching marshes, and was difficult to navigate on a falling tide, while at low tide it was impossible to navigate at all. So, with the tide already half-ebbed, it was necessary for us to make time. This the heavy junk prevented, lumbering along behind and holding the *Reindeer* back by just so much dead weight.

"Tell those coolies to get up that sail," Charley finally called to me. "We don't want to hang up on the mud flats for the rest of the night."

I repeated the order to Yellow Handkerchief, who mumbled it huskily to his men. He was suffering from a bad cold, which doubled him up in convulsive coughing spells and made his eyes heavy and bloodshot. This made him more evil-looking than ever, and when he glared viciously at me I remembered with a shiver the close shave I had had with him at the time of his previous arrest.

His crew sullenly tailed on to the halyards, and the strange, outlandish sail, lateen in rig and dyed a warm brown, rose in the air. We were sailing on the wind, and when Yellow Handkerchief flattened down the sheet the junk forged ahead and the tow-line went slack. Fast as the *Reindeer* could sail, the junk outsailed her; and to avoid running her down I hauled a little closer on the wind. But the junk likewise outpointed, and in a couple of minutes I was abreast of the *Reindeer* and to windward. The tow-line had now tautened, at right angles to the two boats, and the predicament was laughable.

"Cast off!" I shouted.

Charley hesitated.

"It's all right," I added. "Nothing can happen. We'll make the creek on this tack, and you'll be right behind me all the way up to San Rafael."

At this Charley cast off, and Yellow Handkerchief sent one of his men forward to haul in the line. In the gathering darkness I could just make out the mouth of San Rafael Creek, and by the time we entered it I could barely see its banks. The *Reindeer* was fully five minutes astern, and we continued to leave her astern as we beat up the narrow, winding channel. With Charley behind us, it seemed I had little to fear from my five prisoners; but the darkness prevented my keeping a sharp eye on them, so I transferred my revolver from my trousers pocket to the side pocket of my coat, where I could more quickly put my hand on it.

Yellow Handkerchief was the one I feared, and that he

knew it and made use of it, subsequent events will show. He was sitting a few feet away from me, on what then happened to be the weather side of the junk. I could scarcely see the outlines of his form, but I soon became convinced that he was slowly, very slowly, edging closer to me. I watched him carefully. Steering with my left hand, I slipped my right into my pocket and got hold of the revolver.

I saw him shift along for a couple of inches, and I was just about to order him back—the words were trembling on the tip of my tongue—when I was struck with great force by a heavy figure that had leaped through the air upon me from the lee side. It was one of the crew. He pinioned my right arm so that I could not withdraw my hand from my pocket, and at the same time clapped his other hand over my mouth. Of course, I could have struggled away from him and freed my hand or gotten my mouth clear so that I might cry an alarm, but in a trice Yellow Handkerchief was on top of me.

I struggled around to no purpose in the bottom of the junk, while my legs and arms were tied and my mouth securely bound in what I afterward found to be a cotton shirt. Then I was left lying in the bottom. Yellow Handkerchief took the tiller, issuing his orders in whispers; and from our position at the time, and from the alteration of the sail, which I could dimly make out above me as a blot against the stars, I knew the junk was being headed into the mouth of a small slough which emptied at that point into San Rafael Creek.

In a couple of minutes, we ran softly alongside the bank, and the sail was silently lowered. The Chinese kept very quiet. Yellow Handkerchief sat down in the bottom alongside of me, and I could feel him straining to repress his raspy, hacking cough. Possibly seven or eight minutes later I heard Charley's voice as the *Reindeer* went past the mouth of the slough.

"I can't tell you how relieved I am," I could plainly hear him saying to Neil, "that the lad has finished with the fish patrol without accident."

Here Neil said something which I could not catch, and then Charley's voice went on:

"The youngster takes naturally to the water, and if, when he finishes high school, he takes a course in navigation and goes deep sea, I see no reason why he shouldn't rise to be master of the finest and biggest ship afloat."

It was all very flattering to me, but lying there, bound and gagged by my own prisoners, with the voices growing faint and fainter as the *Reindeer* slipped on through the darkness toward San Rafael, I must say I was not in quite the proper situation to enjoy my smiling future. With the *Reindeer* went my last hope. What was to happen next I could not imagine, for the Chinese were a different race from mine, and from what I knew I was confident that fair play was no part of their make-up.

After waiting a few minutes longer, the crew hoisted the lateen sail, and Yellow Handkerchief steered down toward the mouth of San Rafael Creek. The tide was getting lower, and he had difficulty in escaping the mud-banks. I was hoping he would run aground, but he succeeded in making the Bay without accident.

As we passed out of the creek a noisy discussion arose,

which I knew related to me. Yellow Handkerchief was vehement, but the other four as vehemently opposed him. It was very evident that he advocated doing away with me and that they were afraid of the consequences. I was familiar enough with the Chinese character to know that fear alone restrained them. But what plan they offered in place of Yellow Handkerchief's murderous one, I could not make out.

My feelings, as my fate hung in the balance, may be guessed. The discussion developed into a quarrel, in the midst of which Yellow Handkerchief unshipped the heavy tiller and sprang toward me. But his four companions threw themselves between, and a clumsy struggle took place for possession of the tiller. In the end Yellow Handkerchief was overcome, and sullenly returned to the steering, while they soundly berated him for his rashness.

Not long after, the sail was run down and the junk slowly urged forward by means of the sweeps. I felt it ground gently on the soft mud. Three of the Chinese—they all wore long sea-boots—got over the side, and the other two passed me across the rail. With Yellow Handkerchief at my legs and his two companions at my shoulders, they began to flounder along through the mud. After some time their feet struck firmer footing, and I knew they were carrying me up some beach. The location of this beach was not doubtful in my mind. It could be none other than one of the Marin Islands, a group of rocky islets which lay off the Marin County shore.

When they reached the firm sand that marked high tide, I was dropped, and none too gently. Yellow Handkerchief kicked me spitefully in the ribs, and then the trio floundered back through the mud to the junk. A moment later I heard the sail go up and slat in the wind as they drew in the sheet. Then silence fell, and I was left to my own devices for getting free.

I remembered having seen tricksters writhe and squirm out of ropes with which they were bound, but though I writhed and squirmed like a good fellow, the knots remained as hard as ever, and there was no appreciable slack. In the course of my squirming, however, I rolled over upon a heap of clam-shells—the remains, evidently, of some yachting party's clam-bake. This gave me an idea. My hands were tied behind my back; and, clutching a shell in them, I rolled over and over, up the beach, till I came to the rocks I knew to be there.

Rolling around and searching, I finally discovered a narrow crevice, into which I shoved the shell. The edge of it was sharp, and across the sharp edge I proceeded to saw the rope that bound my wrists. The edge of the shell was also brittle, and I broke it by bearing too heavily upon it. Then I rolled back to the heap and returned with as many shells as I could carry in both hands. I broke many shells, cut my hands a number of times, and got cramps in my legs from my strained position and my exertions.

While I was suffering from the cramps, and resting, I heard a familiar halloo drift across the water. It was Charley, searching for me. The gag in my mouth prevented me from replying, and I could only lie there, helplessly fuming, while he rowed past the island and his voice slowly lost itself in the distance.

I returned to the sawing process, and at the end of half an hour succeeded in severing the rope. The rest was easy.

My hands once free, it was a matter of minutes to loosen my legs and to take the gag out of my mouth. I ran around the island to make sure it was an island and not by any chance a portion of the mainland. An island it certainly was, one of the Marin group, fringed with a sandy beach and surrounded by a sea of mud. Nothing remained but to wait till daylight and to keep warm; for it was a cold, raw night for California, with just enough wind to pierce the skin and cause one to shiver.

To keep up the circulation, I ran around the island a dozen times or so and clambered across its rocky backbone as many times more—all of which was of greater service to me, as I afterward discovered, than merely to warm me up. In the midst of this exercise, I wondered if I had lost anything out of my pockets while rolling over and over in the sand. A search showed the absence of my revolver and pocket-knife. The first Yellow Handkerchief had taken; but the knife had been lost in the sand.

I was hunting for it when the sound of rowlocks came to my ears. At first, of course, I thought of Charley; but on second thought I knew Charley would be calling out as he rowed along. A sudden premonition of danger seized me. The Marin Islands are lonely places; chance visitors in the dead of night are hardly to be expected. What if it were Yellow Handkerchief? The sound made by the rowlocks grew more distinct. I crouched in the sand and listened intently. The boat, which I judged a small skiff from the quick stroke of the oars, was landing in the mud about fifty yards up the beach. I heard a raspy, hacking cough, and my heart stood still. It was Yellow Handkerchief. Not to be robbed of his revenge by his more cautious companions, he had stolen away from the village and come back alone.

I did some swift thinking. I was unarmed and helpless on a tiny islet, and a yellow barbarian, whom I had reason to fear, was coming after me. Any place was safer than the island, and I turned instinctively to the water, or rather to the mud. As he began to flounder ashore through the mud, I started to flounder out into it, going over the same course which the Chinese had taken in landing me and in returning to the junk.

Yellow Handkerchief, believing me to be lying tightly bound, exercised no care, but came ashore noisily. This helped me, for, under the shield of his noise and making no more myself than necessary, I managed to cover fifty feet by the time he had made the beach. Here I lay down in the mud. It was cold and clammy, and made me shiver, but I did not care to stand up and run the risk of being discovered by his sharp eyes.

He walked down the beach straight to where he had left me lying, and I had a fleeting feeling of regret at not being able to see his surprise when he did not find me. But it was a very fleeting regret, for my teeth were chattering with the cold.

What his movements were after that I had largely to deduce from the facts of the situation, for I could scarcely see him in the dim starlight. But I was sure that the first thing he did was to make the circuit of the beach to learn if landings had been made by other boats. This he would have known at once by the tracks through the mud.

Convinced that no boat had removed me from the

island, he next started to find out what had become of me. Beginning at the pile of clamshells, he lighted matches to trace my tracks in the sand. At such times I could see his villainous face plainly, and, when the sulfur from the matches irritated his lungs, between the raspy cough that followed and the clammy mud in which I was lying, I confess I shivered harder than ever.

The multiplicity of my footprints puzzled him. Then the idea that I might be out in the mud must have struck him, for he waded out a few yards in my direction, and, stooping, with his eyes searched the dim surface long and carefully. He could not have been more than fifteen feet from me and had he lighted a match he would surely have discovered me.

He returned to the beach and clambered about, over the rocky backbone, again hunting for me with lighted matches, The closeness of the shave impelled me to further flight. Not daring to wade upright, on account of the noise made by floundering and by the suck of the mud, I remained lying down in the mud and propelled myself over its surface by means of my hands. Still keeping the trail made by the Chinese in going from and to the junk, I held on until I reached the water. Into this I waded to a depth of three feet, and then I turned off to the side on a line parallel with the beach.

The thought came to me of going toward Yellow Handkerchief's skiff and escaping in it, but at that very moment he returned to the beach, and, as though fearing the very thing I had in mind, he slushed out through the mud to assure himself that the skiff was safe. This turned me in the opposite direction. Half swimming, half wading, with my head just out of water and avoiding splashing, I succeeded in putting about a hundred feet between myself and the spot where the Chinese had begun to wade ashore from the junk. I drew myself out on the mud and remained lying flat.

Again, Yellow Handkerchief returned to the beach and made a search of the island, and again he returned to the heap of clam-shells. I knew what was running in his mind as well as he did himself. No one could leave or land without making tracks in the mud. The only tracks to be seen were those leading from his skiff and from where the junk had been. I was not on the island. I must have left it by one or the other of those two tracks. He had just been over the one to his skiff and was certain I had not left that way. Therefore, I could have left the island only by going over the tracks of the junk landing. This he proceeded to verify by wading out over them himself, lighting matches as he came along.

When he arrived at the point where I had first lain, I knew, by the matches he burned and the time he took, that he had discovered the marks left by my body. These he followed straight to the water and into it, but in three feet of water he could no longer see them. On the other hand, as the tide was still falling, he could easily make out the impression made by the junk's bow, and could have likewise made out the impression of any other boat if it had landed at that particular spot. But there was no such mark; and I knew that he was absolutely convinced that I was hiding somewhere in the mud.

But to hunt on a dark night for a boy in a sea of mud would be like hunting for a needle in a haystack, and he did not attempt it. Instead, he went back to the beach and prowled around for some time. I was hoping he would give me up and go, for by this time I was suffering severely from the cold. At last, he waded out to his skiff and rowed away. What if this departure of Yellow Handkerchief's were a sham? What if he had done it merely to entice me ashore?

The more I thought of it the more certain I became that he had made a little too much noise with his oars as he rowed away. So I remained, lying in the mud and shivering. I shivered till the muscles of the small of my back ached and pained me as badly as the cold, and I had need of all my self-control to force myself to remain in my miserable situation.

It was well that I did, however, for, possibly an hour later, I thought I could make out something moving on the beach. I watched intently, but my ears were rewarded first, by a raspy cough I knew only too well. Yellow Handkerchief had sneaked back, landed on the other side of the island, and crept around to surprise me if I had returned.

After that, though hours passed without sign of him, I was afraid to return to the island at all. On the other hand, I was almost equally afraid that I should die of the exposure I was undergoing. I had never dreamed one could suffer so. I grew so cold and numb, finally, that I ceased to shiver. But my muscles and bones began to ache in a way that was agony. The tide had long since begun to rise, and, foot by foot, it drove me in toward the beach. High water came at three o'clock, and at three o'clock I drew myself up on the beach, more dead than alive, and too helpless to have offered any resistance had Yellow Handkerchief swooped down upon me.

But no Yellow Handkerchief appeared. He had given me up and gone back to Point Pedro. Nevertheless, I was in a deplorable, not to say dangerous, condition. I could not stand upon my feet, much less walk. My clammy, muddy garments clung to me like sheets of ice. I thought I should never get them off. So numb and lifeless were my fingers, and so weak was I, that it seemed to take an hour to get off my shoes. I had not the strength to break the porpoise- hide laces, and the knots defied me. I repeatedly beat my hands upon the rocks to get some sort of life into them. Sometimes I felt sure I was going to die.

But in the end—after several centuries, it seemed to me—I got off the last of my clothes. The water was now close at hand, and I crawled painfully into it and washed the mud from my naked body. Still, I could not get on my feet and walk, and I was afraid to lie still. Nothing remained but to crawl weakly, like a snail, and at the cost of constant pain, up and down the sand. I kept this up as long as possible, but as the east paled with the coming of dawn, I began to succumb. The sky grew rosy-red, and the golden rim of the sun, showing above the horizon, found me lying helpless and motionless among the clam-shells.

As in a dream, I saw the familiar mainsail of the *Reindeer* as she slipped out of San Rafael Creek on a light puff of morning air. This dream was very much broken. There are intervals I can never recollect on looking back over it. Three things, however, I distinctly remember: the first sight of the *Reindeer*'s mainsail; her lying at anchor a few hundred feet away and a small boat leaving her side; and the cabin stove roaring red-hot, myself swathed all over with blankets, except on the chest and shoulders, which Charley was pounding and mauling unmercifully, and my mouth and throat burning with the coffee which Neil Partington was pouring down a trifle too hot.

But burn or no burn, I tell you it felt good. By the time we arrived in Oakland I was as limber and strong as ever—though Charlie and Neil Partington were afraid I was going to have pneumonia, and Mrs. Partington, for my first six months of school, kept an anxious eye upon me to discover the first symptoms of consumption.

Time flies. It seems but yesterday that I was a lad of sixteen on the fish patrol. Yet I know that I arrived this very morning from China, with a quick passage to my credit, and master of the barkentine Harvester. And I know that tomorrow morning I shall run over to Oakland to see Neil Partington and his wife and family, and later on up to Benicia to see Charley Le Grant and talk over old times. No; I shall not go to Benicia, now that I think about it. I expect to be a highly interested party to a wedding, shortly to take place. Her name is Alice Partington, and, since Charley has promised to be best man, he will have to come down to Oakland instead.

MAKE WESTING

MAKE WESTING
(1908)

FOR SEVEN WEEKS the *Mary Rogers* had been between 50 degrees south in the Atlantic and 50 degrees south in the Pacific, which meant that for seven weeks she had been struggling to round Cape Horn. For seven weeks she had been either in dirt, or close to dirt, save once, and then, following upon six days of excessive dirt, which she had ridden out under the shelter of the redoubtable Terra del Fuego coast, she had almost gone ashore during a heavy swell in the dead calm that had suddenly fallen. For seven weeks she had wrestled with the Cape Horn graybeards, and in return been buffeted and smashed by them. She was a wooden ship, and her ceaseless straining had opened her seams, so that twice a day the watch took its turn at the pumps.

The *Mary Rogers* was strained, the crew was strained, and big Dan Cullen, master, was likewise strained. Perhaps he was strained most of all, for upon him rested the responsibility of that titanic struggle. He slept most of the time in his clothes, though he rarely slept. He haunted the deck at night, a great, burly, robust ghost, black with the sunburn of thirty years of sea and hairy as an orang-outang. He, in turn, was haunted by one thought of action, a sailing direction for the Horn: Whatever you do, make westing! make westing! It was an obsession. He thought of nothing else, except, at times, to blaspheme God for sending such bitter weather.

Make westing! He hugged the Horn, and a dozen times lay hove to with the iron Cape bearing east-by-north, or north-north-east, a score of miles away. And each time the eternal west wind smote him back and he made easting. He fought gale after gale, south to 64 degrees, inside the Antarctic drift-ice, and pledged his immortal soul to the Powers of Darkness for a bit of westing, for a slant to take him around. And he made easting. In despair, he had tried to make the passage through the Straits of Le Maire. Halfway through, the wind hauled to the north'ard of north- west, the glass dropped to 28.88, and he turned and ran before a gale of cyclonic fury, missing, by a hair's-breadth, piling up the *Mary Rogers* on the black-toothed rocks. Twice he had made west to the Diego Ramirez Rocks, one of the times saved between two snow-squalls by sighting the gravestones of ships a quarter of a mile dead ahead.

Blow! Captain Dan Cullen instanced all his thirty years at sea to prove that never had it blown so before. The *Mary Rogers* was hove to at the time he gave the evidence, and, to clinch it, inside half an hour the *Mary Rogers* was hove down to the hatches. Her new maintopsail and brand new spencer were blown away like tissue paper; and five sails, furled and fast under double gaskets, were blown loose and stripped from the yards. And before morning the *Mary Rogers* was hove down twice again, and holes were knocked in her bulwarks to ease her decks from the weight of ocean that pressed her down.

On an average of once a week, Captain Dan Cullen caught glimpses of the sun. Once, for ten minutes, the sun shone at midday, and ten minutes afterward a new gale was piping up, both watches were shortening sail, and all was buried in the obscurity of a driving snow-squall. For a fortnight, once, Captain Dan Cullen was without a meridian or a chronometer sight. Rarely did he know his position within half of a degree, except when in sight of land; for sun and stars remained hidden behind the sky, and it was so gloomy that even at the best the horizons were poor for accurate observations. A gray gloom shrouded the world. The clouds were gray; the great driving seas were leaden gray; the smoking crests were a gray churning; even the occasional albatrosses were gray, while the snow- flurries were not white, but gray, under the somber pall of the heavens.

Life on board the *Mary Rogers* was gray—gray and gloomy. The faces of the sailors were blue-gray; they were afflicted with sea-cuts and sea-boils, and suffered exquisitely. They were shadows of men. For seven weeks, in the forecastle or on deck, they had not known what it was to be dry. They had forgotten what it was to sleep out a watch, and all watches it was, "All hands on deck!" They caught snatches of agonized sleep, and they slept in their oilskins ready for the everlasting call. So weak and worn were they that it took both watches to do the work of one. That was why both watches were on deck so much of the time. And no shadow of a man could shirk duty. Nothing less than a broken leg could enable a man to knock off work; and there were two such, who had been mauled and pulped by the seas that broke aboard.

One other man who was the shadow of a man was George Dorety. He was the only passenger on board, a friend of the firm, and he had elected to make the voyage for his health. But seven weeks of Cape Horn had not bettered his health. He gasped and panted in his bunk through the long, heaving nights; and when on deck he was so bundled up for warmth that he resembled a peripatetic old-clothes shop. At midday, eating at the cabin table in a gloom so deep that the swinging sea-lamps burned always, he looked as blue- gray as the sickest, saddest man for'ard. Nor did gazing across the table at Captain Dan Cullen have any cheering effect upon him. Captain Cullen chewed and scowled and kept silent. The scowls were for God, and with every chew he reiterated the sole thought of his existence, which was make westing. He was a big, hairy brute, and the sight of him was not stimulating to the other's appetite. He looked upon George Dorety as a Jonah, and told him so, once each meal, savagely transferring the scowl from God to the passenger and back again.

Nor did the mate prove a first aid to a languid appetite. Joshua Higgins by name, a seaman by profession and pull, but a pot-wolloper by capacity, he was a loose-jointed, sniffling creature, heartless and selfish and cowardly, without a soul, in fear of his life of Dan Cullen, and a bully over the sailors, who knew that behind the mate was Captain Cullen, the law-giver and compeller, the driver and the destroyer, the incarnation of a dozen bucko mates. In that wild weather at the southern end of the earth, Joshua Higgins ceased washing. His grimy face usually robbed George Dorety of what little appetite he managed to accumulate. Ordinarily this lavatorial dereliction would have caught Captain Cullen's eye and vocabulary, but in the present his mind was filled with making westing, to the exclusion of all other things not contributory thereto. Whether the mate's face was clean or dirty had no bearing upon westing. Later on, when 50 degrees south in the Pacific had been reached, Joshua Higgins would wash his face very abruptly. In the meantime, at the cabin table, where gray twilight alternated with lamplight while the lamps were being filled, George Dorety sat between the two men, one a tiger and the other a hyena, and wondered why God had made them. The second mate, Matthew Turner, was a true sailor and a man, but George Dorety did not have the solace of his company, for he ate by himself, solitary, when they had finished.

On Saturday morning, July 24, George Dorety awoke to a feeling of life and headlong movement. On deck he found the *Mary Rogers* running off before a howling south-easter. Nothing was set but the lower topsails and the foresail. It was all she could stand, yet she was making fourteen knots, as Mr. Turner shouted in Dorety's ear when he came on deck. And it was all westing. She was going around the Horn at last... if the wind held. Mr. Turner looked happy. The end of the struggle was in sight. But Captain Cullen did not look happy. He scowled at Dorety in passing. Captain Cullen did not want God to know that he was pleased with that wind. He had a conception of a malicious God and believed in his secret soul that if God knew it was a desirable wind, God would promptly efface it and send a snorter from the west. So he walked softly before God, smothering his joy down under scowls and muttered curses, and, so, fooling God, for God was the only thing in the universe of which Dan Cullen was afraid.

All Saturday and Saturday night the *Mary Rogers* raced her westing. Persistently she logged her fourteen knots, so that by Sunday morning she had covered three hundred and fifty miles. If the wind held, she would make around. If it failed, and the snorter came from anywhere between south-west and north, back the *Mary Rogers* would be hurled and be no better off than she had been seven weeks before. And on Sunday morning the wind was failing. The big sea was going down and running smooth. Both watches were on deck setting sail after sail as fast as the ship could stand it. And now Captain Cullen went around brazenly before God, smoking a big cigar, smiling jubilantly, as if the failing wind delighted him, while down underneath he was raging against God for taking the life out of the blessed wind. Make westing! So he would, if God would only leave him alone. Secretly, he pledged himself anew to the Powers of Darkness, if they would let him make westing. He pledged himself so easily because he did not believe in the Powers of Darkness. He really believed only in God, though he did not know it. And in his inverted theology God was really the

Prince of Darkness. Captain Cullen was a devil-worshipper, but he called the devil by another name, that was all.

At midday, after calling eight bells, Captain Cullen ordered the royals on. The men went aloft faster than they had gone in weeks. Not alone were they nimble because of the westing, but a benignant sun was shining down and limbering their stiff bodies. George Dorety stood aft, near Captain Cullen, less bundled in clothes than usual, soaking in the grateful warmth as he watched the scene. Swiftly and abruptly the incident occurred. There was a cry from the foreroyal-yard of "Man overboard!" Somebody threw a life-buoy over the side, and at the same instant the second mate's voice came aft, ringing and peremptory—

"Hard down your helm!"

The man at the wheel never moved a spoke. He knew better, for Captain Dan Cullen was standing alongside of him. He wanted to move a spoke, to move all the spokes, to grind the wheel down, hard down, for his comrade drowning in the sea. He glanced at Captain Dan Cullen, and Captain Dan Cullen gave no sign.

"Down! Hard down!" the second mate roared, as he sprang aft.

But he ceased springing and commanding, and stood still, when he saw Dan Cullen by the wheel. And big Dan Cullen puffed at his cigar and said nothing. Astern, and going astern fast, could be seen the sailor. He had caught the life-buoy and was clinging to it. Nobody spoke. Nobody moved. The men aloft clung to the royal yards and watched with terror-stricken faces. And the *Mary Rogers* raced on, making her westing. A long, silent minute passed.

"Who was it?" Captain Cullen demanded.

"Mops, sir," eagerly answered the sailor at the wheel.

Mops topped a wave astern and disappeared temporarily in the trough. It was a large wave, but it was no graybeard. A small boat could live easily in such a sea, and in such a sea the *Mary Rogers* could easily come to. But she could not come to and make westing at the same time.

For the first time in all his years, George Dorety was seeing a real drama of life and death—a sordid little drama in which the scales balanced an unknown sailor named Mops against a few miles of longitude. At first he had watched the man astern, but now he watched big Dan Cullen, hairy and black, vested with power of life and death, smoking a cigar.

Captain Dan Cullen smoked another long, silent minute. Then he removed the cigar from his mouth. He glanced aloft at the spars of the *Mary Rogers*, and overside at the sea.

"Sheet home the royals!" he cried.

Fifteen minutes later they sat at table, in the cabin, with food served before them. On one side of George Dorety sat Dan Cullen, the tiger, on the other side, Joshua Higgins, the hyena. Nobody spoke. On deck the men were sheeting home the sky-sails. George Dorety could hear their cries, while a persistent vision haunted him of a man called Mops, alive and well, clinging to a life-buoy miles astern in that lonely ocean. He glanced at Captain Cullen, and experienced a feeling of nausea, for the man was eating his food with relish, almost bolting it.

"Captain Cullen," Dorety said, "you are in command of

this ship, and it is not proper for me to comment now upon what you do. But I wish to say one thing. There is a hereafter, and yours will be a hot one."

Captain Cullen did not even scowl. In his voice was regret as he said—

"It was blowing a living gale. It was impossible to save the man."

"He fell from the royal-yard," Dorety cried hotly. "You were setting the royals at the time. Fifteen minutes afterward you were setting the sky-sails."

"It was a living gale, wasn't it, Mr. Higgin?" Captain Cullen said, turning to the mate.

"If you'd brought her to, it'd have taken the sticks out of her," was the mate's answer. "You did the proper thing, Captain Cullen. The man hadn't a ghost of a show."

George Dorety made no answer, and to the meal's end no one spoke. After that, Dorety had his meals served in his state-room. Captain Cullen scowled at him no longer, though no speech was exchanged between them, while the *Mary Rogers* sped north toward warmer latitudes. At the end of the week, Dan Cullen cornered Dorety on deck.

"What are you going to do when we get to 'Frisco?" he demanded bluntly.

"I am going to swear out a warrant for your arrest," Dorety answered quietly. "I am going to charge you with murder, and I am going to see you hanged for it."

"You're almighty sure of yourself," Captain Cullen sneered, turning on his heel.

A second week passed, and one morning found George Dorety standing in the coach-house companionway at the for'ard end of the long poop, taking his first gaze around the deck. The *Mary Rogers* was reaching full-and-by, in a stiff breeze. Every sail was set and drawing, including the staysails. Captain Cullen strolled for'ard along the poop. He strolled carelessly, glancing at the passenger out of the corner of his eye. Dorety was looking the other way, standing with head and shoulders outside the companionway, and only the back of his head was to be seen. Captain Cullen, with swift eye, embraced the mainstaysail-block and the head and estimated the distance. He glanced about him. Nobody was looking. Aft, Joshua Higgins, pacing up and down, had just turned his back and was going the other way. Captain Cullen bent over suddenly and cast the staysail-sheet off from its pin. The heavy block hurtled through the air, smashing Dorety's head like an egg-shell and hurtling on and back and forth as the staysail whipped and slatted in the wind. Joshua Higgins turned around to see what had carried away and met the full blast of the vilest portion of Captain Cullen's profanity.

"I made the sheet fast myself," whimpered the mate in the first lull, "with an extra turn to make sure. I remember it distinctly."

"Made fast?" the Captain snarled back, for the benefit of the watch as it struggled to capture the flying sail before it tore to ribbons. "You couldn't make your grandmother fast, you useless hell's scullion. If you made that sheet fast with an extra turn, why in hell didn't it stay fast? That's what I want to know. Why in hell didn't it stay fast?"

The mate whined inarticulately.

"Oh, shut up!" was the final word of Captain Cullen.

Half an hour later he was as surprised as any when the body of George Dorety was found inside the companionway on the floor. In the afternoon, alone in his room, he doctored up the log.

"Ordinary seaman, Karl Brun," he wrote, "lost overboard from foreroyal-yard in a gale of wind. Was running at the time, and for the safety of the ship did not dare come up to the wind. Nor could a boat have lived in the sea that was running."

On another page, he wrote

"Had often warned Mr. Dorety about the danger he ran because of his carelessness on deck. I told him, once, that someday he would get his head knocked off by a block. A carelessly fastened mainstaysail sheet was the cause of the accident, which was deeply to be regretted because Mr. Dorety was a favorite with all of us."

Captain Dan Cullen read over his literary effort with admiration, blotted the page, and closed the log. He lighted a cigar and stared before him. He felt the *Mary Rogers* lift, and heel, and surge along, and knew that she was making nine knots. A smile of satisfaction slowly dawned on his black and hairy face. Well, anyway, he had made his westing and fooled God.

THE "FRANCIS SPAIGHT"

THE "FRANCIS SPAIGHT" (1911)

A TRUE TALE RETOLD

THE FRANCIS SPAIGHT WAS running before it solely under a mizzentopsail, when the thing happened. It was not due to carelessness so much as to the lack of discipline of the crew and to the fact that they were indifferent seamen at best. The man at the wheel in particular, a Limerick man, had had no experience with salt water beyond that of rafting timber on the *Shannon* between the Quebec vessels and the shore. He was afraid of the huge seas that rose out of the murk astern and bore down upon him, and he was more given to cowering away from their threatened impact than he was to meeting their blows with the wheel and checking the ship's rush to broach to.

It was three in the morning when his unseamanlike conduct precipitated the catastrophe. At sight of a sea far

377

larger than its fellows, he crouched down, releasing his hands from the spokes. The *Francis Spaight* sheered as her stern lifted on the sea, receiving the full fling of the cap on her quarter. The next instant she was in the trough, her lee-rail buried till the ocean was level with her hatch-coamings, sea after sea breaking over her weather rail and sweeping what remained exposed of the deck with icy deluges.

The men were out of hand, helpless and hopeless, stupid in their bewilderment and fear, and resolute only in that they would not obey orders. Some wailed, others clung silently in the weather shrouds, and still others muttered prayers or shrieked vile imprecations; and neither captain nor mate could get them to bear a hand at the pumps or at setting patches of sails to bring the vessel up to the wind and sea. Inside the hour the ship was over on her beam ends, the lubberly cowards climbing up her side and hanging on in the rigging. When she went over, the mate was caught and drowned in the after-cabin, as were two sailors who had sought refuge in the forecastle.

The mate had been the ablest man on board, and the captain was now scarcely less helpless than his men. Beyond cursing them for their worthlessness, he did nothing; and it remained for a man named Mahoney, a Belfast man, and a boy, O'Brien, of Limerick, to cut away the fore and main masts. This they did at great risk on the perpendicular wall of the wreck, sending the mizzentopmast overside along in the general crash. The *Francis Spaight* righted, and it was well that she was lumber laden, else she would have sunk, for she was already water-logged. The mainmast, still fast by the shrouds, beat like a thunderous sledge-hammer against the ship's side, every stroke bringing groans from the men.

Day dawned on the savage ocean, and in the cold gray light all that could be seen of the *Francis Spaight* emerging from the sea were the poop, the shattered mizzenmast, and a ragged line of bulwarks. It was midwinter in the North Atlantic, and the wretched men were half-dead from cold. But there was no place where they could find rest. Every sea breached clean over the wreck, washing away the salt incrustations from their bodies and depositing fresh incrustations. The cabin under the poop was awash to the knees, but here at least was shelter from the chill wind, and here the survivors congregated, standing upright, holding on by the cabin furnishings, and leaning against one another for support.

In vain Mahoney strove to get the men to take turns in watching aloft from the mizzenmast for any chance vessel. The icy gale was too much for them, and they preferred the shelter of the cabin. O'Brien, the boy, who was only fifteen, took turns with Mahoney on the freezing perch. It was the boy, at three in the afternoon, who called down that he had sighted a sail. This did bring them from the cabin, and they crowded the poop rail and weather mizzen shrouds as they watched the strange ship. But its course did not lie near, and when it disappeared below the skyline, they returned shivering to the cabin, not one offering to relieve the watch at the mast head.

By the end of the second day, Mahoney and O'Brien gave up their attempt, and thereafter the vessel drifted in the gale uncared for and without a lookout. There were thirteen alive, and for seventy-two hours they stood knee-deep in the sloshing water on the cabin floor, half-frozen, without food, and with but three bottles of wine shared among them. All food and fresh water were below, and there was no getting at such supplies in the water-logged condition of the wreck. As the days went by, no food whatever passed their lips. Fresh water, in small quantities, they were able to obtain by holding a cover of a tureen under the saddle of the mizzenmast. But the rain fell infrequently, and they were hard put. When it rained, they also soaked their handkerchiefs, squeezing them out into their mouths or into their shoes. As the wind and sea went down, they were even able to mop the exposed portions of the deck that were free from brine and so add to their water supply. But food they had none, and no way of getting it, though sea-birds flew repeatedly overhead.

In the calm weather that followed the gale, after having remained on their feet for ninety-six hours, they were able to find dry planks in the cabin on which to lie. But the long hours of standing in the salt water had caused sores to form on their legs. These sores were extremely painful. The slightest contact or scrape caused severe anguish, and in their weak condition and crowded situation they were continually hurting one another in this manner. Not a man could move about without being followed by volleys of abuse, curses, and groans. So great was their misery that the strong oppressed the weak, shoving them aside from the dry planks to shift for themselves in the cold and wet. The boy, O'Brien, was specially maltreated. Though there were three other boys, it was O'Brien who came in for most of the abuse. There was no explaining it, except on the ground that his was a stronger and more dominant spirit than those of the other boys, and that he stood up more for his rights, resenting the petty injustices that were meted out to all the boys by the men. Whenever O'Brien came near the men in search of a dry place to sleep, or merely moved about, he was kicked and cuffed away. In return, he cursed them for their selfish brutishness, and blows and kicks and curses were rained upon him. Miserable as were all of them, he was thus made far more miserable; and it was only the flame of life, unusually strong in him, that enabled him to endure.

As the days went by and they grew weaker, their peevishness and ill-temper increased, which, in turn, increased the ill-treatment and sufferings of O'Brien. By the sixteenth day all hands were far gone with hunger, and they stood together in small groups, talking in undertones and occasionally glancing at O'Brien. It was at high noon that the conference came to a head. The captain was the spokesman. All were collected on the poop.

"Men," the captain began, "we have been a long time without food—two weeks and two days it is, though it seems more like two years and two months. We can't hang out much longer. It is beyond human nature to go on hanging out with nothing in our stomachs. There is a serious question to consider: whether it is better for all to die, or for one to die. We are standing with our feet in our graves. If one of us dies, the rest may live until a ship is sighted. What say you?"

Michael Behane, the man who had been at the wheel when the *Francis Spaight* broached to, called out that it was well. The others joined in the cry.

"Let it be one of the b'ys!" cried Sullivan, a Tarbert man, glancing at the same time significantly at O'Brien.

"It is my opinion," the captain went on, "that it will be a good deed for one of us to die for the rest."

"A good deed! A good deed!" the men interjected.

"And it is my opinion that 'tis best for one of the boys to die. They have no families to support, nor would they be considered so great a loss to their friends as those who have wives and children."

"'Tis right." "Very right." "Very fit it should be done," the men muttered one to another.

But the four boys cried out against the injustice of it.

"Our lives is just as dear to us as the rest iv yez," O'Brien protested. "An' our famblies, too. As for wives an' childer, who is there savin' meself to care for me old mother that's a widow, as you know well, Michael Behane, that comes from Limerick? 'Tis not fair. Let the lots be drawn between all of us, men and b'ys."

Mahoney was the only man who spoke in favor of the boys, declaring that it was the fair thing for all to share alike. Sullivan and the captain insisted on the drawing of lots being confined to the boys. There were high words, in the midst of which Sullivan turned upon O'Brien, snarling—

"'Twould be a good deed to put you out of the way. You deserve it. 'Twould be the right way to serve you, an' serve you we will."

He started toward O'Brien, with intent to lay hands on him and proceed at once with the killing, while several others likewise shuffled toward him and reached for him. He stumbled backwards to escape them, at the same time crying that he would submit to the drawing of the lots among the boys.

The captain prepared four sticks of different lengths and handed them to Sullivan.

"You're thinkin' the drawin'll not be fair," the latter sneered to O'Brien. "So it's yerself'll do the drawin'."

To this O'Brien agreed. A handkerchief was tied over his eyes, blindfolding him, and he knelt down on the deck with his back to Sullivan.

"Whoever you name for the shortest stick'll die," the captain said.

Sullivan held up one of the sticks. The rest were concealed in his hand so that no one could see whether it was the short stick or not.

"An' whose stick will it be?" Sullivan demanded.

"For little Johnny Sheehan," O'Brien answered.

Sullivan laid the stick aside. Those who looked could not tell if it were the fatal one. Sullivan held up another stick.

"Whose will it be?"

"For George Burns," was the reply.

The stick was laid with the first one, and a third held up.

"An' whose is this wan?"

"For myself," said O'Brien.

With a quick movement, Sullivan threw the four sticks together. No one had seen.

"'Tis for yourself ye've drawn it," Sullivan announced.

"A good deed," several of the men muttered.

O'Brien was very quiet. He arose to his feet, took the

bandage off, and looked around.

"Where is ut?" he demanded. "The short stick? The wan for me?"

The captain pointed to the four sticks lying on the deck.

"How do you know the stick was mine?" O'Brien questioned. "Did you see ut, Johnny Sheehan?"

Johnny Sheehan, who was the youngest of the boys, did not answer.

"Did you see ut?" O'Brien next asked Mahoney.

"No, I didn't see ut."

The men were muttering and growling.

"'Twas a fair drawin'," Sullivan said. "Ye had yer chanct an' ye lost, that's all iv ut."

"A fair drawin'," the captain added. "Didn't I behold it myself? The stick was yours, O'Brien, an' ye may as well get ready. Where's the cook? Gorman, come here. Fetch the tureen cover, some of ye. Gorman, do your duty like a man."

"But how'll I do it," the cook demanded. He was a weak-eyed, weak-chinned, indecisive man.

"'Tis a damned murder!" O'Brien cried out.

"I'll have none of ut," Mahoney announced. "Not a bite shall pass me lips."

"Then 'tis yer share for better men than yerself," Sullivan sneered. "Go on with yer duty, cook."

"'Tis not me duty, the killin' of b'ys," Gorman protested irresolutely.

"If yez don't make mate for us, we'll be makin' mate of yerself," Behane threatened. "Somebody must die, an' as well you as another."

Johnny Sheehan began to cry. O'Brien listened anxiously. His face was pale. His lips trembled, and at times his whole body shook.

"I signed on as cook," Gorman enounced. "An' cook I wud if galley there was. But I'll not lay me hand to murder. 'Tis not in the articles. I'm the cook—"

"An' cook ye'll be for wan minute more only," Sullivan said grimly, at the same moment gripping the cook's head from behind and bending it back till the windpipe and jugular were stretched taut. "Where's yer knife, Mike? Pass it along."

At the touch of the steel, Gorman whimpered.

"I'll do ut, if yez'll hold the b'y."

The pitiable condition of the cook seemed in some fashion to nerve up O'Brien.

"It's all right, Gorman," he said. "Go on with ut. 'Tis meself knows yer not wantin' to do ut. It's all right, sir"—this to the captain, who had laid a hand heavily on his arm. "Ye won't have to hold me, sir. I'll stand still."

"Stop yer blitherin', an' go an' get the tureen cover," Behane commanded Johnny Sheehan, at the same time dealing him a heavy cuff alongside the head.

The boy, who was scarcely more than a child, fetched the cover. He crawled and tottered along the deck, so weak was he from hunger. The tears still ran down his cheeks. Behane took the cover from him, at the same time administering another cuff.

O'Brien took off his coat and bared his right arm. His under lip still trembled, but he held a tight grip on himself. The captain's penknife was opened and passed to Gorman.

"Mahoney, tell me mother what happened to me, if ever ye get back," O'Brien requested.

Mahoney nodded.

"'Tis black murder, black an' damned," he said. "The b'y's flesh'll do none iv yez anny good. Mark me words. Ye'll not profit by it, none iv yez."

"Get ready," the captain ordered. "You, Sullivan, hold the cover—that's it—close up. Spill nothing. It's precious stuff."

Gorman made an effort. The knife was dull. He was weak. Besides, his hand was shaking so violently that he nearly dropped the knife. The three boys were crouched apart, in a huddle, crying and sobbing. With the exception of Mahoney, the men were gathered about the victim, craning their necks to see.

"Be a man, Gorman," the captain cautioned.

The wretched cook was seized with a spasm of resolution, sawing back and forth with the blade on O'Brien's wrist. The veins were severed. Sullivan held the tureen cover close underneath. The cut veins gaped wide, but no ruddy flood gushed forth. There was no blood at all. The veins were dry and empty. No one spoke. The grim and silent figures swayed in unison with each heave of the ship. Every eye was turned fixedly upon that inconceivable and monstrous thing, the dry veins of a creature that was alive.

"'Tis a warnin'," Mahoney cried. "Lave the b'y alone. Mark me words. His death'll do none iv yez anny good."

"Try at the elbow—the left elbow, 'tis nearer the heart," the captain said finally, in a dim and husky voice that was unlike his own.

"Give me the knife," O'Brien said roughly, taking it out of the cook's hand. "I can't be lookin' at ye puttin' me to hurt."

Quite coolly he cut the vein at the left elbow, but, like the cook, he failed to bring blood.

"This is all iv no use," Sullivan said. "'Tis better to put him out iv his misery by bleedin' him at the throat."

The strain had been too much for the lad.

"Don't be doin' ut," he cried. "There'll be no blood in me throat. Give me a little time. 'Tis cold an' weak I am. Be lettin' me lay down an' slape a bit. Then I'll be warm an' the blood'll flow."

"'Tis no use," Sullivan objected. "As if ye cud be slapin' at a time like this. Ye'll not slape, and ye'll not warm up. Look at ye now. You've an ague."

"I was sick at Limerick wan night," O'Brien hurried on, "an' the dochtor cudn't bleed me. But after slapin' a few hours an' gettin' warm in bed the blood came freely. It's God's truth I'm tellin' yez. Don't be murderin' me!"

"His veins are open now," the captain said. "'Tis no use leavin' him in his pain. Do it now an' be done with it."

They started to reach for O'Brien, but he backed away.

"I'll be the death iv yez!" he screamed. "Take yer hands off iv me, Sullivan! I'll come back! I'll haunt yez! Wakin' or slapin', I'll haunt yez till you die!"

"'Tis disgraceful!" yelled Behane. "If the short stick'd ben mine, I'd a- let me mates cut the head off iv me an' died happy."

Sullivan leaped in and caught the unhappy lad by the hair. The rest of the men followed, O'Brien kicked and struggled, snarling and snapping at the hands that clutched him from every side. Little Johnny Sheehan broke out into wild screaming, but the men took no notice of him. O'Brien was bent backward to the deck, the tureen cover under his neck. Gorman was shoved forward. Someone had thrust a large sheath-knife into his hand.

"Do yer duty! Do yer duty!" the men cried.

The cook bent over, but he caught the boy's eyes and faltered.

"If ye don't, I'll kill ye with me own hands," Behane shouted.

From every side a torrent of abuse and threats poured in upon the cook. Still he hung back.

"Maybe there'll be more blood in his veins than O'Brien's," Sullivan suggested significantly.

Behane caught Gorman by the hair and twisted his head back, while Sullivan attempted to take possession of the sheath-knife. But Gorman clung to it desperately.

"Lave go, an' I'll do ut!" he screamed frantically. "Don't be cuttin' me throat! I'll do the deed! I'll do the deed!"

"See that you do it, then," the captain threatened him.

Gorman allowed himself to be shoved forward. He looked at the boy, closed his eyes, and muttered a prayer. Then, without opening his eyes, he did the deed that had been appointed him. O'Brien emitted a shriek that sank swiftly to a gurgling sob. The men held him till his struggles ceased, when he was laid upon the deck. They were eager and impatient, and with oaths and threats they urged Gorman to hurry with the preparation of the meal.

"Lave ut, you bloody butchers," Mahoney said quietly.

"Lave ut, I tell yez. Ye'll not be needin' anny iv ut now. 'Tis as I said: ye'll not be profitin' by the lad's blood. Empty ut overside, Behane. Empty ut overside."

Behane, still holding the tureen cover in both his hands, glanced to windward. He walked to the rail and threw the cover and contents into the sea. A full-rigged ship was bearing down upon them a short mile away. So occupied had they been with the deed just committed, that none had had eyes for a lookout. All hands watched her coming on—the brightly coppered forefoot parting the water like a golden knife, the headsails flapping lazily and emptily at each downward surge, and the towering canvas tiers dipping and curtsying with each stately swing of the sea. No man spoke.

As she hove to, a cable length away, the captain of the *Francis Spaight* bestirred himself and ordered a tarpaulin to be thrown over O'Brien's corpse. A boat was lowered from the stranger's side and began to pull toward them. John Gorman laughed. He laughed softly at first, but he accompanied each stroke of the oars with spasmodically increasing glee. It was this maniacal laughter that greeted the rescue boat as it hauled alongside and the first officer clambered on board.